HEROES OF OLYMPUS

THE HOUSE OF HADES

RICK RIORDAN

PUFFIN

PUFFIN BOOKS

UK | USA | Canada | Ireland | Australia
India | New Zealand | South Africa

Puffin Books is part of the Penguin Random House group of companies
whose addresses can be found at global.penguinrandomhouse.com.

www.penguin.co.uk   www.puffin.co.uk   www.ladybird.co.uk

First published in the USA by Disney·Hyperion Books, an imprint of Disney Book Group, 2013
Published simultaneously in Great Britain in Puffin Books 2013
This edition published 2017
001

Text copyright © Rick Riordan, 2013

The moral right of the author has been asserted

Printed in Great Britain by Clays Ltd, St Ives plc
A CIP catalogue record for this book is available from the British Library

ISBN: 978–0–241–33555–0

All correspondence to:
Puffin Books, Penguin Random House Children's
80 Strand, London WC2R 0RL

PUFFIN BOOKS

THE HOUSE OF HADES

Praise for *Heroes of Olympus: The Lost Hero*:

'Another cracking read' – *Sunday Express*

'Action-packed' – Nicolette Jones, *Daily Telegraph*

Praise for the Percy Jackson series:
'One of the best books of the year . . . vastly
entertaining' – *Independent*

'A fantastic blend of myth and modern. Rick Riordan
takes the reader back to the stories we love, then shakes the
cobwebs out of them' – Eoin Colfer, author of *Artemis Fowl*

'Witty and inspired. Gripping, touching and deliciously
satirical' – Amanda Craig, *The Times*

To my wonderful readers:
Sorry about that last cliff-hanger.
Well, no, not really. HAHAHAHA.
But, seriously, I love you guys.

HAZEL

DURING THE THIRD ATTACK, Hazel almost ate a boulder. She was peering into the fog, wondering how it could be so difficult to fly across one stupid mountain range, when the ship's alarm bells sounded.

'Hard to port!' Nico yelled from the foremast of the flying ship.

Back at the helm, Leo yanked the wheel. The *Argo II* veered left, its aerial oars slashing through the clouds like rows of knives.

Hazel made the mistake of looking over the rail. A dark spherical shape hurtled towards her. She thought, *Why is the moon coming at us?* Then she yelped and hit the deck. The huge rock passed so close overhead it blew her hair out of her face.

CRACK!

The foremast collapsed – sail, spars and Nico all crashing to the deck. The boulder, roughly the size of a pickup truck, tumbled off into the fog like it had important business elsewhere.

'Nico!' Hazel scrambled over to him as Leo brought the ship level.

'I'm fine,' Nico muttered, kicking folds of canvas off his legs.

She helped him up, and they stumbled to the bow. Hazel peeked over more carefully this time. The clouds parted just long enough to reveal the top of the mountain below them: a spearhead of black rock jutting from mossy green slopes. Standing at the summit was a mountain god – one of the *numina montanum*, Jason had called them. Or *ourae*, in Greek. Whatever you called them, they were nasty.

Like the others they had faced, this one wore a simple white tunic over skin as rough and dark as basalt. He was about twenty feet tall and extremely muscular, with a flowing white beard, scraggly hair and a wild look in his eyes, like a crazy hermit. He bellowed something Hazel didn't understand, but it obviously wasn't welcoming. With his bare hands, he prised another chunk of rock from his mountain and began shaping it into a ball.

The scene disappeared in the fog, but when the mountain god bellowed again other *numina* answered in the distance, their voices echoing through the valleys.

'Stupid rock gods!' Leo yelled from the helm. 'That's the *third* time I've had to replace that mast! You think they grow on trees?'

Nico frowned. 'Masts *are* from trees.'

'That's not the point!' Leo snatched up one of his controls, rigged from a Nintendo Wii stick, and spun it in a circle. A few feet away, a trapdoor opened in the deck. A Celestial bronze cannon rose. Hazel just had time to cover her ears before it discharged into the sky, spraying a dozen metal spheres that trailed green fire. The spheres grew spikes in midair, like helicopter blades, and hurtled away into the fog.

A moment later, a series of explosions crackled across the mountains, followed by the outraged roars of mountain gods.

'Ha!' Leo yelled.

Unfortunately, Hazel guessed, judging from their last two encounters, Leo's newest weapon had only annoyed the *numina*.

Another boulder whistled through the air off to their starboard side.

Nico yelled, 'Get us out of here!'

Leo muttered some unflattering comments about *numina*, but he turned the wheel. The engines hummed. Magical rigging lashed itself tight, and the ship tacked to port. The *Argo II* picked up speed, retreating north-west, as they'd been doing for the past two days.

Hazel didn't relax until they were out of the mountains. The fog cleared. Below them, morning sunlight illuminated the Italian countryside – rolling green hills and golden fields not too different from those in northern California. Hazel could almost imagine she was sailing home to Camp Jupiter.

The thought weighed on her chest. Camp Jupiter had only been her home for nine months, since Nico had brought her back from the Underworld. But she missed it more than her birthplace of New Orleans, and *definitely* more than Alaska, where she'd died back in 1942.

She missed her bunk in the Fifth Cohort barracks. She missed dinners in the mess hall, with wind spirits whisking platters through the air and legionnaires joking about the war games. She wanted to wander the streets of New Rome, holding hands with Frank Zhang. She wanted to experience just being a regular girl for once, with an actual sweet, caring boyfriend.

Most of all, she wanted to feel safe. She was tired of being scared and worried all the time.

She stood on the quarterdeck as Nico picked mast splinters out of his arms and Leo punched buttons on the ship's console.

'Well, *that* was sucktastic,' Leo said. 'Should I wake the others?'

Hazel was tempted to say yes, but the other crew members had taken the night shift and had earned their rest. They were exhausted from defending the ship. Every few hours, it seemed, some Roman monster had decided the *Argo II* looked like a tasty treat.

A few weeks ago, Hazel wouldn't have believed that anyone could sleep through a *numina* attack, but now she imagined her friends were still snoring away belowdecks. Whenever *she* got a chance to crash, she slept like a coma patient.

'They need rest,' she said. 'We'll have to figure out another way on our own.'

'Huh.' Leo scowled at his monitor. In his tattered work shirt and grease-splattered jeans, he looked like he'd just lost a wrestling match with a locomotive.

Ever since their friends Percy and Annabeth had fallen into Tartarus, Leo had been working almost non-stop. He'd been acting angrier and even more driven than usual.

Hazel worried about him. But part of her was relieved by the change. Whenever Leo smiled and joked, he looked *too* much like Sammy, his great-grandfather . . . Hazel's first boyfriend, back in 1942.

Ugh, why did her life have to be so complicated?

'Another way,' Leo muttered. 'Do you see one?'

On his monitor glowed a map of Italy. The Apennine Mountains ran down the middle of the boot-shaped country. A green dot for the *Argo II* blinked on the western side of the range, a few hundred miles north of Rome. Their path should have been simple. They needed to get to a place called Epirus in Greece and find an old temple called the House of Hades (or Pluto, as the Romans called him; or as Hazel liked to think of him: the World's Worst Absent Father).

To reach Epirus, all they had to do was go straight east – over the Apennines and across the Adriatic Sea. But it hadn't worked out that way. Each time they tried to cross the spine of Italy, the mountain gods attacked.

For the past two days they'd skirted north, hoping to find a safe pass, with no luck. The *numina montanum* were sons of Gaia, Hazel's least favourite goddess. That made them *very* determined enemies. The *Argo II* couldn't fly high enough to avoid their attacks and, even with all its defences, the ship couldn't make it across the range without being smashed to pieces.

'It's our fault,' Hazel said. 'Nico's and mine. The *numina* can sense us.'

She glanced at her half-brother. Since they'd rescued him from the giants, he'd started to regain his strength, but he was still painfully thin. His black shirt and jeans hung off his skeletal frame. Long dark hair framed his sunken eyes. His olive complexion had turned a sickly greenish white, like the colour of tree sap.

In human years, he was barely fourteen, just a year older than Hazel, but that didn't tell the whole story. Like Hazel, Nico di Angelo was a demigod from another era. He radiated a kind of *old* energy – a melancholy that came from knowing he didn't belong in the modern world.

Hazel hadn't known him very long, but she understood, even shared, his sadness. The children of Hades (Pluto – whichever) rarely had happy lives. And, judging from what Nico had told her the night before, their biggest challenge was yet to come when they reached the House of Hades – a challenge he'd implored her to keep secret from the others.

Nico gripped the hilt of his Stygian iron sword. 'Earth spirits don't like children of the Underworld. That's true. We get under their skin – *literally*. But I think the *numina* could sense this ship anyway. We're carrying the Athena Parthenos. That thing is like a magical beacon.'

Hazel shivered, thinking of the massive statue that took up most of the hold. They'd sacrificed so much saving it from the cavern under Rome, but they had no idea what to do with it. So far the only thing it seemed to be good for was alerting more monsters to their presence.

Leo traced his finger down the map of Italy. 'So crossing the mountains is out. Thing is they go a long way in either direction.'

'We could go by sea,' Hazel suggested. 'Sail around the southern tip of Italy.'

'That's a long way,' Nico said. 'Plus, we don't have . . .' His voice cracked. 'You know . . . our sea expert, Percy.'

The name hung in the air like an impending storm.

Percy Jackson, son of Poseidon . . . probably the demigod Hazel admired most. He'd saved her life so many times on their quest to Alaska, but when he had needed Hazel's help in Rome she'd failed him. She'd watched, powerless, as he and Annabeth had plunged into that pit.

Hazel took a deep breath. Percy and Annabeth were still alive. She knew that in her heart. She could *still* help them if she could get to the House of Hades, if she could survive the challenge Nico had warned her about . . .

'What about continuing north?' she asked. 'There *has* to be a break in the mountains, or something.'

Leo fiddled with the bronze Archimedes sphere that he'd installed on the console – his newest and most dangerous toy. Every time Hazel looked at the thing, her mouth went dry. She worried that Leo would turn the wrong combination on the sphere and accidentally eject them all from the deck, or blow up the ship, or turn the *Argo II* into a giant toaster.

Fortunately, they got lucky. The sphere grew a camera lens and projected a 3-D image of the Apennine Mountains above the console.

'I dunno.' Leo examined the hologram. 'I don't see any good passes to the north. But I like that idea better than backtracking south. I'm done with Rome.'

No one argued with that. Rome had not been a good experience.

'Whatever we do,' Nico said, 'we have to hurry. Every day that Annabeth and Percy are in Tartarus . . .'

He didn't need to finish. They had to hope Percy and Annabeth could survive long enough to find the Tartarus side of the Doors of Death. Then, assuming the *Argo II* could reach the House of Hades, they *might* be able to open the Doors on the mortal side, save their friends and seal the entrance, stopping Gaia's forces from being reincarnated in the mortal world over and over.

Yes . . . nothing could go wrong with *that* plan.

Nico scowled at the Italian countryside below them. 'Maybe we *should* wake the others. This decision affects us all.'

'No,' Hazel said. 'We can find a solution.'

She wasn't sure why she felt so strongly about it, but since leaving Rome the crew had started to lose its cohesion. They'd been learning to work as a team. Then *bam* . . . their two most important members had fallen into Tartarus. Percy had been their backbone. He'd given them confidence as they sailed across the Atlantic and into the Mediterranean. As for Annabeth – she'd been the de facto leader of the quest. She'd recovered the Athena Parthenos single-handedly. She was the smartest of the seven, the one with the answers.

If Hazel woke up the rest of the crew every time they had a problem, they'd just start arguing again, feeling more and more hopeless.

She had to make Percy and Annabeth proud of her. She had to take the initiative. She couldn't believe her only role in this quest would be what Nico had warned her about – removing the obstacle waiting for them in the House of Hades. She pushed the thought aside.

'We need some creative thinking,' she said. 'Another way to cross those mountains, or a way to hide ourselves from the *numina*.'

Nico sighed. 'If I was on my own, I could shadow-travel. But that won't work for an entire ship. And, honestly, I'm not sure I have the strength to even transport *myself* any more.'

'I could maybe rig some kind of camouflage,' Leo said, 'like a smoke screen to hide us in the clouds.' He didn't sound very enthusiastic.

Hazel stared down at the rolling farmland, thinking about what lay beneath it – the realm of her father, lord of the Underworld. She'd only met Pluto once, and she hadn't even realized who he was. She certainly had never expected help from him – not when she was alive the first time, not during her time as a spirit in the Underworld, not since Nico had brought her back to the world of the living.

Her dad's servant Thanatos, god of death, had suggested that Pluto might be doing Hazel a favour by ignoring her.

After all, she wasn't supposed to be alive. If Pluto took notice of her, he might have to return her to the land of the dead.

Which meant calling on Pluto would be a very bad idea. And yet . . .

Please, Dad, she found herself praying. *I* have *to find a way to your temple in Greece – the House of Hades. If you're down there, show me what to do.*

At the edge of the horizon, a flicker of movement caught her eye – something small and beige racing across the fields at incredible speed, leaving a vapour trail like a plane's.

Hazel couldn't believe it. She didn't dare hope, but it *had* to be . . . 'Arion.'

'What?' Nico asked.

Leo let out a happy whoop as the dust cloud got closer. 'It's her horse, man! You missed that whole part. We haven't seen him since Kansas!'

Hazel laughed – the first time she'd laughed in days. It felt so good to see her old friend.

About a mile to the north, the small beige dot circled a hill and stopped at the summit. He was difficult to make out, but when the horse reared and whinnied the sound carried all the way to the *Argo II*. Hazel had no doubt – it was Arion.

'We have to meet him,' she said. 'He's here to help.'

'Yeah, okay.' Leo scratched his head. 'But, uh, we talked about not landing the ship on the ground any more, remember? You know, with Gaia wanting to destroy us and all.'

'Just get me close, and I'll use the rope ladder.' Hazel's heart was pounding. 'I think Arion wants to tell me something.'

HAZEL

HAZEL HAD NEVER FELT SO HAPPY. Well, except for maybe on the night of the victory feast at Camp Jupiter, when she'd kissed Frank for the first time . . . but this was a close second.

As soon as she reached the ground, she ran to Arion and threw her arms around his neck. 'I missed you!' She pressed her face into the horse's warm flank, which smelled of sea salt and apples. 'Where have you been?'

Arion nickered. Hazel wished she could speak Horse like Percy could, but she got the general idea. Arion sounded impatient, as if saying, *No time for sentiment, girl! Come on!*

'You want me to go with you?' she guessed.

Arion bobbed his head, trotting on the spot. His dark brown eyes gleamed with urgency.

Hazel still couldn't believe he was actually here. He could run across any surface, even the sea, but she'd been afraid he wouldn't follow them into the ancient lands. The

Mediterranean was too dangerous for demigods and their allies.

He wouldn't have come unless Hazel was in dire need. And he seemed so agitated . . . Anything that could make a fearless horse skittish should have terrified Hazel.

Instead, she felt elated. She was *so* tired of being seasick and airsick. Aboard the *Argo II*, she felt about as useful as a box of ballast. She was glad to be back on solid ground, even if it *was* Gaia's territory. She was ready to ride.

'Hazel!' Nico called down from the ship. 'What's going on?'

'It's fine!' She crouched down and summoned a gold nugget from the earth. She was getting better at controlling her power. Precious stones hardly ever popped up around her by accident any more, and pulling gold from the ground was easy.

She fed Arion the nugget . . . his favourite snack. Then she smiled up at Leo and Nico, who were watching her from the top of the ladder a hundred feet above. 'Arion wants to take me somewhere.'

The boys exchanged nervous looks.

'Uh . . .' Leo pointed north. 'Please tell me he's not taking you into *that*?'

Hazel had been so focused on Arion she hadn't noticed the disturbance. A mile away, on the crest of the next hill, a storm had gathered over some old stone ruins – maybe the remains of a Roman temple or a fortress. A funnel cloud snaked its way down towards the hill like an inky black finger.

Hazel's mouth tasted like blood. She looked at Arion. 'You want to go *there*?'

Arion whinnied, as if to say, *Uh, duh!*

Well . . . Hazel had asked for help. Was this her dad's answer?

She hoped so, but she sensed something besides Pluto at work in that storm . . . something dark, powerful and not necessarily friendly.

Still, this was her chance to help her friends – to lead instead of follow.

She tightened the straps of her Imperial gold cavalry sword and climbed onto Arion's back.

'I'll be okay!' she called up to Nico and Leo. 'Stay put and wait for me.'

'Wait for how long?' Nico asked. 'What if you don't come back?'

'Don't worry, I will,' she promised, hoping it was true.

She spurred Arion, and they shot across the countryside, heading straight for the growing tornado.

III

HAZEL

THE STORM SWALLOWED THE HILL in a swirling cone of black vapour.

Arion charged straight into it.

Hazel found herself at the summit, but it felt like a different dimension. The world lost its colour. The walls of the storm encircled the hill in murky black. The sky churned grey. The crumbling ruins were bleached so white that they almost glowed. Even Arion had turned from caramel brown to a dark shade of ash.

In the eye of the tempest, the air was still. Hazel's skin tingled coolly, as if she'd been rubbed with alcohol. In front of her, an arched gateway led through mossy walls into some sort of enclosure.

Hazel couldn't see much through the gloom, but she felt a presence within, as if she were a chunk of iron close to a large magnet. Its pull was irresistible, dragging her forward.

Yet she hesitated. She reined in Arion, and he clopped

impatiently, the ground crackling under his hooves. Wherever he stepped, the grass, dirt and stones turned white like frost. Hazel remembered the Hubbard Glacier in Alaska – how the surface had cracked under their feet. She remembered the floor of that horrible cavern in Rome crumbling to dust, plunging Percy and Annabeth into Tartarus.

She hoped this black-and-white hilltop wouldn't dissolve under her, but she decided it was best to keep moving.

'Let's go, then, boy.' Her voice sounded muffled, as if she were speaking into a pillow.

Arion trotted through the stone archway. Ruined walls bordered a square courtyard about the size of a tennis court. Three other gateways, one in the middle of each wall, led north, east and west. In the centre of the yard, two cobble-stone paths intersected, making a cross. Mist hung in the air – hazy shreds of white that coiled and undulated as if they were alive.

Not mist, Hazel realized. *The Mist.*

All her life, she'd heard about the Mist – the supernatural veil that obscured the world of myth from the sight of mortals. It could deceive humans, even demigods, into seeing monsters as harmless animals, or gods as regular people.

Hazel had never thought of it as actual smoke, but as she watched it curling around Arion's legs, floating through the broken arches of the ruined courtyard, the hairs stood up on her arms. Somehow she knew: this white stuff was pure magic.

In the distance, a dog howled. Arion wasn't usually scared of anything, but he reared, huffing nervously.

'It's okay.' Hazel stroked his neck. 'We're in this together. I'm going to get down, all right?'

She slid off Arion's back. Instantly he turned and ran.

'Arion, wai–'

But he'd already disappeared the way he'd come.

So much for being in this together.

Another howl cut through the air – closer this time.

Hazel stepped towards the centre of the courtyard. The Mist clung to her like freezer fog.

'Hello?' she called.

'Hello,' a voice answered.

The pale figure of a woman appeared at the northern gateway. No, wait . . . she stood at the eastern entrance. No, the western. *Three* smoky images of the same woman moved in unison towards the centre of the ruins. Her form was blurred, made from Mist, and she was trailed by two smaller wisps of smoke, darting at her heels like animals. Some sort of pets?

She reached the centre of the courtyard and her three forms merged into one. She solidified into a young woman in a dark sleeveless gown. Her golden hair was gathered into a high-set ponytail, Ancient Greek style. Her dress was so silky it seemed to ripple, as if the cloth were ink spilling off her shoulders. She looked no more than twenty, but Hazel knew that meant nothing.

'Hazel Levesque,' said the woman.

She was beautiful, but deathly pale. Once, back in New Orleans, Hazel had been forced to attend a wake for a dead classmate. She remembered the lifeless body of the young girl in the open casket. Her face had been made up prettily, as if she were resting, which Hazel had found terrifying.

This woman reminded Hazel of that girl – except the woman's eyes were open and completely black. When she tilted her head, she seemed to break into three different people again . . . misty after-images blurring together, like a photograph of someone moving too fast to capture.

'Who are you?' Hazel's fingers twitched at the hilt of her sword. 'I mean . . . which goddess?'

Hazel was sure of that much. This woman radiated power. Everything around them – the swirling Mist, the monochromatic storm, the eerie glow of the ruins – was because of her presence.

'Ah.' The woman nodded. 'Let me give you some light.'

She raised her hands. Suddenly she was holding two old-fashioned reed torches, guttering with fire. The Mist receded to the edges of the courtyard. At the woman's sandalled feet, the two wispy animals took on solid form. One was a black Labrador retriever. The other was a long, grey furry rodent with a white mask around its face. A weasel, maybe?

The woman smiled serenely.

'I am Hecate,' she said. 'Goddess of magic. We have much to discuss if you're to live through tonight.'

IV

HAZEL

HAZEL WANTED TO RUN, but her feet seemed to be stuck to the white-glazed ground.

On either side of the crossroads, two dark metal torch-stands erupted from the dirt like plant stalks. Hecate fixed her torches in them, then walked a slow circle around Hazel, regarding her as if they were partners in some eerie dance.

The black dog and the weasel followed in her wake.

'You are like your mother,' Hecate decided.

Hazel's throat constricted. 'You knew her?'

'Of course. Marie was a fortune-teller. She dealt in charms and curses and *gris-gris*. I am the goddess of magic.'

Those pure black eyes seemed to pull at Hazel, as if trying to extract her soul. During her *first* lifetime in New Orleans, Hazel had been tormented by the kids at St Agnes School because of her mother. They'd called Marie Levesque a witch. The nuns had muttered that Hazel's mother was trading with the Devil.

If the nuns were scared of my mom, Hazel wondered, what would they make of this goddess?

'Many fear me,' Hecate said, as if reading her thoughts. 'But magic is neither good nor evil. It is a tool, like a knife. Is a knife evil? Only if the wielder is evil.'

'My – my mother . . .' Hazel stammered. 'She didn't believe in magic. Not really. She was just faking it, for the money.'

The weasel chittered and bared its teeth. Then it made a squeaking sound from its back end. Under other circumstances, a weasel passing gas might have been funny, but Hazel didn't laugh. The rodent's red eyes glared at her balefully, like tiny coals.

'Peace, Gale,' said Hecate. She gave Hazel an apologetic shrug. 'Gale does not like hearing about nonbelievers and con artists. She herself was once a witch, you see.'

'Your weasel was a witch?'

'She's a polecat, actually,' Hecate said. 'But, yes – Gale was once a disagreeable human witch. She had terrible personal hygiene, plus extreme – ah, digestive issues.' Hecate waved her hand in front of her nose. 'It gave my other followers a bad name.'

'Okay.' Hazel tried not to look at the weasel. She really didn't want to know about the rodent's intestinal problems.

'At any rate,' Hecate said, 'I turned her into a polecat. She's much better as a polecat.'

Hazel swallowed. She looked at the black dog, which was affectionately nuzzling the goddess's hand. 'And your Labrador . . . ?'

'Oh, she's Hecuba, the former queen of Troy,' Hecate said, as if that should be obvious.

The dog grunted.

'You're right, Hecuba,' the goddess said. 'We don't have time for long introductions. The point is, Hazel Levesque, your mother may have claimed not to believe, but she had true magic. Eventually, she realized this. When she searched for a spell to summon the god Pluto, *I* helped her find it.'

'You . . . ?'

'Yes.' Hecate continued circling Hazel. 'I saw potential in your mother. I see even *more* potential in you.'

Hazel's head spun. She remembered her mother's confession just before she had died: how she'd summoned Pluto, how the god had fallen in love with her and how, because of her greedy wish, her daughter Hazel had been born with a curse. Hazel could summon riches from the earth, but anyone who used them would suffer and die.

Now this goddess was saying that *she* had made all that happen.

'My mother suffered because of that magic. My whole life –'

'Your life wouldn't have happened without me,' Hecate said flatly. 'I have no time for your anger. Neither do you. Without my help, you will die.'

The black dog snarled. The polecat snapped its teeth and passed gas.

Hazel felt like her lungs were filling with hot sand.

'What kind of help?' she demanded.

Hecate raised her pale arms. The three gateways she'd come from – north, east and west – began to swirl with Mist. A flurry of black-and-white images glowed and flickered, like the old silent movies that were still playing in theatres when Hazel was small.

In the western doorway, Roman and Greek demigods in full armour fought one another on a hillside under a large pine tree. The grass was strewn with the wounded and the dying. Hazel saw herself riding Arion, charging through the melee and shouting – trying to stop the violence.

In the gateway to the east, Hazel saw the *Argo II* plunging through the sky above the Apennines. Its rigging was in flames. A boulder smashed into the quarterdeck. Another punched through the hull. The ship burst like a rotten pumpkin, and the engine exploded.

The images in the northern doorway were even worse. Hazel saw Leo, unconscious – or dead – falling through the clouds. She saw Frank staggering alone down a dark tunnel, clutching his arm, his shirt soaked in blood. And Hazel saw herself in a vast cavern filled with strands of light like a luminous web. She was struggling to break through while, in the distance, Percy and Annabeth lay sprawled and unmoving at the foot of two black-and-silver metal doors.

'Choices,' said Hecate. 'You stand at the crossroads, Hazel Levesque. And I am the goddess of crossroads.'

The ground rumbled at Hazel's feet. She looked down and saw the glint of silver coins . . . thousands of old Roman denarii breaking the surface all around her, as if the entire hilltop was coming to a boil. She'd been so agitated by the visions in the doorways that she must have summoned every bit of silver in the surrounding countryside.

'The past is close to the surface in this place,' Hecate said. 'In ancient times, two great Roman roads met here. News was exchanged. Markets were held. Friends met, and enemies fought. Entire armies had to choose a direction. Crossroads are always places of decision.'

'Like . . . like Janus.' Hazel remembered the shrine of Janus on Temple Hill back at Camp Jupiter. Demigods would go there to make decisions. They would flip a coin, heads or tails, and hope the two-faced god would guide them well. Hazel had always hated that place. She'd never understood why her friends were so willing to let a god take away their responsibility for choosing. After all Hazel had been through, she trusted the wisdom of the gods about as much as she trusted a New Orleans slot machine.

The goddess of magic made a disgusted hiss. 'Janus and his doorways. He would have you believe that all choices are black or white, yes or no, in or out. In fact, it's not that simple. Whenever you reach the crossroads, there are always at least *three* ways to go . . . four, if you count going backwards. You are at such a crossing now, Hazel.'

Hazel looked again at each swirling gateway: a demigod war, the destruction of the *Argo II*, disaster for herself and her friends. 'All the choices are bad.'

'All choices have risks,' the goddess corrected. 'But what is your goal?'

'My goal?' Hazel waved helplessly at the doorways. 'None of these.'

The dog Hecuba snarled. Gale the polecat skittered around the goddess's feet, farting and gnashing her teeth.

'You could go backwards,' Hecate suggested, 'retrace your steps to Rome . . . but Gaia's forces are expecting that. None of you will survive.'

'So . . . what are you saying?'

Hecate stepped to the nearest torch. She scooped a handful of fire and sculpted the flames until she was holding a miniature relief map of Italy.

'You could go west.' Hecate let her finger drift away from her fiery map. 'Go back to America with your prize, the Athena Parthenos. Your comrades back home, Greek and Roman, are on the brink of war. Leave now, and you might save many lives.'

'*Might*,' Hazel repeated. 'But Gaia is supposed to wake in Greece. That's where the giants are gathering.'

'True. Gaia has set the date of August first, the Feast of Spes, goddess of hope, for her rise to power. By waking on the Day of Hope, she intends to destroy all hope forever. Even if you reached Greece by then, could you stop her? I do not know.' Hecate traced her finger along the tops of the fiery Apennines. 'You could go east, across the mountains, but Gaia will do anything to stop you from crossing Italy. She has raised her mountain gods against you.'

'We noticed,' Hazel said.

'Any attempt to cross the Apennines will mean the

destruction of your ship. Ironically, this might be the *safest* option for your crew. I foresee that all of you would survive the explosion. It is possible, though unlikely, that you could still reach Epirus and close the Doors of Death. You might find Gaia and prevent her rise. But by then both demigod camps would be destroyed. You would have no home to return to.' Hecate smiled. 'More likely, the destruction of your ship would strand you in the mountains. It would mean the end of your quest, but it would spare you and your friends much pain and suffering in the days to come. The war with the giants would have to be won or lost without you.'

Won or lost without us.

A small guilty part of Hazel found that appealing. She'd been wishing for the chance to be a normal girl. She didn't want any more pain or suffering for herself and her friends. They'd already been through so much.

She looked behind Hecate at the middle gateway. She saw Percy and Annabeth sprawled helplessly before those black-and-silver doors. A massive dark shape, vaguely humanoid, now loomed over them, its foot raised as if to crush Percy.

'What about them?' Hazel asked, her voice ragged. 'Percy and Annabeth?'

Hecate shrugged. 'West, east or south . . . they die.'

'Not an option,' Hazel said.

'Then you have only one path, though it is the most dangerous.'

Hecate's finger crossed her miniature Apennines, leaving

a glowing white line in the red flames. 'There is a secret pass here in the north, a place where I hold sway, where Hannibal once crossed when he marched against Rome.'

The goddess made a wide loop . . . to the top of Italy, then east to the sea, then down along the western coast of Greece. 'Once through the pass, you would travel north to Bologna and then to Venice. From there, sail the Adriatic to your goal, here: Epirus in Greece.'

Hazel didn't know much about geography. She had no idea what the Adriatic Sea was like. She'd never heard of Bologna, and all she knew about Venice was vague stories about canals and gondolas. But one thing was obvious. 'That's so far out of the way.'

'Which is why Gaia will not expect you to take this route,' Hecate said. 'I can obscure your progress somewhat, but the success of your journey will depend on you, Hazel Levesque. You must learn to use the Mist.'

'Me?' Hazel's heart felt like it was tumbling down her rib cage. 'Use the Mist how?'

Hecate extinguished her map of Italy. She flicked her hand at the black dog Hecuba. Mist collected around the Labrador until she was completely hidden in a cocoon of white. The fog cleared with an audible *poof!* Where the dog had stood was a disgruntled-looking black kitten with golden eyes.

'Mew,' it complained.

'I am the goddess of the Mist,' Hecate explained. 'I am responsible for keeping the veil that separates the world of the gods from the world of mortals. My children learn to use the Mist to their advantage, to create illusions or influence the minds of mortals. Other demigods can do this as well. And so must you, Hazel, if you are to help your friends.'

'But . . .' Hazel looked at the cat. She knew it was actually Hecuba, the black Labrador, but she couldn't convince herself. The cat seemed so real. 'I can't do that.'

'Your mother had the talent,' Hecate said. 'You have even more. As a child of Pluto who has returned from the dead, you understand the veil between worlds better than most. You *can* control the Mist. If you do not . . . well, your brother Nico has already warned you. The spirits have whispered to him, told him of your future. When you reach the House of Hades, you will meet a formidable enemy. She cannot be overcome by strength or sword. You alone can defeat her, and you will require magic.'

Hazel's legs felt wobbly. She remembered Nico's grim expression, his fingers digging into her arm. *You can't tell the others. Not yet. Their courage is already stretched to the limit.*

'Who?' Hazel croaked. 'Who is this enemy?'

'I will not speak her name,' Hecate said. 'That would alert her to your presence before you are ready to face her. Go north, Hazel. As you travel, practise summoning the Mist. When you arrive in Bologna, seek out the two dwarfs. They will lead you to a treasure that may help you survive in the House of Hades.'

'I don't understand.'

'Mew,' the kitten complained.

'Yes, yes, Hecuba.' The goddess flicked her hand again,

and the cat disappeared. The black Labrador was back in its place.

'You *will* understand, Hazel,' the goddess promised. 'From time to time, I will send Gale to check on your progress.'

The polecat hissed, its beady red eyes full of malice.

'Wonderful,' Hazel muttered.

'Before you reach Epirus, you must be prepared,' Hecate said. 'If you succeed, then perhaps we will meet again . . . for the final battle.'

A final battle, Hazel thought. Oh, joy.

Hazel wondered if she could prevent the revelations she saw in the Mist – Leo falling through the sky; Frank stumbling through the dark, alone and gravely wounded; Percy and Annabeth at the mercy of a dark giant.

She hated the gods' riddles and their unclear advice. She was starting to despise crossroads.

'Why are you helping me?' Hazel demanded. 'At Camp Jupiter, they said you sided with the *Titans* in the last war.'

Hecate's dark eyes glinted. 'Because I *am* a Titan – daughter of Perses and Asteria. Long before the Olympians came to power, I ruled the Mist. Despite this, in the First Titan War, millennia ago, I sided with Zeus against Kronos. I was not blind to Kronos's cruelty. I hoped Zeus would prove a better king.'

She gave a small, bitter laugh. 'When Demeter lost her daughter Persephone, kidnapped by *your* father, I guided Demeter through the darkest night with my torches, helping her search. And when the giants rose the first time I again sided with the gods. I fought my arch-enemy Clytius, made by Gaia to absorb and defeat all my magic.'

'Clytius.' Hazel had never heard that name – *Clai-tee-us* – but saying it made her limbs feel heavy. She glanced at the images in the northern doorway – the massive dark shape looming over Percy and Annabeth. 'Is he the threat in the House of Hades?'

'Oh, he waits for you there,' Hecate said. 'But first you must defeat the witch. Unless you manage that . . .'

She snapped her fingers, and all of the gateways turned dark. The Mist dissolved, the images gone.

'We all face choices,' the goddess said. 'When Kronos arose the second time, I made a mistake. I supported him. I had grown tired of being ignored by the so-called *major* gods. Despite my years of faithful service, they mistrusted me, refused me a seat in their hall . . .'

The polecat Gale chittered angrily.

'It does not matter any more.' The goddess sighed. 'I have made peace again with Olympus. Even now, when they are laid low – their Greek and Roman personas fighting each other – I will help them. Greek or Roman, I have always been only Hecate. I will assist you against the giants, if you prove yourself worthy. So now it is your choice, Hazel Levesque. Will you trust me . . . or will you shun me, as the Olympian gods have done too often?'

Blood roared in Hazel's ears. Could she trust this dark goddess, who'd given her mother the magic that ruined her life? Sorry, no. She didn't much like Hecate's dog nor her gassy polecat either.

But she also knew she couldn't let Percy and Annabeth die.

'I'll go north,' she said. 'We'll take your secret pass through the mountains.'

Hecate nodded, the slightest hint of satisfaction in her face. 'You have chosen well, though the path will not be easy. Many monsters will rise against you. Even some of my *own* servants have sided with Gaia, hoping to destroy your mortal world.'

The goddess took her double torches from their stands. 'Prepare yourself, daughter of Pluto. If you succeed against the witch, we will meet again.'

'I'll succeed,' Hazel promised. 'And Hecate? I'm not choosing one of your paths. I'm making my own.'

The goddess arched her eyebrows. Her polecat writhed, and her dog snarled.

'We're going to find a way to stop Gaia,' Hazel said. 'We're going to rescue our friends from Tartarus. We're going keep the crew and the ship together *and* we're going to stop Camp Jupiter and Camp Half-Blood from going to war. We're going to do it all.'

The storm howled, the black walls of the funnel cloud swirling faster.

'Interesting,' Hecate said, as if Hazel were an unexpected result in a science experiment. 'That would be magic worth seeing.'

A wave of darkness blotted out the world. When Hazel's sight returned, the storm, the goddess and her minions were gone. Hazel stood on the hillside in the morning sunlight, alone in the ruins except for Arion, who paced next to her, nickering impatiently.

'I agree,' Hazel told the horse. 'Let's get out of here.'

'What happened?' Leo asked as Hazel climbed aboard the *Argo II*.

Hazel's hands still shook from her talk with the goddess. She glanced over the rail and saw the dust of Arion's wake stretching across the hills of Italy. She had hoped her friend would stay, but couldn't blame him for wanting to get away from this place as fast as possible.

The countryside sparkled as the summer sun hit the morning dew. On the hill, the old ruins stood white and silent – no sign of ancient paths, or goddesses, or farting weasels.

'Hazel?' Nico asked.

Her knees buckled. Nico and Leo grabbed her arms and helped her to the steps of the foredeck. She felt embarrassed, collapsing like some fairy-tale damsel, but her energy was gone. The memory of those glowing scenes at the crossroads filled her with dread.

'I met Hecate,' she managed.

She didn't tell them everything. She remembered what Nico had said: *Their courage is already stretched to the limit.* But she told them about the secret northern pass through the mountains, and the detour Hecate had described that could take them to Epirus.

When she was done, Nico took her hand. His eyes were full of concern. 'Hazel, you met Hecate at a crossroads. That's . . .

that's something many demigods don't survive. And the ones who *do* survive are never the same. Are you sure you're –'

'I'm fine,' she insisted.

But she knew she wasn't. She remembered how bold and angry she'd felt, telling the goddess she'd find her own path and succeed at everything. Now her boast seemed ridiculous. Her courage had abandoned her.

'What if Hecate is tricking us?' Leo asked. 'This route could be a trap.'

Hazel shook her head. 'If it was a trap, I think Hecate would've made the northern route sound tempting. Believe me, she didn't.'

Leo pulled a calculator out of his tool belt and punched in some numbers. 'That's . . . something like three hundred miles out of our way to get to Venice. Then we'd have to backtrack down the Adriatic. And you said something about baloney dwarfs?'

'Dwarfs in Bologna,' Hazel said. 'I guess Bologna is a city. But why we have to find dwarfs there . . . I have no idea. Some sort of treasure to help us with the quest.'

'Huh,' Leo said. 'I mean, I'm all about treasure, but –'

'It's our best option.' Nico helped Hazel to her feet. 'We have to make up for lost time, travel as fast as we can. Percy's and Annabeth's lives might depend on it.'

'Fast?' Leo grinned. 'I can do fast.'

He hurried to the console and started flipping switches.

Nico took Hazel's arm and guided her out of earshot. 'What else did Hecate say? Anything about –'

'I can't.' Hazel cut him off. The images she'd seen had

almost overwhelmed her: Percy and Annabeth helpless at the feet of those black metal doors, the dark giant looming over them, Hazel herself trapped in a glowing maze of light, unable to help.

You must defeat the witch, Hecate had said. *You alone can defeat her. Unless you manage that . . .*

The end, Hazel thought. All gateways closed. All hope extinguished.

Nico had warned her. He'd communed with the dead, heard them whispering hints about their future. Two children of the Underworld would enter the House of Hades. They would face an impossible foe. Only one of them would make it to the Doors of Death.

Hazel couldn't meet her brother's eyes.

'I'll tell you later,' she promised, trying to keep her voice from trembling. 'Right now, we should rest while we can. Tonight, we cross the Apennines.'

V

ANNABETH

Nine days.

As she fell, Annabeth thought about Hesiod, the old Greek poet who'd speculated it would take nine days to fall from earth to Tartarus.

She hoped Hesiod was wrong. She'd lost track of how long she and Percy had been falling – hours? A day? It felt like an eternity. They'd been holding hands ever since they'd dropped into the chasm. Now Percy pulled her close, hugging her tight as they tumbled through absolute darkness.

Wind whistled in Annabeth's ears. The air grew hotter and damper, as if they were plummeting into the throat of a massive dragon. Her recently broken ankle throbbed, though she couldn't tell if it was still wrapped in spiderwebs.

That cursed monster Arachne. Despite having been trapped in her own webbing, smashed by a car and plunged into Tartarus, the spider lady had got her revenge. Somehow her silk had entangled Annabeth's leg and dragged her over the side of the pit, with Percy in tow.

Annabeth couldn't imagine that Arachne was still alive, somewhere below them in the darkness. She didn't want to meet that monster again when they reached the bottom. On the bright side, assuming there *was* a bottom, Annabeth and Percy would probably be flattened on impact, so giant spiders were the least of their worries.

She wrapped her arms around Percy and tried not to sob. She'd never expected her life to be easy. Most demigods died young at the hands of terrible monsters. That was the way it had been since ancient times. The Greeks *invented* tragedy. They knew the greatest heroes didn't get happy endings.

Still, this wasn't *fair*. She'd gone through so much to retrieve that statue of Athena. Just when she'd succeeded, when things had been looking up and she'd been reunited with Percy, they had plunged to their deaths.

Even the gods couldn't devise a fate so twisted.

But Gaia wasn't like other gods. The Earth Mother was older, more vicious, more bloodthirsty. Annabeth could imagine her laughing as they fell into the depths.

Annabeth pressed her lips to Percy's ear. 'I love you.'

She wasn't sure he could hear her – but if they were going to die she wanted those to be her last words.

She tried desperately to think of a plan to save them. She was a daughter of Athena. She'd proven herself in the tunnels under Rome, beaten a whole series of challenges with only her wits. But she couldn't think of any way to reverse or even slow their fall.

Neither of them had the power to fly – not like Jason, who could control the wind, or Frank, who could turn into a winged animal. If they reached the bottom at terminal velocity . . . well, she knew enough science to know it would be *terminal*.

She was seriously wondering whether they could fashion a parachute out of their shirts – *that's* how desperate she was – when something about their surroundings changed. The darkness took on a grey-red tinge. She realized she could see Percy's hair as she hugged him. The whistling in her ears turned into more of a roar. The air became intolerably hot, permeated with a smell like rotten eggs.

Suddenly, the chute they'd been falling through opened into a vast cavern. Maybe half a mile below them, Annabeth could see the bottom. For a moment she was too stunned to think properly. The entire island of Manhattan could have fitted inside this cavern – and she couldn't even see its full extent. Red clouds hung in the air like vaporized blood. The landscape – at least what she could see of it – was rocky black plains, punctuated by jagged mountains and fiery chasms. To Annabeth's left, the ground dropped away in a series of cliffs, like colossal steps leading deeper into the abyss.

The stench of sulphur made it hard to concentrate, but she focused on the ground directly below them and saw a ribbon of glittering black liquid – a *river*.

'Percy!' she yelled in his ear. 'Water!'

She gestured frantically. Percy's face was hard to read in the dim red light. He looked shell-shocked and terrified, but he nodded as if he understood.

Percy could control water – assuming that *was* water below them. He might be able to cushion their fall somehow. Of course Annabeth had heard horrible stories about the rivers of the Underworld. They could take away your memories, or burn your body and soul to ashes. But she decided not to think about that. This was their only chance.

The river hurtled towards them. At the last second, Percy yelled defiantly. The water erupted in a massive geyser and swallowed them whole.

VI

ANNABETH

THE IMPACT DIDN'T KILL HER, but the cold nearly did.

Freezing water shocked the air right out of her lungs. Her limbs turned rigid, and she lost her grip on Percy. She began to sink. Strange wailing sounds filled her ears – millions of heartbroken voices, as if the river were made of distilled sadness. The voices were worse than the cold. They weighed her down and made her numb.

What's the point of struggling? they told her. *You're dead anyway. You'll never leave this place.*

She could sink to the bottom and drown, let the river carry her body away. That would be easier. She could just close her eyes . . .

Percy gripped her hand and jolted her back to reality. She couldn't see him in the murky water, but suddenly she didn't want to die. Together they kicked upward and broke the surface.

Annabeth gasped, grateful for the air, no matter how

sulphurous. The water swirled around them, and she realized Percy was creating a whirlpool to buoy them up.

Though she couldn't make out their surroundings, she knew this was a river. Rivers had shores.

'Land,' she croaked. 'Go sideways.'

Percy looked near dead with exhaustion. Usually water reinvigorated him, but not *this* water. Controlling it must have taken every bit of his strength. The whirlpool began to dissipate. Annabeth hooked one arm around his waist and struggled across the current. The river worked against her: thousands of weeping voices whispering in her ears, getting inside her brain.

Life is despair, they said. *Everything is pointless, and then you die.*

'Pointless,' Percy murmured. His teeth chattered from the cold. He stopped swimming and began to sink.

'Percy!' she shrieked. 'The river is messing with your mind. It's the Cocytus – the River of Lamentation. It's made of pure misery!'

'Misery,' he agreed.

'Fight it!'

She kicked and struggled, trying to keep both of them afloat. Another cosmic joke for Gaia to laugh at: *Annabeth dies trying to keep her boyfriend, the son of Poseidon, from drowning.*

Not going to happen, you hag, Annabeth thought.

She hugged Percy tighter and kissed him. 'Tell me about New Rome,' she demanded. 'What were your plans for us?'

'New Rome . . . For us . . .'

'Yeah, Seaweed Brain. You said we could have a future there! Tell me!'

Annabeth had never wanted to leave Camp Half-Blood. It was the only real home she'd ever known. But days ago, on the *Argo II*, Percy had told her that he imagined a future for the two of them among the Roman demigods. In their city of New Rome, veterans of the legion could settle down safely, go to college, get married, even have kids.

'Architecture,' Percy murmured. The fog started to clear from his eyes. 'Thought you'd like the houses, the parks. There's one street with all these cool fountains.'

Annabeth started making progress against the current. Her limbs felt like bags of wet sand, but Percy was helping her now. She could see the dark line of the shore about a stone's throw away.

'College,' she gasped. 'Could we go there together?'

'Y-yeah,' he agreed, a little more confidently.

'What would you study, Percy?'

'Dunno,' he admitted.

'Marine science,' she suggested. 'Oceanography?'

'Surfing?' he asked.

She laughed, and the sound sent a shock wave through the water. The wailing faded to background noise. Annabeth wondered if anyone had ever laughed in Tartarus before – just a pure, simple laugh of pleasure. She doubted it.

She used the last of her strength to reach the riverbank. Her feet dug into the sandy bottom. She and Percy hauled themselves ashore, shivering and gasping, and collapsed on the dark sand.

Annabeth wanted to curl up next to Percy and go to sleep. She wanted to shut her eyes, hope all of this was just a bad dream and wake up to find herself back on the *Argo II*, safe with her friends (well . . . as safe as a demigod can ever be).

But, no. They were really in Tartarus. At their feet, the River Cocytus roared past, a flood of liquid wretchedness. The sulphurous air stung Annabeth's lungs and prickled her skin. When she looked at her arms, she saw they were already covered with an angry rash. She tried to sit up and gasped in pain.

The beach wasn't sand. They were sitting on a field of jagged black-glass chips, some of which were now embedded in Annabeth's palms.

So the air was acid. The water was misery. The ground was broken glass. Everything here was designed to hurt and kill. Annabeth took a rattling breath and wondered if the voices in the Cocytus were right. Maybe fighting for survival was pointless. They would be dead within the hour.

Next to her, Percy coughed. 'This place smells like my ex-stepfather.'

Annabeth managed a weak smile. She'd never met Smelly Gabe, but she'd heard enough stories. She loved Percy for trying to lift her spirits.

If she'd fallen into Tartarus by herself, Annabeth thought, she would have been doomed. After all she'd been through beneath Rome, finding the Athena Parthenos, this was simply too much. She would've curled up and cried until she became another ghost, melting into the Cocytus.

But she wasn't alone. She had Percy. And that meant she couldn't give up.

She forced herself to take stock. Her foot was still wrapped in its makeshift cast of board and bubble wrap, still tangled in cobwebs. But when she moved it, it didn't hurt. The ambrosia she'd eaten in the tunnels under Rome must have finally mended her bones.

Her backpack was gone – lost during the fall, or maybe washed away in the river. She hated losing Daedalus's laptop, with all its fantastic programs and data, but she had worse problems. Her Celestial bronze dagger was missing – the weapon she'd carried since she was seven years old.

The realization almost broke her, but she couldn't let herself dwell on it. Time to grieve later. What else did they have?

No food, no water . . . basically no supplies at all.

Yep. Off to a promising start.

Annabeth glanced at Percy. He looked pretty bad. His dark hair was plastered across his forehead, his T-shirt ripped to shreds. His fingers were scraped raw from holding on to that ledge before they fell. Most worrisome of all, he was shivering and his lips were blue.

'We should keep moving or we'll get hypothermia,' Annabeth said. 'Can you stand?'

He nodded. They both struggled to their feet.

Annabeth put her arm around his waist, though she wasn't sure who was supporting whom. She scanned their surroundings. Above, she saw no sign of the tunnel they'd fallen down. She couldn't even see the cavern roof – just blood-coloured clouds floating in the hazy grey air. It was like staring through a thin mix of tomato soup and cement.

The black-glass beach stretched inland about fifty yards, then dropped off the edge of a cliff. From where she stood, Annabeth couldn't see what was below, but the edge flickered with red light as if illuminated by huge fires.

A distant memory tugged at her – something about Tartarus and fire. Before she could think too much about it, Percy inhaled sharply.

'Look.' He pointed downstream.

A hundred feet away, a familiar-looking baby-blue Italian car had crashed headfirst into the sand. It looked just like the Fiat that had smashed into Arachne and sent her plummeting into the pit.

Annabeth hoped she was wrong, but how many Italian sports cars could there be in Tartarus? Part of her didn't want to go anywhere near it, but she had to find out. She gripped Percy's hand, and they stumbled towards the wreckage. One of the car's tyres had come off and was floating in a backwater eddy of the Cocytus. The Fiat's windows had shattered, sending brighter glass like frosting across the dark beach. Under the crushed hood lay the tattered, glistening remains of a giant silk cocoon – the trap that Annabeth had tricked Arachne into weaving. It was unmistakably empty. Slash marks in the sand made a trail downriver . . . as if something heavy, with multiple legs, had scuttled into the darkness.

'She's alive.' Annabeth was so horrified, so outraged by the unfairness of it all, she had to suppress the urge to throw up.

'It's Tartarus,' Percy said. 'Monster home court. Down here, maybe they can't be killed.'

He gave Annabeth an embarrassed look, as if realizing he wasn't helping team morale. 'Or maybe she's badly wounded, and she crawled away to die.'

'Let's go with that,' Annabeth agreed.

Percy was still shivering. Annabeth wasn't feeling any warmer either, despite the hot, sticky air. The glass cuts on her hands were still bleeding, which was unusual for her. Normally, she healed fast. Her breathing got more and more laboured.

'This place is killing us,' she said. 'I mean, it's *literally* going to kill us, unless . . .'

Tartarus. Fire. That distant memory came into focus. She gazed inland towards the cliff, illuminated by flames from below.

It was an absolutely crazy idea. But it might be their only chance.

'Unless what?' Percy prompted. 'You've got a brilliant plan, haven't you?'

'It's a plan,' Annabeth murmured. 'I don't know about brilliant. We need to find the River of Fire.'

VII

ANNABETH

WHEN THEY REACHED THE LEDGE, Annabeth was sure she'd signed their death warrants.

The cliff dropped more than eighty feet. At the bottom stretched a nightmarish version of the Grand Canyon: a river of fire cutting a path through a jagged obsidian crevasse, the glowing red current casting horrible shadows across the cliff faces.

Even from the top of the canyon, the heat was intense. The chill of the River Cocytus hadn't left Annabeth's bones, but now her face felt raw and sunburnt. Every breath took more effort, as if her chest were filled with styrofoam peanuts. The cuts on her hands bled more rather than less. Annabeth's ankle, which had almost healed, now seemed to be broken again. She'd taken off her makeshift cast, but now she regretted it. Each step made her wince.

Assuming they could make it down to the fiery river, which she doubted, her plan seemed certifiably insane.

'Uh . . .' Percy examined the cliff. He pointed to a tiny fissure running diagonally from the edge to the bottom. 'We can try that ledge there. Might be able to climb down.'

He didn't say they'd be crazy to try. He managed to sound hopeful. Annabeth was grateful for that, but she also worried that she was leading him to his doom.

Of course if they stayed here they would die anyway. Blisters had started to form on their arms from exposure to the Tartarus air. The whole environment was about as healthy as a nuclear blast zone.

Percy went first. The ledge was barely wide enough to allow a toehold. Their hands clawed for any crack in the glassy rock. Every time Annabeth put pressure on her bad foot, she wanted to yelp. She'd ripped off the sleeves of her T-shirt and used the cloth to wrap her bloody palms, but her fingers were still slippery and weak.

A few steps below her, Percy grunted as he reached for another handhold. 'So . . . what is this fire river called?'

'The Phlegethon,' she said. 'You should concentrate on going down.'

'The *Phlegethon*?' He shinned along the ledge. They'd made it roughly a third of the way down the cliff – still high enough up to die if they fell. 'Sounds like a marathon for hawking spitballs.'

'Please don't make me laugh,' she said.

'Just trying to keep things light.'

'Thanks,' she grunted, nearly missing the ledge with her bad foot. 'I'll have a smile on my face as I plummet to my death.'

They kept going, one step at a time. Annabeth's eyes stung with sweat. Her arms trembled. But, to her amazement, they finally made it to the bottom of the cliff.

When she reached the ground, she stumbled. Percy caught her. She was alarmed by how feverish his skin felt. Red boils had erupted on his face, so he looked like a smallpox victim.

Her own vision was blurry. Her throat felt blistered, and her stomach was clenched tighter than a fist.

We have to hurry, she thought.

'Just to the river,' she told Percy, trying to keep the panic out of her voice. 'We can do this.'

They staggered over slick glass ledges, around massive boulders, avoiding stalagmites that would've impaled them with any slip of the foot. Their tattered clothes steamed from the heat of the river, but they kept going until they crumpled to their knees at the banks of the Phlegethon.

'We have to drink,' Annabeth said.

Percy swayed, his eyes half-closed. It took him three counts to respond. 'Uh . . . drink fire?'

'The Phlegethon flows from Hades's realm down into Tartarus.' Annabeth could barely talk. Her throat was closing up from the heat and the acidic air. 'The river is used to punish the wicked. But also . . . some legends call it the River of Healing.'

'*Some* legends?'

Annabeth swallowed, trying to stay conscious. 'The Phlegethon keeps the wicked in one piece so that they can endure the torments of the Fields of Punishment. I think . . . it might be the Underworld equivalent of ambrosia and nectar.'

Percy winced as cinders sprayed from the river, curling around his face. 'But it's fire. How can we –'

'Like this.' Annabeth thrust her hands into the river.

Stupid? Yes, but she was convinced they had no choice. If they waited any longer, they would pass out and die. Better to try something foolish and hope it worked.

On first contact, the fire wasn't painful. It felt cold, which probably meant it was *so* hot it was overloading Annabeth's nerves. Before she could change her mind, she cupped the fiery liquid in her palms and raised it to her mouth.

She expected a taste like gasoline. It was *so* much worse. Once, at a restaurant back in San Francisco, she'd made the mistake of tasting a ghost chilli pepper that had come with a plate of Indian food. After barely nibbling it, she'd thought her respiratory system was going to implode. Drinking from the Phlegethon was like gulping down a ghost chilli smoothie. Her sinuses filled with liquid flame. Her mouth felt like it was being deep-fried. Her eyes shed boiling tears, and every pore on her face popped. She collapsed, gagging and retching, her whole body shaking violently.

'Annabeth!' Percy grabbed her arms and just managed to stop her from rolling into the river.

The convulsions passed. She took a ragged breath and managed to sit up. She felt horribly weak and nauseous, but her next breath came more easily. The blisters on her arms were starting to fade.

'It worked,' she croaked. 'Percy, you've got to drink.'

'I . . .' His eyes rolled up in his head, and he slumped against her.

Desperately, she cupped more fire in her palm. Ignoring the pain, she dripped the liquid into Percy's mouth. He didn't respond.

She tried again, pouring a whole handful down his throat. This time he spluttered and coughed. Annabeth held him as he trembled, the magical fire coursing through his system. His fever disappeared. His boils faded. He managed to sit up and smack his lips.

'Ugh,' he said. 'Spicy, yet disgusting.'

Annabeth laughed weakly. She was so relieved she felt light-headed. 'Yeah. That pretty much sums it up.'

'You saved us.'

'For now,' she said. 'The problem is we're still in Tartarus.'

Percy blinked. He looked around as if just coming to terms with where they were. 'Holy Hera. I never thought . . . well, I'm not sure *what* I thought. Maybe that Tartarus was empty space, a pit with no bottom. But this is a *real* place.'

Annabeth recalled the landscape she'd seen while they fell – a series of plateaus leading ever downwards into the gloom.

'We haven't seen all of it,' she warned. 'This could be just the first tiny part of the abyss, like the front steps.'

'The welcome mat,' Percy muttered.

They both gazed up at the blood-coloured clouds swirling in the grey haze. No way would they have the strength to climb back up that cliff, even if they wanted to. Now there were only two choices: downriver or upriver, skirting the banks of the Phlegethon.

'We'll find a way out,' Percy said. 'The Doors of Death.'

Annabeth shuddered. She remembered what Percy had said just before they fell into Tartarus. He'd made Nico di Angelo promise to lead the *Argo II* to Epirus, to the mortal side of the Doors of Death.

We'll see you there, Percy had said.

That idea seemed even crazier than drinking fire. How could the two of them wander through Tartarus and find the Doors of Death? They'd barely been able to stumble a hundred yards in this poisonous place without dying.

'We have to,' Percy said. 'Not just for us. For everybody we love. The Doors have to be closed on both sides, or the monsters will just keep coming through. Gaia's forces will overrun the world.'

Annabeth knew he was right. Still . . . when she tried to imagine a plan that could succeed, the logistics overwhelmed her. They had no way of locating the Doors. They didn't know how much time it would take, or even if time flowed at the same speed in Tartarus. How could they possibly synchronize a meeting with their friends? And Nico had mentioned a legion of Gaia's strongest monsters guarding the Doors on the Tartarus side. Annabeth and Percy couldn't exactly launch a frontal assault.

She decided not to mention any of that. They both knew the odds were bad. Besides, after swimming in the River Cocytus, Annabeth had heard enough whining and moaning to last a lifetime. She promised herself never to complain again.

'Well.' She took a deep breath, grateful at least that her

lungs didn't hurt. 'If we stay close to the river, we'll have a way to heal ourselves. If we go downstream –'

It happened so fast that Annabeth would have been dead if she'd been on her own.

Percy's eyes locked on something behind her. Annabeth spun as a massive dark shape hurtled down at her – a snarling, monstrous blob with spindly barbed legs and glinting eyes.

She had time to think: *Arachne.* But she was frozen in terror, her senses smothered by the sickly sweet smell.

Then she heard the familiar *SHINK* of Percy's ballpoint pen transforming into a sword. His blade swept over her head in a glowing bronze arc. A horrible wail echoed through the canyon.

Annabeth stood there, stunned, as yellow dust – the remains of Arachne – rained around her like tree pollen.

'You okay?' Percy scanned the cliffs and boulders, alert for more monsters, but nothing else appeared. The golden dust of the spider settled on the obsidian rocks.

Annabeth stared at her boyfriend in amazement. Riptide's Celestial bronze blade glowed even brighter in the gloom of Tartarus. As it passed through the thick hot air, it made a defiant hiss like a riled snake.

'She . . . she would've killed me,' Annabeth stammered.

Percy kicked the dust on the rocks, his expression grim and dissatisfied. 'She died too easily, considering how much torture she put you through. She deserved worse.'

Annabeth couldn't argue with that, but the hard edge in Percy's voice made her unsettled. She'd never seen someone get so angry or vengeful on her behalf. It almost made her glad Arachne had died quickly. 'How did you move so fast?'

Percy shrugged. 'Gotta watch each other's backs, right? Now, you were saying . . . downstream?'

Annabeth nodded, still in a daze. The yellow dust dissipated on the rocky shore, turning to steam. At least now they knew that monsters could be killed in Tartarus . . . though she had no idea how long Arachne would remain dead. Annabeth didn't plan on staying long enough to find out.

'Yeah, downstream,' she managed. 'If the river comes from the upper levels of the Underworld, it should flow deeper into Tartarus –'

'So it leads into more dangerous territory,' Percy finished. 'Which is probably where the Doors are. Lucky us.'

VIII

ANNABETH

THEY'D ONLY TRAVELLED a few hundred yards when Annabeth heard voices.

Annabeth plodded along, half in a stupor, trying to form a plan. Since she was a daughter of Athena, plans were supposed to be her speciality, but it was hard to strategize with her stomach growling and her throat baking. The fiery water of the Phlegethon may have healed her and given her strength, but it hadn't done anything for her hunger or thirst. The river wasn't about making you feel good, Annabeth guessed. It just kept you going so you could experience more excruciating pain.

Her head started to droop with exhaustion. Then she heard them – female voices having some sort of argument – and she was instantly alert.

She whispered, 'Percy, down!'

She pulled him behind the nearest boulder, wedging

herself so close against the riverbank that her shoes almost touched the river's fire. On the other side, on the narrow path between the river and the cliffs, voices snarled, getting louder as they approached from upstream.

Annabeth tried to steady her breathing. The voices sounded vaguely human, but that meant nothing. She assumed anything in Tartarus was their enemy. She didn't know how the monsters could have failed to spot them already. Besides, monsters could *smell* demigods – especially powerful ones like Percy, son of Poseidon. Annabeth doubted that hiding behind a boulder would do any good when the monsters caught their scent.

Still, as the monsters got nearer, their voices didn't change in tone. Their uneven footsteps – *scrap, clump, scrap, clump* – didn't get any faster.

'Soon?' one of them asked in a raspy voice, as if she'd been gargling in the Phlegethon.

'Oh my gods!' said another voice. This one sounded much younger and much more human, like a teenaged mortal girl getting exasperated with her friends at the mall. For some reason, she sounded familiar to Annabeth. 'You guys are *totally* annoying! I told you, it's like three *days* from here.'

Percy gripped Annabeth's wrist. He looked at her with alarm, as if he recognized the mall girl's voice too.

There was a chorus of growling and grumbling. The creatures – maybe half a dozen, Annabeth guessed – had paused just on the other side of the boulder, but still they gave no indication that they'd caught the demigods' scent.

Annabeth wondered if demigods didn't smell the same in Tartarus, or if the other scents here were so powerful they masked a demigod's aura.

'I wonder,' said a third voice, gravelly and ancient like the first, 'if perhaps you do not know the way, young one.'

'Oh, shut your fang hole, Serephone,' said the mall girl. 'When's the last time *you* escaped to the mortal world? I was there a couple of years ago. I know the way! Besides, *I* understand what we're facing up there. You don't have a clue!'

'The Earth Mother did not make you boss!' shrieked a fourth voice.

More hissing, scuffling and feral moans – like giant alley cats fighting. At last the one called Serephone yelled, 'Enough!'

The scuffling died down.

'We will follow for now,' Serephone said. 'But if you do *not* lead us well, if we find you have *lied* about the summons of Gaia –'

'I don't lie!' snapped the mall girl. 'Believe me, I've got good reason to get into this battle. I have some enemies to devour, and you'll feast on the blood of heroes. Just leave one special morsel for me – the one named Percy Jackson.'

Annabeth fought down a snarl of her own. She forgot about her fear. She wanted to jump over the boulder and slash the monsters to dust with her knife . . . except she didn't have it any more.

'Believe me,' said the mall girl. 'Gaia has called us, and we're going to have *so* much fun. Before this war is over,

mortals and demigods will tremble at the sound of my name
– Kelli!'

Annabeth almost yelped aloud. She glanced at Percy. Even
in the red light of the Phlegethon, his face seemed waxy.

Empousai, she mouthed. *Vampires.*

Percy nodded grimly.

She remembered Kelli. Two years ago, at Percy's freshman
orientation, he and their friend Rachel Dare had been
attacked by *empousai* disguised as cheerleaders. One of them
had been Kelli. Later, the same *empousa* had attacked them in
Daedalus's workshop. Annabeth had stabbed her in the back
and sent her . . . here. To Tartarus.

The creatures shuffled off, their voices getting fainter.
Annabeth crept to the edge of the boulder and risked a
glimpse. Sure enough, five women staggered along on mismatched legs – mechanical bronze on the left, shaggy and
cloven-hooved on the right. Their hair was made of fire, their
skin as white as bone. Most of them wore tattered Ancient
Greek dresses, except for the one in the lead, Kelli, who wore
a burnt and torn blouse with a short pleated skirt . . . her
cheerleader's outfit.

Annabeth gritted her teeth. She had faced a lot of bad
monsters over the years, but she hated *empousai* more than
most.

In addition to their nasty claws and fangs, they had a
powerful ability to manipulate the Mist. They could change
shape and charmspeak, tricking mortals into letting down
their guard. Men were especially susceptible. The *empousa*'s

favourite tactic was to make a guy fall in love with her, then drink his blood and devour his flesh. Not a great first date.

Kelli had almost killed Percy. She had manipulated Annabeth's oldest friend, Luke, urging him to commit darker and darker deeds in the name of Kronos.

Annabeth *really* wished she still had her dagger.

Percy rose. 'They're heading for the Doors of Death,' he murmured. 'You know what that means?'

Annabeth didn't want to think about it, but sadly this squad of flesh-eating horror-show women might be the closest thing to good luck they were going to get in Tartarus.

'Yeah,' she said. 'We need to follow them.'

LEO

LEO SPENT THE NIGHT WRESTLING with a forty-foot-tall Athena.

Ever since they'd brought the statue aboard, Leo had been obsessed with figuring out how it worked. He was sure it had primo powers. There had to be a secret switch or a pressure plate or something.

He was supposed to be sleeping, but he just couldn't. He spent hours crawling over the statue, which took up most of the lower deck. Athena's feet stuck into sickbay, so you had to squeeze past her ivory toes if you wanted some painkillers. Her body ran the length of the port corridor, her outstretched hand jutting into the engine room, offering the life-sized figure of Nike that stood in her palm, like, *Here, have some Victory!* Athena's serene face took up most of the aft pegasus stables, which were fortunately unoccupied. If Leo were a magic horse, he wouldn't have wanted to live in a stall with an oversized goddess of wisdom staring at him.

The statue was wedged tight in the corridor, so Leo had to climb over the top and wriggle under her limbs, searching for levers and buttons.

As usual, he found nothing.

He'd done some research on the statue. He knew it was made from a hollow wooden frame covered in ivory and gold, which explained why it was so light. It was in pretty good shape, considering it was more than two thousand years old and had been pillaged from Athens, toted to Rome and secretly stored in a spider's cavern for most of the past two millennia. Magic must've kept it intact, Leo figured, combined with really good craftsmanship.

Annabeth had said . . . well, he tried not to think about Annabeth. He still felt guilty about her and Percy falling into Tartarus. Leo knew it was *his* fault. He should have got everyone safely on board the *Argo II* before he started securing the statue. He should have realized the cavern floor was unstable.

Still, moping around wasn't going to get Percy and Annabeth back. He had to concentrate on fixing the problems he could fix.

Anyway, Annabeth had said the statue was the key to defeating Gaia. It could heal the rift between Greek and Roman demigods. Leo figured there had to be more to it than just symbolism. Maybe Athena's eyes shot lasers, or the snake behind her shield could spit poison. Or maybe the smaller figure of Nike came to life and busted out some ninja moves.

Leo could think of all kinds of fun things the statue might do if *he* had designed it, but the more he examined it, the more frustrated he got. The Athena Parthenos radiated magic. Even *he* could feel that. But it didn't seem to do anything except look impressive.

The ship careened to one side, taking evasive manoeuvres. Leo resisted the urge to run to the helm. Jason, Piper and Frank were on duty with Hazel now. They could handle whatever was going on. Besides, Hazel had insisted on taking the wheel to guide them through the secret pass that the magic goddess had told her about.

Leo hoped Hazel was right about the long detour north. He didn't trust this Hecate lady. He didn't see why such a creepy goddess would suddenly decide to be helpful.

Of course, he didn't trust magic in general. That's why he was having so much trouble with the Athena Parthenos. It had no moving parts. Whatever it did, it apparently operated on pure sorcery . . . and Leo didn't appreciate that. He wanted it to make sense, like a machine.

Finally he got too exhausted to think straight. He curled up with a blanket in the engine room and listened to the soothing hum of the generators. Buford the mechanical table sat in the corner in sleep mode, making little steamy snores: *Shhh, pfft, shh, pfft.*

Leo liked his quarters okay, but he felt safest here in the heart of the ship – in a room filled with mechanisms he knew how to control. Besides, maybe if he spent more time close to the Athena Parthenos, he would eventually soak in its secrets.

'It's you or me, Big Lady,' he murmured as he pulled the blanket up to his chin. 'You're gonna cooperate eventually.'

He closed his eyes and slept. Unfortunately, that meant dreams.

He was running for his life through his mother's old workshop, where she'd died in a fire when Leo was eight.

He wasn't sure what was chasing him, but he sensed it closing fast – something large and dark and full of hate.

He stumbled into workbenches, knocked over toolboxes and tripped on electrical cords. He spotted the exit and sprinted towards it, but a figure loomed in front of him – a woman in robes of dry swirling earth, her face covered in a veil of dust.

Where are you going, little hero? Gaia asked. *Stay and meet my favourite son.*

Leo darted to the left, but the earth goddess's laughter followed him.

The night your mother died, I warned you. I said the Fates would not allow me to kill you then. But now *you have chosen your path. Your death is near, Leo Valdez.*

He ran into a drafting table – his mother's old workstation. The wall behind it was decorated with Leo's crayon drawings. He sobbed in desperation and turned, but the thing pursuing him now stood in his path – a colossal being wrapped in shadows, its shape vaguely humanoid, its head almost scraping the ceiling twenty feet above.

Leo's hands burst into flame. He blasted the giant, but the darkness consumed his fire. Leo reached for his tool belt. The pockets were sewn shut. He tried to speak – to say anything that would save his life – but he couldn't make a sound, as if the air had been stolen from his lungs.

My son will not allow any fires tonight, Gaia said from the depths of the warehouse. *He is the void that consumes all magic, the cold that consumes all fire, the silence that consumes all speech.*

Leo wanted to shout: *And I'm the dude that's all out of here!*

His voice didn't work, so he used his feet. He dashed to the right, ducking under the shadowy giant's grasping hands, and burst through the nearest doorway.

Suddenly, he found himself at Camp Half-Blood, except the camp was in ruins. The cabins were charred husks. Burnt fields smouldered in the moonlight. The dining pavilion had collapsed into a pile of white rubble, and the Big House was on fire, its windows glowing like demon eyes.

Leo kept running, sure the shadow giant was still behind him.

He weaved around the bodies of Greek and Roman demigods. He wanted to check if they were alive. He wanted to help them. But somehow he knew he was running out of time.

He jogged towards the only living people he saw – a group of Romans standing at the volleyball pit. Two centurions leaned casually on their javelins, chatting with a tall skinny blond guy in a purple toga. Leo stumbled. It was that freak Octavian, the augur from Camp Jupiter, who was always screaming for war.

Octavian turned to face him, but he seemed to be in a trance. His features were slack, his eyes closed. When he spoke, it was in Gaia's voice: *This cannot be prevented. The*

Romans move east from New York. They advance on your camp, and nothing can slow them down.

Leo was tempted to punch Octavian in the face. Instead he kept running.

He climbed Half-Blood Hill. At the summit, lightning had splintered the giant pine tree.

He faltered to a stop. The back of the hill was shorn away. Beyond it, the entire world was gone. Leo saw nothing but clouds far below – a rolling silver carpet under the dark sky.

A sharp voice said, 'Well?'

Leo flinched.

At the shattered pine tree, a woman knelt at a cave entrance that had cracked open between the tree's roots.

The woman wasn't Gaia. She looked more like a living Athena Parthenos, with the same golden robes and bare ivory arms. When she rose, Leo almost stumbled off the edge of the world.

Her face was regally beautiful, with high cheekbones, large dark eyes and braided liquorice-coloured hair piled in a fancy Greek hairdo, set with a spiral of emeralds and diamonds so that it reminded Leo of a Christmas tree. Her expression radiated pure hatred. Her lip curled. Her nose wrinkled.

'The tinkerer god's child,' she sneered. 'You are no threat, but I suppose my vengeance must start somewhere. Make your choice.'

Leo tried to speak, but he was about to crawl out of his skin with panic. Between this hate queen and the giant chasing him, he had no idea what to do.

'He'll be here soon,' the woman warned. 'My dark friend will not give you the luxury of a choice. It's the cliff or the cave, boy!'

Suddenly Leo understood what she meant. He was cornered. He could jump off the cliff, but that was suicide. Even if there was land under those clouds, he would die in the fall, or maybe he would just keep falling forever.

But the cave . . . He stared at the dark opening between the tree roots. It smelled of rot and death. He heard bodies shuffling inside, voices whispering in the shadows.

The cave was the home of the dead. If he went down there, he would never come back.

'Yes,' the woman said. Around her neck hung a strange bronze-and-emerald pendant, like a circular labyrinth. Her eyes were so angry, Leo finally understood why *mad* was a word for *crazy*. This lady had been driven nuts by hatred. 'The House of Hades awaits. You will be the first puny rodent to die in my maze. You have only one chance to escape, Leo Valdez. Take it.'

She gestured towards the cliff.

'You're bonkers,' he managed.

That was the wrong thing to say. She seized his wrist. 'Perhaps I should kill you now, before my dark friend arrives?'

Steps shook the hillside. The giant was coming, wrapped in shadows, huge and heavy and bent on murder.

'Have you heard of dying in a dream, boy?' the woman asked. 'It is possible, at the hands of a sorceress!'

Leo's arm started to smoke. The woman's touch was acid. He tried to free himself, but her grip was like steel.

He opened his mouth to scream. The massive shape of the giant loomed over him, obscured by layers of black smoke.

The giant raised his fist, and a voice cut through the dream.

'Leo!' Jason was shaking his shoulder. 'Hey, man, why are you hugging Nike?'

Leo's eyes fluttered open. His arms were wrapped around the human-sized statue in Athena's hand. He must have been thrashing in his sleep. He clung to the victory goddess like he used to cling to his pillow when he had nightmares as a kid. (Man, that had been *so* embarrassing in the foster homes.)

He disentangled himself and sat up, rubbing his face.

'Nothing,' he muttered. 'We were just cuddling. Um, what's going on?'

Jason didn't tease him. That's one thing Leo appreciated about his friend. Jason's ice-blue eyes were level and serious. The little scar on his mouth twitched like it always did when he had bad news to share.

'We made it through the mountains,' he said. 'We're almost to Bologna. You should join us in the mess hall. Nico has new information.'

LEO

LEO HAD DESIGNED the mess hall's walls to show real-time scenes from Camp Half-Blood. At first he had thought that was a pretty awesome idea. Now he wasn't so sure.

The scenes from back home – the campfire sing-alongs, dinners at the pavilion, volleyball games outside the Big House – just seemed to make his friends sad. The further they got from Long Island, the worse it got. The time zones kept changing, making Leo *feel* the distance every time he looked at the walls. Here in Italy the sun had just come up. Back at Camp Half-Blood it was the middle of the night. Torches sputtered at the cabin doorways. Moonlight glittered on the waves of Long Island Sound. The beach was covered in footprints, as if a big crowd had just left.

With a start, Leo realized that yesterday – last night, whatever – had been the Fourth of July. They'd missed Camp Half-Blood's annual party at the beach with awesome fireworks prepared by Leo's siblings in Cabin Nine.

He decided not to mention that to the crew, but he hoped their buddies back home had had a good celebration. They needed something to keep their spirits up, too.

He remembered the images he'd seen in his dream – the camp in ruins, littered with bodies; Octavian standing at the volleyball pit, casually talking in Gaia's voice.

He stared down at his eggs and bacon. He wished he could turn off the wall videos.

'So,' Jason said, 'now that we're here . . .'

He sat at the head of the table, kind of by default. Since they'd lost Annabeth, Jason had done his best to act as the group's leader. Having been praetor back at Camp Jupiter, he was probably used to that, but Leo could tell his friend was stressed. His eyes were more sunken than usual. His blond hair was uncharacteristically messy, like he'd forgotten to comb it.

Leo glanced at the others around the table. Hazel was bleary-eyed, too, but of course she'd been up all night guiding the ship through the mountains. Her curly cinnamon-coloured hair was tied back in a bandanna, which gave her a commando look that Leo found kind of hot – and then immediately felt guilty about.

Next to her sat her boyfriend Frank Zhang, dressed in black workout pants and a Roman tourist T-shirt that said *CIAO!* (was that even a word?). Frank's old centurion badge was pinned to his shirt, despite the fact that the demigods of the *Argo II* were now Public Enemies Numbers 1 through 7 back at Camp Jupiter. His grim expression just reinforced his unfortunate resemblance to a sumo wrestler. Then there was Hazel's half-brother, Nico di Angelo. Dang, that kid gave Leo the freaky-deakies. He sat back in his leather aviator jacket, his black T-shirt and jeans, that wicked silver skull ring on his finger and the Stygian sword at his side. His tufts of black hair stuck up in curls like baby bat wings. His eyes were sad and kind of empty, as if he'd stared into the depths of Tartarus – which he had.

The only absent demigod was Piper, who was taking her turn at the helm with Coach Hedge, their satyr chaperone.

Leo wished Piper were here. She had a way of calming things down with that Aphrodite charm of hers. After his dreams last night, Leo could use some calm.

On the other hand, it was probably good she was above deck chaperoning their chaperone. Now that they were in the ancient lands, they had to be constantly on guard. Leo was nervous about letting Coach Hedge fly solo. The satyr was a little trigger-happy, and the helm had plenty of bright, dangerous buttons that could cause the picturesque Italian villages below them to go BOOM!

Leo had zoned out so totally he didn't realize Jason was still talking.

'– the House of Hades,' he was saying. 'Nico?'

Nico sat forward. 'I communed with the dead last night.'

He just tossed that line out there, like he was saying he got a text from a buddy.

'I was able to learn more about what we'll face,' Nico continued. 'In ancient times, the House of Hades was a major site for Greek pilgrims. They would come to speak with the dead and honour their ancestors.'

Leo frowned. 'Sounds like Día de los Muertos. My Aunt Rosa took that stuff seriously.'

He remembered being dragged by her to the local cemetery in Houston, where they'd clean up their relatives' gravesites and put out offerings of lemonade, cookies and fresh marigolds. Aunt Rosa would force Leo to stay for a picnic, as if hanging out with dead people were good for his appetite.

Frank grunted. 'Chinese have that, too – ancestor worship, sweeping the graves in the springtime.' He glanced at Leo. 'Your Aunt Rosa would've got along with my grandmother.'

Leo had a terrifying image of his Aunt Rosa and some old Chinese woman in wrestlers' outfits, whaling on each other with spiked clubs.

'Yeah,' Leo said. 'I'm sure they would've been best buds.'

Nico cleared his throat. 'A lot of cultures have seasonal traditions to honour the dead, but the House of Hades was open year round. Pilgrims could actually *speak* to the ghosts. In Greek, the place was called the Necromanteion, the Oracle of Death. You'd work your way through different levels of tunnels, leaving offerings and drinking special potions –'

'Special potions,' Leo muttered. 'Yum.'

Jason flashed him a look like, *Dude, enough.* 'Nico, go on.'

'The pilgrims believed that each level of the temple brought you closer to the Underworld, until the dead would appear before you. If they were pleased with your offerings, they would answer your questions, maybe even tell you the future.'

Frank tapped his mug of hot chocolate. 'And if the spirits *weren't* pleased?'

'Some pilgrims found nothing,' Nico said. 'Some went insane or died after leaving the temple. Others lost their way in the tunnels and were never seen again.'

'The point is,' Jason said quickly, 'Nico found some information that might help us.'

'Yeah.' Nico didn't sound very enthusiastic. 'The ghost I spoke to last night . . . he was a former priest of Hecate. He confirmed what the goddess told Hazel yesterday at the crossroads. In the first war with the giants, Hecate fought for the gods. She slew one of the giants – one who'd been designed as the *anti*-Hecate. A guy named Clytius.'

'Dark dude,' Leo guessed. 'Wrapped in shadows.'

Hazel turned towards him, her gold eyes narrowing. 'Leo, how did you know that?'

'Kind of had a dream.'

No one looked surprised. Most demigods had vivid nightmares about what was going on in the world.

His friends paid close attention as Leo explained. He tried not to look at the wall images of Camp Half-Blood as he described the place in ruins. He told them about the dark giant and the strange woman on Half-Blood Hill, offering him a multiple-choice death.

Jason pushed away his plate of pancakes. 'So the giant is Clytius. I suppose he'll be waiting for us, guarding the Doors of Death.'

Frank rolled up one of the pancakes and started munching – not a guy to let impending death stand in the way of a hearty breakfast. 'And the woman in Leo's dream?'

'She's my problem.' Hazel passed a diamond between her fingers in a sleight of hand. 'Hecate mentioned a formidable enemy in the House of Hades – a witch who couldn't be defeated except by me, using magic.'

'Do you know magic?' Leo asked.

'Not yet.'

'Ah.' He tried to think of something hopeful to say, but he recalled the angry woman's eyes, the way her steely grip made his skin smoke. 'Any idea who she is?'

Hazel shook her head. 'Only that . . .' She glanced at Nico, and some sort of silent argument happened between them. Leo got the feeling that the two of them had had private conversations about the House of Hades and they weren't sharing all the details. 'Only that she won't be easy to defeat.'

'But there *is* some good news,' Nico said. 'The ghost I talked to explained how Hecate defeated Clytius in the first war. She used her torches to set his hair on fire. He burned to death. In other words, fire is his weakness.'

Everybody looked at Leo.

'Oh,' he said. 'Okay.'

Jason nodded encouragingly, like this was great news – like he expected Leo to walk up to a towering mass of darkness, shoot a few fireballs and solve all their problems. Leo didn't want to bring him down, but he could still hear Gaia's voice: *He is the void that consumes all magic, the cold that consumes all fire, the silence that consumes all speech.*

Leo was pretty sure it would take more than a few matches to set that giant ablaze.

'It's a good lead,' Jason insisted. 'At least we know how to kill the giant. And this sorceress . . . well, if Hecate believes Hazel can defeat her, then so do I.'

Hazel dropped her eyes. 'Now we just have to reach the House of Hades, battle our way through Gaia's forces –'

'Plus a bunch of ghosts,' Nico added grimly. 'The spirits in that temple may not be friendly.'

'– and find the Doors of Death,' Hazel continued. 'Assuming we can somehow arrive at the same time as Percy and Annabeth and rescue them.'

Frank swallowed a bite of pancake. 'We can do it. We *have* to.'

Leo admired the big guy's optimism. He wished he shared it.

'So, with this detour,' Leo said, 'I'm estimating four or five days to arrive at Epirus, assuming no delays for, you know, monster attacks and stuff.'

Jason smiled sourly. 'Yeah. Those never happen.'

Leo looked at Hazel. 'Hecate told you that Gaia was planning her big Wake Up party on August first, right? The Feast of Whatever?'

'Spes,' Hazel said. 'The goddess of hope.'

Jason turned his fork. 'Theoretically, that leaves us enough time. It's only July fifth. We should be able to close the Doors of Death, then find the giants' HQ and stop them from waking Gaia before August first.'

'Theoretically,' Hazel agreed. 'But I'd still like to know

how we make our way through the House of Hades without going insane or dying.'

Nobody volunteered any ideas.

Frank set down his pancake roll like it suddenly didn't taste so good. 'It's July fifth. Oh, jeez, I hadn't even thought of that . . .'

'Hey, man, it's cool,' Leo said. 'You're Canadian, right? I didn't expect you to get me an Independence Day present or anything . . . unless you wanted to.'

'It's not that. My grandmother . . . she always told me that seven was an unlucky number. It was a *ghost* number. She didn't like it when I told her there would be seven demigods on our quest. And July is the seventh month.'

'Yeah, but . . .' Leo tapped his fingers nervously on the table. He realized he was doing the Morse code for *I love you*, the way he used to do with his mom, which would have been pretty embarrassing if his friends understood Morse code. 'But that's just coincidence, right?'

Frank's expression didn't reassure him.

'Back in China,' Frank said, 'in the old days, people called the seventh month the *ghost month*. That's when the spirit world and the human world were closest. The living and the dead could go back and forth. Tell me it's a coincidence we're searching for the Doors of Death during the ghost month.'

No one spoke.

Leo wanted to think that an old Chinese belief couldn't have anything to do with the Romans and the Greeks. Totally different, right? But Frank's existence was proof that the cultures were tied together. The Zhang family went all the way back to Ancient Greece. They'd found their way through Rome and China and finally to Canada.

Also, Leo kept thinking about his meeting with the revenge goddess Nemesis at the Great Salt Lake. Nemesis had called him the *seventh wheel*, the odd man out on the quest. She didn't mean seventh as in *ghost*, did she?

Jason pressed his hands against the arms of his chair. 'Let's focus on the things we can deal with. We're getting close to Bologna. Maybe we'll get more answers once we find these dwarfs that Hecate –'

The ship lurched as if it had hit an iceberg. Leo's breakfast plate slid across the table. Nico fell backwards out of his chair and banged his head against the sideboard. He collapsed on the floor, with a dozen magic goblets and platters crashing down on top of him.

'Nico!' Hazel ran to help him.

'What –?' Frank tried to stand, but the ship pitched in the other direction. He stumbled into the table and went face-first into Leo's plate of scrambled eggs.

'Look!' Jason pointed at the walls. The images of Camp Half-Blood were flickering and changing.

'Not possible,' Leo murmured.

No way those enchantments could show anything other than scenes from camp, but suddenly a huge, distorted face filled the entire port-side wall: crooked yellow teeth, a scraggly red beard, a warty nose and two mismatched eyes – one much larger and higher than the other. The face seemed to be trying to eat its way into the room.

The other walls flickered, showing scenes from above

deck. Piper stood at the helm, but something was wrong. From the shoulders down she was wrapped in duct tape, her mouth gagged and her legs bound to the control console.

At the mainmast, Coach Hedge was similarly bound and gagged, while a bizarre-looking creature – a sort of gnome/chimpanzee combo with poor fashion sense – danced around him, doing the coach's hair in tiny pigtails with pink rubber bands.

On the port-side wall, the huge ugly face receded so that Leo could see the entire creature – another gnome chimp, in even crazier clothes. This one began leaping around the deck, stuffing things into a burlap bag – Piper's dagger, Leo's Wii controllers. Then he prised the Archimedes sphere out of the command console.

'No!' Leo yelled.

'Uhhh,' Nico groaned from the floor.

'Piper!' Jason cried.

'Monkey!' Frank yelled.

'Not monkeys,' Hazel grumbled. 'I think those are dwarfs.'

'Stealing my stuff!' Leo yelled, and he ran for the stairs.

LEO

LEO WAS VAGUELY AWARE OF HAZEL SHOUTING, 'Go! I'll take care of Nico!'

As if Leo was going to turn back. Sure, he'd hoped di Angelo was okay, but he had headaches of his own.

Leo bounded up the steps, with Jason and Frank behind him.

The situation on deck was even worse than he'd feared.

Coach Hedge and Piper were struggling against their duct-tape bonds while one of the demon monkey dwarfs danced around the deck, picking up whatever wasn't tied down and sticking it in his bag. He was maybe four feet tall, even shorter than Coach Hedge, with bowed legs and chimp-like feet, his clothes so loud they gave Leo vertigo. His green-plaid trousers were pinned at the cuffs and held up with bright-red suspenders over a striped pink-and-black woman's blouse. He wore half a dozen gold watches on each arm and a zebra-patterned cowboy hat with a price tag dangling from the brim.

His skin was covered with patches of scraggly red fur, though ninety percent of his body hair seemed to be concentrated in his magnificent eyebrows.

Leo was just forming the thought *Where's the other dwarf?* when he heard a *click* behind him and realized he'd led his friends into a trap.

'Duck!' He hit the deck as the explosion blasted his eardrums.

Note to self, Leo thought groggily. Do not leave boxes of magic grenades where dwarfs can reach them.

At least he was alive. Leo had been experimenting with all sorts of weapons based on the Archimedes sphere that he'd recovered in Rome. He'd built grenades that could spray acid, fire, shrapnel or freshly buttered popcorn. (Hey, you never knew when you'd get hungry in battle.) Judging from the ringing in Leo's ears, the dwarf had detonated the flash-bang grenade, which Leo had filled with a rare vial of Apollo's music, pure liquid extract. It didn't kill, but it left Leo feeling like he'd just done a belly flop off the deep end.

He tried to get up. His limbs were useless. Someone was tugging at his waist, maybe a friend trying to help him up? No. His friends didn't smell like heavily perfumed monkey cages.

He managed to turn over. His vision was out of focus and tinted pink, like the world had been submerged in strawberry jelly. A grinning, grotesque face loomed over him. The brown-furred dwarf was dressed even worse than his friend, in a green bowler hat like a leprechaun's, dangly diamond earrings and a white-and-black referee's shirt. He showed off the prize he'd just stolen – Leo's tool belt – then danced away.

Leo tried to grab him, but his fingers were numb. The dwarf frolicked over to the nearest ballista, which his red-furred friend was priming to launch.

The brown-furred dwarf jumped onto the projectile like it was a skateboard, and his friend shot him into the sky.

Red Fur pranced over to Coach Hedge. He gave the satyr a big smack on the cheek, then skipped to the rail. He bowed to Leo, doffing his zebra cowboy hat, and did a backflip over the side.

Leo managed to get up. Jason was already on his feet, stumbling and running into things. Frank had turned into a silverback gorilla (why, Leo wasn't sure; maybe to commune with the monkey dwarfs?) but the flash grenade had hit him hard. He was sprawled on the deck with his tongue hanging out and his gorilla eyes rolled up in his head.

'Piper!' Jason staggered to the helm and carefully pulled the gag out of her mouth.

'Don't waste your time on me!' she said. 'Go after *them*!'

At the mast, Coach Hedge mumbled, 'HHHmmmmm-hmmm!'

Leo figured that meant: 'KILL THEM!' Easy translation, since most of the coach's sentences involved the word *kill*.

Leo glanced at the control console. His Archimedes sphere was gone. He put his hand to his waist, where his tool belt should have been. His head started to clear, and his sense of outrage came to a boil. Those dwarfs had attacked his ship. They'd stolen his most precious possessions.

Below him spread the city of Bologna – a jigsaw puzzle of red-tiled buildings in a valley hemmed in by green hills.

Unless Leo could find the dwarfs somewhere in that maze of streets . . . Nope. Failure wasn't an option. Neither was waiting for his friends to recover.

He turned to Jason. 'You feeling good enough to control the winds? I need a lift.'

Jason frowned. 'Sure, but –'

'Good,' Leo said. 'We've got some monkey dudes to catch.'

Jason and Leo touched down in a big piazza lined with white marble government buildings and outdoor cafés. Bikes and Vespas clogged the surrounding streets, but the square itself was empty except for pigeons and a few old men drinking espressos.

None of the locals seemed to notice the huge Greek warship hovering over the piazza, nor the fact that Jason and Leo had just flown down – Jason wielding a gold sword, and Leo . . . well, Leo pretty much empty-handed.

'Where to?' Jason asked.

Leo stared at him. 'Well, I dunno. Let me pull my dwarf-tracking GPS out of my tool belt . . . Oh, wait! I don't have a dwarf-tracking GPS – or my tool belt!'

'Fine,' Jason grumbled. He glanced up at the ship as if to get his bearings, then pointed across the piazza. 'The ballista fired the first dwarf in *that* direction, I think. Come on.'

They waded through a lake of pigeons, then manoeuvred down a side street of clothing stores and gelato shops. The sidewalks were lined with white columns covered in graffiti.

A few panhandlers asked for change (Leo didn't know Italian, but he got the message loud and clear).

He kept patting his waist, hoping his tool belt would magically reappear. It didn't. He tried not to freak, but he'd come to depend on that belt for almost everything. He felt like somebody had stolen one of his hands.

'We'll find it,' Jason promised.

Usually, Leo would have felt reassured. Jason had a talent for staying levelheaded in a crisis, and he'd got Leo out of plenty of bad scrapes. Today, though, all Leo could think about was the stupid fortune cookie he had opened in Rome. The goddess Nemesis had promised him help, and he'd got it: the code to activate the Archimedes sphere. At the time, Leo had had no choice but to use it if he wanted to save his friends – but Nemesis had warned that her help came with a price.

Leo wondered if that price would ever be paid. Percy and Annabeth were gone. The ship was hundreds of miles off course, heading towards an impossible challenge. Leo's friends were counting on him to beat a terrifying giant. And now he didn't even have his tool belt or his Archimedes sphere.

He was so absorbed with feeling sorry for himself that he didn't notice where they were until Jason grabbed his arm. 'Check it out.'

Leo looked up. They'd arrived in a smaller piazza. Looming over them was a huge bronze statue of a buck-naked Neptune.

'Ah, jeez.' Leo averted his eyes. He really didn't need to see a godly groin this early in the morning.

The sea god stood on a big marble column in the middle of a fountain that wasn't working (which seemed kind of ironic). On either side of Neptune, little winged Cupid dudes were sitting, kind of chillin', like, *What's up?* Neptune himself (avoid the groin) was throwing his hip to one side in an Elvis Presley move. He gripped his trident loosely in his right hand and stretched his left hand out like he was blessing Leo, or possibly attempting to levitate him.

'Some kind of clue?' Leo wondered.

Jason frowned. 'Maybe, maybe not. There are statues of the gods all over the place in Italy. I'd just feel better if we ran across Jupiter. Or Minerva. Anybody but Neptune, really.'

Leo climbed into the dry fountain. He put his hand on the statue's pedestal, and a rush of impressions surged through his fingertips. He sensed Celestial bronze gears, magical levers, springs and pistons.

'It's mechanical,' he said. 'Maybe a doorway to the dwarfs' secret lair?'

'Ooooo!' shrieked a nearby voice. 'Secret lair?'

'I want a secret lair!' yelled another voice from above.

Jason stepped back, his sword ready. Leo almost got whiplash trying to look in two places at once. The red-furred dwarf in the cowboy hat was sitting about thirty feet away at the nearest café table, sipping an espresso held by his monkey-like foot. The brown-furred dwarf in the green bowler was perched on the marble pedestal at Neptune's feet, just above Leo's head.

'If we had a secret lair,' said Red Fur, 'I would want a firehouse pole.'

'And a waterslide!' said Brown Fur, who was pulling random tools out of Leo's belt, tossing aside wrenches, hammers and staple guns.

'Stop that!' Leo tried to grab the dwarf's feet, but he couldn't reach the top of the pedestal.

'Too short?' Brown Fur sympathized.

'You're calling *me* short?' Leo looked around for something to throw, but there was nothing but pigeons, and he doubted he could catch one. 'Give me my belt, you stupid –'

'Now, now!' said Brown Fur. 'We haven't even introduced ourselves. I'm Akmon. And my brother over there –'

'– is the handsome one!' The red-furred dwarf lifted his espresso. Judging from his dilated eyes and his maniacal grin, he didn't need any more caffeine. 'Passalos! Singer of songs! Drinker of coffee! Stealer of shiny stuff!'

'Please!' shrieked his brother, Akmon. 'I steal *much* better than you.'

Passalos snorted. 'Stealing naps, maybe!' He took out a knife – Piper's knife – and started picking his teeth with it.

'Hey!' Jason yelled. 'That's my girlfriend's knife!'

He lunged at Passalos, but the red-furred dwarf was too quick. He sprang from his chair, bounced off Jason's head, did a flip and landed next to Leo, his hairy arms around Leo's waist.

'Save me?' the dwarf pleaded.

'Get off!' Leo tried to shove him away, but Passalos did a backwards somersault and landed out of reach. Leo's trousers promptly fell around his knees.

He stared at Passalos, who was now grinning and holding

a small zigzaggy strip of metal. Somehow, the dwarf had stolen the zipper right off Leo's trousers.

'Give – stupid – zipper!' Leo stuttered, trying to shake his fist and hoist up his trousers at the same time.

'Eh, not shiny enough.' Passalos tossed it away.

Jason lunged with his sword. Passalos launched himself straight up and was suddenly sitting on the statue's pedestal next to his brother.

'Tell me I don't have moves,' Passalos boasted.

'Okay,' Akmon said. 'You don't have moves.'

'Bah!' Passalos said. 'Give me the tool belt. I want to see.'

'No!' Akmon elbowed him away. 'You got the knife and the shiny ball.'

'Yes, the shiny ball is nice.' Passalos took off his cowboy hat. Like a magician producing a rabbit, he pulled out the Archimedes sphere and began tinkering with the ancient bronze dials.

'Stop!' Leo yelled. 'That's a delicate machine.'

Jason came to his side and glared up at the dwarfs. 'Who *are* you two, anyway?'

'The Kerkopes!' Akmon narrowed his eyes at Jason. 'I bet you're a son of Jupiter, eh? I can always tell.'

'Just like Black Bottom,' Passalos agreed.

'Black Bottom?' Leo resisted the urge to jump at the dwarfs' feet again. He was sure Passalos was going to ruin the Archimedes sphere any second now.

'Yes, you know.' Akmon grinned. 'Hercules. We called him Black Bottom because he used to go around without clothes. He got so tanned that his backside, well –'

'At least he had a sense of humour!' Passalos said. 'He was going to kill us when we stole from him, but he let us go because he liked our jokes. Not like you two. Grumpy, grumpy!'

'Hey, I've got a sense of humour,' Leo snarled. 'Give me back our stuff, and I'll tell you a joke with a good punch line.'

'Nice try!' Akmon pulled a ratchet wrench from the tool belt and spun it like a noisemaker. 'Oh, very nice! I'm definitely keeping this! Thanks, Blue Bottom!'

Blue Bottom?

Leo glanced down. His trousers had slipped around his ankles again, revealing his blue boxer shorts. 'That's it!' he shouted. 'My stuff. Now. Or I'll show you how funny a flaming dwarf is.'

His hands caught fire.

'Now we're talking.' Jason thrust his sword into the sky. Dark clouds began to gather over the piazza. Thunder boomed.

'Oh, scary!' Akmon shrieked.

'Yes,' Passalos agreed. 'If only we had a secret lair to hide in.'

'Alas, this statue isn't the doorway to a secret lair,' Akmon said. 'It has a different purpose.'

Leo's gut twisted. The fires died in his hands, and he realized something was very wrong. He yelled, 'Trap!' and dived out of the fountain. Unfortunately, Jason was too busy summoning his storm.

Leo rolled on his back as five golden cords shot from the Neptune statue's fingers. One barely missed Leo's feet. The rest homed in on Jason, wrapping him like a rodeo calf and yanking him upside down.

A bolt of lightning blasted the tines of Neptune's trident, sending arcs of electricity up and down the statue, but the Kerkopes had already disappeared.

'Bravo!' Akmon applauded from a nearby café table. 'You make a wonderful piñata, son of Jupiter!'

'Yes!' Passalos agreed. 'Hercules hung us upside down once, you know. Oh, revenge is sweet!'

Leo summoned a fireball. He lobbed it at Passalos, who was trying to juggle two pigeons and the Archimedes sphere.

'Eek!' The dwarf jumped free of the explosion, dropping the sphere and letting the pigeons fly.

'Time to leave!' Akmon decided.

He tipped his bowler and sprang away, jumping from table to table. Passalos glanced at the Archimedes sphere, which had rolled between Leo's feet.

Leo summoned another fireball. 'Try me,' he snarled.

'Bye!' Passalos did a backflip and ran after his brother.

Leo scooped up the Archimedes sphere and ran over to Jason, who was still hanging upside down, thoroughly hog-tied except for his sword arm. He was trying to cut the cords with his gold blade but having no luck.

'Hold on,' Leo said. 'If I can find a release switch –'

'Just go!' Jason growled. 'I'll follow you when I get out of this.'

'But –'

'Don't lose them!'

The last thing Leo wanted was some alone time with the monkey dwarfs, but the Kerkopes were already disappearing around the far corner of the piazza. Leo left Jason hanging and ran after them.

XII

LEO

THE DWARFS DIDN'T TRY VERY HARD TO LOSE HIM, which made Leo suspicious. They stayed just at the edge of his vision, scampering over red-tiled rooftops, knocking over window boxes, whooping and hollering and leaving a trail of screws and nails from Leo's tool belt – almost as if they *wanted* Leo to follow.

He jogged after them, cursing every time his trousers fell down. He turned a corner and saw two ancient stone towers jutting into the sky, side by side, much taller than anything else in the neighbourhood – maybe mediaeval watchtowers? They leaned in different directions like gearshifts on a race car.

The Kerkopes scaled the tower on the right. When they reached the top, they climbed around the back and disappeared.

Had they gone inside? Leo could see some tiny windows at the top, covered with metal grates, but he doubted those would stop the dwarfs. He watched for a minute, but the Kerkopes didn't reappear. Which meant Leo had to get up there and look for them.

'Great,' he muttered. No flying friend to carry him up. The ship was too far away to call for help. He could rig the Archimedes sphere into some sort of flying device, maybe, but only if he had his tool belt – which he didn't. He scanned the neighbourhood, trying to think. Half a block down, a set of double glass doors opened and an old lady hobbled out, carrying plastic shopping bags.

A grocery store? Hmm . . .

Leo patted his pockets. To his amazement, he still had some euro notes from his time in Rome. Those stupid dwarfs had taken everything *except* his money.

He ran for the store as fast as his zipperless trousers allowed.

Leo scoured the aisles, looking for things he could use. He didn't know the Italian for *Hello, where are your dangerous chemicals, please?* But that was probably just as well. He didn't want to end up in an Italian jail.

Fortunately, he didn't need to read labels. He could tell just from picking up a toothpaste tube whether it contained potassium nitrate. He found charcoal. He found sugar and baking soda. The store sold matches and bug spray and aluminium foil. Pretty much everything he needed, plus a laundry cord he could use as a belt. He added some Italian junk food to the basket, just to sort of disguise his more suspicious purchases, then dumped his stuff at the till. A wide-eyed checkout lady asked him some questions he didn't understand, but he managed to pay, get a bag and race out.

He ducked into the nearest doorway where he could keep an eye on the towers. He started to work, summoning fire to dry out materials and do a little cooking that otherwise would have taken days to complete.

Every once in a while he sneaked a look at the tower, but there was no sign of the dwarfs. Leo could only hope they were still up there. Making his arsenal took just a few minutes – he was *that* good – but it felt like hours.

Jason didn't show. Maybe he was still tangled at the Neptune fountain or scouring the streets looking for Leo. No one else from the ship came to help. Probably it was taking them a long time to get all those pink rubber bands out of Coach Hedge's hair.

That meant Leo had only himself, his bag of junk food and a few highly improvised weapons made from sugar and toothpaste. Oh, and the Archimedes sphere. That was kind of important. He hoped he hadn't ruined it by filling it with chemical powder.

He ran to the tower and found the entrance. He started up the winding stairs inside, only to be stopped at a ticket booth by some caretaker who yelled at him in Italian.

'Seriously?' Leo asked. 'Look, man, you've got dwarfs in your belfry. I'm the exterminator.' He held up his can of bug spray. 'See? Exterminator *Molto Buono*. Squirt, squirt. Ahhh!' He pantomimed a dwarf melting in terror, which for some reason the Italian didn't seem to understand.

The guy just held out his palm for money.

'Dang, man,' Leo grumbled, 'I just spent all my cash on homemade explosives and whatnot.' He dug around in his grocery bag. 'Don't suppose you'd accept . . . uh . . . whatever these are?'

Leo held up a yellow-and-red bag of junk food called Fonzies. He assumed they were some kind of potato chips. To his surprise, the caretaker shrugged and took the bag. *'Avanti!'*

Leo kept climbing, but he made a mental note to stock up on Fonzies. Apparently they were better than cash in Italy.

The stairs went on and on and on. The whole tower seemed to be nothing but an excuse to build a staircase.

He stopped on a landing and slumped against a narrow barred window, trying to catch his breath. He was sweating like crazy, and his heart thumped against his ribs. Stupid Kerkopes. Leo figured that as soon as he reached the top they would jump away before he could use his weapons, but he had to try.

He kept climbing.

Finally, his legs feeling like overcooked noodles, he reached the top.

The room was about the size of a broom closet, with barred windows on all four walls. Shoved in the corners were sacks of treasure, shiny goodies spilling all over the floor. Leo spotted Piper's knife, an old leather-bound book, a few interesting-looking mechanical devices and enough gold to give Hazel's horse a stomachache.

At first, he thought the dwarfs had left. Then he looked up. Akmon and Passalos were hanging upside down from the rafters by their chimp feet, playing antigravity poker. When they saw Leo, they threw their cards like confetti and broke out in applause.

'I told you he'd do it!' Akmon shrieked in delight.

Passalos shrugged and took off one of his gold watches and handed it to his brother. 'You win. I didn't think he was that dumb.'

They both dropped to the floor. Akmon was wearing Leo's tool belt – he was so close that Leo had to resist the urge to lunge for it.

Passalos straightened his cowboy hat and kicked open the grate on the nearest window. 'What should we make him climb next, brother? The dome of San Luca?'

Leo wanted to throttle the dwarfs, but he forced a smile. 'Oh, that sounds fun! But, before you guys go, you forgot something shiny.'

'Impossible!' Akmon scowled. 'We were very thorough.'

'You sure?' Leo held up his grocery bag.

The dwarfs inched closer. As Leo had hoped, their curiosity was so strong that they couldn't resist.

'Look.' Leo brought out his first weapon – a lump of dried chemicals wrapped in aluminium foil – and lit it with his hand.

He knew enough to turn away when it popped, but the dwarfs were staring right at it. Toothpaste, sugar and bug spray weren't as good as Apollo's music, but they made a pretty decent flash-bang.

The Kerkopes wailed, clawing at their eyes. They stumbled towards the window, but Leo set off his homemade firecrackers – snapping them around the dwarfs' bare feet to keep them off balance. Then, for good measure, Leo turned the dial on his Archimedes sphere, which unleashed a plume of foul white fog that filled the room.

Leo wasn't bothered by smoke. Being immune to fire, he'd stood in smoky bonfires, endured dragon breath and cleaned out blazing forges plenty of times. While the dwarfs were hacking and wheezing, he grabbed his tool belt from Akmon, calmly summoned some bungee cords and tied up the dwarfs.

'My eyes!' Akmon coughed. 'My tool belt!'

'My feet are on fire!' Passalos wailed. 'Not shiny! Not shiny at all!'

After making sure they were securely bound, Leo dragged the Kerkopes into one corner and began rifling through their treasures. He retrieved Piper's dagger, a few of his prototype grenades and a dozen other odds and ends the dwarfs had taken from the *Argo II*.

'Please!' Akmon wailed. 'Don't take our shinies!'

'We'll make you a deal!' Passalos suggested. 'We'll cut you in for ten percent if you let us go!'

'Afraid not,' Leo muttered. 'It's all mine now.'

'Twenty percent!'

Just then, thunder boomed overhead. Lightning flashed, and the bars on the nearest window burst into sizzling, melted stubs of iron.

Jason flew in like Peter Pan, electricity sparking around him and his gold sword steaming.

Leo whistled appreciatively. 'Man, you just wasted an *awesome* entrance.'

Jason frowned. He noticed the hog-tied Kerkopes. 'What the –'

'All by myself,' Leo said. 'I'm special that way. How did you find me?'

'Uh, the smoke,' Jason managed. 'And I heard popping noises. Were you having a gunfight in here?'

'Something like that.' Leo tossed him Piper's dagger, then kept rummaging through the bags of dwarf shinies. He remembered what Hazel had said about finding a treasure that would help them with the quest, but he wasn't sure what he was looking for. There were coins, gold nuggets, jewellery, paper clips, foil wrappers, cuff links.

He kept coming back to a couple of things that didn't seem to belong. One was an old bronze navigation device, like an astrolabe from a ship. It was badly damaged and seemed to be missing some pieces, but Leo still found it fascinating.

'Take it!' Passalos offered. 'Odysseus made it, you know! Take it and let us go.'

'Odysseus?' Jason asked. 'Like, *the* Odysseus?'

'Yes!' Passalos squeaked. 'Made it when he was an old man in Ithaca. One of his last inventions, and we stole it!'

'How does it work?' Leo asked.

'Oh, it doesn't,' Akmon said. 'Something about a missing crystal?' He glanced at his brother for help.

'"My biggest what-if",' Passalos said. '"Should've taken a crystal." That's what he kept muttering in his sleep, the night we stole it.' Passalos shrugged. 'No idea what he meant. But the shiny is yours! Can we go now?'

Leo wasn't sure why he wanted the astrolabe. It was obviously broken, and he didn't get the sense that this was what Hecate meant them to find. Still, he slipped it into one of his tool belt's magic pockets.

He turned his attention to the other strange piece of

loot – the leather-bound book. Its title was in gold leaf, in a language Leo couldn't understand, but nothing else about the book seemed shiny. He didn't figure the Kerkopes for big readers.

'What's this?' He wagged it at the dwarfs, who were still teary-eyed from the smoke.

'Nothing!' Akmon said. 'Just a book. It had a pretty gold cover, so we took it from him.'

'Him?' Leo asked.

Akmon and Passalos exchanged a nervous look.

'Minor god,' Passalos said. 'In Venice. Really, it's nothing.'

'Venice.' Jason frowned at Leo. 'Isn't that where we're supposed to go next?'

'Yeah.' Leo examined the book. He couldn't read the text, but it had lots of illustrations: scythes, different plants, a picture of the sun, a team of oxen pulling a cart. He didn't see how any of that was important, but if the book had been stolen from a minor god in Venice – the next place Hecate had told them to visit – then this *had* to be what they were looking for.

'Where exactly can we find this minor god?' Leo asked.

'No!' Akmon shrieked. 'You can't take it back to him! If he finds out we stole it –'

'He'll destroy you,' Jason guessed. 'Which is what we'll do if you don't tell us, and we're a *lot* closer.' He pressed the point of his sword against Akmon's furry throat.

'Okay, okay!' the dwarf shrieked. 'La Casa Nera! Calle Frezzeria!'

'Is that an address?' Leo asked.

The dwarfs both nodded vigorously.

'*Please* don't tell him we stole it,' Passalos begged. 'He isn't nice at all!'

'Who is he?' Jason asked. 'What god?'

'I – I can't say,' Passalos stammered.

'You'd better,' Leo warned.

'No,' Passalos said miserably. 'I mean, I *really* can't say. I can't pronounce it! Tr – Tri – It's too hard!'

'Truh,' Akmon said. 'Tru-toh – Too many syllables!'

They both burst into tears.

Leo didn't know if the Kerkopes were telling them the truth, but it was hard to stay mad at weeping dwarfs, no matter how annoying and badly dressed they were.

Jason lowered his sword. 'What do you want to do with them, Leo? Send them to Tartarus?'

'Please, no!' Akmon wailed. 'It might take us weeks to come back.'

'Assuming Gaia even lets us!' Passalos sniffled. 'She controls the Doors of Death now. She'll be very cross with us.'

Leo looked at the dwarfs. He'd fought lots of monsters before and never felt bad about dissolving them, but this was different. He had to admit he sort of admired these little guys. They played cool pranks and liked shiny things. Leo could relate. Besides, Percy and Annabeth were in Tartarus right now, hopefully still alive, trudging towards the Doors of Death. The idea of sending these twin monkey boys there to face the same nightmarish problem . . . well, it didn't seem right.

He imagined Gaia laughing at his weakness – a demigod

too softhearted to kill monsters. He remembered his dream about Camp Half-Blood in ruins, Greek and Roman bodies littering the fields. He remembered Octavian speaking with the earth goddess's voice: *The Romans move east from New York. They advance on your camp, and nothing can slow them down.*

'Nothing can slow them down,' Leo mused. 'I wonder . . .'

'What?' Jason asked.

Leo looked at the dwarfs. 'I'll make you a deal.'

Akmon's eyes lit up. 'Thirty percent?'

'We'll leave you all your treasure,' Leo said, 'except the stuff that belongs to us and the astrolabe and this book, which we'll take back to the dude in Venice.'

'But he'll destroy us!' Passalos wailed.

'We won't say where we got it,' Leo promised. 'And we won't kill you. We'll let you go free.'

'Uh, Leo . . . ?' Jason asked nervously.

Akmon squealed with delight. 'I knew you were as smart as Hercules! I will call you Black Bottom, the Sequel!'

'Yeah, no thanks,' Leo said. 'But in return for us sparing your lives, you have to do something for us. I'm going to send you somewhere to steal from some people, harass them, make life hard for them any way you can. You have to follow my directions exactly. You have to swear on the River Styx.'

'We swear!' Passalos said. 'Stealing from people is our speciality!'

'I love harassment!' Akmon agreed. 'Where are we going?'

Leo grinned. 'Ever heard of New York?'

XIII

PERCY

PERCY HAD TAKEN HIS GIRLFRIEND on some romantic walks before. This wasn't one of them.

They followed the River Phlegethon, stumbling over the glassy black terrain, jumping crevices and hiding behind rocks whenever the vampire girls slowed in front of them.

It was tricky to stay far enough back to avoid getting spotted but close enough to keep Kelli and her comrades in view through the dark hazy air. The heat from the river baked Percy's skin. Every breath was like inhaling sulphur-scented fibreglass. When they needed a drink, the best they could do was sip some refreshing liquid fire.

Yep. Percy definitely knew how to show a girl a good time.

At least Annabeth's ankle seemed to have healed. She was hardly limping at all. Her various cuts and scrapes had faded. She'd tied her blonde hair back with a strip of denim torn from her jeans, and in the fiery light of the river her grey eyes flickered. Despite being beat-up, sooty and dressed like a homeless person, she looked great to Percy.

So what if they were in Tartarus? So what if they stood a slim chance of surviving? He was so glad that they were together he had the ridiculous urge to smile.

Physically, Percy felt better too, though his clothes looked like he'd been through a hurricane of broken glass. He was thirsty, hungry and scared out of his mind (though he wasn't going to tell Annabeth that), but he'd shaken off the hopeless cold of the River Cocytus. And as nasty as the firewater tasted it seemed to keep him going.

Time was impossible to judge. They trudged along, following the river as it cut through the harsh landscape. Fortunately the *empousai* weren't exactly speed walkers. They shuffled on their mismatched bronze and donkey legs, hissing and fighting with each other, apparently in no hurry to reach the Doors of Death.

Once, the demons sped up in excitement and swarmed something that looked like a beached carcass on the riverbank. Percy couldn't tell what it was – a fallen monster? An animal of some kind? The *empousai* attacked it with relish.

When the demons moved on, Percy and Annabeth reached the spot and found nothing left except a few splintered bones and glistening stains drying in the heat of the river. Percy had no doubt the *empousai* would devour demigods with the same gusto.

'Come on.' He led Annabeth gently away from the scene. 'We don't want to lose them.'

As they walked, Percy thought about the first time he'd

fought the *empousa* Kelli at Goode High School's freshman orientation, when he and Rachel Elizabeth Dare got trapped in the band hall. At the time, it had seemed like a hopeless situation. Now, he'd give anything to have a problem that simple. At least he'd been in the mortal world then. Here, there was nowhere to run.

Wow. When he started looking back on the war with Kronos as the good old days – that was sad. He kept hoping things would get better for Annabeth and him, but their lives just got more and more dangerous, as if the Three Fates were up there spinning their futures with barbed wire instead of thread just to see how much two demigods could tolerate.

After a few more miles, the *empousai* disappeared over a ridge. When Percy and Annabeth caught up, they found themselves at the edge of another massive cliff. The River Phlegethon spilled over the side in jagged tiers of fiery waterfalls. The demon ladies were picking their way down the cliff, jumping from ledge to ledge like mountain goats.

Percy's heart crept into his throat. Even if he and Annabeth reached the bottom of the cliff alive, they didn't have much to look forward to. The landscape below them was a bleak ash-grey plain bristling with black trees, like insect hair. The ground was pocked with blisters. Every once in a while, a bubble would swell and burst, disgorging a monster like a larva from an egg.

Suddenly Percy wasn't hungry any more.

All the newly formed monsters were crawling and hobbling in the same direction – towards a bank of black fog that swallowed the horizon like a storm front. The Phlegethon flowed in the same direction until about halfway across the plain, where it met another river of black water – maybe the Cocytus? The two floods combined in a steaming, boiling cataract and flowed on as one towards the black fog.

The longer Percy looked into that storm of darkness, the less he wanted to go there. It could be hiding anything – an ocean, a bottomless pit, an army of monsters. But if the Doors of Death were in that direction it was their only chance to get home.

He peered over the edge of the cliff.

'Wish we could fly,' he muttered.

Annabeth rubbed her arms. 'Remember Luke's winged shoes? I wonder if they're still down here somewhere.'

Percy remembered. Those shoes had been cursed to drag their wearer into Tartarus. They'd almost taken his best friend, Grover. 'I'd settle for a hang-glider.'

'Maybe not a good idea.' Annabeth pointed. Above them, dark winged shapes spiralled in and out of the blood-red clouds.

'Furies?' Percy wondered.

'Or some other kind of demon,' Annabeth said. 'Tartarus has thousands.'

'Including the kind that eats hang-gliders,' Percy guessed. 'Okay, so we climb.'

He couldn't see the *empousai* below them any more. They'd disappeared behind one of the ridges, but that didn't matter. It was clear where he and Annabeth needed to go. Like all the maggot monsters crawling over the plains of Tartarus, they should head towards the dark horizon. Percy was just brimming with enthusiasm for that.

XIV

PERCY

As **THEY STARTED DOWN THE CLIFF,** Percy concentrated on the challenges at hand: keeping his footing, avoiding rock-slides that would alert the *empousai* to their presence and of course making sure he and Annabeth didn't plummet to their deaths.

About halfway down the precipice, Annabeth said, 'Stop, okay? Just a quick break.'

Her legs wobbled so badly, Percy cursed himself for not calling a rest earlier.

They sat together on a ledge next to a roaring fiery water-fall. Percy put his arm around Annabeth, and she leaned against him, shaking from exhaustion.

He wasn't much better. His stomach felt like it had shrunk to the size of a gumdrop. If they came across any more monster carcasses, he was afraid he might pull an *empousa* and try to devour it.

At least he had Annabeth. They would find a way out of

Tartarus. They *had* to. He didn't think much of fates and prophecies, but he did believe in one thing: Annabeth and he were supposed to be together. They hadn't survived so much just to get killed now.

'Things could be worse,' Annabeth ventured.

'Yeah?' Percy didn't see how, but he tried to sound upbeat.

She snuggled against him. Her hair smelled of smoke, and if he closed his eyes he could almost imagine they were at the campfire at Camp Half-Blood.

'We could've fallen into the River Lethe,' she said. 'Lost all our memories.'

Percy's skin crawled just thinking about it. He'd had enough trouble with amnesia for one lifetime. Only last month, Hera had erased his memories to put him among the Roman demigods. Percy had stumbled into Camp Jupiter with no idea who he was or where he came from. And a few years before that he'd fought a Titan on the banks of the Lethe, near Hades's palace. He'd blasted the Titan with water from that river and completely wiped his memory clean. 'Yeah, the Lethe,' he muttered. 'Not my favourite.'

'What was the Titan's name?' Annabeth asked.

'Uh . . . Iapetus. He said it meant the *Impaler* or something.'

'No, the name you gave him after he lost his memory. Steve?'

'Bob,' Percy said.

Annabeth managed a weak laugh. 'Bob the Titan.'

Percy's lips were so parched, it hurt to smile. He wondered what had happened to Iapetus after they'd left him in Hades's palace . . . if he was still content being Bob, friendly, happy and clueless. Percy hoped so, but the Underworld seemed to bring out the worst in everyone – monsters, heroes and gods.

He gazed across the ashen plains. The other Titans were supposed to be here in Tartarus – maybe bound in chains, or roaming aimlessly, or hiding in some of those dark crevices. Percy and his allies had destroyed the worst Titan, Kronos, but even *his* remains might be down here somewhere – a billion angry Titan particles floating through the blood-coloured clouds or lurking in that dark fog.

Percy decided not to think about that. He kissed Annabeth's forehead. 'We should keep moving. You want some more fire to drink?'

'Ugh. I'll pass.'

They struggled to their feet. The rest of the cliff looked impossible to descend – nothing more than a crosshatching of tiny ledges – but they kept climbing down.

Percy's body went on autopilot. His fingers cramped. He felt blisters popping up on his ankles. He got shaky from hunger.

He wondered if they would die of starvation, or if the fire-water would keep them going. He remembered the punishment of Tantalus, who'd been permanently stuck in a pool of water under a fruit tree but couldn't reach either food or drink.

Jeez, Percy hadn't thought about Tantalus in years. That stupid guy had been paroled briefly to serve as director at Camp Half-Blood. Probably he was back in the Fields of Punishment. Percy had never felt sorry for the jerk before, but now he was starting to sympathize. He could imagine what it would be like, getting hungrier and hungrier for eternity but never being able to eat.

Keep climbing, he told himself.

Cheeseburgers, his stomach replied.

Shut up, he thought.

With fries, his stomach complained.

A billion years later, with a dozen new blisters on his feet, Percy reached the bottom. He helped Annabeth down, and they collapsed on the ground.

Ahead of them stretched miles of wasteland, bubbling with monstrous larvae and big insect-hair trees. To their right, the Phlegethon split into branches that etched the plain, widening into a delta of smoke and fire. To the north, along the main route of the river, the ground was riddled with cave entrances. Here and there, spires of rock jutted up like exclamation points.

Under Percy's hand, the soil felt alarmingly warm and smooth. He tried to grab a handful, then realized that, under a thin layer of dirt and debris, the ground was a single vast membrane . . . like skin.

He almost threw up, but forced himself not to. There was nothing in his stomach but fire.

He didn't mention it to Annabeth, but he started to feel like something was watching them – something vast and malevolent. He couldn't zero in on it, because the presence was all around them. *Watching* was the wrong word, too. That implied eyes, and this thing was simply aware of them. The ridges above them now looked less like steps and more like rows of massive teeth. The spires of rock looked like broken ribs. And if the ground was skin . . .

Percy forced those thoughts aside. This place was just freaking him out. That was all.

Annabeth stood, wiping soot from her face. She gazed towards the darkness on the horizon. 'We're going to be completely exposed, crossing this plain.'

About a hundred yards ahead of them, a blister burst on the ground. A monster clawed its way out . . . a glistening telkhine with slick fur, a seal-like body and stunted human limbs. It managed to crawl a few yards before something shot out of the nearest cave, so fast that Percy could only register a dark green reptilian head. The monster snatched the squealing telkhine in its jaws and dragged it into the darkness.

Reborn in Tartarus for two seconds, only to be eaten. Percy wondered if that telkhine would pop up in some other place in Tartarus, and how long it would take to re-form.

He swallowed down the sour taste of firewater. 'Oh, yeah. This'll be fun.'

Annabeth helped him to his feet. He took one last look at the cliffs, but there was no going back. He would've given a thousand golden drachmas to have Frank Zhang with them right now – good old Frank, who always seemed to show up when needed and could turn into an eagle or a dragon to fly them across this stupid wasteland.

They started walking, trying to avoid the cave entrances, sticking close to the bank of the river.

They were just skirting one of the spires when a glint of

movement caught Percy's eye – something darting between the rocks to their right.

A monster following them? Or maybe it was just some random baddie, heading for the Doors of Death.

Suddenly he remembered why they'd started following this route, and he froze in his tracks.

'The *empousai*.' He grabbed Annabeth's arm. 'Where are they?'

Annabeth scanned a three-sixty, her grey eyes bright with alarm.

Maybe the demon ladies had been snapped up by that reptile in the cave. If the *empousai* were still ahead of them, they should've been visible somewhere on the plains.

Unless they were hiding . . .

Too late, Percy drew his sword.

The *empousai* emerged from the rocks all around them – five of them forming a ring. A perfect trap.

Kelli limped forward on her mismatched legs. Her fiery hair burned across her shoulders like a miniature Phlegethon waterfall. Her tattered cheerleader outfit was splattered with rusty-brown stains, and Percy was pretty sure they weren't ketchup. She fixed him with her glowing red eyes and bared her fangs.

'Percy Jackson,' she cooed. 'How awesome! I don't even have to return to the mortal world to destroy you!'

XV

PERCY

PERCY RECALLED HOW DANGEROUS Kelli had been the last time they'd fought in the Labyrinth. Despite those mismatched legs, she could move fast when she wanted to. She'd dodged his sword strikes and would have eaten his face if Annabeth hadn't stabbed her from behind.

Now she had four friends with her.

'And your friend *Annabeth* is with you!' Kelli hissed with laughter. 'Oh, yeah, I totally remember her.'

Kelli touched her own sternum, where the tip of the knife had exited when Annabeth had stabbed her in the back. 'What's the matter, daughter of Athena? Don't have your weapon? Bummer. I'd use it to kill you.'

Percy tried to think. He and Annabeth stood shoulder to shoulder as they had many times before, ready to fight. But neither of them was in good shape for battle. Annabeth was empty-handed. They were hopelessly outnumbered. There was nowhere to run. No help coming.

Briefly Percy considered calling for Mrs O'Leary, his hellhound friend who could shadow-travel. Even if she heard him, could she make it into Tartarus? This was where monsters went when they died. Calling her here might kill her, or turn her back to her natural state as a fierce monster. No . . . he couldn't do that to his dog.

So, no help. Fighting was a long shot.

That left Annabeth's favourite tactics: trickery, talk, delay.

'So . . .' he started, 'I guess you're wondering what we're doing in Tartarus.'

Kelli snickered. 'Not really. I just want to kill you.'

That would've been it, but Annabeth chimed in.

'Too bad,' she said. 'Because you have no idea what's going on in the mortal world.'

The other *empousai* circled, watching Kelli for a cue to attack, but the ex-cheerleader only snarled, crouching out of reach of Percy's sword.

'We know enough,' Kelli said. 'Gaia has spoken.'

'You're heading towards a major defeat.' Annabeth sounded so confident, even Percy was impressed. She glanced at the other *empousai*, one by one, then pointed accusingly at Kelli. 'This one claims she's leading you to a victory. She's lying. The last time she was in the mortal world, Kelli was in charge of keeping my friend Luke Castellan faithful to Kronos. In the end, Luke rejected him. He gave his life to expel Kronos. The Titans lost because Kelli *failed*. Now Kelli wants to lead you to another disaster.'

The other *empousai* muttered and shifted uneasily.

'Enough!' Kelli's fingernails grew into long black talons.

She glared at Annabeth as if imagining her sliced into small pieces.

Percy was pretty sure Kelli had had a thing for Luke Castellan. Luke had that effect on girls – even donkey-legged vampires – and Percy wasn't sure bringing up his name was such a good idea.

'The girl lies,' Kelli said. 'So the Titans lost. Fine! That was part of the plan to wake Gaia! Now the Earth Mother and her giants will destroy the mortal world, and we will *totally* feast on demigods!'

The other vampires gnashed their teeth in a frenzy of excitement. Percy had been in the middle of a school of sharks when the water was full of blood. That wasn't nearly as scary as *empousai* ready to feed.

He prepared to attack, but how many could he dispatch before they overwhelmed him? It wouldn't be enough.

'The demigods have united!' Annabeth yelled. 'You'd better think twice before you attack us. Romans and Greeks will fight you together. You don't stand a chance!'

The *empousai* backed up nervously, hissing, '*Romani*.'

Percy guessed they'd had experience with the Twelfth Legion before and it hadn't worked out well for them.

'Yeah, you bet *Romani*.' Percy bared his forearm and showed them the brand he'd got at Camp Jupiter – the SPQR mark, with the trident of Neptune. 'You mix Greek and Roman, and you know what you get? You get *BAM*!'

He stomped his foot, and the *empousai* scrambled back. One fell off the boulder where she'd been perched.

That made Percy feel good, but they recovered quickly and closed in again.

'Bold talk,' Kelli said, 'for two demigods lost in Tartarus. Lower your sword, Percy Jackson, and I'll kill you quickly. Believe me, there are worse ways to die down here.'

'Wait!' Annabeth tried again. 'Aren't *empousai* the servants of Hecate?'

Kelli curled her lip. 'So?'

'So Hecate is on *our* side now,' Annabeth said. 'She has a cabin at Camp Half-Blood. Some of her demigod children are my friends. If you fight us, she'll be angry.'

Percy wanted to hug Annabeth, she was so brilliant.

One of the other *empousai* growled. 'Is this true, Kelli? Has our mistress made peace with Olympus?'

'Shut up, Serephone!' Kelli screeched. '*Gods*, you're annoying!'

'I will not cross the Dark Lady.'

Annabeth took the opening. 'You'd all be better following Serephone. She's older and wiser.'

'Yes!' Serephone shrieked. 'Follow me!'

Kelli struck so fast, Percy didn't have the chance to raise his sword. Fortunately, she didn't attack him. Kelli lashed out at Serephone. For half a second, the two demons were a blur of slashing claws and fangs.

Then it was over. Kelli stood triumphant over a pile of dust. From her claws hung the tattered remains of Serephone's dress.

'Any more *issues*?' Kelli snapped at her sisters. 'Hecate

is the goddess of the Mist! Her ways are mysterious. Who knows which side she truly favours? She is also the goddess of the crossroads, and she expects us to make our own choices. I choose the path that will bring us the most demigod blood! I choose Gaia!'

Her friends hissed in approval.

Annabeth glanced at Percy, and he saw that she was out of ideas. She'd done what she could. She'd got Kelli to eliminate one of her own. Now there was nothing left but to fight.

'For two years I churned in the void,' Kelli said. 'Do you know how completely *annoying* it is to be vaporized, Annabeth Chase? Slowly re-forming, fully conscious, in searing pain for months and years as your body regrows, then finally breaking the crust of this hellish place and clawing your way back to daylight? All because some *little girl* stabbed you in the back?'

Her baleful eyes held Annabeth's. 'I wonder what happens if a demigod is killed in Tartarus. I doubt it's ever happened before. Let's find out.'

Percy sprang, slashing Riptide in a huge arc. He cut one of the demons in half, but Kelli dodged and charged Annabeth. The other two *empousai* launched themselves at Percy. One grabbed his sword arm. Her friend jumped on his back.

Percy tried to ignore them and staggered towards Annabeth, determined to go down defending her if he had to, but Annabeth was doing pretty well. She tumbled to one side, evading Kelli's claws, and came up with a rock in her hand, which she smacked into Kelli's nose.

Kelli wailed. Annabeth scooped up gravel and flung it in the *empousa's* eyes.

Meanwhile Percy thrashed from side to side, trying to throw off his *empousa* hitch-hiker, but her claws sank deeper into his shoulders. The second *empousa* held his arm, preventing him from using Riptide.

Out of the corner of his eye, he saw Kelli lunge, raking her talons across Annabeth's arm. Annabeth screamed and fell.

Percy stumbled in her direction. The vampire on his back sank her teeth into his neck. Searing pain coursed through his body. His knees buckled.

Stay on your feet, he told himself. *You have to beat them.*

Then the other vampire bit his sword arm, and Riptide clattered to the ground.

That was it. His luck had finally run out. Kelli loomed over Annabeth, savouring her moment of triumph. The other two *empousai* circled Percy, their mouths slavering, ready for another taste.

Then a shadow fell across Percy. A deep war cry bellowed from somewhere above, echoing across the plains of Tartarus, and a Titan dropped onto the battlefield.

XVI

PERCY

PERCY THOUGHT HE WAS HALLUCINATING. It just wasn't possible that a huge silvery figure could drop out of the sky and stomp Kelli flat, trampling her into a mound of monster dust.

But that's exactly what happened. The Titan was ten feet tall, with wild silver Einstein hair, pure silver eyes and muscular arms protruding from a ripped-up blue janitor's uniform. In his hand was a massive push broom. His name tag, incredibly, read BOB.

Annabeth yelped and tried to crawl away, but the giant janitor wasn't interested in her. He turned to the two remaining *empousai*, who stood over Percy.

One was foolish enough to attack. She lunged with the speed of a tiger, but she never stood a chance. A spearhead jutted from the end of Bob's broom. With a single deadly swipe, he cut her to dust. The last vampire tried to run. Bob threw his broom like a massive boomerang (was there such a thing as a broomerang?). It sliced through the vampire and returned to Bob's hand.

'SWEEP!' The Titan grinned with delight and did a victory dance. 'Sweep, sweep, sweep!'

Percy couldn't speak. He couldn't bring himself to believe that something good had actually happened. Annabeth looked just as shocked.

'H-how . . . ?' she stammered.

'Percy called me!' the janitor said happily. 'Yes, he did.'

Annabeth crawled a little further away. Her arm was bleeding badly. 'Called you? He – wait. You're Bob? *The* Bob?'

The janitor frowned when he noticed Annabeth's wounds. 'Owie.'

Annabeth flinched as he knelt next to her.

'It's okay,' Percy said, still woozy with pain. 'He's friendly.'

He remembered when he'd first met Bob. The Titan had healed a bad wound on Percy's shoulder just by touching it. Sure enough, the janitor tapped Annabeth's forearm and it mended instantly.

Bob chuckled, pleased with himself, then bounded over to Percy and healed his bleeding neck and arm. The Titan's hands were surprisingly warm and gentle.

'All better!' Bob declared, his eerie silver eyes crinkling with pleasure. 'I am Bob, Percy's friend!'

'Uh . . . yeah,' Percy managed. 'Thanks for the help, Bob. It's *really* good to see you again.'

'Yes!' the janitor agreed. 'Bob. That's me. Bob, Bob, Bob.' He shuffled around, obviously pleased with his name. 'I am helping. I heard my name. Upstairs in Hades's palace, nobody calls for Bob unless there is a mess. Bob, sweep up these bones. Bob, mop up these tortured souls. Bob, a zombie exploded in the dining room.'

Annabeth gave Percy a puzzled look, but he had no explanation.

'Then I heard my friend call!' The Titan beamed. 'Percy said, *Bob*!'

He grabbed Percy's arm and hoisted him to his feet.

'That's awesome,' Percy said. 'Seriously. But how did you –'

'Oh, time to talk later.' Bob's expression turned serious. 'We must go before they find you. They are coming. Yes, indeed.'

'*They?*' Annabeth asked.

Percy scanned the horizon. He saw no approaching monsters – nothing but the stark grey wasteland.

'Yes,' Bob agreed. 'But Bob knows a way. Come on, friends! We will have fun!'

XVII

FRANK

FRANK WOKE UP AS A PYTHON, which puzzled him.

Changing into an animal wasn't confusing. He did that all the time. But he had never changed from one animal to another in his sleep before. He was pretty sure he hadn't dozed off as a snake. Usually, he slept like a dog.

He'd discovered that he got through the night much better if he curled up on his bunk in the shape of a bulldog. For whatever reason, his nightmares didn't bother him as much. The constant screaming in his head almost disappeared.

He had no idea why he'd become a reticulated python, but it did explain his dream about slowly swallowing a cow. His jaw was still sore.

He braced himself and changed back to human form. Immediately, his splitting headache returned, along with the voices.

Fight them! yelled Mars. *Take this ship! Defend Rome!*

The voice of Ares shouted back: *Kill the Romans! Blood and death! Large guns!*

His father's Roman and Greek personalities screamed back and forth in Frank's mind with the usual soundtrack of battle noises – explosions, assault rifles, roaring jet engines – all throbbing like a subwoofer behind Frank's eyes.

He sat up on his berth, dizzy with pain. As he did every morning, he took a deep breath and stared at the lamp on his desk – a tiny flame that burned night and day, fuelled by magic olive oil from the supply room.

Fire . . . Frank's biggest fear. Keeping an open flame in his room terrified him, but it also helped him focus. The noise in his head faded into the background, allowing him to think.

He'd got better at this, but for days he'd been almost worthless. As soon as the fighting broke out at Camp Jupiter, the war god's two voices had started screaming non-stop. Ever since, Frank had been stumbling around in a daze, barely able to function. He'd acted like a fool, and he was sure his friends thought he'd lost his marbles.

He couldn't tell them what was wrong. There was nothing they could do and, from listening to them talk, Frank was pretty sure they didn't have the same problem with their godly parents yelling in their ears.

Just Frank's luck, but he *had* to pull it together. His friends *needed* him – especially now, with Annabeth gone.

Annabeth had been kind to him. Even when he was so distracted he'd acted like a buffoon, Annabeth had been patient and helpful. While Ares screamed that Athena's children couldn't be trusted and Mars bellowed at him to kill all the Greeks, Frank had grown to respect Annabeth.

Now that they were without her, Frank was the next best thing the group had to a military strategist. They would need him for the trip ahead.

He rose and got dressed. Fortunately he'd managed to buy some new clothes in Siena a couple of days ago, replacing the laundry that Leo had sent flying away on Buford the table. (Long story.) He tugged on some Levi's and an army-green T-shirt, then reached for his favourite pullover before remembering he didn't need it. The weather was too warm. More important, he didn't need the pockets any more to protect the magical piece of firewood that controlled his life span. Hazel was keeping it safe for him.

Maybe that should have made him nervous. If the firewood burned, Frank died: end of story. But he trusted Hazel more than he trusted himself. Knowing she was safeguarding his big weakness made him feel better – like he'd fastened his seat belt for a high-speed chase.

He slung his bow and quiver over his shoulder. Immediately they morphed into a regular backpack. Frank loved that. He never would've known about the quiver's camouflage power if Leo hadn't figured it out for him.

Leo! Mars raged. *He must die!*

Throttle him! Ares cried. *Throttle everyone! Who are we talking about again?*

The two began shouting at each other again, over the sound of bombs exploding in Frank's skull.

He steadied himself against the wall. For days, Frank had listened to those voices demanding Leo Valdez's death.

After all, Leo had started the war with Camp Jupiter by firing a ballista into the Forum. Sure, he'd been possessed at the time, but still Mars demanded vengeance. Leo made things harder by constantly teasing Frank, and Ares demanded that Frank retaliate for every insult.

Frank kept the voices at bay, but it wasn't easy.

On their trip across the Atlantic, Leo had said something that still stuck in Frank's mind. When they'd learned that Gaia the evil earth goddess had put a bounty on their heads, Leo had wanted to know for how much.

I can understand not being as pricey as Jason or Percy, he'd said, *but am I worth, like, two or three Franks?*

Just another one of Leo's stupid jokes, but the comment hit a little too close to home. On the *Argo II*, Frank definitely felt like the LVP – Least Valuable Player. Sure, he could turn into animals. So what? His biggest claim to helpfulness so far had been changing into a weasel to escape from an underground workshop, and even *that* had been Leo's idea. Frank was better known for the Giant Goldfish Fiasco in Atlanta and, just yesterday, for turning into a two-hundred-kilo gorilla only to get knocked senseless by a flash-bang grenade.

Leo hadn't made any gorilla jokes at his expense yet. But it was only a matter of time.

Kill him!

Torture him! Then *kill him!*

The two sides of the war god seemed to be kicking and

punching each other inside Frank's head, using his sinuses as a wrestling mat.

Blood! Guns!

Rome! War!

Quiet down, Frank ordered.

Amazingly, the voices obeyed.

Okay, then, Frank thought.

Maybe he could finally get those annoying screaming mini-gods under control. Maybe today would be a good day.

That hope was shattered as soon as he climbed above deck.

'What *are* they?' Hazel asked.

The *Argo II* was docked at a busy wharf. On one side stretched a shipping channel about half a kilometre wide. On the other spread the city of Venice – red-tiled roofs, metal church domes, steepled towers and sun-bleached buildings in all the colours of Valentine candy hearts – red, white, ochre, pink and orange.

Everywhere there were statues of lions – on top of pedestals, over doorways, on the porticoes of the largest buildings. There were so many, Frank figured the lion must be the city's mascot.

Where streets should have been, green canals etched their way through the neighbourhoods, each one jammed with motorboats. Along the docks, the sidewalks were mobbed with tourists shopping at the T-shirt kiosks, overflowing from stores, and lounging across acres of outdoor café tables, like pods of sea lions. Frank had thought Rome was full of tourists. This place was insane.

Hazel and the rest of his friends weren't paying attention to any of that, though. They had gathered at the starboard rail to stare at the dozens of weird shaggy monsters milling through the crowds.

Each monster was about the size of a cow, with a bowed back like a broken-down horse, matted grey fur, skinny legs and black cloven hooves. The creatures' heads seemed much too heavy for their necks. Their long anteater-like snouts drooped to the ground. Their overgrown grey manes completely covered their eyes.

Frank watched as one of the creatures lumbered across the promenade, snuffling and licking the pavement with its long tongue. The tourists parted around it, unconcerned. A few even petted it. Frank wondered how the mortals could be so calm. Then the monster's appearance flickered. For a moment it turned into an old, fat beagle.

Jason grunted. 'The mortals think they're stray dogs.'

'Or pets roaming around,' Piper said. 'My dad shot a film in Venice once. I remember him telling me there were dogs everywhere. Venetians love dogs.'

Frank frowned. He kept forgetting that Piper's dad was Tristan McLean, A-list movie star. She didn't talk about him much. She seemed pretty down-to-earth for a kid raised in Hollywood. That was fine with Frank. The last thing they needed on this quest was paparazzi taking pictures of all Frank's epic fails.

'But what are they?' he asked, repeating Hazel's question.

'They look like . . . starving, shaggy cows with sheepdog hair.'

He waited for someone to enlighten him. Nobody volunteered any information.

'Maybe they're harmless,' Leo suggested. 'They're ignoring the mortals.'

'Harmless!' Gleeson Hedge laughed. The satyr wore his usual gym shorts, sports shirt and coach's whistle. His expression was as gruff as ever, but he still had one pink rubber band stuck in his hair from the prankster dwarfs in Bologna. Frank was kind of scared to mention it to him. 'Valdez, how many *harmless* monsters have we met? We should just aim the ballistae and see what happens!'

'Uh, no,' Leo said.

For once, Frank agreed with Leo. There were too many monsters. It would be impossible to target one without causing collateral damage to the crowds of tourists. Besides, if those creatures panicked and stampeded . . .

'We'll have to walk through them and hope they're peaceful,' Frank said, hating the idea already. 'It's the only way we're going to track down the owner of that book.'

Leo pulled the leather-bound manual from underneath his arm. He'd slapped a sticky note on the cover with the address the dwarfs in Bologna had given him.

'*La Casa Nera*,' he read. '*Calle Frezzeria.*'

'The Black House,' Nico di Angelo translated. 'Calle Frezzeria is the street.'

Frank tried not to flinch when he realized Nico was at his shoulder. The guy was so quiet and brooding he almost seemed to dematerialize when he wasn't speaking. Hazel might have been the one who came back from the dead, but Nico was *way* more ghost-like.

'You speak Italian?' Frank asked.

Nico shot him a warning look, like: *Watch the questions.* He spoke calmly, though. 'Frank is right. We have to find that address. The only way to do it is to walk the city. Venice is a maze. We'll have to risk the crowds and those . . . whatever they are.'

Thunder rumbled in the clear summer sky. They'd passed through some storms the night before. Frank had thought they were over, but now he wasn't sure. The air felt as thick and warm as sauna steam.

Jason frowned at the horizon. 'Maybe I should stay on board. Lots of *venti* in that storm last night. If they decide to attack the ship again . . .'

He didn't need to finish. They'd all had experiences with angry wind spirits. Jason was the only one who had much luck fighting them.

Coach Hedge grunted. 'Well, I'm out, too. If you soft-hearted cupcakes are going to stroll through Venice without even whacking those furry animals on the head, forget it. I don't like *boring* expeditions.'

'It's okay, Coach.' Leo grinned. 'We still have to repair the foremast. Then I need your help in the engine room. I've got an idea for a new installation.'

Frank didn't like the gleam in Leo's eye. Since Leo had found that Archimedes sphere, he'd been trying out a lot of 'new installations'. Usually, they exploded or sent smoke billowing upstairs into Frank's cabin.

'Well . . .' Piper shifted her feet. 'Whoever goes should be good with animals. I, uh . . . I'll admit I'm not great with cows.'

Frank figured there was a story behind that comment, but he decided not to ask.

'I'll go,' he said.

He wasn't sure why he volunteered – maybe because he was anxious to be useful for a change. Or maybe he didn't want anyone beating him to the punch. *Animals? Frank can turn into animals! Send him!*

Leo patted him on shoulder and handed him the leather-bound book. 'Awesome. If you pass a hardware store, could you get me some two-by-fours and a gallon of tar?'

'Leo,' Hazel chided, 'it's not a shopping trip.'

'I'll go with Frank,' Nico offered.

Frank's eye started twitching. The war gods' voices rose to a crescendo in his head: *Kill him! Graecus scum!*

No! I love Graecus scum!

'Uh . . . you're good with animals?' he asked.

Nico smiled without humour. 'Actually, most animals hate me. They can sense death. But there's something about this city . . .' His expression turned grim. 'Lots of death. Restless spirits. If I go, I may be able to keep them at bay. Besides, as you noticed, I speak Italian.'

Leo scratched his head. 'Lots of death, huh? Personally, I'm trying to avoid lots of death, but you guys have fun!'

Frank wasn't sure what scared him more: shaggy-cow monsters, hordes of restless ghosts or going somewhere alone with Nico di Angelo.

'I'll go, too.' Hazel slipped her arm through Frank's. 'Three is the best number for a demigod quest, right?'

Frank tried not to look too relieved. He didn't want to offend Nico. But he glanced at Hazel and told her with his eyes: *Thank you thank you thank you.*

Nico stared at the canals, as if wondering what new and interesting forms of evil spirits might be lurking there. 'All right, then. Let's go find the owner of that book.'

XVIII

FRANK

FRANK MIGHT HAVE LIKED VENICE if it hadn't been summertime and tourist season, and if the city wasn't overrun with large hairy creatures. Between the rows of old houses and the canals, the stone pavements were already too narrow for the crowds jostling one another and stopping to take pictures. The monsters made things worse. They shuffled around with their heads down, bumping into mortals and sniffing the ground.

One seemed to find something it liked at the edge of a canal. It nibbled and licked at a crack between the stones until it dislodged some sort of greenish root. The monster sucked it up happily and shambled along.

'Well, they're plant-eaters,' Frank said. 'That's good news.'

Hazel slipped her hand into his. 'Unless they supplement their diet with demigods. Let's hope not.'

Frank was so pleased to be holding her hand that the crowds and the heat and the monsters suddenly didn't seem so bad. He felt *needed* – useful.

Not that Hazel required his protection. Anybody who'd seen her charging on Arion with her sword drawn would know she could take care of herself. Still, Frank liked being next to her, imagining he was her bodyguard. If any of these monsters tried to hurt her, Frank would gladly turn into a rhinoceros and push them into the canal.

Could he do a rhino? Frank had never tried that before.

Nico stopped. 'There.'

They'd turned onto a smaller street, leaving the canal behind. Ahead of them was a small plaza lined with five-storey buildings. The area was strangely deserted – as if the mortals could sense it wasn't safe. In the middle of the cobblestone courtyard, a dozen shaggy cow creatures were sniffing around the mossy base of an old stone well.

'A lot of cows in one place,' Frank said.

'Yeah, but look,' Nico said. 'Past that archway.'

Nico's eyes must've been better than his. Frank squinted. At the far end of the plaza, a stone archway carved with lions led into a narrow street. Just past the arch, one of the town houses was painted black – the only black building Frank had seen so far in Venice.

'La Casa Nera,' he guessed.

Hazel's grip tightened on his fingers. 'I don't like that plaza. It feels . . . cold.'

Frank wasn't sure what she meant. He was still sweating like crazy.

But Nico nodded. He studied the town-house windows, most of which were covered with wooden shutters. 'You're right, Hazel. This neighbourhood is filled with *lemures*.'

'Lemurs?' Frank asked nervously. 'I'm guessing you don't mean the furry little guys from Madagascar?'

'Angry ghosts,' Nico said. '*Lemures* go back to Roman times. They hang around a lot of Italian cities, but I've never felt so many in one place. My mom told me . . .' He hesitated. 'She used to tell me stories about the ghosts of Venice.'

Again Frank wondered about Nico's past, but he was afraid to ask. He caught Hazel's eye.

Go ahead, she seemed to be saying. *Nico needs practice talking to people.*

The sounds of assault rifles and atom bombs got louder in Frank's head. Mars and Ares were trying to outsing each other with 'Dixie' and 'The Battle Hymn of the Republic'. Frank did his best to push that aside.

'Nico, your mom was Italian?' he guessed. 'She was from Venice?'

Nico nodded reluctantly. 'She met Hades here, back in the 1930s. As World War Two got closer, she fled to the U.S. with my sister and me. I mean . . . Bianca, my other sister. I don't remember much about Italy, but I can still speak the language.'

Frank tried to think of a response. *Oh, that's nice* didn't seem to cut it.

He was hanging out with not one but *two* demigods who'd been pulled out of time. They were both, technically, about seventy years older than he was.

'Must've been hard on your mom,' Frank said. 'I guess we'll do anything for someone we love.'

Hazel squeezed his hand appreciatively. Nico stared at the cobblestones. 'Yeah,' he said bitterly. 'I guess we will.'

Frank wasn't sure what Nico was thinking. He had a hard time imagining Nico di Angelo acting out of love for anybody, except maybe Hazel. But Frank decided he'd gone as far as he dared with the personal questions.

'So, the *lemures* . . .' He swallowed. 'How do we avoid them?'

'I'm already on it,' Nico said. 'I'm sending out the message that they should stay away and ignore us. Hopefully that's enough. Otherwise . . . things could get messy.'

Hazel pursed her lips. 'Let's get going,' she suggested.

Halfway across the piazza, everything went wrong, but it had nothing to do with ghosts.

They were skirting the well in the middle of the square, trying to give the cow monsters some distance, when Hazel stumbled on a loose piece of cobblestone. Frank caught her. Six or seven of the big grey beasts turned to look at them. Frank glimpsed a glowing green eye under one's mane, and instantly he was hit with a wave of nausea, the way he felt when he ate too much cheese or ice cream.

The creatures made deep throbbing sounds in their throats like angry foghorns.

'Nice cows,' Frank murmured. He put himself between his friends and the monsters. 'Guys, I'm thinking we should back out of here slowly.'

'I'm such a klutz,' Hazel whispered. 'Sorry.'

'It's not your fault,' Nico said. 'Look at your feet.'

Frank glanced down and caught his breath.

Under their shoes, the paving stones were moving – spiky plant tendrils were pushing up from the cracks.

Nico stepped back. The roots snaked out in his direction, trying to follow. The tendrils got thicker, exuding a steamy green vapour that smelled of boiled cabbage.

'These roots seem to like demigods,' Frank noted.

Hazel's hand drifted to her sword hilt. 'And the cow creatures like the roots.'

The entire herd was now looking their direction, making foghorn growls and stamping their hooves. Frank understood animal behaviour well enough to get the message: *You are standing on our food. That makes you enemies.*

Frank tried to think. There were too many monsters to fight. Something about their eyes hidden under those shaggy manes . . . Frank had got sick from the barest glimpse. He had a bad feeling that if those monsters made direct eye contact, he might get a lot worse than nauseous.

'Don't meet their eyes,' Frank warned. 'I'll distract them. You two back up slowly towards that black house.'

The creatures tensed, ready to attack.

'Never mind,' Frank said. 'Run!'

As it turned out, Frank could *not* turn into a rhino, and he lost valuable time trying.

Nico and Hazel bolted for the side street. Frank stepped in front of the monsters, hoping to keep their attention. He yelled at the top of his lungs, imagining himself as a fearsome rhinoceros, but with Ares and Mars screaming in his head he couldn't concentrate. He remained regular-old Frank.

Two of the cow monsters peeled off from the herd to chase Nico and Hazel.

'No!' Frank yelled after them. 'Me! I'm the rhino!'

The rest of the herd surrounded Frank. They growled, emerald-green gas billowing from their nostrils. Frank stepped back to avoid the stuff, but the stench nearly knocked him over.

Okay, so not a rhino. Something else. Frank knew he had only seconds before the monsters trampled or poisoned him, but he couldn't think. He couldn't hold the image of any animal long enough to change form.

Then he glanced up at one of the town-house balconies and saw a stone carving – the symbol of Venice.

The next instant, Frank was a full-grown lion. He roared in challenge, then sprang from the middle of the monster herd and landed eight metres away, on top of the old stone well.

The monsters growled in reply. Three of them sprang at once, but Frank was ready. His lion reflexes were built for speed in combat.

He slashed the first two monsters into dust with his claws, then sank his fangs into the third one's throat and tossed it aside.

There were seven left, plus the two chasing his friends. Not great odds, but Frank had to keep the bulk of herd focused on him. He roared at the monsters, and they edged away.

They outnumbered him, yes. But Frank was a top-of-the-chain predator. The herd monsters knew it. They had also just watched him send three of their friends to Tartarus.

He pressed his advantage and leaped off the well, still baring his fangs. The herd backed off.

If he could just manoeuvre around them, then turn and run after his friends . . .

He was doing all right, until he took his first backwards step towards the arch. One of cows, either the bravest or the stupidest, took that as a sign of weakness. It charged and blasted Frank in the face with green gas.

He slashed the monster to dust, but the damage was already done. He forced himself not to breathe. Regardless, he could feel the fur burning off his snout. His eyes stung. He staggered back, half-blind and dizzy, dimly aware of Nico screaming his name.

'Frank! *Frank!*'

He tried to focus. He was back in human form, retching and stumbling. His face felt like it was peeling off. In front of him, the green cloud of gas floated between him and the herd. The remaining cow monsters eyed him warily, probably wondering if Frank had any more tricks up his sleeve.

He glanced behind him. Under the stone arch, Nico di Angelo was holding his black Stygian iron sword, gesturing at Frank to hurry. At Nico's feet, two puddles of darkness stained the ground – no doubt the remains of the cow monsters that had chased them.

And Hazel . . . she was propped against the wall behind her brother. She wasn't moving.

Frank ran towards them, forgetting about the monster herd. He rushed past Nico and grabbed Hazel's shoulders. Her head slumped against her chest.

'She got a blast of green gas right in the face,' Nico said miserably. 'I – I wasn't fast enough.'

Frank couldn't tell if she was breathing. Rage and despair battled inside him. He'd always been scared of Nico. Now he wanted to drop-kick the son of Hades into the nearest canal. Maybe that wasn't fair, but Frank didn't care. Neither did the war gods screaming in his head.

'We need to get her back to the ship,' Frank said.

The cow monster herd prowled cautiously just beyond the archway. They bellowed their foghorn cries. From nearby streets, more monsters answered. Reinforcements would soon have the demigods surrounded.

'We'll never make it on foot,' Nico said. 'Frank, turn into a giant eagle. Don't worry about me. Get her back to the *Argo II*!'

With his face burning and the voices screaming in his mind, Frank wasn't sure he could change shape, but he was about to try when a voice behind them said, 'Your friends can't help you. They don't know the cure.'

Frank spun round. Standing on the threshold of the Black House was a young man in jeans and a denim shirt. He had curly black hair and a friendly smile, though Frank doubted he was friendly. Probably he wasn't even human.

At the moment, Frank didn't care.

'Can you cure her?' he asked.

'Of course,' the man said. 'But you'd better hurry inside. I think you've angered every *katobleps* in Venice.'

XIX

FRANK

THEY BARELY MADE IT INSIDE.

As soon as their host threw the bolts, the cow monsters bellowed and slammed into the door, making it shudder on its hinges.

'Oh, they can't get in,' the man in denim promised. 'You're safe now!'

'Safe?' Frank demanded. 'Hazel is dying!'

Their host frowned as if he didn't appreciate Frank ruining his good mood. 'Yes, yes. Bring her this way.'

Frank carried Hazel as they followed the man further into the building. Nico offered to help, but Frank didn't need it. Hazel weighed nothing, and Frank's body hummed with adrenalin. He could feel Hazel shivering, so at least he knew she was alive, but her skin was cold. Her lips had taken on a greenish tinge – or was that just Frank's blurry vision?

His eyes still burned from the monster's breath. His lungs felt like he'd inhaled a flaming cabbage. He didn't know why the gas had affected him less than it had Hazel. Maybe she'd got more of it in her lungs. He would have given anything to change places if it meant saving her.

The voices of Mars and Ares yelled in his head, urging him to kill Nico and the man in denim and anyone else he could find, but Frank forced down the noise.

The house's front room was some sort of greenhouse. The walls were lined with tables of plant trays under fluorescent lights. The air smelled of fertilizer solution. Maybe Venetians did their gardening inside, since they were surrounded by water instead of soil? Frank wasn't sure, but he didn't spend much time worrying about it.

The back room looked like a combination garage, college dorm and computer lab. Against the left wall glowed a bank of servers and laptops, their screen savers flashing pictures of ploughed fields and tractors. Against the right wall was a single bed, a messy desk and an open wardrobe filled with extra denim clothes and a stack of farm implements, like pitchforks and rakes.

The back wall was a huge garage door. Parked next to it was a red-and-gold chariot with an open carriage and a single axle, like the chariots Frank had raced at Camp Jupiter. Sprouting from the sides of the driver's box were giant feathery wings. Wrapped around the rim of the left wheel, a spotted python snored loudly.

Frank hadn't known that pythons could snore. He hoped he hadn't done that himself in python form last night.

'Set your friend here,' said the man in denim.

Frank placed Hazel gently on the bed. He removed her

sword and tried to make her comfortable, but she was as limp as a scarecrow. Her complexion definitely had a greenish tint.

'What were those cow things?' Frank demanded. 'What did they do to her?'

'*Katoblepones*,' said their host. 'Singular: *katobleps*. In English, it means *down-looker*. Called that because –'

'They're always looking down.' Nico smacked his forehead. 'Right. I remember reading about them.'

Frank glared at him. '*Now* you remember?'

Nico hung his head almost as low as a *katobleps*. 'I, uh . . . used to play this stupid card game when I was younger. Mythomagic. The *katobleps* was one of the monster cards.'

Frank blinked. 'I played Mythomagic. I never saw that card.'

'It was in the *Africanus Extreme* expansion deck.'

'Oh.'

Their host cleared his throat. 'Are you two done, ah, *geeking out*, as they say?'

'Right, sorry,' Nico muttered. 'Anyway, *katoblepones* have poison breath and a poison gaze. I thought they only lived in Africa.'

The man in denim shrugged. 'That's their native land. They were accidentally imported to Venice hundreds of years ago. You've heard of Saint Mark?'

Frank wanted to scream with frustration. He didn't see how any of this was relevant, but, if their host could heal Hazel, Frank decided maybe it would be best not to make him angry. 'Saints? They're not part of Greek mythology.'

The man in denim chuckled. 'No, but Saint Mark is the

patron saint of this city. He died in Egypt, oh, a long time ago. When the Venetians became powerful . . . well, the relics of saints were a big tourist attraction back in the Middle Ages. The Venetians decided to steal Saint Mark's remains and bring them to their big church of San Marco. They smuggled out his body in a barrel of pickled pig parts.'

'That's . . . disgusting,' Frank said.

'Yes,' the man agreed with a smile. 'The point is you can't do something like that and not have consequences. The Venetians unintentionally smuggled something *else* out of Egypt – the *katoblepones*. They came here aboard that ship and have been breeding like rats ever since. They love the magical poison roots that grow here – swampy, foul-smelling plants that creep up from the canals. It makes their breath even more poisonous! Usually the monsters ignore mortals, but demigods . . . especially demigods who get in their way –'

'Got it,' Frank snapped. 'Can you cure her?'

The man shrugged. 'Possibly.'

'*Possibly?*' Frank had to use all his willpower not to throttle the guy.

He put his hand under Hazel's nose. He couldn't feel her breath. 'Nico, please tell me she's doing that death-trance thing, like you did in the bronze jar.'

Nico grimaced. 'I don't know if Hazel can do that. Her dad is technically Pluto, not Hades, so –'

'Hades!' cried their host. He backed away, staring at Nico with distaste. 'So *that's* what I smell. Children of the Underworld? If I'd known *that*, I would never have let you in!'

Frank rose. 'Hazel's a good person. You promised you would *help* her!'

'I did *not* promise.'

Nico drew his sword. 'She's my sister,' he growled. 'I don't know who you are, but if you can cure her you have to, or so help me by the River Styx –'

'Oh, blah, blah, blah!' The man waved his hand. Suddenly where Nico di Angelo had been standing was a potted plant about five feet tall, with drooping green leaves, tufts of silk and half a dozen ripe yellow ears of corn.

'There,' the man huffed, wagging his finger at the corn plant. 'Children of Hades can't order me around! You should talk less and listen more. Now at least you have *ears*.'

Frank stumbled against the bed. 'What did you – why –?'

The man raised an eyebrow. Frank made a squeaky noise that wasn't very courageous. He'd been so focused on Hazel, he'd forgotten what Leo had told them about the guy they were looking for. 'You're a god,' he remembered.

'Triptolemus.' The man bowed. 'My friends call me Trip, so don't call me that. And if you're another child of Hades –'

'Mars!' Frank said quickly. 'Child of Mars!'

Triptolemus sniffed. 'Well . . . not much better. But perhaps you deserve to be something better than a corn plant. Sorghum? Sorghum is very nice.'

'Wait!' Frank pleaded. 'We're here on a friendly mission. We brought a gift.' Very slowly, he reached into his backpack and brought out the leather-bound book. 'This belongs to you?'

'My almanac!' Triptolemus grinned and seized the book. He thumbed through the pages and started bouncing on the balls of his feet. 'Oh, this is fabulous! Where did you find it?'

'Um, Bologna. There were these –' Frank remembered that he wasn't supposed to mention the dwarfs – 'terrible monsters. We risked our lives, but we knew this was important to you. So could you maybe, you know, turn Nico back to normal and heal Hazel?'

'Hmm?' Trip looked up from his book. He'd been happily reciting lines to himself – something about turnip-planting schedules. Frank wished that Ella the harpy were here. She would get along great with this guy.

'Oh, *heal* them?' Triptolemus clucked disapprovingly. 'I'm grateful for the book, of course. I can definitely let *you* go free, son of Mars. But I have a long-standing problem with Hades. After all, I owe my godly powers to Demeter!'

Frank racked his brain, but it was hard with the voices screaming in his head and the *katobleps* poison making him dizzy.

'Uh, Demeter,' he said, 'the plant goddess. She – she didn't like Hades because . . .' Suddenly he recalled an old story he'd heard at Camp Jupiter. 'Her daughter, Proserpine –'

'Persephone,' Trip corrected. 'I prefer the Greek, if you don't mind.'

Kill him! Mars screamed.

I love this guy! Ares yelled back. *Kill him anyway!*

Frank decided not to take offence. He didn't want to

get turned into a sorghum plant. 'Okay. Hades kidnapped Persephone.'

'Exactly!' Trip said.

'So . . . Persephone was a friend of yours?'

Trip snorted. 'I was just a mortal prince back then. Persephone wouldn't have noticed me. But when her mother, Demeter, went searching for her, scouring the whole earth, not many people would help her. Hecate lit her way at night with her torches. And I . . . well, when Demeter came to my part of Greece, I gave her a place to stay. I comforted her, gave her a meal, and offered my assistance. I didn't know she was a goddess at the time, but my good deed paid off. Later, Demeter rewarded me by making me a god of farming!'

'Wow,' Frank said. 'Farming. Congratulations.'

'I know! Pretty awesome, right? Anyway, Demeter never got along with Hades. So naturally, you know, I have to side with my patron goddess. Children of Hades – forget it! In fact, one of them – this Scythian king named Lynkos? When I tried to teach his countrymen about farming, he killed my right python!'

'Your . . . right python?'

Trip marched over to his winged chariot and hopped in. He pulled a lever, and the wings began to flap. The spotted python on the left wheel opened his eyes. He started to writhe, coiling around the axle like a spring. The chariot whirred into motion, but the right wheel stayed in place, so Triptolemus spun in circles, the chariot beating its wings and bouncing up and down like a defective merry-go-round.

'You see?' he said as he spun. 'No good! Ever since I lost my right python, I haven't been able to spread the word about farming – at least not in person. Now I have to resort to giving online courses.'

'What?' As soon as he said it, Frank was sorry he'd asked.

Trip hopped off the chariot while it was still spinning. The python slowed to a stop and went back to snoring. Trip jogged over to the line of computers. He tapped the keyboards and the screens woke up, displaying a website in maroon and gold, with a picture of a happy farmer in a toga and a farmer's hat, standing with his bronze scythe in a field of wheat.

'Triptolemus Farming University!' he announced proudly. 'In just six weeks, you can get your bachelor's degree in the exciting and vibrant career of the future – farming!'

Frank felt a bead of sweat trickle down his cheek. He didn't care about this crazy god or his snake-powered chariot or his online degree programme. But Hazel was turning greener by the moment. Nico was a corn plant. And he was alone.

'Look,' he said. 'We *did* bring you the almanac. And my friends are really nice. They're not like those other children of Hades you've met. So if there's any way –'

'Oh!' Trip snapped his fingers. 'I see where you're going!'

'Uh . . . you do?'

'Absolutely! If I cure your friend Hazel and return the other one, Nicholas –'

'Nico.'

'– if I return him to normal . . .'

Frank hesitated. 'Yes?'

'Then, in exchange, you stay with me and take up farming! A child of Mars as my apprentice? It's perfect! What a spokesman you'll be. We can beat swords into ploughshares and have so much fun!'

'Actually . . .' Frank tried frantically to come up with a plan. Ares and Mars screamed in his head, *Swords! Guns! Massive ka-booms!*

If he declined Trip's offer, Frank figured he would offend the guy and end up as sorghum or wheat or some other cash crop.

If it was the only way to save Hazel, then, sure, he could agree to Trip's demands and become a farmer. But that *couldn't* be the only way. Frank refused to believe he'd been chosen by the Fates to go on this quest just so he could take online courses in turnip cultivation.

Frank's eyes wandered to the broken chariot. 'I have a better offer,' he blurted out. 'I can fix that.'

Trip's smile melted. 'Fix . . . my chariot?'

Frank wanted to kick himself. What was he *thinking*? He wasn't Leo. He couldn't even figure out a stupid pair of Chinese handcuffs. He could barely change the batteries in a TV remote. He couldn't fix a magical chariot!

But something told him it was his only chance. That chariot was the one thing Triptolemus might really want.

'I'll go find a way to fix the chariot,' he said. 'In return, you fix Nico and Hazel. Let us go in peace. And – and give us whatever aid you can to defeat Gaia's forces.'

Triptolemus laughed. 'What makes you think I can aid you with *that*?'

'Hecate told us so,' Frank said. 'She sent us here. She – she decided Hazel is one of her favourites.'

The colour drained from Trip's face. 'Hecate?'

Frank hoped he wasn't overstating things. He didn't need Hecate mad at him too. But, if Triptolemus and Hecate were both friends of Demeter, maybe that would convince Trip to help.

'The goddess guided us to your almanac in Bologna,' Frank said. 'She wanted us to return it to you, because . . . well, she must've known you had some knowledge that would help us get through the House of Hades in Epirus.'

Trip nodded slowly. 'Yes. I see. I know why Hecate sent you to me. Very well, son of Mars. Go find a way to fix my chariot. If you succeed, I will do all you ask. If not –'

'I know,' Frank grumbled. 'My friends die.'

'Yes,' Trip said cheerfully. 'And you'll make a lovely patch of sorghum!'

FRANK

FRANK STUMBLED OUT OF THE BLACK HOUSE. The door shut behind him, and he collapsed against the wall, overcome with guilt. Fortunately the *katoblepones* had cleared off, or he might have just sat there and let them trample him. He deserved nothing better. He'd left Hazel inside, dying and defenceless, at the mercy of a crazy farmer god.

Kill farmers! Ares screamed in his head.

Return to the legion and fight Greeks! Mars said. *What are we doing here?*

Killing farmers! Ares screamed back.

'Shut up!' Frank yelled aloud. 'Both of you!'

A couple of old ladies with shopping bags shuffled past. They gave Frank a strange look, muttered something in Italian and kept going.

Frank stared miserably at Hazel's cavalry sword, lying at his feet next to his backpack. He could run back to the *Argo II* and get Leo. Maybe Leo could fix the chariot.

But Frank somehow knew this wasn't a problem for Leo. It was Frank's task. He had to prove himself. Besides, the chariot wasn't exactly broken. There was no mechanical problem. It was missing a serpent.

Frank could turn himself into a python. When he'd woken up that morning as a giant snake, perhaps it had been a sign from the gods. He didn't want to spend the rest of his life turning the wheel of a farmer's chariot, but if it meant saving Hazel . . .

No. There had to be another way.

Serpents, Frank thought. Mars.

Did his father have some connection to snakes? Mars's sacred animal was the wild boar, not the serpent. Still, Frank was sure he'd heard something once . . .

He could think of only one person to ask. Reluctantly, he opened his mind to the voices of the war god.

I need a snake, he told them. *How?*

Ha, ha! Ares screamed. *Yes, the serpent!*

Like that vile Cadmus, Mars said. *We punished him for killing our dragon!*

They both started yelling, until Frank thought his brain would split in half.

'Okay! Stop!'

The voices quieted.

'Cadmus,' Frank muttered. 'Cadmus . . .'

The story came back to him. The demigod Cadmus had slain a dragon that happened to be a child of Ares. How Ares had ended up with a dragon for a son, Frank didn't want to know, but as punishment for the dragon's death Ares turned Cadmus into a snake.

'So you can turn your enemies into snakes,' Frank said. 'That's what I need. I need to find an enemy. Then I need you to turn him into a snake.'

You think I would do that for you? Ares roared. *You have not proven your worth!*

Only the greatest hero could ask such a boon, Mars said. *A hero like Romulus!*

Too Roman! Ares shouted. *Diomedes!*

Never! Mars shouted back. *That coward fell to Heracles!*

Horatius, then, Ares suggested.

Mars went silent. Frank sensed a grudging agreement.

'Horatius,' Frank said. 'Fine. If that's what it takes, I'll prove I'm as good as Horatius. Uh . . . what did he do?'

Images flooded into Frank's mind. He saw a lone warrior standing on a stone bridge, facing an entire army massed on the far side of the Tiber River.

Frank remembered the legend. Horatius, the Roman general, had single-handedly held off a horde of invaders, sacrificing himself on that bridge to keep the barbarians from crossing the Tiber. By giving his fellow Romans time to finish their defences, he'd saved the Republic.

Venice is overrun, Mars said, *as Rome was about to be. Cleanse it!*

Destroy them all! Ares said. *Put them to the sword!*

Frank pushed the voices to the back of his mind. He looked at his hands and was amazed they weren't trembling.

For the first time in days, his thoughts were clear. He knew exactly what he needed to do. He didn't know how he would pull it off. The odds of dying were excellent, but he had to try. Hazel's life depended on him.

He strapped Hazel's sword to his belt, morphed his backpack into a quiver and bow, and raced towards the piazza where he'd fought the cow monsters.

The plan had three phases: dangerous, really dangerous and insanely dangerous.

Frank stopped at the old stone well. No *katoblepones* in sight. He drew Hazel's sword and used it to prise up some cobblestones, unearthing a big tangle of spiky roots. The tendrils unfurled, exuding their stinky green fumes as they crept towards Frank's feet.

In the distance, a *katobleps*'s foghorn moan filled the air. Others joined in from all different directions. Frank wasn't sure how the monsters could tell he was harvesting their favourite food – maybe they just had an excellent sense of smell.

He had to move fast now. He sliced off a long cluster of vines and laced them through one of his belt loops, trying to ignore the burning and itching in his hands. Soon he had a glowing, stinking lasso of poisonous weeds. Hooray.

The first few *katoblepones* lumbered into the piazza, bellowing in anger. Green eyes glowed under their manes. Their long snouts blew clouds of gas, like furry steam engines.

Frank nocked an arrow. He had a momentary pang of guilt. These were not the worst monsters he'd met. They were basically grazing animals that happened to be poisonous.

Hazel is dying because of them, he reminded himself.

He let the arrow fly. The nearest *katobleps* collapsed, crumbling to dust. He nocked a second arrow, but the rest of the herd was almost on top of him. More were charging into the square from the opposite direction.

Frank turned into a lion. He roared defiantly and leaped towards the archway, straight over the heads of the second herd. The two groups of *katoblepones* slammed into each other, but quickly recovered and ran after him.

Frank hadn't been sure the roots would still smell when he changed form. Usually his clothes and possessions just sort of melted into his animal shape, but apparently he still smelled like a yummy poison dinner. Each time he raced past a *katobleps*, it roared with outrage and joined the *Kill Frank!* Parade.

He turned onto a larger street and pushed through the crowds of tourists. What the mortals saw, he had no idea – a cat being chased by a pack of dogs? People cursed Frank in about twelve different languages. Gelato cones went flying. A woman spilled a stack of carnival masks. One dude toppled into the canal.

When Frank glanced back, he had at least two dozen monsters on his tail, but he needed more. He needed *all* the monsters in Venice, and he had to keep the ones behind him enraged.

He found an open spot in the crowd and turned back into a human. He drew Hazel's *spatha* – never his preferred weapon, but he was big enough and strong enough that the heavy cavalry sword didn't bother him. In fact he was glad for the extra reach. He slashed the golden blade, destroying the first *katobleps* and letting the others bunch up in front of him.

He tried to avoid their eyes, but he could feel their gaze burning into him. He figured that if all these monsters breathed on him at once their combined noxious cloud would be enough to melt him into a puddle. The monsters crowded forward and slammed into one another.

Frank yelled, 'You want my poison roots? Come and get them!'

He turned into a dolphin and jumped into the canal. He hoped *katoblepones* couldn't swim. At the very least, they seemed reluctant to follow him in, and he couldn't blame them. The canal was disgusting – smelly and salty and as warm as soup – but Frank forged through it, dodging gondolas and speedboats, pausing occasionally to chitter dolphin insults at the monsters who followed him on the sidewalks. When he reached the nearest gondola dock, Frank turned back into a human again, stabbed a few more *katoblepones* to keep them angry and took off running.

So it went.

After a while, Frank fell into a kind of daze. He attracted more monsters, scattered more crowds of tourists and led his now massive following of *katoblepones* through the winding streets of the old city. Whenever he needed a quick escape, he dived into a canal as a dolphin or turned into an eagle and soared overhead, but he never got too far ahead of his pursuers.

Whenever he felt like the monsters might be losing interest, he stopped on a rooftop and drew his bow, picking off a few of

the *katoblepones* in the centre of the herd. He shook his lasso
of poison vines and insulted the monsters' bad breath, stirring
them into a fury. Then he continued the race.

He backtracked. He lost his way. Once he turned a corner
and ran into the tail end of his own monster mob. He should
have been exhausted, yet somehow he found the strength to
keep going – which was good. The hardest part was yet to
come.

He spotted a couple of bridges, but they didn't look right.
One was elevated and completely covered; no way could he get
the monsters to funnel through it. Another was too crowded
with tourists. Even if the monsters ignored the mortals, that
noxious gas couldn't be good for anyone to breathe. The
bigger the monster herd got, the more mortals would get
pushed aside, knocked into the water or trampled.

Finally Frank saw something that would work. Just ahead,
past a big piazza, a wooden bridge spanned one of the widest
canals. The bridge itself was a latticed arc of timber, like an
old-fashioned roller coaster, about fifty metres long.

From above, in eagle form, Frank saw no monsters on
the far side. Every *katobleps* in Venice seemed to have joined
the herd and was pushing through the streets behind him as
tourists screamed and scattered, maybe thinking they were
caught in the midst of a stray dog stampede.

The bridge was empty of foot traffic. It was perfect.

Frank dropped like a stone and turned back to human
form. He ran to the middle of the bridge – a natural choke
point – and threw his bait of poisonous roots on the deck
behind him.

As the front of the *katobleps* herd reached the base of the bridge, Frank drew Hazel's golden *spatha*.

'Come on!' he yelled. 'You want to know what Frank Zhang is worth? Come on!'

He realized he wasn't just shouting at the monsters. He was venting weeks of fear, rage and resentment. The voices of Mars and Ares screamed right along with him.

The monsters charged. Frank's vision turned red.

Later, he couldn't remember the details clearly. He sliced through monsters until he was ankle-deep in yellow dust. Whenever he got overwhelmed and the clouds of gas began to choke him, he changed shape – became an elephant, a dragon, a lion – and each transformation seemed to clear his lungs, giving him a fresh burst of energy. His shape-shifting became so fluid, he could start an attack in human form with his sword and finish as a lion, raking his claws across a *katobleps*'s snout.

The monsters kicked with their hooves. They breathed noxious gas and glared straight at Frank with their poisonous eyes. He should have died. He should have been trampled. But somehow he stayed on his feet, unharmed, and unleashed a hurricane of violence.

He didn't feel any sort of pleasure in this, but he didn't hesitate, either. He stabbed one monster and beheaded another. He turned into a dragon and bit a *katobleps* in half, then changed into an elephant and trampled three at once under his feet. His vision was still tinted red, and he realized his eyes weren't playing tricks on him. He was actually glowing – surrounded by a rosy aura.

He didn't understand why, but he kept fighting until there was only one monster left.

Frank faced it with his sword drawn. He was out of breath, sweaty and caked in monster dust, but he was unharmed.

The *katobleps* snarled. It must not have been the smartest monster. Despite the fact that several hundred of its brethren had just died, it did not back down.

'Mars!' Frank yelled. 'I've proven myself. Now I need a snake!'

Frank doubted anyone had ever shouted those words before. It was kind of a weird request. He got no answer from the skies. For once, the voices in his head were silent.

The *katobleps* lost patience. It launched itself at Frank and left him no choice. He slashed upward. As soon as his blade hit the monster, the *katobleps* disappeared in a flash of blood-red light. When Frank's vision cleared, a mottled brown Burmese python was coiled at his feet.

'Well done,' said a familiar voice.

Standing a few feet away was his dad, Mars, wearing a red beret and olive fatigues with the insignia of the Italian Special Forces, an assault rifle slung over his shoulder. His face was hard and angular, his eyes covered with dark sunglasses.

'Father,' Frank managed.

He couldn't believe what he'd just done. The terror started to catch up with him. He felt like sobbing, but he guessed that would not be a good idea in front of Mars.

'It's natural to feel fear.' The war god's voice was surprisingly warm, full of pride. 'All great warriors are afraid. Only the stupid and the delusional are not. But you faced your fear, my son. You did what you had to do, like Horatius. This was your bridge, and you defended it.'

'I –' Frank wasn't sure what to say. 'I . . . I just needed a snake.'

A tiny smile tugged at Mars's mouth. 'Yes. And now you have one. Your bravery has united my forms, Greek and Roman, if only for a moment. Go. Save your friends. But hear me, Frank. Your greatest test is yet to come. When you face the armies of Gaia at Epirus, your leadership –'

Suddenly the god doubled over, clutching his head. His form flickered. His fatigues turned into a toga, then a biker's jacket and jeans. His rifle changed into a sword and then a rocket launcher.

'Agony!' Mars bellowed. 'Go! Hurry!'

Frank didn't ask questions. Despite his exhaustion, he turned into a giant eagle, snatched up the python in his massive claws and launched himself into the air.

When he glanced back, a miniature mushroom cloud erupted from the middle of the bridge, rings of fire washing outwards, and a pair of voices – Mars and Ares – screamed, 'Noooo!'

Frank wasn't sure what had just happened, but he had no time to think about it. He flew over the city – now completely empty of monsters – and headed for the house of Triptolemus.

'You found one!' the farmer god exclaimed.

Frank ignored him. He stormed into La Casa Nera, dragging the python by its tail like a very strange Santa Claus bag, and dropped it next to the bed.

He knelt at Hazel's side.

She was still alive – green and shivering, barely breathing, but alive. As for Nico, he was still a corn plant.

'Heal them,' Frank said. 'Now.'

Triptolemus crossed his arms. 'How do I know the snake will work?'

Frank gritted his teeth. Since the explosion on the bridge, the voices of the war god had gone silent in his head, but he still felt their combined anger churning inside him. He felt physically different, too. Had Triptolemus got shorter?

'The snake is a gift from Mars,' Frank growled. 'It will work.'

As if on cue, the Burmese python slithered over to the chariot and wrapped itself around the right wheel. The other snake woke up. The two serpents checked each other out, touching noses, then turned their wheels in unison. The chariot inched forward, its wings flapping.

'You see?' Frank said. 'Now, heal my friends!'

Triptolemus tapped his chin. 'Well, thank you for the snake, but I'm not sure I like your tone, demigod. Perhaps I'll turn you into –'

Frank was faster. He lunged at Trip and slammed him into the wall, his fingers locked around the god's throat.

'Think about your next words,' Frank warned, deadly calm. 'Or, instead of beating my sword into a ploughshare, I will beat it into your head.'

Triptolemus gulped. 'You know . . . I think I'll heal your friends.'

'Swear it on the River Styx.'

'I swear it on the River Styx.'

Frank released him. Triptolemus touched his throat, as if making sure it was still there. He gave Frank a nervous smile, edged around him and scurried off to the front room. 'Just – just gathering herbs!'

Frank watched as the god picked leaves and roots and crushed them in a mortar. He rolled a pill-sized ball of green goop and jogged to Hazel's side. He placed the gunk ball under Hazel's tongue.

Instantly, she shuddered and sat up, coughing. Her eyes flew open. The greenish tint in her skin disappeared.

She looked around, bewildered, until she saw Frank. 'What –?'

Frank tackled her in a hug. 'You're going to be fine,' he said fiercely. 'Everything is fine.'

'But . . .' Hazel gripped his shoulders and stared at him in amazement. 'Frank, what *happened* to you?'

'To *me*?' He stood, suddenly self-conscious. 'I don't . . .'

He looked down and realized what she meant. Triptolemus hadn't got shorter. Frank was taller. His gut had shrunk. His chest seemed bulkier.

Frank had had growth spurts before. Once he'd woken up two centimetres taller than when he'd gone to sleep. But this was nuts. It was as if some of the dragon and lion had stayed with him when he'd turned back to human.

'Uh . . . I don't . . . Maybe I can fix it.'

Hazel laughed with delight. 'Why? You look amazing!'

'I – I do?'

'I mean, you were handsome before! But you look older, and taller, and so distinguished –'

Triptolemus heaved a dramatic sigh. 'Yes, obviously some sort of blessing from Mars. Congratulations, blah, blah, blah. Now, if we're done here . . . ?'

Frank glared at him. 'We're not done. Heal Nico.'

The farm god rolled his eyes. He pointed at the corn plant, and BAM! Nico di Angelo appeared in an explosion of corn silk.

Nico looked around in a panic. 'I – I had the weirdest nightmare about popcorn.' He frowned at Frank. 'Why are you *taller*?'

'Everything's fine,' Frank promised. 'Triptolemus was about to tell us how to survive the House of Hades. Weren't you, Trip?'

The farm god raised his eyes to the ceiling, like, *Why me, Demeter?*

'Fine,' Trip said. 'When you arrive at Epirus, you will be offered a chalice to drink from.'

'Offered by whom?' Nico asked.

'Doesn't matter,' Trip snapped. 'Just know that it is filled with deadly poison.'

Hazel shuddered. 'So you're saying that we shouldn't drink it.'

'No!' Trip said. 'You *must* drink it, or you'll never be able to make it through the temple. The poison connects you to the world of the dead, lets you pass into the lower levels. The secret to surviving is –' his eyes twinkled – '*barley*.'

Frank stared at him. 'Barley.'

'In the front room, take some of my special barley. Make it into little cakes. Eat these before you step into the House of Hades. The barley will absorb the worst of the poison, so it will *affect* you, but not kill you.'

'That's it?' Nico demanded. 'Hecate sent us halfway across Italy so you could tell us to eat barley?'

'Good luck!' Triptolemus sprinted across the room and hopped in his chariot. 'And, Frank Zhang, I forgive you! You've got spunk. If you ever change your mind, my offer is open. I'd love to see you get a degree in farming!'

'Yeah,' Frank muttered. 'Thanks.'

The god pulled a lever on his chariot. The snake-wheels turned. The wings flapped. At the back of the room, the garage doors rolled open.

'Oh, to be mobile again!' Trip cried. 'So many ignorant lands in need of my knowledge. I will teach them the glories of tilling, irrigation, fertilizing!' The chariot lifted off and zipped out of the house, Triptolemus shouting to the sky, 'Away, my serpents! Away!'

'That,' Hazel said, 'was very strange.'

'The glories of fertilizing.' Nico brushed some corn silk off his shoulder. 'Can we get out of here now?'

Hazel put her hand on Frank's shoulder. 'Are you okay, really? You bartered for our lives. What did Triptolemus make you do?'

Frank tried to hold it together. He scolded himself for feeling so weak. He could face an army of monsters, but as soon as Hazel showed him kindness he wanted to break down and cry. 'Those cow monsters . . . the *katoblepones* that poisoned you . . . I had to destroy them.'

'That was brave,' Nico said. 'There must have been, what, six or seven left in that herd.'

'No.' Frank cleared his throat. 'All of them. I killed *all* of them in the city.'

Nico and Hazel stared at him in stunned silence. Frank was afraid they might doubt him, or start to laugh. How many monsters had he killed on that bridge – two hundred? Three hundred?

But he saw in their eyes that they believed him. They were children of the Underworld. Maybe they could sense the death and carnage he'd unleashed.

Hazel kissed his cheek. She had to stand on her tiptoes to do it now. Her eyes were incredibly sad, as if she realized something had changed in Frank – something much more important than the physical growth spurt.

Frank knew it too. He would never be the same. He just wasn't sure if that was a good thing.

'Well,' Nico said, breaking the tension, 'does anyone know what barley looks like?'

ANNABETH

ANNABETH DECIDED THE MONSTERS wouldn't kill her. Neither would the poisonous atmosphere, nor the treacherous landscape with its pits, cliffs and jagged rocks.

Nope. Most likely she would die from an overload of *weirdness* that would make her brain explode.

First, she and Percy had had to drink fire to stay alive. Then they were attacked by a gaggle of vampires, led by a cheerleader Annabeth had killed two years ago. Finally, they were rescued by a Titan janitor named Bob who had Einstein hair, silver eyes and wicked broom skills.

Sure. Why not?

They followed Bob through the wasteland, tracing the route of the Phlegethon as they approached the storm front of darkness. Every so often they stopped to drink firewater, which kept them alive, but Annabeth wasn't happy about it. Her throat felt like she was constantly gargling with battery acid.

Her only comfort was Percy. Every so often he would glance over and smile, or squeeze her hand. He had to be just as scared and miserable as she was, and she loved him for trying to make her feel better.

'Bob knows what he's doing,' Percy promised.

'You have interesting friends,' Annabeth murmured.

'Bob is interesting!' The Titan turned and grinned. 'Yes, thank you!'

The big guy had good ears. Annabeth would have to remember that.

'So, Bob . . .' She tried to sound casual and friendly, which wasn't easy with a throat scorched by firewater. 'How did you get to Tartarus?'

'I jumped,' he said, like it was obvious.

'You jumped into Tartarus,' she said, 'because Percy said your name?'

'He needed me.' Those silver eyes gleamed in the darkness. 'It is okay. I was tired of sweeping the palace. Come along! We are almost at a rest stop.'

A rest stop.

Annabeth couldn't imagine what those words meant in Tartarus. She remembered all the times she, Luke and Thalia had relied on highway rest stops when they were homeless demigods, trying to survive.

Wherever Bob was taking them, she hoped it had clean restrooms and a snack machine. She repressed the giggles. Yes, she was definitely losing it.

Annabeth hobbled along, trying to ignore the rumble in her stomach. She stared at Bob's back as he led them towards the wall of darkness, now only a few hundred yards away. His blue janitor's coveralls were ripped between the shoulder blades, as if someone had tried to stab him. Cleaning rags stuck out of his pocket. A squirt bottle swung from his belt, the blue liquid inside sloshing hypnotically.

Annabeth remembered Percy's story about meeting the Titan. Thalia Grace, Nico di Angelo and Percy had worked together to defeat Bob on the banks of the Lethe. After wiping his memory, they didn't have the heart to kill him. He became so gentle and sweet and cooperative that they left him at the palace of Hades, where Persephone promised he would be looked after.

Apparently, the Underworld king and queen thought 'looking after' someone meant giving him a broom and having him sweep up their messes. Annabeth wondered how even Hades could be so callous. She'd never felt sorry for a Titan before, but it didn't seem right taking a brainwashed immortal and turning him into an unpaid janitor.

He's not your friend, she reminded herself.

She was terrified that Bob would suddenly remember himself. Tartarus was where monsters came to regenerate. What if it healed his memory? If he became Iapetus again . . . well, Annabeth had seen the way he had dealt with those *empousai*. Annabeth had no weapon. She and Percy were in no condition to fight a Titan.

She glanced nervously at Bob's broom handle, wondering how long it would be before that hidden spearhead jutted out and was pointed at her.

Following Bob through Tartarus was a crazy risk. Unfortunately, she couldn't think of a better plan.

They picked their way across the ashen wasteland as red lightning flashed overhead in the poisonous clouds. Just another lovely day in the dungeon of creation. Annabeth couldn't see far in the hazy air, but the longer they walked, the more certain she became that the entire landscape was a downward curve.

She'd heard conflicting descriptions of Tartarus. It was a bottomless pit. It was a fortress surrounded by brass walls. It was nothing but an endless void.

One story described it as the inverse of the sky – a huge, hollow, upside-down dome of rock. That seemed the most accurate, though if Tartarus was a dome Annabeth guessed it was like the sky – with no real bottom but made of multiple layers, each one darker and less hospitable than the last.

And even *that* wasn't the full, horrible truth . . .

They passed a blister in the ground – a writhing, translucent bubble the size of a minivan. Curled inside was the half-formed body of a drakon. Bob speared the blister without a second thought. It burst in a geyser of steaming yellow slime, and the drakon dissolved into nothing.

Bob kept walking.

Monsters are zits on the skin of Tartarus, Annabeth thought. She shuddered. Sometimes she wished she didn't have such a good imagination, because now she was certain they were walking across a living thing. This whole twisted landscape – the dome, pit or whatever you called it – was the body of the god Tartarus – the most ancient incarnation of evil. Just as Gaia inhabited the surface of the earth, Tartarus inhabited the pit.

If that god noticed them walking across his skin, like fleas on a dog . . . Enough. No more thinking.

'Here,' Bob said.

They stopped at the top of a ridge. Below them, in a sheltered depression like a moon crater, stood a ring of broken black marble columns surrounding a dark stone altar.

'Hermes's shrine,' Bob explained.

Percy frowned. 'A Hermes shrine in *Tartarus*?'

Bob laughed in delight. 'Yes. It fell from somewhere long ago. Maybe mortal world. Maybe Olympus. Anyway, monsters steer clear. Mostly.'

'How did you know it was here?' Annabeth asked.

Bob's smile faded. He got a vacant look in his eyes. 'Can't remember.'

'That's okay,' Percy said quickly.

Annabeth felt like kicking herself. Before Bob became Bob, he had been Iapetus the Titan. Like all his brethren, he'd been imprisoned in Tartarus for aeons. Of *course* he knew his way around. If he remembered this shrine, he might start recalling other details of his old prison and his old life. That would *not* be good.

They climbed into the crater and entered the circle of columns. Annabeth collapsed on a broken slab of marble, too exhausted to take another step. Percy stood over her protectively, scanning their surroundings. The inky storm front was less than a hundred feet away now, obscuring everything ahead of them. The crater's rim blocked their view of the wasteland behind. They'd be well hidden here, but if monsters *did* stumble across them they would have no warning.

'You said someone was chasing us,' Annabeth said. 'Who?'

Bob swept his broom around the base of the altar, occasionally crouching to study the ground as if looking for something. 'They are following, yes. They know you are here. Giants and Titans. The defeated ones. They know.'

The defeated ones . . .

Annabeth tried to control her fear. How many Titans and giants had she and Percy fought over the years? Each one had seemed like an impossible challenge. If *all* of them were down here in Tartarus, and if they were actively hunting Percy and Annabeth . . .

'Why are we stopping, then?' she said. 'We should keep moving.'

'Soon,' Bob said. 'But mortals need rest. Good place here. Best place for . . . oh, long, long way. I will guard you.'

Annabeth glanced at Percy, sending him the silent message: *Uh, no.* Hanging out with a Titan was bad enough. Going to sleep while the Titan guarded you . . . she didn't need to be a daughter of Athena to know that was one hundred percent unwise.

'You sleep,' Percy told her. 'I'll keep the first watch with Bob.'

Bob rumbled in agreement. 'Yes, good. When you wake, food should be here!'

Annabeth's stomach did a rollover at the mention of food.

She didn't see how Bob could summon food in the midst of Tartarus. Maybe he was a caterer as well as a janitor.

She didn't want to sleep, but her body betrayed her. Her eyelids turned to lead. 'Percy, wake me for second watch. Don't be a hero.'

He gave her that smirk she'd come to love. 'Who, me?'

He kissed her, his lips parched and feverishly warm. 'Sleep.'

Annabeth felt like she was back in the Hypnos cabin at Camp Half-Blood, overcome with drowsiness. She curled up on the hard ground and closed her eyes.

XXII

ANNABETH

LATER, SHE MADE A RESOLUTION: never *EVER* sleep in Tartarus.

Demigod dreams were always bad. Even in the safety of her bunk at camp, she'd had horrible nightmares. In Tartarus, they were a thousand times more vivid.

First, she was a little girl again, struggling to climb Half-Blood Hill. Luke Castellan held her hand, pulling her along. Their satyr guide Grover Underwood pranced nervously at the summit, yelling, 'Hurry! Hurry!'

Thalia Grace stood behind them, holding back an army of hellhounds with her terror-invoking shield, Aegis.

From the top of the hill, Annabeth could see the camp in the valley below – the warm lights of the cabins, the possibility of sanctuary. She stumbled, twisting her ankle, and Luke scooped her up to carry her. When they looked back, the monsters were only a few yards away – dozens of them surrounding Thalia.

'Go!' Thalia yelled. 'I'll hold them off.'

She brandished her spear, and forked lightning slashed through the monsters' ranks, but as the hellhounds fell more took their place.

'We have to run!' Grover cried.

He led the way into camp. Luke followed, with Annabeth crying, beating at his chest and screaming that they couldn't leave Thalia alone. But it was too late.

The scene shifted.

Annabeth was older, climbing to the summit of Half-Blood Hill. Where Thalia had made her last stand, a tall pine tree now rose. Overhead a storm was raging.

Thunder shook the valley. A blast of lightning split the tree down to its roots, opening a smoking crevice. In the darkness below stood Reyna, the praetor of New Rome. Her cloak was the colour of blood fresh from a vein. Her gold armour glinted. She stared up, her face regal and distant, and spoke directly into Annabeth's mind.

You have done well, Reyna said, but the voice was Athena's. *The rest of my journey must be on the wings of Rome.*

The praetor's dark eyes turned as grey as storm clouds.

I must stand here, Reyna told her. *The Roman must bring me.*

The hill shook. The ground rippled as the grass became folds of silk – the dress of a massive goddess. Gaia rose over Camp Half-Blood – her sleeping face as large as a mountain.

Hellhounds poured over the hills. Giants, six-armed Earthborn and wild Cyclopes charged from the beach, tearing down the dining pavilion, setting fire to the cabins and the Big House.

Hurry, said the voice of Athena. *The message must be sent.*

The ground split at Annabeth's feet and she fell into darkness.

Her eyes flew open. She cried out, grasping Percy's arms. She was still in Tartarus, at the shrine of Hermes.

'It's okay,' Percy promised. 'Bad dreams?'

Her body tingled with dread. 'Is it – is it my turn to watch?'

'No, no. We're good. I let you sleep.'

'Percy!'

'Hey, it's fine. Besides, I was too excited to sleep. Look.'

Bob the Titan sat cross-legged by the altar, happily munching a piece of pizza.

Annabeth rubbed her eyes, wondering if she was still dreaming. 'Is that . . . pepperoni?'

'Burnt offerings,' Percy said. 'Sacrifices to Hermes from the mortal world, I guess. They appeared in a cloud of smoke. We've got half a hot dog, some grapes, a plate of roast beef and a package of peanut M&M's.'

'M&M's for Bob!' Bob said happily. 'Uh, that okay?'

Annabeth didn't protest. Percy brought her the plate of roast beef, and she wolfed it down. She'd never tasted anything so good. The brisket was still hot, with exactly the same spicy sweet glaze as the barbecue at Camp Half-Blood.

'I know,' said Percy, reading her expression. 'I think it *is* from Camp Half-Blood.'

The idea made Annabeth giddy with homesickness. At every meal, the campers would burn a portion of their food to honour their godly parents. The smoke supposedly pleased the gods, but Annabeth had never thought about where the food went when it was burned. Maybe the offerings reappeared on the gods' altars in Olympus . . . or even here in the middle of Tartarus.

'Peanut M&M's,' Annabeth said. 'Connor Stoll always burned a pack for his dad at dinner.'

She thought about sitting in the dining pavilion, watching the sunset over Long Island Sound. That was the first place she and Percy had truly kissed. Her eyes smarted.

Percy put his hand on her shoulder. 'Hey, this is *good*. Actual food from home, right?'

She nodded. They finished eating in silence.

Bob chomped down the last of his M&M's. 'Should go now. They will be here in a few minutes.'

'A few *minutes*?' Annabeth reached for her dagger, then remembered she didn't have it.

'Yes . . . well, I *think* minutes . . .' Bob scratched his silvery hair. 'Time is hard in Tartarus. Not the same.'

Percy crept to the edge of the crater. He peered back the way they'd come. 'I don't see anything, but that doesn't mean much. Bob, which giants are we talking about? Which Titans?'

Bob grunted. 'Not sure of names. Six, maybe seven. I can sense them.'

'*Six or seven?*' Annabeth wasn't sure her barbecue would stay down. 'And can they sense *you*?'

'Don't know.' Bob smiled. 'Bob is different! But they can smell demigods, yes. You two smell very strong. Good strong. Like . . . hmm. Like buttery bread!'

'Buttery bread,' Annabeth said. 'Well, that's great.'

Percy climbed back to the altar. 'Is it possible to kill a giant in Tartarus? I mean, since we don't have a god to help us?'

He looked at Annabeth as if she actually had an answer.

'Percy, I don't know. Travelling in Tartarus, fighting monsters here . . . it's never been done before. Maybe Bob could help us kill a giant? Maybe a Titan would count as a god? I just don't know.'

'Yeah,' Percy said. 'Okay.'

She could see the worry in his eyes. For years, he'd depended on her for answers. Now, when he needed her most, she couldn't help. She hated being so clueless, but nothing she'd ever learned at camp had prepared her for Tartarus. There was only one thing she was sure of: they had to keep moving. They couldn't be caught by six or seven hostile immortals.

She stood, still disoriented from her nightmares. Bob started cleaning up, collecting their trash in a little pile, using his squirt bottle to wipe off the altar.

'Where to now?' Annabeth asked.

Percy pointed at the stormy wall of darkness. 'Bob says that way. Apparently the Doors of Death –'

'You *told* him?' Annabeth didn't mean it to come out so harsh, but Percy winced.

'While you were asleep,' he admitted. 'Annabeth, Bob can help. We need a guide.'

'Bob helps!' Bob agreed. 'Into the Dark Lands. The Doors of Death . . . hmm, walking straight to them would be bad. Too many monsters gathered there. Even Bob could not sweep that many. They would kill Percy and Annabeth in about two seconds.' The Titan frowned. 'I *think* seconds. Time is hard in Tartarus.'

'Right,' Annabeth grumbled. 'So is there another way?'

'Hiding,' said Bob. 'The Death Mist could hide you.'

'Oh . . .' Annabeth suddenly felt very small in the shadow of the Titan. 'Uh, what is Death Mist?'

'It is dangerous,' Bob said. 'But if the lady will give you Death Mist it might hide you. If we can avoid Night. The lady is *very* close to Night. That is bad.'

'The lady,' Percy repeated.

'Yes.' Bob pointed ahead of them into the inky blackness. 'We should go.'

Percy glanced at Annabeth, obviously hoping for guidance, but she had none. She was thinking about her nightmare – Thalia's tree splintered by lightning, Gaia rising on the hillside and unleashing her monsters on Camp Half-Blood.

'Okay, then,' Percy said. 'I guess we'll see a lady about some Death Mist.'

'Wait,' Annabeth said.

Her mind was buzzing. She thought of her dream about Luke and Thalia. She recalled the stories Luke had told her about his father, Hermes – god of travellers, guide to the spirits of the dead, god of communication.

She stared at the black altar.

'Annabeth?' Percy sounded concerned.

She walked to the pile of trash and picked out a reasonably clean paper napkin.

She remembered her vision of Reyna, standing in the

smoking crevice beneath the ruins of Thalia's pine tree, speaking with the voice of Athena:

I must stand here. The Roman must bring me.

Hurry. The message must be sent.

'Bob,' she said, 'offerings burned in the mortal world appear on this altar, right?'

Bob frowned uncomfortably, like he wasn't ready for a pop quiz. 'Yes?'

'So what happens if I burn something on the altar here?'

'Uh . . .'

'That's all right,' Annabeth said. 'You don't know. Nobody knows, because it's never been done.'

There was a chance, she thought, just the slimmest chance that an offering burned on this altar might appear at Camp Half-Blood.

Doubtful, but if it *did* work . . .

'Annabeth?' Percy said again. 'You're planning something. You've got that *I'm planning something* look.'

'I don't have an *I'm planning something* look.'

'Yeah, you totally do. Your eyebrows knit and your lips press together and –'

'Do you have a pen?' she asked him.

'You're kidding, right?' He brought out Riptide.

'Yes, but can you actually write with it?'

'I – I don't know,' he admitted. 'Never tried.'

He uncapped the pen. As usual, it sprang into a full-sized sword. Annabeth had watched him do this hundreds of times. Normally when he fought, Percy simply discarded the cap. It always appeared in his pocket later, as needed. When he touched the cap to the point of the sword, it would turn back into a ballpoint pen.

'What if you touch the cap to the other end of the sword?' Annabeth said. 'Like where you'd put the cap if you were actually going to write with the pen.'

'Uh . . .' Percy looked doubtful, but he touched the cap to the hilt of the sword. Riptide shrank back into a ballpoint pen, but now the writing point was exposed.

'May I?' Annabeth plucked it from his hand. She flattened the napkin against the altar and began to write. Riptide's ink glowed Celestial bronze.

'What are you doing?' Percy asked.

'Sending a message,' Annabeth said. 'I just hope Rachel gets it.'

'Rachel?' Percy asked. 'You mean *our* Rachel? Oracle of Delphi Rachel?'

'That's the one.' Annabeth suppressed a smile.

Whenever she brought up Rachel's name, Percy got nervous. At one point, Rachel had been interested in dating Percy. That was ancient history. Rachel and Annabeth were good friends now. But Annabeth didn't mind making Percy a little uneasy. You had to keep your boyfriend on his toes.

Annabeth finished her note and folded the napkin. On the outside, she wrote:

Connor,
   Give this to Rachel. Not a prank. Don't be a moron.
      Love,
      Annabeth

She took a deep breath. She was asking Rachel Dare to do something ridiculously dangerous, but it was the only way she could think of to communicate with the Romans – the only way that might avoid bloodshed.

'Now I just need to burn it,' she said. 'Anybody got a match?'

The point of Bob's spear shot from his broom handle. It sparked against the altar and erupted in silvery fire.

'Uh, thanks.' Annabeth lit the napkin and set it on the altar. She watched it crumble to ash and wondered if she was crazy. Could the smoke really make it out of Tartarus?

'We should go now,' Bob advised. 'Really, really go. Before we are killed.'

Annabeth stared at the wall of blackness in front of them. Somewhere in there was a lady who dispensed a Death Mist that *might* hide them from monsters – a plan recommended by a Titan, one of their bitterest enemies. Another dose of weirdness to explode her brain.

'Right,' she said. 'I'm ready.'

XXIII

ANNABETH

ANNABETH LITERALLY STUMBLED over the second Titan.

After entering the storm front, they plodded on for what seemed like hours, relying on the light of Percy's Celestial bronze blade, and on Bob, who glowed faintly in the dark like some sort of crazy janitor angel.

Annabeth could only see about five feet in front of her. In a strange way, the Dark Lands reminded her of San Francisco, where her dad lived – on those summer afternoons when the fog bank rolled in like cold, wet packing material and swallowed Pacific Heights. Except here in Tartarus, the fog was made of ink.

Rocks loomed out of nowhere. Pits appeared at their feet, and Annabeth barely avoided falling in. Monstrous roars echoed in the gloom, but Annabeth couldn't tell where they came from. All she could be certain of was that the terrain was still sloping down.

Down seemed to be the only direction allowed in Tartarus.

If Annabeth backtracked even a step, she felt tired and heavy, as if gravity were increasing to discourage her. Assuming that the entire pit *was* the body of Tartarus, Annabeth had a nasty feeling they were marching straight down his throat.

She was so preoccupied with that thought she didn't notice the ledge until it was too late.

Percy yelled, 'Whoa!' He grabbed for her arm, but she was already falling.

Fortunately, it was only a shallow depression. Most of it was filled with a monster blister. She had a soft landing on a warm bouncy surface and was feeling lucky – until she opened her eyes and found herself staring through a glowing gold membrane at another, much larger face.

She screamed and flailed, toppling sideways off the mound. Her heart did a hundred jumping jacks.

Percy helped her to her feet. 'You okay?'

She didn't trust herself to answer. If she opened her mouth, she might scream again, and that would be undignified. She was a daughter of Athena, not some shrill girlie victim in a horror movie.

But gods of Olympus . . . Curled in the membrane bubble in front of her was a fully formed Titan in golden armour, his skin the colour of polished pennies. His eyes were closed, but he scowled so deeply he appeared to be on the verge of a bloodcurdling war cry. Even through the blister, Annabeth could feel the heat radiating from his body.

'Hyperion,' Percy said. 'I hate that guy.'

Annabeth's shoulder suddenly ached from an old wound. During the Battle of Manhattan, Percy had fought this Titan at the Reservoir – water against fire. It had been the first time Percy had summoned a hurricane – which wasn't something Annabeth would ever forget. 'I thought Grover turned this guy into a maple tree.'

'Yeah,' Percy agreed. 'Maybe the maple tree died, and he wound up back here?'

Annabeth remembered how Hyperion had summoned fiery explosions and how many satyrs and nymphs he'd destroyed before Percy and Grover stopped him.

She was about to suggest that they burst Hyperion's bubble before he woke up. He looked ready to pop out at any moment and start charbroiling everything in his path.

Then she glanced at Bob. The silvery Titan was studying Hyperion with a frown of concentration – maybe recognition. Their faces looked so much alike . . .

Annabeth bit back a curse. Of course they looked alike. Hyperion was his *brother*. Hyperion was the Titan lord of the east. Iapetus, Bob, was the lord of the west. Take away Bob's broom and his janitor's clothes, put him in armour and cut his hair, change his colour scheme from silver to gold, and Iapetus would have been almost indistinguishable from Hyperion.

'Bob,' she said, 'we should go.'

'Gold, not silver,' Bob murmured. 'But he looks like me.'

'Bob,' Percy said. 'Hey, buddy, over here.'

The Titan reluctantly turned.

'Am I your friend?' Percy asked.

'Yes.' Bob sounded dangerously uncertain. 'We are friends.'

'You know that some monsters are good,' Percy said. 'And some are bad.'

'Hmm,' Bob said. 'Like . . . the pretty ghost ladies who serve Persephone are good. Exploding zombies are bad.'

'Right,' Percy said. 'And some mortals are good, and some are bad. Well, the same thing is true for Titans.'

'Titans . . .' Bob loomed over them, glowering. Annabeth was pretty sure her boyfriend had just made a big mistake.

'That's what you are,' Percy said calmly. 'Bob the Titan. You're good. You're awesome, in fact. But some Titans are not. This guy here, Hyperion, is full-on bad. He tried to kill me . . . tried to kill a lot of people.'

Bob blinked his silver eyes. 'But he looks . . . his face is so –'

'He looks like you,' Percy agreed. 'He's a Titan, like you. But he's not good like you are.'

'Bob is good.' His fingers tightened on his broom handle. 'Yes. There is always at least one good one – monsters, Titans, giants.'

'Uh . . .' Percy grimaced. 'Well, I'm not sure about the giants.'

'Oh, yes.' Bob nodded earnestly.

Annabeth sensed they'd already been in this place too long. Their pursuers would be closing in.

'We should go,' she urged. 'What do we do about . . . ?'

'Bob,' Percy said, 'it's your call. Hyperion is your kind. We could leave him alone, but if he wakes up –'

Bob's broom-spear swept into motion. If he'd been aiming at Annabeth or Percy, they would've been cut in half. Instead,

Bob slashed through the monstrous blister, which burst in a geyser of hot golden mud.

Annabeth wiped the Titan sludge out of her eyes. Where Hyperion had been, there was nothing but a smoking crater.

'Hyperion is a bad Titan,' Bob announced, his expression grim. 'Now he can't hurt my friends. He will have to re-form somewhere else in Tartarus. Hopefully it will take a long time.'

The Titan's eyes seemed brighter than usual, as if he were about to cry quicksilver.

'Thank you, Bob,' Percy said.

How was he keeping his cool? The way he talked to Bob left Annabeth awestruck . . . and maybe a little uneasy, too. If Percy had been serious about leaving the choice to Bob, then she didn't like how much he trusted the Titan. If he'd been manipulating Bob into making that choice . . . well, then, Annabeth was stunned that Percy could be so calculating.

He met her eyes, but she couldn't read his expression. That bothered her, too.

'We'd better keep going,' he said.

She and Percy followed Bob, the golden mud flecks from Hyperion's burst bubble glowing on his janitor's uniform.

XXIV

ANNABETH

AFTER A WHILE, Annabeth's feet felt like Titan mush. She marched along, following Bob, listening to the monotonous slosh of liquid in his cleaning bottle.

Stay alert, she told herself, but it was hard. Her thoughts were as numb as her legs. From time to time, Percy took her hand or made an encouraging comment, but she could tell the dark landscape was getting to him as well. His eyes had a dull sheen – like his spirit was being slowly extinguished.

He fell into Tartarus to be with you, said a voice in her head. *If he dies, it will be your fault.*

'Stop it,' she said aloud.

Percy frowned. 'What?'

'No, not you.' She tried for a reassuring smile, but she couldn't quite muster one. 'Talking to myself. This place . . . it's messing with my mind. Giving me dark thoughts.'

The worry lines deepened around Percy's sea-green eyes. 'Hey, Bob, where exactly are we heading?'

'The lady,' Bob said. 'Death Mist.'

Annabeth fought down her irritation. 'But what does that mean? Who is this lady?'

'Naming her?' Bob glanced back. 'Not a good idea.'

Annabeth sighed. The Titan was right. Names had power, and speaking them here in Tartarus was probably very dangerous.

'Can you at least tell us how far?' she asked.

'I do not know,' Bob admitted. 'I can only feel it. We wait for the darkness to get darker. Then we go sideways.'

'Sideways,' Annabeth muttered. 'Naturally.'

She was tempted to ask for a rest, but she didn't want to stop. Not here in this cold, dark place. The black fog seeped into her body, turning her bones into moist Styrofoam.

She wondered if her message would get to Rachel Dare. If Rachel could somehow carry her proposal to Reyna without getting killed in the process . . .

A ridiculous hope, said the voice in her head. *You have only put Rachel in danger. Even if she finds the Romans, why should Reyna trust you after all that has happened?*

Annabeth was tempted to shout back at the voice, but she resisted. Even if she were going crazy, she didn't want to *look* like she was going crazy.

She desperately needed something to lift her spirits. A drink of actual water. A moment of sunlight. A warm bed. A kind word from her mother.

Suddenly Bob stopped. He raised his hand: *Wait.*

'What?' Percy whispered.

'Shh,' Bob warned. 'Ahead. Something moves.'

Annabeth strained her ears. From somewhere in the fog came a deep thrumming noise, like the idling engine of a large construction vehicle. She could feel the vibrations through her shoes.

'We will surround it,' Bob whispered. 'Each of you, take a flank.'

For the millionth time, Annabeth wished she had her dagger. She picked up a chunk of jagged black obsidian and crept to the left. Percy went right, his sword ready.

Bob took the middle, his spearhead glowing in the fog.

The humming got louder, shaking the gravel at Annabeth's feet. The noise seemed to be coming from immediately in front of them.

'Ready?' Bob murmured.

Annabeth crouched, preparing to spring. 'On three?'

'One,' Percy whispered. 'Two –'

A figure appeared in the fog. Bob raised his spear.

'Wait!' Annabeth shrieked.

Bob froze just in time, the point of his spear hovering an inch above the head of a tiny calico kitten.

'Rrow?' said the kitten, clearly unimpressed by their attack plan. It butted its head against Bob's foot and purred loudly.

It seemed impossible, but the deep rumbling sound was coming from the kitten. As it purred, the ground vibrated and pebbles danced. The kitten fixed its yellow, lamp-like eyes on one particular rock, right between Annabeth's feet, and pounced.

The cat could've been a demon or a horrible Underworld monster in disguise. But Annabeth couldn't help it. She picked it up and cuddled it. The little thing was bony under its fur, but otherwise it seemed perfectly normal.

'How did . . . ?' She couldn't even form the question. 'What is a kitten doing . . . ?'

The cat grew impatient and squirmed out of her arms. It landed with a thump, padded over to Bob and started purring again as it rubbed against his boots.

Percy laughed. 'Somebody likes you, Bob.'

'It must be a good monster.' Bob looked up nervously. 'Isn't it?'

Annabeth felt a lump in her throat. Seeing the huge Titan and this tiny kitten together, she suddenly felt insignificant compared to the vastness of Tartarus. This place had no respect for anything – good or bad, small or large, wise or unwise. Tartarus swallowed Titans and demigods and kittens indiscriminately.

Bob knelt down and scooped up the cat. It fitted perfectly in Bob's palm, but it decided to explore. It climbed the Titan's arm, made itself at home on his shoulder and closed its eyes, purring like an earthmover. Suddenly its fur shimmered. In a flash, the kitten became a ghostly skeleton, as if it had stepped behind an X-ray machine. Then it was a regular kitten again.

Annabeth blinked. 'Did you see –?'

'Yeah.' Percy knitted his eyebrows. 'Oh, man . . . I *know* that kitten. It's one of the ones from the Smithsonian.'

Annabeth tried to make sense of that. She'd never been to the Smithsonian with Percy . . . Then she recalled several years ago, when the Titan Atlas had captured her. Percy and Thalia had led a quest to rescue her. Along the way, they'd watched Atlas raise some skeleton warriors from dragon teeth in the Smithsonian Museum.

According to Percy, the Titan's first attempt went wrong. He'd planted sabre-toothed tiger teeth by mistake and raised a batch of skeleton kittens from the soil.

'*That*'s one of them?' Annabeth asked. 'How did it get here?'

Percy spread his hands helplessly. 'Atlas told his servants to take the kittens away. Maybe they destroyed the cats and they were reborn in Tartarus? I don't know.'

'It's cute,' Bob said, as the kitten sniffed his ear.

'But is it safe?' Annabeth asked.

The Titan scratched the kitten's chin. Annabeth didn't know if it was a good idea, carrying around a cat grown from a prehistoric tooth, but obviously it didn't matter now. The Titan and the cat had bonded.

'I will call him Small Bob,' said Bob. 'He is a good monster.'

End of discussion. The Titan hefted his spear and they continued marching into the gloom.

Annabeth walked in a daze, trying not to think about pizza. To keep herself distracted, she watched Small Bob the kitten pacing across Bob's shoulders and purring, occasionally turning into a glowing kitty skeleton and then back to a calico fuzz-ball.

'Here,' Bob announced.

He stopped so suddenly, Annabeth almost ran into him.

Bob stared off to their left, as if deep in thought.

'Is this the place?' Annabeth asked. 'Where we go *sideways*?'

'Yes,' Bob agreed. 'Darker, then sideways.'

Annabeth couldn't tell if it was actually darker, but the air did seem colder and thicker, as if they'd stepped into a different microclimate. Again she was reminded of San Francisco, where you could walk from one neighbourhood to the next and the temperature might drop ten degrees. She wondered if the Titans had built their palace on Mount Tamalpais because the Bay Area reminded them of Tartarus.

What a depressing thought. Only Titans would see such a beautiful place as a potential outpost of the abyss – a hellish home away from home.

Bob struck off to the left. They followed. The air definitely got colder. Annabeth pressed against Percy for warmth. He put his arm around her. It felt good being close to him, but she couldn't relax.

They'd entered some sort of forest. Towering black trees soared into the gloom, perfectly round and bare of branches, like monstrous hair follicles. The ground was smooth and pale.

With our luck, Annabeth thought, we're marching through the armpit of Tartarus.

Suddenly her senses were on high alert, as if somebody had snapped a rubber band against the base of her neck. She rested her hand on the trunk of the nearest tree.

'What is it?' Percy raised his sword.

Bob turned and looked back, confused. 'We are stopping?'

Annabeth held up her hand for silence. She wasn't sure what had set her off. Nothing looked different. Then she realized the tree trunk was quivering. She wondered momentarily if it was the kitten's purr, but Small Bob had fallen asleep on Large Bob's shoulder.

A few yards away, another tree shuddered.

'Something's moving above us,' Annabeth whispered. 'Gather up.'

Bob and Percy closed ranks with her, standing back to back.

Annabeth strained her eyes, trying to see above them in the dark, but nothing moved.

She had almost decided she was being paranoid when the first monster dropped to the ground only five feet away.

Annabeth's first thought: *The Furies.*

The creature looked almost exactly like one: a wrinkled hag with bat-like wings, brass talons and glowing red eyes. She wore a tattered dress of black silk, and her face was twisted and ravenous, like a demonic grandmother in the mood to kill.

Bob grunted as another one dropped in front of him, and then another in front of Percy. Soon there were half a dozen surrounding them. More hissed in the trees above.

They couldn't be Furies, then. There were only *three* of those, and these winged hags didn't carry whips. That didn't comfort Annabeth. The monsters' talons looked plenty dangerous.

'What are you?' she demanded.

The arai, hissed a voice. *The curses!*

Annabeth tried to locate the speaker, but none of the demons had moved their mouths. Their eyes looked dead; their expressions were frozen, like a puppet's. The voice simply floated overhead like a movie narrator's, as if a single mind controlled all the creatures.

'What – what do you want?' Annabeth asked, trying to maintain a tone of confidence.

The voice cackled maliciously. *To curse you, of course! To destroy you a thousand times in the name of Mother Night!*

'Only a thousand times?' Percy murmured. 'Oh, good . . . I thought we were in trouble.'

The circle of demon ladies closed in.

XXV

HAZEL

EVERYTHING SMELLED LIKE POISON. Two days after leaving Venice, Hazel still couldn't get the noxious scent of *eau de cow monster* out of her nose.

The seasickness didn't help. The *Argo II* sailed down the Adriatic, a beautiful glittering expanse of blue, but Hazel couldn't appreciate it, thanks to the constant rolling of the ship. Above deck, she tried to keep her eyes fixed on the horizon – the white cliffs that always seemed just a mile or so to the east. What country was that, Croatia? She wasn't sure. She just wished she were on solid ground again.

The thing that nauseated her most was the weasel.

Last night, Hecate's pet Gale had appeared in her cabin. Hazel woke from a nightmare, thinking, *What is that smell?* She found a furry rodent propped on her chest, staring at her with its beady black eyes.

Nothing like waking up screaming, kicking off your covers

and dancing around your cabin while a weasel scampers between your feet, screeching and farting.

Her friends rushed to her room to see if she was okay. The weasel was difficult to explain. Hazel could tell that Leo was trying hard not to make a joke.

In the morning, once the excitement died down, Hazel decided to visit Coach Hedge, since he could talk to animals.

She'd found his cabin door ajar and heard the coach inside, talking as if he were on the phone with someone – except they had no phones on board. Maybe he was sending a magical Iris-message? Hazel had heard that the Greeks used those a lot.

'Sure, hon,' Hedge was saying. 'Yeah, I know, baby. No, it's great news, but –' His voice broke with emotion. Hazel suddenly felt horrible for eavesdropping.

She would've backed away, but Gale squeaked at her heels. Hazel knocked on the coach's door.

Hedge poked his head out, scowling as usual, but his eyes were red.

'What?' he growled.

'Um . . . sorry,' Hazel said. 'Are you okay?'

The coach snorted and opened his door wide. 'Kinda question is that?'

There was no one else in the room.

'I –' Hazel tried to remember why she was there. 'I wondered if you could talk to my weasel.'

The coach's eyes narrowed. He lowered his voice. 'Are we speaking in code? Is there an intruder aboard?'

'Well, sort of.'

Gale peeked out from behind Hazel's feet and started chattering.

The coach looked offended. He chattered back at the weasel. They had what sounded like a very intense argument.

'What did she say?' Hazel asked.

'A lot of rude things,' grumbled the satyr. 'The gist of it: she's here to see how it goes.'

'How *what* goes?'

Coach Hedge stomped his hoof. 'How am I supposed to know? She's a polecat! They *never* give a straight answer. Now, if you'll excuse me, I've got, uh, stuff . . .'

He closed the door in her face.

After breakfast, Hazel stood at the port rail, trying to settle her stomach. Next to her, Gale ran up and down the railing, passing gas, but the strong wind off the Adriatic helped whisk it away.

Hazel wondered what was wrong with Coach Hedge. He must have been using an Iris-message to talk with someone, but, if he'd got great news, why had he looked so devastated? She'd never seen him so shaken up. Unfortunately, she doubted the coach would ask for help if he needed it. He wasn't exactly the warm and open type.

She stared at the white cliffs in the distance and thought about why Hecate had sent Gale the polecat.

She's here to see how it goes.

Something was about to happen. Hazel would be tested.

She didn't understand how she was supposed to learn magic with no training. Hecate expected her to defeat some super-powerful sorceress – the lady in the gold dress, whom Leo had described from his dream. But *how*?

Hazel had spent all her free time trying to figure that out. She'd stared at her *spatha*, trying to make it look like a walking stick. She'd tried to summon a cloud to hide the full moon. She'd concentrated until her eyes crossed and her ears popped, but nothing happened. She couldn't manipulate the Mist.

The last few nights, her dreams had got worse. She found herself back in the Fields of Asphodel, drifting aimlessly among the ghosts. Then she was in Gaia's cave in Alaska, where Hazel and her mother had died as the ceiling collapsed and the voice of the earth goddess wailed in anger. She was on the stairs of her mother's apartment building in New Orleans, face to face with her father, Pluto. His cold fingers gripped her arm. The fabric of his black wool suit writhed with imprisoned souls. He fixed her with his dark angry eyes and said: *The dead see what they* believe *they will see. So do the living. That is the secret.*

He'd never said that to her in real life. She had no idea what it meant.

The worst nightmares seemed like glimpses of the future. Hazel was stumbling through a dark tunnel while a woman's laughter echoed around her.

Control this if you can, child of Pluto, the woman taunted.

And always Hazel dreamed about the images she'd seen at Hecate's crossroads: Leo falling through the sky; Percy and Annabeth lying unconscious, possibly dead, in front of black metal doors; and a shrouded figure looming above them – the giant Clytius wrapped in darkness.

Next to her on the rail, Gale the weasel chittered impatiently. Hazel was tempted to push the stupid rodent into the sea.

I can't even control my own dreams, she wanted to scream. *How am I supposed to control the Mist?*

She was so miserable that she didn't notice Frank until he was standing at her side.

'Feeling any better?' he asked.

He took her hand, his fingers completely covering hers. She couldn't believe how much taller he'd become. He had changed into so many animals, she wasn't sure why one more transformation should amaze her . . . but suddenly he'd grown into his weight. No one could call him pudgy or cuddly any more. He looked like a football player, solid and strong, with a new centre of gravity. His shoulders had broadened. He walked with more confidence.

What Frank had done on that bridge in Venice . . . Hazel was still in awe. None of them had actually seen the battle, but no one doubted it. Frank's whole bearing had changed. Even Leo had stopped making jokes at his expense.

'I'm – I'm all right,' Hazel managed. 'You?'

He smiled, the corners of his eyes crinkling. 'I'm, uh, *taller*. Otherwise, yeah. I'm good. I haven't really, you know, changed inside . . .'

His voice held a little of the old doubt and awkwardness – the voice of *her* Frank, who always worried about being a klutz and messing up.

Hazel felt relieved. She *liked* that part of him. At first, his new appearance had shocked her. She'd been worried that his personality had changed as well.

Now she was starting to relax about that. Despite all his strength, Frank was the same sweet guy. He was still vulnerable. He still trusted her with his biggest weakness – the piece of magical firewood she carried in her coat pocket, next to her heart.

'I know, and I'm glad.' She squeezed his hand. 'It's . . . it's actually not *you* I'm worried about.'

Frank grunted. 'How's Nico doing?'

She'd been thinking about *herself*, not Nico, but she followed Frank's gaze to the top of the foremast, where Nico was perched on the yardarm.

Nico claimed that he liked to keep watch because he had good eyes. Hazel knew that wasn't the reason. The top of the mast was one of the few places on board where Nico could be alone. The others had offered him the use of Percy's cabin, since Percy was . . . well, absent. Nico had adamantly refused. He spent most of his time up in the rigging, where he didn't have to talk with the rest of the crew.

Since he'd been turned into a corn plant in Venice, he'd only got more reclusive and morose.

'I don't know,' Hazel admitted. 'He's been through a lot. Getting captured in Tartarus, being held prisoner in that bronze jar, watching Percy and Annabeth fall . . .'

'And promising to lead us to Epirus.' Frank nodded. 'I get the feeling Nico doesn't play well with others.'

Frank stood up straight. He was wearing a beige T-shirt

with a picture of a horse and the words PALIO DI SIENA. He'd only bought it a couple of days ago, but now it was too small. When he stretched, his midriff was exposed.

Hazel realized she was staring. She quickly looked away, her face flushed.

'Nico is my only relative,' she said. 'He's not easy to like, but . . . thanks for being kind to him.'

Frank smiled. 'Hey, you put up with my grandmother in Vancouver. Talk about *not easy to like.*'

'I loved your grandmother!'

Gale the polecat scampered up to them, farted and ran away.

'Ugh.' Frank waved away the smell. 'Why is that thing here, anyway?'

Hazel was almost glad she wasn't on dry land. As agitated as she felt, gold and gems would probably be popping up all around her feet.

'Hecate sent Gale to observe,' she said.

'Observe what?'

Hazel tried to take comfort in Frank's presence, his new aura of solidity and strength.

'I don't know,' she said at last. 'Some kind of test.'

Suddenly the boat lurched forward.

XXVI

HAZEL

HAZEL AND FRANK TUMBLED OVER EACH OTHER. Hazel accidentally gave herself the Heimlich manoeuvre with the pommel of her sword and curled on the deck, moaning and coughing up the taste of *katobleps* poison.

Through a fog of pain, she heard the ship's figurehead, Festus the bronze dragon, creaking in alarm and shooting fire.

Dimly, Hazel wondered if they'd hit an iceberg – but in the Adriatic, in the middle of summer?

The ship rocked to port with a massive commotion, like telephone poles snapping in half.

'Gahh!' Leo yelled somewhere behind her. 'It's eating the oars!'

What is? Hazel wondered. She tried to stand, but something large and heavy was pinning her legs. She realized it was Frank, grumbling as he tried to extract himself from a pile of loose rope.

Everyone else was scrambling. Jason jumped over them, his sword drawn, and raced towards the stern. Piper was already on the quarterdeck, shooting food from her cornucopia and yelling, 'Hey! HEY! Eat this, ya stupid turtle!'

Turtle?

Frank helped Hazel to her feet. 'You okay?'

'Yeah,' Hazel lied, clutching her stomach. 'Go!'

Frank sprinted up the steps, slinging off his backpack, which instantly transformed into a bow and quiver. By the time he reached the helm, he had already fired one arrow and was nocking the second.

Leo frantically worked the ship's controls. 'Oars won't retract. Get it away! Get it away!'

Up in the rigging, Nico's face was slack with shock.

'Styx – it's huge!' he yelled. 'Port! Go port!'

Coach Hedge was the last one on deck. He compensated for that with enthusiasm. He bounded up the steps, waving his baseball bat, and without hesitation goat-galloped to the stern and leaped over the rail with a gleeful 'Ha-HA!'

Hazel staggered towards the quarterdeck to join her friends. The boat shuddered. More oars snapped, and Leo yelled, 'No, no, no! Dang slimy-shelled son of a mother!'

Hazel reached the stern and couldn't believe what she saw.

When she heard the word *turtle*, she thought of a cute little thing the size of a jewellery box, sitting on a rock in the middle of a fishpond. When she heard *huge*, her mind tried to adjust – okay, perhaps it was like the Galapagos tortoise she'd seen in the zoo once, with a shell big enough to ride on.

She did *not* envision a creature the size of an island. When she saw the massive dome of craggy black and brown squares, the word *turtle* simply did not compute. Its shell was more like a landmass – hills of bone, shiny pearl valleys, kelp and moss forests, rivers of seawater trickling down the grooves of its carapace.

On the ship's starboard side, another part of the monster rose from the water like a submarine.

Lares of Rome . . . was that its *head*?

Its gold eyes were the size of wading pools, with dark sideways slits for pupils. Its skin glistened like wet army camouflage – brown flecked with green and yellow. Its red, toothless mouth could've swallowed the Athena Parthenos in one bite.

Hazel watched as it snapped off half a dozen oars.

'Stop that!' Leo wailed.

Coach Hedge clambered around the turtle's shell, whacking at it uselessly with his baseball bat and yelling, 'Take that! And that!'

Jason flew from the stern and landed on the creature's head. He stabbed his golden sword straight between its eyes, but the blade slipped sideways, as if the turtle's skin were greased steel. Frank shot arrows at the monster's eyes with no success. The turtle's filmy inner eyelids blinked with uncanny precision, deflecting each shot. Piper shot cantaloupes into the water, yelling, 'Fetch, ya stupid turtle!' But the turtle seemed fixated on eating the *Argo II*.

'How did it get so close?' Hazel demanded.

Leo threw his hands up in exasperation. 'Must be that shell. Guess it's invisible to sonar. It's a freaking stealth turtle!'

'Can the ship fly?' Piper asked.

'With half our oars broken off?' Leo punched some buttons and spun his Archimedes sphere. 'I'll have to try something else.'

'There!' Nico yelled from above. 'Can you get us to those straits?'

Hazel looked where he was pointing. About half a mile to the east, a long strip of land ran parallel to the coastal cliffs. It was hard to be sure from a distance, but the stretch of water between them looked to be only twenty or thirty yards across – possibly wide enough for the *Argo II* to slip through, but definitely not wide enough for the giant turtle's shell.

'Yeah. Yeah.' Leo apparently understood. He turned the Archimedes sphere. 'Jason, get away from that thing's head! I have an idea!'

Jason was still hacking away at the turtle's face, but when he heard Leo say, '*I have an idea*,' he made the only smart choice. He flew away as fast as possible.

'Coach, come on!' Jason said.

'No, I got this!' Hedge said, but Jason grabbed him around the waist and took off. Unfortunately, the coach struggled so much that Jason's sword fell out of his hand and splashed into the sea.

'Coach!' Jason complained.

'What?' Hedge said. 'I was softening him up!'

The turtle head-butted the hull, almost tossing the whole

crew off the port side. Hazel heard a cracking sound, like the keel had splintered.

'Just another minute,' Leo said, his hands flying over the console.

'We might not be here in another minute!' Frank fired his last arrow.

Piper yelled at the turtle, 'Go away!'

For a moment, it actually worked. The turtle turned from the ship and dipped its head underwater. But then it came right back and rammed them even harder.

Jason and Coach Hedge landed on the deck.

'You all right?' Piper asked.

'Fine,' Jason muttered. 'Without a weapon, but fine.'

'Fire in the shell!' Leo cried, spinning his Wii controller.

Hazel thought the stern had exploded. Jets of fire blasted out behind them, washing over the turtle's head. The ship shot forward and threw Hazel to the deck again.

She hauled herself up and saw that the ship was bouncing over the waves at incredible speed, trailing fire like a rocket. The turtle was already a hundred yards behind them, its head charred and smoking.

The monster bellowed in frustration and started after them, its paddle feet scooping through the water with such power that it actually started to gain on them. The entrance to the straits was still a quarter mile ahead.

'A distraction,' Leo muttered. 'We'll never make it unless we get a distraction.'

'A distraction,' Hazel repeated.

She concentrated and thought: *Arion!*

She had no idea whether it would work. But instantly Hazel spotted something on the horizon – a flash of light and steam. It streaked across the surface of the Adriatic. In a heartbeat, Arion stood on the quarterdeck.

Gods of Olympus, Hazel thought. I love this horse.

Arion snorted as if to say, *Of course you do. You're not stupid.*

Hazel climbed on his back. 'Piper, I could use that charmspeak of yours.'

'Once upon a time, I liked turtles,' Piper muttered, accepting a hand up. 'Not any more!'

Hazel spurred Arion. He leaped over the side of the boat, hitting the water at a full gallop.

The turtle was a fast swimmer, but it couldn't match Arion's speed. Hazel and Piper zipped around the monster's head, Hazel slicing with her sword, Piper shouting random commands like, 'Dive! Turn left! Look behind you!'

The sword did no damage. Each command only worked for a moment, but they were making the turtle very annoyed. Arion whinnied derisively as the turtle snapped at him, only to get a mouthful of horse vapour.

Soon the monster had completely forgotten the *Argo II*. Hazel kept stabbing at its head. Piper kept yelling commands and using her cornucopia to bounce coconuts and roasted chickens off the turtle's eyeballs.

As soon as the *Argo II* had passed into the straits, Arion broke off his harassment. They sped after the ship, and a moment later were back on deck.

The rocket fire had extinguished, though smoking bronze exhaust vents still jutted from the stern. The *Argo II* limped forward under sail power, but their plan had paid off. They were safely harboured in the narrow waters, with a long, rocky island to starboard and the sheer white cliffs of the mainland to port. The turtle stopped at the entrance to the straits and glared at them balefully, but it made no attempt to follow. Its shell was obviously much too wide.

Hazel dismounted and got a big hug from Frank. 'Nice work out there!' he said.

Her face flushed. 'Thanks.'

Piper slid down next to her. 'Leo, since when do we have *jet* propulsion?'

'Aw, you know . . .' Leo tried to look modest and failed. 'Just a little something I whipped up in my spare time. Wish I could've given you more than a few seconds of burn, but at least it got us out of there.'

'And roasted the turtle's head,' Jason said appreciatively. 'So what now?'

'Kill it!' Coach said. 'You even have to ask? We got enough distance. We got ballistae. Lock and load, demigods!'

Jason frowned. 'Coach, first of all, you made me lose my sword.'

'Hey! I didn't ask for an evac!'

'Second, I don't think the ballistae will do any good. That shell is like Nemean Lion skin. Its head isn't any softer.'

'So we chuck one right down its throat,' Coach said, 'like you guys did with that shrimp monster thing in the Atlantic. Light it up from the inside.'

Frank scratched his head. 'Might work. But then you've

got a five-million-kilo turtle carcass blocking the entrance to the straits. If we can't fly with the oars broken, how do we get the ship out?'

'You wait and fix the oars!' Coach said. 'Or just sail in the other direction, you big galoot.'

Frank looked confused. 'What's a galoot?'

'Guys!' Nico called down from the mast. 'About sailing in the other direction? I don't think that's going to work.'

He pointed past the prow.

A quarter mile ahead of them, the long rocky strip of land curved in and met the cliffs. The channel ended in a narrow V.

'We're not in a strait,' Jason said. 'We're in a dead end.'

Hazel got a cold feeling in her fingers and toes. On the port rail, Gale the weasel sat up on her haunches, staring at Hazel expectantly.

'This is a trap,' Hazel said.

The others looked at her.

'Nah, it's fine,' Leo said. 'Worst that happens, we make repairs. Might take overnight, but I can get the ship flying again.'

At the mouth of the inlet, the turtle roared. It didn't appear interested in leaving.

'Well . . .' Piper shrugged. 'At least the turtle can't get us. We're safe here.'

That was something no demigod should ever say. The words had barely left Piper's mouth when an arrow sank into the mainmast, six inches from her face.

• • •

The crew scattered for cover, except for Piper, who stood frozen in place, gaping at the arrow that had almost pierced her nose the hard way.

'Piper, duck!' Jason whispered harshly.

But no other missiles rained down.

Frank studied the angle of the bolt in the mast and pointed towards the top of the cliffs.

'Up there,' he said. 'Single shooter. See him?'

The sun was in her eyes, but Hazel spotted a tiny figure standing at the top of the ledge. His bronze armour glinted.

'Who the heck is he?' Leo demanded. 'Why is he firing at us?'

'Guys?' Piper's voice was thin and watery. 'There's a note.'

Hazel hadn't seen it before, but a parchment scroll was tied to the arrow shaft. She wasn't sure why, but that made her angry. She stormed over and untied it.

'Uh, Hazel?' Leo said. 'You sure that's safe?'

She read the note out loud. 'First line: *Stand and deliver.*'

'What does that mean?' Coach Hedge complained. 'We *are* standing. Well, crouching, anyway. And if that guy is expecting a pizza delivery, forget it!'

'There's more,' Hazel said. '*This is a robbery. Send two of your party to the top of the cliff with all your valuables. No more than two. Leave the magic horse. No flying. No tricks. Just climb.*'

'Climb *what?*' Piper asked.

Nico pointed. 'There.'

A narrow set of steps was carved into the cliff, leading to the top. The turtle, the dead-end channel, the cliff . . . Hazel got the feeling this was not the first time the letter writer had ambushed a ship here.

She cleared her throat and kept reading aloud: '*I do mean all your valuables. Otherwise my turtle and I will destroy you. You have five minutes.*'

'Use the catapults!' cried the coach.

'*P.S.*' Hazel read, '*don't even think about using your catapults.*'

'Curse it!' said the coach. 'This guy is good.'

'Is the note signed?' Nico asked.

Hazel shook her head. She'd heard a story back at Camp Jupiter, something about a robber who worked with a giant turtle, but, as usual, as soon as she needed the information it sat annoyingly in the back of her memory, just out of reach.

The weasel Gale watched her, waiting to see what she would do.

The test hasn't happened yet, Hazel thought.

Distracting the turtle hadn't been enough. Hazel hadn't proven anything about how she could manipulate the Mist . . . mostly because she *couldn't* manipulate the Mist.

Leo studied the cliff top and muttered under his breath. 'That's not a good trajectory. Even if I could arm the catapult before that guy pincushioned us with arrows, I don't think I could make the shot. That's hundreds of feet, almost straight up.'

'Yeah,' Frank grumbled. 'My bow is useless too. He's got a huge advantage, being above us like that. I couldn't reach him.'

'And, um . . .' Piper nudged the arrow that was stuck in

the mast. 'I have a feeling he's a good shot. I don't think he *meant* to hit me. But if he did . . .'

She didn't need to elaborate. Whoever that robber was, he could hit a target from hundreds of feet away. He could shoot them all before they could react.

'I'll go,' Hazel said.

She hated the idea, but she was sure Hecate had set this up as some sort of twisted challenge. This was Hazel's test – *her* turn to save the ship. As if she needed confirmation, Gale scampered along the railing and jumped on her shoulder, ready to hitch a ride.

The others stared at her.

Frank gripped his bow. 'Hazel –'

'No, listen,' she said, 'this robber wants valuables. I can go up there, summon gold, jewels, whatever he wants.'

Leo raised an eyebrow. 'If we pay him off, you think he'll actually let us go?'

'We don't have much choice,' Nico said. 'Between that guy and the turtle . . .'

Jason raised his hand. The others fell silent.

'I'll go too,' he said. 'The letter says two people. I'll take Hazel up there and watch her back. Besides, I don't like the look of those steps. If Hazel falls . . . well, I can use the winds to keep us both from coming down the hard way.'

Arion whinnied in protest, as if to say, *You're going without me? You're kidding, right?*

'I have to, Arion,' Hazel said. 'Jason . . . yes. I think you're right. It's the best plan.'

'Only wish I had my sword.' Jason glared at the coach. 'It's back there at the bottom of the sea, and we don't have Percy to retrieve it.'

The name *Percy* passed over them like a cloud. The mood on deck got even darker.

Hazel stretched out her arm. She didn't think about it. She just concentrated on the water and called for Imperial gold.

A stupid idea. The sword was much too far away, probably hundreds of feet underwater. But she felt a quick tug in her fingers, like a bite on a fishing line, and Jason's blade flew out of the water and into her hand.

'Here,' she said, handing it over.

Jason's eyes widened. 'How . . . That was like half a mile!'

'I've been practising,' she said, though it wasn't true.

She hoped she hadn't accidentally cursed Jason's sword by summoning it, the way she cursed jewels and precious metals.

Somehow, though, she thought, weapons were different. After all, she'd raised a bunch of Imperial gold equipment from Glacier Bay and distributed it to the Fifth Cohort. That had worked out okay.

She decided not to worry about it. She felt so angry at Hecate and so tired of being manipulated by the gods that she wasn't going to let any trifling problems stand in her way. 'Now, if there are no other objections, we have a robber to meet.'

XXVII

HAZEL

HAZEL LIKED THE GREAT OUTDOORS – but climbing a two-hundred-foot cliff on a stairway without rails, with a bad-tempered weasel on her shoulder? Not so much. Especially when she could have ridden Arion to the top in a matter of seconds.

Jason walked behind her so he could catch her if she fell. Hazel appreciated that, but it didn't make the sheer drop any less scary.

She glanced to her right, which was a mistake. Her foot almost slipped, sending a spray of gravel over the edge. Gale squeaked in alarm.

'You all right?' Jason asked.

'Yes.' Hazel's heart jackhammered at her ribs. 'Fine.'

She had no room to turn and look at him. She just had to trust he wouldn't let her plummet to her death. Since he could fly, he was the only logical backup. Still, she wished it were Frank at her back, or Nico, or Piper, or Leo. Or even . . . well, okay, maybe not Coach Hedge. But, still, Hazel couldn't get a read on Jason Grace.

Ever since she'd arrived at Camp Jupiter, she'd heard stories about him. The campers spoke with reverence about the son of Jupiter who'd risen from the lowly ranks of the Fifth Cohort to become praetor, led them to victory in the Battle of Mount Tam, then disappeared. Even now, after all the events of the past couple of weeks, Jason seemed more like a legend than a person. She had a hard time warming to him, with those icy blue eyes and that careful reserve, like he was calculating every word before he said it. Also, she couldn't forget how he had been ready to write off her brother, Nico, when they'd learned he was a captive in Rome.

Jason had thought Nico was bait for a trap. He had been right. And maybe, now that Nico was safe, Hazel could see why Jason's caution was a good idea. Still, she didn't quite know what to think of the guy. What if they got themselves into trouble at the top of this cliff and Jason decided that saving *Hazel* wasn't in the best interest of the quest?

She glanced up. She couldn't see the thief from here, but she sensed he was waiting. Hazel was confident she could produce enough gems and gold to impress even the greediest robber. She wondered if the treasures she summoned would still bring bad luck. She'd never been sure whether that curse had been broken when she had died the first time. This seemed like a good opportunity to find out. Anybody who robbed innocent demigods with a giant turtle deserved a few nasty curses.

Gale the weasel jumped off her shoulder and scampered ahead. She glanced back and barked eagerly.

'Going as fast as I can,' Hazel muttered.

She couldn't shake the feeling that the weasel was anxious to watch her fail.

'This, uh, controlling the Mist,' Jason said. 'Have you had any luck?'

'No,' Hazel admitted.

She didn't like to think about her failures – the seagull she couldn't turn into a dragon, Coach Hedge's baseball bat stubbornly refusing to turn into a hot dog. She just couldn't make herself believe any of it was possible.

'You'll get it,' Jason said.

His tone surprised her. It wasn't a throwaway comment just to be nice. He sounded truly convinced. She kept climbing, but she imagined him watching her with those piercing blue eyes, his jaw set with confidence.

'How can you be sure?' she asked.

'Just am. I've got a good instinct for what people can do – demigods, anyway. Hecate wouldn't have picked you if she didn't believe you had power.'

Maybe that should have made Hazel feel better. It didn't.

She had a good instinct for people too. She understood what motivated most of her friends – even her brother, Nico, who wasn't easy to read.

But Jason? She didn't have a clue. Everybody said he was a natural leader. She believed it. Here he was, making her feel like a valued member of the team, telling her she was capable of anything. But what was *Jason* capable of?

She couldn't talk to anyone about her doubts. Frank was in awe of the guy. Piper, of course, was head-over-heels. Leo was his best friend. Even Nico seemed to follow his lead without question.

But Hazel couldn't forget that Jason had been Hera's first move in the war against the giants. The Queen of Olympus had dropped Jason into Camp Half-Blood, which had started this entire chain of events to stop Gaia. Why Jason first? Something told Hazel he was the linchpin. Jason would be the final play, too.

To storm or fire the world must fall. That's what the prophecy said. As much as Hazel feared fire, she feared storms more. Jason Grace could cause some pretty huge storms.

She glanced up and saw the rim of the cliff only a few yards above her.

She reached the top, breathless and sweaty. A long sloping valley marched inland, dotted with scraggly olive trees and limestone boulders. There were no signs of civilization.

Hazel's legs trembled from the climb. Gale seemed anxious to explore. The weasel barked and farted and scampered into the nearest bushes. Far below, the *Argo II* looked like a toy boat in the channel. Hazel didn't understand how anyone could shoot an arrow accurately from this high up, accounting for the wind and the glare of the sun off the water. At the mouth of the inlet, the massive shape of the turtle's shell glinted like a burnished coin.

Jason joined her at the top, looking no worse for the climb.

He started to say, 'Where –'

'Here!' said a voice.

Hazel flinched. Only ten feet away, a man had appeared, a bow and quiver over his shoulder and two old-fashioned flintlock duelling pistols in his hands. He wore high leather boots, leather breeches and a pirate-style shirt. His curly black hair looked like a little kid's do and his sparkly green eyes were friendly enough, but a red bandanna covered the lower half of his face.

'Welcome!' the bandit cried, pointing his guns at them. 'Your money or your life!'

Hazel was certain that he hadn't been there a second ago. He'd simply materialized, as if he'd stepped out from behind an invisible curtain.

'Who are you?' Hazel asked.

The bandit laughed. 'Sciron, of course!'

'Chiron?' Jason asked. 'Like the centaur?'

The bandit rolled his eyes. '*Sky*-ron, my friend. Son of Poseidon! Thief extraordinaire! All-around awesome guy! But that's not important. I'm not seeing any valuables!' he cried, as if this were excellent news. 'I guess that means you want to die?'

'Wait,' Hazel said. 'We've got valuables. But, if we give them up, how can we be sure you'll let us go?'

'Oh, they *always* ask that,' Sciron said. 'I promise you, on the River Styx, that as soon as you surrender what I want, I will *not* shoot you. I will send you right back down that cliff.'

Hazel gave Jason a wary look. River Styx or no, the way Sciron phrased his promise didn't reassure her.

'What if we fought you?' Jason asked. 'You can't attack us and hold our ship hostage at the same –'

BANG! BANG!

It happened so fast that Hazel's brain needed a moment to catch up.

Smoke curled from the side of Jason's head. Just above his left ear, a groove cut through his hair like a racing stripe. One of Sciron's flintlocks was still pointed at his face. The other flintlock was pointed down, over the side of the cliff, as if Sciron's second shot had been fired at the *Argo II*.

Hazel choked from delayed shock. 'What did you do?'

'Oh, don't worry!' Sciron laughed. 'If you could see that far – which you can't – you'd see a hole in the deck between the shoes of the big young man, the one with the bow.'

'Frank!'

Sciron shrugged. 'If you say so. That was just a demonstration. I'm afraid it *could* have been much more serious.'

He spun his flintlocks. The hammers reset, and Hazel had a feeling the guns had just magically reloaded.

Sciron waggled his eyebrows at Jason. 'So! To answer your question – yes, I *can* attack you and hold your ship hostage at the same time. Celestial bronze ammunition. Quite deadly to demigods. You two would die first – *bang, bang*. Then I could take my time picking off your friends on that ship. Target practice is so much more fun with live targets running around screaming!'

Jason touched the new furrow that the bullet had ploughed through his hair. For once, he didn't look very confident.

Hazel's ankles wobbled. Frank was the best shot she knew with a bow, but this bandit Sciron was *inhumanly* good.

'You're a son of Poseidon?' she managed. 'I would've thought Apollo, the way you shoot.'

The smile lines deepened around his eyes. 'Why, thank you! It's just from practice, though. The giant turtle – that's due to my parentage. You can't go around taming giant turtles without being a son of Poseidon! I *could* overwhelm your ship with a tidal wave, of course, but it's terribly difficult work. Not nearly as fun as ambushing and shooting people.'

Hazel tried to collect her thoughts, stall for time, but it was difficult while staring down the smoking barrels of those flintlocks. 'Uh . . . what's the bandanna for?'

'So no one recognizes me!' Sciron said.

'But you introduced yourself,' Jason said. 'You're Sciron.'

The bandit's eyes widened. 'How did you – Oh. Yes, I suppose I did.' He lowered one flintlock and scratched the side of his head with the other. 'Terribly sloppy of me. Sorry. I'm afraid I'm a little rusty. Back from the dead and all that. Let me try again.'

He levelled his pistols. 'Stand and deliver! I am an anonymous bandit and you *do not* need to know my name!'

An anonymous bandit. Something clicked in Hazel's memory. 'Theseus. He killed you once.'

Sciron's shoulders slumped. 'Now, *why* did you have to mention him? We were getting along so well!'

Jason frowned. 'Hazel, you know this guy's story?'

She nodded, though the details were murky. 'Theseus met him on the road to Athens. Sciron would kill his victims by, um . . .'

Something about the turtle. Hazel couldn't remember.

'Theseus was *such* a cheater!' Sciron complained. 'I don't want to talk about him. I'm back from the dead now. Gaia promised me I could stay on the coastline and rob all the demigods I wanted, and that's what I'm going to do! Now . . . where were we?'

'You were about to let us go,' Hazel ventured.

'Hmm . . .' Sciron said. 'No, I'm pretty sure that wasn't it. Ah, right! Money or your life. Where are your valuables? No valuables? Then I'll have to –'

'Wait,' Hazel said. 'I have our valuables. At least, I can get them.'

Sciron pointed a flintlock at Jason's head. 'Well, then, my dear, hop to it, or my next shot will cut off more than your friend's hair!'

Hazel hardly needed to concentrate. She was so anxious, the ground rumbled beneath her and immediately yielded a bumper crop – precious metals popping to the surface as though the earth was anxious to expel them.

She found herself surrounded by a knee-high mound of treasure – Roman denarii, silver drachmas, ancient gold jewellery, glittering diamonds and topaz and rubies – enough to fill several lawn bags.

Sciron laughed with delight. 'How in the *world* did you do that?'

Hazel didn't answer. She thought about all the coins that had appeared at the crossroads with Hecate. Here were even more – centuries' worth of hidden wealth from every empire that had ever claimed this land – Greek, Roman, Byzantine and so many others. Those empires were gone, leaving only a barren coastline for Sciron the bandit.

That thought made her feel small and powerless.

'Just take the treasure,' she said. 'Let us go.'

Sciron chuckled. 'Oh, but I did say *all* your valuables. I understand you're holding something very special on that ship . . . a certain ivory-and-gold statue about, say, forty feet tall?'

The sweat started to dry on Hazel's neck, sending a shiver down her back.

Jason stepped forward. Despite the gun pointed at his face, his eyes were as hard as sapphires. 'The statue isn't negotiable.'

'You're right, it's not!' Sciron agreed. 'I must have it!'

'Gaia told you about it,' Hazel guessed. 'She ordered you to take it.'

Sciron shrugged. 'Maybe. But she told me I could keep it for myself. Hard to pass up that offer! I don't intend to die again, my friends. I intend to live a long life as a very wealthy man!'

'The statue won't do you any good,' Hazel said. 'Not if Gaia destroys the world.'

The muzzles of Sciron's pistols wavered. 'Pardon?'

'Gaia is using you,' Hazel said. 'If you take that statue, we won't be able to defeat her. She's planning on wiping all mortals and demigods off the face of the earth, letting her giants and monsters take over. So where will you spend your gold, Sciron? Assuming Gaia even lets you live.'

Hazel let that sink in. She figured Sciron would have no trouble believing in double-crosses, being a bandit and all.

He was silent for a count of ten.

Finally his smile lines returned.

'All right!' he said. 'I'm not unreasonable. Keep the statue.'

Jason blinked. 'We can go?'

'Just one more thing,' Sciron said. 'I always demand a show of respect. Before I let my victims leave, I insist that they wash my feet.'

Hazel wasn't sure she'd heard him right. Then Sciron kicked off his leather boots, one after the other. His bare feet were the most disgusting things Hazel had ever seen . . . and she had seen some *very* disgusting things.

They were puffy, wrinkled and white as dough, as if they'd been soaking in formaldehyde for a few centuries. Tufts of brown hair sprouted from each misshapen toe. His jagged toenails were green and yellow, like a tortoise's shell.

Then the smell hit her. Hazel didn't know if her father's Underworld palace had a cafeteria for zombies, but if it *did* that cafeteria would smell like Sciron's feet.

'So!' Sciron wriggled his disgusting toes. 'Who wants the left, and who wants the right?'

Jason's face turned almost as white as those feet. 'You've . . . got to be kidding.'

'Not at all!' Sciron said. 'Wash my feet, and we're done. I'll send you back down the cliff. I promise on the River Styx.'

He made that promise so easily, alarm bells rang in Hazel's mind. *Feet. Send you back down the cliff. Tortoise shell.*

The story came back to her, all the missing pieces fitting into place. She remembered how Sciron killed his victims.

'Could we have a moment?' Hazel asked the bandit.

Sciron's eyes narrowed. 'What for?'

'Well, it's a big decision,' she said. 'Left foot, right foot. We need to discuss.'

She could tell he was smiling under the mask.

'Of course,' he said. 'I'm so generous you can have *two* minutes.'

Hazel climbed out of her pile of treasure. She led Jason as far away as she dared – about fifty feet down the cliff, which she hoped was out of earshot.

'Sciron kicks his victims off the cliff,' she whispered.

Jason scowled. 'What?'

'When you kneel down to wash his feet,' Hazel said. 'That's how he kills you. When you're off-balance, woozy from the smell of his feet, he'll kick you over the edge. You'll fall right into the mouth of his giant turtle.'

Jason took a moment to digest that, so to speak. He glanced over the cliff, where the turtle's massive shell glinted just under the water.

'So we have to fight,' Jason said.

'Sciron's too fast,' Hazel said. 'He'll kill us both.'

'Then I'll be ready to fly. When he kicks me over, I'll float halfway down the cliff. Then when he kicks you, I'll catch you.'

Hazel shook her head. 'If he kicks you hard and fast enough, you'll be too dazed to fly. And, even if you can, Sciron's got the eyes of a marksman. He'll watch you fall. If you hover, he'll just shoot you out of the air.'

'Then . . .' Jason clenched his sword hilt. 'I hope you have another idea?'

A few feet away, Gale the weasel appeared from the

bushes. She gnashed her teeth and peered at Hazel as if to say, *Well? Do you?*

Hazel calmed her nerves, trying to avoid pulling more gold from the ground. She remembered the dream she'd had of her father Pluto's voice: *The dead see what they* believe *they will see. So do the living. That is the secret.*

She understood what she had to do. She hated the idea more than she hated that farting weasel, more than she hated Sciron's feet.

'Unfortunately, yes,' Hazel said. 'We have to let Sciron win.'

'What?' Jason demanded.

Hazel told him the plan.

XXVIII

HAZEL

'FINALLY!' SCIRON CRIED. 'That was *much* longer than two minutes!'

'Sorry,' Jason said. 'It was a big decision . . . which foot.'

Hazel tried to clear her mind and imagine the scene through Sciron's eyes – what he desired, what he expected.

That was the key to using the Mist. She couldn't force someone to see the world her way. She couldn't make Sciron's reality appear *less* believable. But if she showed him what he wanted to see . . . well, she was a child of Pluto. She'd spent decades with the dead, listening to them yearn for past lives that were only half-remembered, distorted by nostalgia.

The dead saw what they *believed* they would see. So did the living.

Pluto was the god of the Underworld, the god of wealth. Maybe those two spheres of influence were more connected than Hazel had realized. There wasn't much difference between longing and greed.

If she could summon gold and diamonds, why not summon another kind of treasure – a vision of the world people *wanted* to see?

Of course she could be wrong, in which case she and Jason were about to be turtle food.

She rested her hand on her jacket pocket, where Frank's magical firewood seemed heavier than usual. She wasn't just carrying his lifeline now. She was carrying the lives of the entire crew.

Jason stepped forward, his hands open in surrender. 'I'll go first, Sciron. I'll wash your left foot.'

'Excellent choice!' Sciron wriggled his hairy, corpse-like toes. 'I may have stepped on something with that foot. It felt a little squishy inside my boot. But I'm sure you'll clean it properly.'

Jason's ears reddened. From the tension in his neck, Hazel could tell that he was tempted to drop the charade and attack – one quick slash with his Imperial gold blade. But Hazel knew if he tried, he would fail.

'Sciron,' she broke in, 'do you have water? Soap? How are we supposed to wash –'

'Like this!' Sciron spun his left flintlock. Suddenly it became a squirt bottle with a rag. He tossed it to Jason.

Jason squinted at the label. 'You want me to wash your feet with *glass* cleaner?'

'Of course not!' Sciron knitted his eyebrows. 'It says *multi-surface* cleanser. My feet definitely qualify as *multi-surface*. Besides, it's antibacterial. I need that. Believe me, water won't do the trick on *these* babies.'

Sciron wiggled his toes, and more zombie café odour wafted across the cliffs.

Jason gagged. 'Oh, gods, no . . .'

Sciron shrugged. 'You can always choose what's in my other hand.' He hefted his right flintlock.

'He'll do it,' Hazel said.

Jason glared at her, but Hazel won the staring contest.

'Fine,' he muttered.

'Excellent! Now . . .' Sciron hopped to the nearest chunk of limestone that was the right size for a footstool. He faced the water and planted his foot, so he looked like some explorer who'd just claimed a new country. 'I'll watch the horizon while you scrub my bunions. It'll be much more enjoyable.'

'Yeah,' Jason said. 'I bet.'

Jason knelt in front of the bandit, at the edge of the cliff where he was an easy target. One kick and he'd topple over.

Hazel concentrated. She imagined she was Sciron, the lord of bandits. She was looking down at a pathetic blond-haired kid who was no threat at all – just another defeated demigod about to become his victim.

In her mind, she saw what would happen. She summoned the Mist, calling it from the depths of the earth the way she did with gold or silver or rubies.

Jason squirted the cleaning fluid. His eyes watered. He wiped Sciron's big toe with his rag and turned aside to gag. Hazel could barely watch. When the kick happened, she almost missed it.

Sciron slammed his foot into Jason's chest. Jason tumbled backwards over the edge, his arms flailing, screaming as he fell. When he was about to hit the water, the turtle rose up and swallowed him in one bite, then sank below the surface.

Alarm bells sounded on the *Argo II*. Hazel's friends scrambled on deck, manning the catapults. Hazel heard Piper wailing all the way from the ship.

It was so disturbing that Hazel almost lost her focus. She forced her mind to split into two parts – one intensely focused on her task, one playing the role Sciron needed to see.

She screamed in outrage. 'What did you *do*?'

'Oh, dear . . .' Sciron sounded sad, but Hazel got the impression he was hiding a grin under his bandanna. 'That was an accident, I assure you.'

'My friends will *kill* you now!'

'They can try,' Sciron said. 'But in the meantime I think you have time to wash my other foot! Believe me, my dear. My turtle is full now. He doesn't want you too. You'll be quite safe, unless you refuse.'

He levelled the flintlock pistol at her head.

She hesitated, letting him see her anguish. She couldn't agree too easily, or he wouldn't think she was beaten.

'Don't kick me,' she said, half-sobbing.

His eyes twinkled. This was exactly what he expected. She was broken and helpless. Sciron, the son of Poseidon, had won again.

Hazel could hardly believe this guy had the same father as Percy Jackson. Then she remembered that Poseidon had a changeable personality, like the sea. Maybe his children reflected that. Percy was a child of Poseidon's better nature – powerful, but gentle and helpful, the kind of sea that sped ships safely to distant lands. Sciron was a child of Poseidon's *other* side – the kind of sea that battered relentlessly at the coastline until it crumbled away, or carried the innocents from shore and let them drown, or smashed ships and killed entire crews without mercy.

She snatched up the spray bottle Jason had dropped.

'Sciron,' she growled, 'your feet are the *least* disgusting thing about you.'

His green eyes hardened. 'Just *clean*.'

She knelt, trying to ignore the smell. She shuffled to one side, forcing Sciron to adjust his stance, but she imagined that the sea was still at her back. She held that vision in her mind as she shuffled sideways again.

'Just get on with it!' Sciron said.

Hazel suppressed a smile. She'd managed to turn Sciron one-hundred-and-eighty degrees, but he still saw the water in front of him, the rolling countryside at his back.

She started to clean.

Hazel had done plenty of ugly work before. She'd cleaned the unicorn stables at Camp Jupiter. She'd filled and dug latrines for the legion.

This is nothing, she told herself. But it was hard not to retch when she looked at Sciron's toes.

When the kick came, she flew backwards, but she didn't go far. She landed on her butt in the grass a few yards away.

Sciron stared at her. 'But . . .'

Suddenly the world shifted. The illusion melted, leaving Sciron totally confused. The sea was at *his* back. He'd only succeeded in kicking Hazel away from the ledge.

He lowered his flintlock. 'How –'

'Stand and deliver,' Hazel told him.

Jason swooped out of the sky, right over her head, and body-slammed the bandit over the cliff.

Sciron screamed as he fell, firing his flintlock wildly, but for once hitting nothing. Hazel got to her feet. She reached the cliff's edge in time to see the turtle lunge and snap Sciron out of the air.

Jason grinned. 'Hazel, that was *amazing*. Seriously . . . Hazel? Hey, Hazel?'

Hazel collapsed to her knees, suddenly dizzy.

Distantly, she could hear her friends cheering from the ship below. Jason stood over her, but he was moving in slow motion, his outline blurry, his voice nothing but static.

Frost crept across the rocks and grass around her. The mound of riches she'd summoned sank back into the earth. The Mist swirled.

What have I done? she thought in a panic. *Something went wrong.*

'No, Hazel,' said a deep voice behind her. 'You have done well.'

She hardly dared to breathe. She'd only heard that voice once before, but she had replayed it in her mind thousands of times.

She turned and found herself looking up at her father.

He was dressed in Roman style – his dark hair close-cropped, his pale angular face clean-shaven. His tunic and toga were of black wool, embroidered with threads of gold. The faces of tormented souls shifted in the fabric. The edge of his toga was lined with the crimson of a senator or a praetor, but the stripe rippled like a river of blood. On Pluto's ring finger was a massive opal, like a chunk of polished frozen Mist.

His wedding ring, Hazel thought. But Pluto had never married Hazel's mother. Gods did not marry mortals. That ring would signify his marriage to Persephone.

The thought made Hazel so angry, she shook off her dizziness and stood.

'What do you want?' she demanded.

She hoped her tone would hurt him – jab him for all the pain he'd caused her. But a faint smile played across his mouth.

'My daughter,' he said. 'I am impressed. You have grown strong.'

No thanks to you, she wanted to say. She didn't want to take any pleasure in his compliment, but her eyes still prickled.

'I thought you major gods were incapacitated,' she managed. 'Your Greek and Roman personalities fighting against one another.'

'We are,' Pluto agreed. 'But you invoked me so strongly that you allowed me to appear . . . if only for a moment.'

'I didn't invoke you.'

But, even as she said it, she knew it wasn't true. For the first time, willingly, she'd embraced her lineage as a child of Pluto. She'd tried to understand her father's powers and use them to the fullest.

'When you come to my house in Epirus,' Pluto said, 'you must be prepared. The dead will not welcome you. And the sorceress Pasiphaë –'

'Pacify?' Hazel asked. Then she realized that must be the woman's name.

'She will not be fooled as easily as Sciron.' Pluto's eyes glittered like volcanic stone. 'You succeeded in your first test, but Pasiphaë intends to rebuild her domain, which will endanger *all* demigods. Unless you stop her at the House of Hades . . .'

His form flickered. For a moment he was bearded, in Greek robes with a golden laurel wreath in his hair. Around his feet, skeletal hands broke through the earth.

The god gritted his teeth and scowled.

His Roman form stabilized. The skeletal hands dissolved back into the earth.

'We do not have much time.' He looked like a man who'd just been violently ill. 'Know that the Doors of Death are at the lowest level of the Necromanteion. You must make Pasiphaë see what she wants to see. You are right. That is the secret to all magic. But it will not be easy when you are in her maze.'

'What do you mean? What maze?'

'You will understand,' he promised. 'And, Hazel Levesque . . . you will not believe me, but I am proud of your strength. Sometimes . . . sometimes the only way I can care for my children is to keep my distance.'

Hazel bit back an insult. Pluto was just another deadbeat godly dad making weak excuses. But her heart pounded as she replayed his words: *I am proud of your strength.*

'Go to your friends,' Pluto said. 'They will be worried. The journey to Epirus still holds many perils.'

'Wait,' Hazel said.

Pluto raised an eyebrow.

'When I met Thanatos,' she said, 'you know . . . *Death* . . . he told me I wasn't on your list of rogue spirits to capture. He said maybe that's why you were keeping your distance. If you acknowledged me, you'd have to take me back to the Underworld.'

Pluto waited. 'What is your question?'

'You're here. Why don't you take me to the Underworld? Return me to the dead?'

Pluto's form started to fade. He smiled, but Hazel couldn't tell if he was sad or pleased. 'Perhaps that is not what *I* want to see, Hazel. Perhaps I was never here.'

XXIX

PERCY

PERCY WAS RELIEVED when the demon grandmothers closed in for the kill.

Sure, he was terrified. He didn't like the odds of three against several dozen. But at least he understood *fighting*. Wandering through the darkness, waiting to be attacked – that had been driving him crazy.

Besides, he and Annabeth had fought together many times. And now they had a Titan on their side.

'Back off.' Percy jabbed Riptide at the nearest shrivelled hag, but she only sneered.

We are the arai, said that weird voice-over, like the entire forest was speaking. *You cannot destroy us.*

Annabeth pressed against his shoulder. 'Don't touch them,' she warned. 'They're the spirits of curses.'

'Bob doesn't like curses,' Bob decided. The skeleton kitten Small Bob disappeared inside his coveralls. Smart cat.

The Titan swept his broom in a wide arc, forcing the

spirits back, but they came in again like the tide.

We serve the bitter and the defeated, said the *arai*. *We serve the slain who prayed for vengeance with their final breath. We have many curses to share with you.*

The firewater in Percy's stomach started crawling up his throat. He wished Tartarus had better beverage options, or maybe a tree that dispensed antacid fruit.

'I appreciate the offer,' he said. 'But my mom told me not to accept curses from strangers.'

The nearest demon lunged. Her claws extended like bony switchblades. Percy cut her in two, but as soon as she vaporized the sides of his chest flared with pain. He stumbled back, clamping his hand to his rib cage. His fingers came away wet and red.

'Percy, you're bleeding!' Annabeth cried, which was kind of obvious to him at that point. 'Oh, gods, on *both* sides.'

It was true. The left and right hems of his tattered shirt were sticky with blood, as if a javelin had run him through.

Or an arrow . . .

Queasiness almost knocked him over. *Vengeance. A curse from the slain.*

He flashed back to an encounter in Texas two years ago – a fight with a monstrous rancher who could only be killed if each of his three bodies was cut through simultaneously.

'Geryon,' Percy said. 'This is how I killed him . . .'

The spirits bared their fangs. More *arai* leaped from the black trees, flapping their leathery wings.

Yes, they agreed. *Feel the pain you inflicted upon Geryon. So many curses have been levelled at you, Percy Jackson. Which will you die from? Choose, or we will rip you apart!*

Somehow he stayed on his feet. The blood stopped spreading, but he still felt like he had a hot metal curtain rod sticking through his ribs. His sword arm was heavy and weak.

'I don't understand,' he muttered.

Bob's voice seemed to echo from the end of a long tunnel: 'If you kill one, it gives you a curse.'

'But if we *don't* kill them . . .' Annabeth said.

'They'll kill us anyway,' Percy guessed.

Choose! the *arai* cried. *Will you be crushed like Kampê? Or disintegrated like the young telkhines you slaughtered under Mount St Helens? You have spread so much death and suffering, Percy Jackson. Let us repay you!*

The winged hags pressed in, their breath sour, their eyes burning with hatred. They looked like Furies, but Percy decided these things were even worse. At least the three Furies were under the control of Hades. These things were wild, and they just kept multiplying.

If they really embodied the dying curses of every enemy Percy had ever destroyed . . . then Percy was in serious trouble. He'd faced a *lot* of enemies.

One of the demons lunged at Annabeth. Instinctively, she dodged. She brought her rock down on the old lady's head and broke her into dust.

It wasn't like Annabeth had a choice. Percy would've done the same thing. But instantly Annabeth dropped her rock and cried in alarm.

'I can't see!' She touched her face, looking around wildly. Her eyes were pure white.

Percy ran to her side as the *arai* cackled.

Polyphemus cursed you when you tricked him with your invisibility in the Sea of Monsters. You called yourself Nobody. He could not see you. Now you will not see your attackers.

'I've got you,' Percy promised. He put his arm around Annabeth, but as the *arai* advanced he didn't know how he could protect either of them.

A dozen demons leaped from every direction, but Bob yelled, 'SWEEP!'

His broom whooshed over Percy's head. The entire *arai* offensive line toppled backwards like bowling pins.

More surged forward. Bob whacked one over the head and speared another, blasting them to dust. The others backed away.

Percy held his breath, waiting for their Titan friend to be laid low with some terrible curse, but Bob seemed fine – a massive silvery bodyguard keeping death at bay with the world's most terrifying cleaning implement.

'Bob, you okay?' Percy asked. 'No curses?'

'No curses for Bob!' Bob agreed.

The *arai* snarled and circled, eying the broom. *The Titan is already cursed. Why should we torture him further? You, Percy Jackson, have already destroyed his memory.*

Bob's spearhead dipped.

'Bob, don't listen to them,' Annabeth said. 'They're evil!'

Time slowed. Percy wondered if the spirit of Kronos was somewhere nearby, swirling in the darkness, enjoying this moment so much that he wanted it to last forever. Percy felt exactly like he had at twelve years old, battling Ares on that beach in Los Angeles, when the shadow of the Titan lord had first passed over him.

Bob turned. His wild white hair looked like an exploded halo. 'My memory . . . It was you?'

Curse him, Titan! the *arai* urged, their red eyes gleaming. *Add to our numbers!*

Percy's heart pressed against his spine. 'Bob, it's a long story. I didn't want you to be my enemy. I tried to make you a friend.'

By stealing your life, the *arai* said. *Leaving you in the palace of Hades to scrub floors!*

Annabeth gripped Percy's hand. 'Which way?' she whispered. 'If we have to run?'

He understood. If Bob wouldn't protect them, their only chance was to run – but that wasn't any chance at all.

'Bob, listen,' he tried again, 'the *arai* want you to get angry. They spawn from bitter thoughts. Don't give them what they want. We *are* your friends.'

Even as he said it, Percy felt like a liar. He'd left Bob in the Underworld and hadn't given him a thought since. What made them friends? The fact that Percy needed him now? Percy always hated it when the gods used him for their errands. Now Percy was treating Bob the same way.

You see his face? the *arai* growled. *The boy cannot even convince himself. Did he visit you, after he stole your memory?*

'No,' Bob murmured. His lower lip quivered. 'The other one did.'

Percy's thoughts moved sluggishly. 'The other one?'

'Nico.' Bob scowled at him, his eyes full of hurt. 'Nico visited. Told me about Percy. Said Percy was good. Said he was a friend. *That* is why Bob helped.'

'But . . .' Percy's voice disintegrated like someone had hit it with a Celestial bronze blade. He'd never felt so low and dishonourable, so unworthy of having a friend.

The *arai* attacked, and this time Bob did not stop them.

XXX

PERCY

'LEFT!' PERCY DRAGGED ANNABETH, slicing through the *arai* to clear a path. He probably brought down a dozen curses on himself, but he didn't feel them right away, so he kept running.

The pain in his chest flared with every step. He weaved between the trees, leading Annabeth at a full sprint despite her blindness.

Percy realized how much she trusted him to get her out of this. He couldn't let her down, yet how could he save her? And if she was permanently blind . . . No. He suppressed a surge of panic. He would figure out how to cure her later. First they had to escape.

Leathery wings beat the air above them. Angry hissing and the scuttling of clawed feet told him the demons were at their backs.

As they ran past one of the black trees, he slashed his sword across the trunk. He heard it topple, followed by the satisfying crunch of several dozen *arai* as they were smashed flat.

If a tree falls in the forest and crushes a demon, does the tree get cursed?

Percy slashed down another trunk, then another. It bought them a few seconds, but not enough.

Suddenly the darkness in front of them became thicker. Percy realized what it meant just in time. He grabbed Annabeth right before they both charged off the side of the cliff.

'What?' she cried. 'What is it?'

'Cliff,' he gasped. 'Big cliff.'

'Which way, then?'

Percy couldn't see how far the cliff dropped. It could be ten feet or a thousand. There was no telling what was at the bottom. They could jump and hope for the best, but he doubted 'the best' ever happened in Tartarus.

So, two options: right or left, following the edge.

He was about to choose randomly when a winged demon descended in front of him, hovering over the void on her bat wings, just out of sword reach.

Did you have a nice walk? asked the collective voice, echoing all around them.

Percy turned. The *arai* poured out of the woods, making a crescent around them. One grabbed Annabeth's arm. Annabeth wailed in rage, judo-flipping the monster and dropping on its neck, putting her whole body weight into an elbow strike that would've made any pro wrestler proud.

The demon dissolved, but when Annabeth got to her feet she looked stunned and afraid as well as blind.

'Percy?' she called, panic creeping into her voice.

'I'm right here.'

He tried to put his hand on her shoulder, but she wasn't standing where he thought. He tried again, only to find she was several feet further away. It was like trying to grab something in a tank of water, with the light shifting the image away.

'Percy!' Annabeth's voice cracked. 'Why did you leave me?'

'I didn't!' He turned on the *arai*, his arms shaking with anger. 'What did you do to her?'

We did nothing, the demons said. *Your beloved has unleashed a special curse – a bitter thought from someone you abandoned. You punished an innocent soul by leaving her in her solitude. Now her most hateful wish has come to pass: Annabeth feels her despair. She, too, will perish alone and abandoned.*

'Percy?' Annabeth spread her arms, trying to find him. The *arai* backed up, letting her stumble blindly through their ranks.

'Who did I abandon?' Percy demanded. 'I never –'

Suddenly his stomach felt like it had dropped off the cliff.

The words rang in his head: *An innocent soul. Alone and abandoned.* He remembered an island, a cave lit with soft glowing crystals, a dinner table on the beach tended by invisible air spirits.

'She wouldn't,' he mumbled. 'She'd never curse me.'

The eyes of the demons blurred together like their voices.

Percy's sides throbbed. The pain in his chest was worse, as if someone were slowly twisting a dagger.

Annabeth wandered among the demons, desperately calling his name. Percy longed to run to her, but he knew the *arai* wouldn't allow it. The only reason they hadn't killed her yet was that they were enjoying her misery.

Percy clenched his jaw. He didn't care how many curses he suffered. He had to keep these leathery old hags focused on him and protect Annabeth as long as he could.

He yelled in fury and attacked them all.

XXXI

PERCY

FOR ONE EXCITING MINUTE, Percy felt like he was winning. Riptide cut through the *arai* as though they were made of powdered sugar. One panicked and ran face-first into a tree. Another screeched and tried to fly away, but Percy sliced off her wings and sent her spiralling into the chasm.

Each time a demon disintegrated, Percy felt a heavier sense of dread as another curse settled on him. Some were harsh and painful: a stabbing in the gut, a burning sensation like he was being blasted by a blowtorch. Some were subtle: a chill in the blood, an uncontrollable tic in his right eye.

Seriously, who curses you with their dying breath and says: *I hope your eye twitches!*

Percy knew that he'd killed a lot of monsters, but he'd never really thought about it from the monsters' point of view. Now all their pain and anger and bitterness poured over him, sapping his strength.

The *arai* just kept coming. For every one he cut down, six more seemed to appear.

His sword arm grew tired. His body ached, and his vision blurred. He tried to make his way towards Annabeth, but she was just out of reach, calling his name as she wandered among the demons.

As Percy blundered towards her, a demon pounced and sank its teeth into his thigh. Percy roared. He sliced the demon to dust, but immediately fell to his knees.

His mouth burned worse than when he had swallowed the firewater of the Phlegethon. He doubled over, shuddering and retching, as a dozen fiery snakes seemed to work their way down his oesophagus.

You have chosen, said the voice of the *arai*, *the curse of Phineas . . . an excellent painful death.*

Percy tried to speak. His tongue felt like it was being microwaved. He remembered the old blind king who had chased harpies through Portland with a weed whacker. Percy had challenged him to a contest, and the loser had drunk a deadly vial of gorgon's blood. Percy didn't remember the old blind man muttering a final curse, but as Phineas had dissolved and returned to the Underworld he probably hadn't wished Percy a long and happy life.

After Percy's victory then, Gaia had warned him: *Do not press your luck. When your death comes, I promise it will be much more painful than gorgon's blood.*

Now he was in Tartarus, dying from gorgon's blood plus a dozen other agonizing curses, while he watched his girlfriend stumble around, helpless and blind and believing he'd abandoned her. He clutched his sword. His knuckles started to steam. White smoke curled off his forearms.

I won't die like this, he thought.

Not only because it was painful and insultingly lame, but because Annabeth needed him. Once he was dead, the demons would turn their attention to her. He couldn't leave her alone.

The *arai* clustered around him, snickering and hissing.

His head will erupt first, the voice speculated.

No, the voice answered itself from another direction. *He will combust all at once*.

They were placing bets on how he would die . . . what sort of scorch mark he would leave on the ground.

'Bob,' he croaked. 'I need you.'

A hopeless plea. He could barely hear himself. Why should Bob answer his call twice? The Titan knew the truth now. Percy was no friend.

He raised his eyes one last time. His surroundings seemed to flicker. The sky boiled and the ground blistered.

Percy realized that what he *saw* of Tartarus was only a watered-down version of its true horror – only what his demigod brain could handle. The worst of it was veiled, the same way the Mist veiled monsters from mortal sight. Now as Percy died he began to see the truth.

The air was the breath of Tartarus. All these monsters were just blood cells circulating through his body. Everything Percy saw was a dream in the mind of the dark god of the pit.

This must have been the way *Nico* had seen Tartarus, and it had almost destroyed his sanity. Nico . . . one of the many people Percy hadn't treated well enough. He and Annabeth had only made it this far through Tartarus because Nico di Angelo had behaved like Bob's *true* friend.

You see the horror of the pit? the *arai* said soothingly. *Give up, Percy Jackson. Isn't death better than enduring this place?*

'I'm sorry,' Percy murmured.

He apologizes! The *arai* shrieked with delight. *He regrets his failed life, his crimes against the children of Tartarus!*

'No,' Percy said. 'I'm sorry, Bob. I should've been honest with you. Please . . . forgive me. Protect Annabeth.'

He didn't expect Bob to hear him or care, but it felt right to clear his conscience. He couldn't blame anyone else for his troubles. Not the gods. Not Bob. He couldn't even blame Calypso, the girl he'd left alone on that island. Maybe she'd turned bitter and cursed Percy's girlfriend out of despair. Still . . . Percy should have followed up with Calypso, made sure the gods sprang her from her exile on Ogygia like they'd promised. He hadn't treated her any better than he'd treated Bob. He hadn't even thought much about her, though her moonlace plant still bloomed in his mom's window box.

It took all his remaining effort, but he got to his feet. Steam rose from his whole body. His legs shook. His insides churned like a volcano.

At least Percy could go out fighting. He raised Riptide.

But, before he could strike, all the *arai* in front of him exploded into dust.

XXXII

PERCY

BOB SERIOUSLY KNEW HOW TO USE A BROOM.

He slashed back and forth, destroying the demons one after the other while Small Bob the kitten sat on his shoulder, arching its back and hissing.

In a matter of seconds, the *arai* were gone. Most had been vaporized. The smart ones had flown off into the darkness, shrieking in terror.

Percy wanted to thank the Titan, but his voice wouldn't work. His legs buckled. His ears rang. Through a red glow of pain, he saw Annabeth a few yards away, wandering blindly towards the edge of the cliff.

'Uh!' Percy grunted.

Bob followed his gaze. He bounded towards Annabeth and scooped her up. She yelled and kicked, pummelling Bob's gut, but Bob didn't seem to care. He carried her over to Percy and put her down gently.

The Titan touched her forehead. 'Owie.'

Annabeth stopped fighting. Her eyes cleared. 'Where – what –?'

She saw Percy, and a series of expressions flashed across her face – relief, joy, shock, horror. 'What's wrong with him?' she cried. 'What happened?'

She cradled his shoulders and wept into his scalp.

Percy wanted to tell her it was okay, but of course it wasn't. He couldn't even feel his body any more. His consciousness was like a small helium balloon, loosely tied to the top of his head. It had no weight, no strength. It just kept expanding, getting lighter and lighter. He knew that soon it would either burst or the string would break, and his life would float away.

Annabeth took his face in her hands. She kissed him and tried to wipe the dust and sweat from his eyes.

Bob loomed over them, his broom planted like a flag. His face was unreadable, luminously white in the dark.

'Lots of curses,' Bob said. 'Percy has done bad things to monsters.'

'Can you fix him?' Annabeth pleaded. 'Like you did with my blindness? Fix *Percy!*'

Bob frowned. He picked at the name tag on his uniform like it was a scab.

Annabeth tried again. 'Bob –'

'Iapetus,' Bob said, his voice a low rumble. 'Before Bob. It was Iapetus.'

The air was absolutely still. Percy felt helpless, barely connected to the world.

'I like Bob better.' Annabeth's voice was surprisingly calm. 'Which do you like?'

The Titan regarded her with his pure silver eyes. 'I do not know any more.'

He crouched next to her and studied Percy. Bob's face looked haggard and careworn, as if he suddenly felt the weight of all his centuries.

'I promised,' he murmured. 'Nico asked me to help. I do not think Iapetus or Bob likes breaking promises.' He touched Percy's forehead.

'Owie,' the Titan murmured. 'Very big owie.'

Percy sank back into his body. The ringing in his ears faded. His vision cleared. He still felt like he had swallowed a deep fryer. His insides bubbled. He could sense that the poison had only been slowed, not removed.

But he was alive.

He tried to meet Bob's eyes, to express his gratitude. His head lolled against his chest.

'Bob cannot cure this,' Bob said. 'Too much poison. Too many curses piled up.'

Annabeth hugged Percy's shoulders. He wanted to say: *I can feel that now. Ow. Too tight.*

'What can we do, Bob?' Annabeth asked. 'Is there water anywhere? Water might heal him.'

'No water,' Bob said. 'Tartarus is bad.'

I noticed, Percy wanted to yell.

At least the Titan called himself *Bob*. Even if he blamed Percy for taking his memory, maybe he would help Annabeth if Percy didn't make it.

'No,' Annabeth insisted. 'No, there *has* to be a way. *Something* to heal him.'

Bob placed his hand on Percy's chest. A cold tingle like eucalyptus oil spread across his sternum, but as soon as Bob lifted his hand the relief stopped. Percy's lungs felt as hot as lava again.

'Tartarus kills demigods,' Bob said. 'It heals monsters, but you do not belong. Tartarus will not heal Percy. The pit hates your kind.'

'I don't care,' Annabeth said. 'Even here, there *has* to be someplace he can rest, some kind of cure he can take. Maybe back at the altar of Hermes, or –'

In the distance, a deep voice bellowed – a voice that Percy recognized, unfortunately.

'I SMELL HIM!' roared the giant. 'BEWARE, SON OF POSEIDON! I COME FOR YOU!'

'Polybotes,' Bob said. 'He hates Poseidon and his children. He is very close now.'

Annabeth struggled to get Percy to his feet. He hated making her work so hard, but he felt like a sack of billiard balls. Even with Annabeth supporting almost all his weight, he could barely stand.

'Bob, I'm going on, with or without you,' she said. 'Will you help?'

The kitten Small Bob mewed and began to purr, rubbing against Bob's chin.

Bob looked at Percy, and Percy wished he could read the Titan's expression. Was he angry or just thoughtful? Was he planning revenge, or was he just feeling hurt because Percy had lied about being his friend?

'There is one place,' Bob said at last. 'There is a giant who might know what to do.'

Annabeth almost dropped Percy. 'A giant. Uh, Bob, giants are bad.'

'One is good,' Bob insisted. 'Trust me, and I will take you . . . unless Polybotes and the others catch us first.'

XXXIII

JASON

JASON FELL ASLEEP ON THE JOB. Which was bad, since he was a thousand feet in the air.

He should have known better. It was the morning after their encounter with Sciron the bandit, and Jason was on duty, fighting some wild *venti* who were threatening the ship. When he slashed through the last one, he forgot to hold his breath.

A stupid mistake. When a wind spirit disintegrates, it creates a vacuum. Unless you're holding your breath, the air gets sucked right out of your lungs. The pressure in your inner ears drops so fast that you black out.

That's what happened to Jason.

Even worse, he instantly plunged into a dream. In the back of his subconscious, he thought: *Really? Now?*

He needed to wake up or he would die, but he wasn't able to hold on to that thought. In the dream, he found himself on the roof of a tall building, the night-time skyline of Manhattan spread around him. A cold wind whipped through his clothes.

A few blocks away, clouds gathered above the Empire State Building – the entrance to Mount Olympus itself. Lightning flashed. The air was metallic with the smell of oncoming rain. The top of the skyscraper was lit up as usual, but the lights seemed to be malfunctioning. They flickered from purple to orange as if the colours were fighting for dominance.

On the roof of Jason's building stood his old comrades from Camp Jupiter: an array of demigods in combat armour, their Imperial gold weapons and shields glinting in the dark. He saw Dakota and Nathan, Leila and Marcus. Octavian stood to one side, thin and pale, his eyes red-rimmed from sleeplessness or anger, a string of sacrificial stuffed animals around his waist. His augur's white robe was draped over a purple T-shirt and cargo pants.

In the centre of the line stood Reyna, her metal dogs Aurum and Argentum at her side. Upon seeing her, Jason felt an incredible pang of guilt. He'd let her believe they had a future together. He had never been in love with her, and he hadn't led her on, exactly . . . but he also hadn't shut her down.

He'd disappeared, leaving her to run the camp on her own. (Okay, that hadn't exactly been Jason's idea, but still . . .) Then he had returned to Camp Jupiter with his new girlfriend Piper and a whole bunch of Greek friends in a warship. They'd fired on the Forum and run away, leaving Reyna with a war on her hands.

In his dream she looked tired. Others might not notice, but

he'd worked with her long enough to recognize the weariness in her eyes, the tightness in her shoulders under the straps of her armour. Her dark hair was wet, like she'd taken a hasty shower.

The Romans stared at the roof-access door as if they were waiting for someone.

When the door opened, two people emerged. One was a faun – no, Jason thought – a *satyr*. He'd learned the difference at Camp Half-Blood, and Coach Hedge was always correcting him if he made that mistake. Roman fauns tended to hang around and beg and eat. Satyrs were more helpful, more engaged with demigod affairs. Jason didn't think he'd seen this particular satyr before, but he was sure the guy was from the Greek side. No faun would look so purposeful walking up to an armed group of Romans in the middle of the night.

He wore a green Nature Conservancy T-shirt with pictures of endangered whales and tigers and stuff. Nothing covered his shaggy legs and hooves. He had a bushy goatee, curly brown hair tucked into a Rasta-style cap and a set of reed pipes around his neck. His hands fidgeted with the hem of his shirt, but considering the way he studied the Romans, noting their positions and their weapons, Jason figured this satyr had been in combat before.

At his side was a red-headed girl Jason recognized from Camp Half-Blood – their oracle, Rachel Elizabeth Dare. She had long frizzy hair, a plain white blouse and jeans covered with hand-drawn ink designs. She held a blue plastic hairbrush that she tapped nervously against her thigh like a good luck talisman.

Jason remembered her at the campfire, reciting lines of prophecy that sent Jason, Piper and Leo on their first quest together. She was a regular mortal teenager – not a demigod – but, for reasons Jason never understood, the spirit of Delphi had chosen her as its host.

The real question: What was she doing with the Romans?

She stepped forward, her eyes fixed on Reyna. 'You got my message.'

Octavian snorted. 'That's the only reason you made it this far alive, *Graecus*. I hope you've come to discuss surrender terms.'

'Octavian . . .' Reyna warned.

'At least search them!' Octavian protested.

'No need,' Reyna said, studying Rachel Dare. 'Do you bring weapons?'

Rachel shrugged. 'I hit Kronos in the eye with this hairbrush once. Otherwise, no.'

The Romans didn't seem to know what to make of that. The mortal didn't sound like she was kidding.

'And your friend?' Reyna nodded to the satyr. 'I thought you were coming alone.'

'This is Grover Underwood,' Rachel said. 'He's a leader of the Council.'

'What *council*?' Octavian demanded.

'Cloven Elders, man.' Grover's voice was high and reedy, as if he were terrified, but Jason suspected the satyr had more steel than he let on. 'Seriously, don't you Romans have nature and trees and stuff? I've got some news you need to hear. Plus, I'm a card-carrying protector. I'm here to, you know, protect Rachel.'

Reyna looked like she was trying not to smile. 'But no weapons?'

'Just the pipes.' Grover's expression became wistful. 'Percy always said my cover of "Born to be Wild" should count as a dangerous weapon, but I don't think it's *that* bad.'

Octavian sneered. 'Another friend of Percy Jackson. That's all *I* need to hear.'

Reyna held up her hand for silence. Her gold and silver dogs sniffed the air, but they remained calm and attentive at her side.

'So far, our guests speak the truth,' Reyna said. 'Be warned, Rachel and Grover, if you start to lie, this conversation will not go well for you. Say what you came to say.'

From her jeans pocket, Rachel dug out a piece of paper like a napkin. 'A message. From Annabeth.'

Jason wasn't sure he'd heard her right. Annabeth was in Tartarus. She couldn't send anyone a note on a napkin.

Maybe I've hit the water and died, his subconscious said. *This isn't a real vision. It's some sort of after-death hallucination.*

But the dream seemed very real. He could feel the wind sweeping across the roof. He could smell the storm. Lightning flickered over the Empire State Building, making the Romans' armour flash.

Reyna took the note. As she read it, her eyebrows crept

higher. Her mouth parted in shock. Finally, she looked up at Rachel. 'Is this a joke?'

'I wish,' Rachel said. 'They're really in Tartarus.'

'But how –'

'I don't know,' Rachel said. 'The note appeared in the sacrificial fire at our dining pavilion. That's Annabeth's handwriting. She asks for you by name.'

Octavian stirred. 'Tartarus? What do you mean?'

Reyna handed him the letter.

Octavian muttered as he read: 'Rome, Arachne, Athena – *Athena Parthenos*?' He looked around in outrage, as if waiting for someone to contradict what he was reading. 'A Greek trick! Greeks are *infamous* for their tricks!'

Reyna took back the note. 'Why ask this of me?'

Rachel smiled. 'Because Annabeth is wise. She believes you can do this, Reyna Avila Ramírez-Arellano.'

Jason felt like he'd been slapped. Nobody *ever* used Reyna's full name. She hated telling anyone what it was. The only time Jason had ever said it aloud, just trying to pronounce it correctly, she'd given him a murderous look. *That was the name of a little girl in San Juan*, she told him. *I left it behind when I left Puerto Rico.*

Reyna scowled. 'How did you –'

'Uh,' Grover Underwood interrupted. 'You mean your initials are RA-RA?'

Reyna's hand drifted towards her dagger.

'But that's not important!' the satyr said quickly. 'Look, we wouldn't have risked coming here if we didn't trust

Annabeth's instincts. A Roman leader returning the most important Greek statue to Camp Half-Blood – she knows that could prevent a war.'

'This isn't a trick,' Rachel added. 'We're not lying. Ask your dogs.'

The metallic greyhounds didn't react. Reyna stroked Aurum's head thoughtfully. 'The Athena Parthenos . . . so the legend is true.'

'Reyna!' Octavian cried. 'You can't seriously be considering this! Even if the statue still exists, you see what they're doing. We're on the verge of attacking them – destroying the stupid Greeks once and for all – and they concoct this stupid errand to divert your attention. They want to send you to your death!'

The other Romans muttered, glaring at their visitors. Jason remembered how persuasive Octavian could be, and he was winning the officers to his side.

Rachel Dare faced the augur. 'Octavian, son of Apollo, you should take this more seriously. Even Romans respected your father's Oracle of Delphi.'

'Ha!' Octavian said. 'You're the Oracle of Delphi? Right. And I'm the Emperor Nero!'

'At least Nero could play music,' Grover muttered.

Octavian balled his fists.

Suddenly the wind shifted. It swirled around the Romans with a hissing sound, like a nest of snakes. Rachel Dare glowed in a green aura, as if hit by a soft emerald spotlight. Then the wind faded and the aura was gone.

The sneer melted from Octavian's face. The Romans rustled uneasily.

'It's your decision,' Rachel said, as if nothing had happened. 'I have no specific prophecy to offer you, but I *can* see glimpses of the future. I see the Athena Parthenos on Half-Blood Hill. I see *her* bringing it.' She pointed at Reyna. 'Also, Ella has been murmuring lines from your Sibylline Books –'

'What?' Reyna interrupted. 'The Sibylline Books were destroyed centuries ago.'

'I *knew* it!' Octavian pounded his fist into his palm. 'That harpy they brought back from the quest – *Ella*. I knew she was spouting prophecies! Now I understand. She – she somehow memorized a copy of the Sibylline Books.'

Reyna shook her head in disbelief. 'How is that possible?'

'We don't know,' Rachel admitted. 'But, yes, that seems to be the case. Ella has a perfect memory. She loves books. Somewhere, somehow, she read your Roman book of prophecies. Now she's the only source for them.'

'Your friends lied,' Octavian said. 'They told us the harpy was just muttering gibberish. They stole her!'

Grover huffed indignantly. 'Ella isn't your property! She's a free creature. Besides, she wants to be at Camp Half-Blood. She's dating one of my friends, Tyson.'

'The Cyclops,' Reyna remembered. 'A harpy dating a Cyclops . . .'

'That's not relevant!' Octavian said. 'The harpy has valuable Roman prophecies. If the Greeks won't return her, we should take their Oracle hostage! Guards!'

Two centurions advanced, their *pila* levelled. Grover brought his pipes to his lips, played a quick jig and their spears turned into Christmas trees. The guards dropped them in surprise.

'Enough!' Reyna shouted.

She didn't often raise her voice. When she did, everyone listened.

'We've strayed from the point,' she said. 'Rachel Dare, you're telling me that Annabeth is in Tartarus, yet she's found a way to send this message. She wants *me* to bring this statue from the ancient lands to your camp.'

Rachel nodded. 'Only a Roman can return it and restore peace.'

'And why would the Romans want peace,' Reyna asked, 'after your ship attacked our city?'

'You know why,' Rachel said. 'To avoid this war. To reconcile the gods' Greek and Roman sides. We have to work together to defeat Gaia.'

Octavian stepped forward to speak, but Reyna shot him a withering look.

'According to Percy Jackson,' Reyna said, 'the battle with Gaia will be fought in the ancient lands. In Greece.'

'That's where the giants are,' Rachel agreed. 'Whatever magic, whatever ritual the giants are planning to wake the Earth Mother, I sense it will happen in Greece. But . . . well, our problems aren't limited to the ancient lands. That's why I brought Grover to talk to you.'

The satyr tugged his goatee. 'Yeah . . . see, over the last few months, I've been talking to satyrs and nature spirits across the continent. They're all saying the same thing. Gaia is stirring – I mean, she's *right* on the edge of consciousness. She's whispering in the minds of naiads, trying to turn them. She's causing earthquakes, uprooting the dryads' trees. Last week alone, she appeared in human form in a dozen different places, scaring the horns off some of my friends. In Colorado, a giant stone fist rose out of a mountain and swatted some Party Ponies like flies.'

Reyna frowned. '*Party Ponies?*'

'Long story,' Rachel said. 'The point is: Gaia will rise *everywhere*. She's already stirring. No place will be safe from the battle. And we know that her first targets are going to be the demigod camps. She wants us destroyed.'

'Speculation,' Octavian said. 'A distraction. The Greeks fear our attack. They're trying to confuse us. It's the Trojan Horse all over again!'

Reyna twisted the silver ring she always wore, with the sword and torch symbols of her mother, Bellona.

'Marcus,' she said, 'bring Scipio from the stables.'

'Reyna, no!' Octavian protested.

She faced the Greeks. 'I will do this for Annabeth, for the hope of peace between our camps, but do not think I have forgotten the insults to Camp Jupiter. Your ship fired on our city. *You* declared war – not us. Now, leave.'

Grover stamped his hoof. 'Percy would never –'

'Grover,' Rachel said, 'we should go.'

Her tone said: *Before it's too late.*

After they had retreated back down the stairs, Octavian wheeled on Reyna. 'Are you *mad*?'

'I am praetor of the legion,' Reyna said. 'I judge this to be in the best interest of Rome.'

'To get yourself killed? To break our oldest laws and travel to the ancient lands? How will you even find their ship, assuming you survive the journey?'

'I will find them,' Reyna said. 'If they are sailing for Greece, I know a place Jason will stop. To face the ghosts in the House of Hades, he will need an army. There is only one place where he can find that sort of help.'

In Jason's dream, the building seemed to tilt under his feet. He remembered a conversation he'd had with Reyna years ago, a promise they had made to each other. He knew what she was talking about.

'This is insanity,' Octavian muttered. 'We're already under attack. We must take the offensive! Those hairy dwarfs have been stealing our supplies, sabotaging our scouting parties – you *know* the Greeks sent them.'

'Perhaps,' Reyna said. 'But you will *not* launch an attack without my orders. Continue scouting the enemy camp. Secure your positions. Gather all the allies you can, and if you catch those dwarfs you have my blessing to send them back to Tartarus. But do *not* attack Camp Half-Blood until I return.'

Octavian narrowed his eyes. 'While you're gone, the augur is the senior officer. I will be in charge.'

'I know.' Reyna didn't sound happy about it. 'But you have my orders. You all heard them.' She scanned the faces of the centurions, daring them to question her.

She stormed off, her purple cloak billowing and her dogs at her heels.

Once she was gone, Octavian turned to the centurions. 'Gather all the senior officers. I want a meeting as soon as Reyna has left on her fool's quest. There will be a few changes in the legion's plans.'

One of the centurions opened his mouth to respond, but for some reason he spoke in Piper's voice: '*WAKE UP!*'

Jason's eyes snapped open, and he saw the ocean's surface hurtling towards him.

XXXIV

JASON

JASON SURVIVED – BARELY.

Later, his friends explained that they hadn't seen him falling from the sky until the last second. There was no time for Frank to turn into an eagle and catch him; no time to formulate a rescue plan.

Only Piper's quick thinking and charmspeak had saved his life. She'd yelled *WAKE UP!* with so much force that Jason felt like he'd been hit with defibrillator paddles. With a millisecond to spare, he'd summoned the winds and avoided becoming a floating patch of demigod grease on the surface of the Adriatic.

Back on board, he had pulled Leo aside and suggested a course correction. Fortunately, Leo trusted him enough not to ask why.

'Weird vacation spot.' Leo grinned. 'But, hey, you're the boss!'

Now, sitting with his friends in the mess hall, Jason felt *so* awake he doubted he would sleep for a week. His hands were jittery. He couldn't stop tapping his feet. He guessed that this was how Leo felt all the time, except that Leo had a sense of humour.

After what Jason had seen in his dream, he didn't feel much like joking.

While they ate lunch, Jason reported on his midair vision. His friends were quiet long enough for Coach Hedge to finish a peanut butter and banana sandwich, along with the ceramic plate.

The ship creaked as it sailed through the Adriatic, its remaining oars still out of alignment from the giant turtle attack. Every once in a while Festus the figurehead creaked and squeaked through the speakers, reporting the autopilot status in that weird machine language that only Leo could understand.

'A note from Annabeth.' Piper shook her head in amazement. 'I don't see how that's possible, but if it is –'

'She's alive,' Leo said. 'Thank the gods and pass the hot sauce.'

Frank frowned. 'What does that mean?'

Leo wiped the chip crumbs off his face. 'It means pass the hot sauce, Zhang. I'm still hungry.'

Frank slid over a jar of salsa. 'I can't believe Reyna would try to find us. It's taboo, coming to the ancient lands. She'll be stripped of her praetorship.'

'If she lives,' Hazel said. 'It was hard enough for us to make it this far with seven demigods and a warship.'

'And me.' Coach Hedge belched. 'Don't forget, cupcake, you got the *satyr* advantage.'

Jason had to smile. Coach Hedge could be pretty ridiculous, but Jason *was* glad he'd come along. He thought about the satyr he'd seen in his dream – Grover Underwood. He couldn't imagine a satyr more different from Coach Hedge, but they both seemed brave in their own way.

It made Jason wonder about the fauns back at Camp Jupiter – whether they could be like that if the Roman demigods expected more from them. Another thing to add to his list . . .

His list. He hadn't realized that he *had* one until that moment, but ever since leaving Camp Half-Blood he'd been thinking of ways to make Camp Jupiter more . . . *Greek.*

He had grown up at Camp Jupiter. He'd done well there. But he had always been a little unconventional. He chafed under the rules.

He'd joined the Fifth Cohort because everyone told him not to. They warned him it was the worst unit. So he'd thought, *Fine, I'll make it the best.*

Once he'd become praetor, he'd campaigned to rename the legion the First Legion rather than the Twelfth Legion, to symbolize a new start for Rome. The idea had almost caused a mutiny. New Rome was all about tradition and legacies; the rules didn't change easily. Jason had learned to live with that and even rose to the top.

But now that he had seen both camps he couldn't shake the feeling that Camp Half-Blood might have taught him more about himself. If he survived this war with Gaia and returned to Camp Jupiter as a praetor, could he change things for the better?

That was his duty.

So why did the idea fill him with dread? He felt guilty about leaving Reyna to rule without him, but still . . . part of him wanted to go back to Camp Half-Blood with Piper and Leo. He guessed that that made him a pretty terrible leader.

'Jason?' Leo asked. '*Argo II* to Jason. Come in.'

He realized his friends were looking at him expectantly. They needed reassurance. Whether or not he made it back to New Rome after the war, Jason had to step up now and act like a praetor.

'Yeah, sorry.' He touched the groove that Sciron the bandit had cut in his hair. 'Crossing the Atlantic is a hard journey, no doubt. But I'd never bet against Reyna. If anyone can make it, she will.'

Piper circled her spoon through her soup. Jason was still a little nervous about her getting jealous of Reyna, but when she looked up she gave him a dry smile that seemed more teasing than insecure.

'Well, I'd *love* to see Reyna again,' she said. 'But how is she supposed to find us?'

Frank raised his hand. 'Can't you just send her an Iris-message?'

'They're not working very well,' Coach Hedge put in. 'Horrible reception. Every night, I swear, I could *kick* that rainbow goddess . . .'

He faltered. His face turned bright red.

'Coach?' Leo grinned. 'Who have you been calling every night, you old goat?'

'No one!' Hedge snapped. 'Nothing! I just meant –'

'He means we've already tried,' Hazel intervened, and the coach gave her a grateful look. 'Some magic is interfering . . . maybe Gaia. Contacting the Romans is even harder. I think they're shielding themselves.'

Jason looked from Hazel to the coach, wondering what was going on with the satyr and how Hazel knew about it. Now that Jason thought about it, the coach hadn't mentioned his cloud nymph girlfriend Mellie in a long time . . .

Frank drummed his fingers on the table. 'I don't suppose Reyna has a cell phone . . . ? Nah. Never mind. She'd probably have bad reception on a pegasus flying over the Atlantic.'

Jason thought about the *Argo II*'s journey across the ocean, the dozens of encounters that had nearly killed them. Thinking about Reyna making that journey alone – he couldn't decide whether it was terrifying or awe-inspiring.

'She'll find us,' he said. 'She mentioned something in the dream – she's expecting me to go to a certain place on our way to the House of Hades. I – I'd forgotten about it, actually, but she's right. It's a place I need to visit.'

Piper leaned towards him, her caramel braid falling over her shoulder. Her multicoloured eyes made it hard for him to think straight.

'And where is this place?' she asked.

'A . . . uh, a town called Split.'

'Split.' She smelled really good – like blooming honeysuckle.

'Um, yeah.' Jason wondered if Piper was working some sort of Aphrodite magic on him – like maybe every time he mentioned Reyna's name she would befuddle him so much he couldn't think about anything but Piper. He supposed it wasn't the worst sort of revenge. 'In fact, we should be getting close. Leo?'

Leo punched the intercom button. 'How's it going up there, buddy?'

Festus the figurehead creaked and steamed.

'He says maybe ten minutes to the harbour,' Leo reported. 'Though I still don't get why you want to go to Croatia, especially a town called *Split*. I mean, you name your city *Split*, you gotta figure it's a warning to, you know, *split*. Kind of like naming your city *Get Out!*'

'Wait,' Hazel said. 'Why are we going to Croatia?'

Jason noticed that the others were reluctant to meet her eyes. Since her trick with the Mist against Sciron the bandit, even Jason felt a little nervous around her. He knew that wasn't fair to Hazel. It was hard enough being a child of Pluto, but she'd pulled off some *serious* magic on that cliff. And afterwards, according to Hazel, Pluto himself had appeared to her. That was something Romans typically called a *bad omen*.

Leo pushed his chips and hot sauce aside. 'Well, technically we've been in Croatian territory for the past day or so. All that coastline we've been sailing past is *it*, but I guess back in the Roman times it was called . . . what'd you say, Jason? Bodacious?'

'Dalmatia,' Nico said, making Jason jump.

Holy Romulus . . . Jason wished he could put a bell around Nico di Angelo's neck to remind him the guy was there. Nico had this disturbing habit of standing silently in the corner, blending into the shadows.

He stepped forward, his dark eyes fixed on Jason. Since they'd rescued him from the bronze jar in Rome, Nico had slept very little and eaten even less, as if he were still subsisting on those emergency pomegranate seeds from the Underworld. He reminded Jason a little too much of a flesh-eating ghoul he'd once fought in San Bernardino.

'Croatia used to be Dalmatia,' Nico said. 'A major Roman province. You want to visit Diocletian's Palace, don't you?'

Coach Hedge managed another heroic belch. '*Whose* palace? And is Dalmatia where those Dalmatian dogs come from? That *101 Dalmatians* movie – I still have nightmares.'

Frank scratched his head. 'Why would you have nightmares about that?'

Coach Hedge looked like he was about to launch into a major speech about the evils of cartoon Dalmatians, but Jason decided he didn't want to know.

'Nico is right,' he said. 'I need to go to Diocletian's Palace. It's where Reyna will go first, because she knows *I* would go there.'

Piper raised an eyebrow. 'And why would Reyna think that? Because you've always had a mad fascination with Croatian culture?'

Jason stared at his uneaten sandwich. It was hard to talk about his life before Juno wiped his memory. His years at

Camp Jupiter seemed made up, like a movie he'd acted in decades before.

'Reyna and I used to talk about Diocletian,' he said. 'We both kind of idolized the guy as a leader. We talked about how we'd like to visit Diocletian's Palace. Of course we knew that was impossible. No one could travel to the ancient lands. But still we made this pact that if we ever *did* that's where we'd go.'

'Diocletian . . .' Leo considered the name, then shook his head. 'I got nothing. Why was he so important?'

Frank looked offended. 'He was the last great pagan emperor!'

Leo rolled his eyes. 'Why am I not surprised you know that, Zhang?'

'Why wouldn't I? He was the last one who worshipped the Olympian gods, before Constantine came along and adopted Christianity.'

Hazel nodded. 'I remember something about that. The nuns at St Agnes taught us that Diocletian was a huge villain, right along with Nero and Caligula.' She looked askance at Jason. 'Why would you idolize him?'

'He wasn't a *total* villain,' Jason said. 'Yeah, he persecuted Christians, but otherwise he was a good ruler. He worked his way up from nothing by joining the legion. His parents were former slaves . . . or at least his *mom* was. Demigods know he was a son of Jupiter – the last demigod to rule Rome. He was also the first emperor ever to retire, like, *peacefully*, and give up his power. He was from Dalmatia, so he moved back there and built a retirement palace. The town of Split grew up around . . .'

He faltered when he looked at Leo, who was mimicking taking notes with an air pencil.

'Go on, Professor Grace!' he said, wide-eyed. 'I wanna get an A on the test.'

'Shut up, Leo.'

Piper sipped another spoonful of soup. 'So why is Diocletian's Palace so special?'

Nico leaned over and plucked a grape. Probably that was the guy's entire diet for the day. 'It's said to be haunted by the ghost of Diocletian.'

'Who was a son of Jupiter, like me,' Jason said. 'His tomb was destroyed centuries ago, but Reyna and I used to wonder if we could find Diocletian's ghost and ask where he was buried . . . well, according to the legends, his sceptre was buried with him.'

Nico gave him a thin, creepy smile. 'Ah . . . *that* legend.'

'What legend?' Hazel asked.

Nico turned to his sister. 'Supposedly Diocletian's sceptre could summon the ghosts of the Roman legions, any of them who worshipped the old gods.'

Leo whistled. 'Okay, *now* I'm interested. Be nice to have a booty-kicking army of pagan zombies on our side when we enter the House of Hades.'

'Not sure I would've put it that way,' Jason muttered, 'but yeah.'

'We don't have much time,' Frank warned. 'It's already July ninth. We have to get to Epirus, close the Doors of Death –'

'Which are guarded,' Hazel murmured, 'by a smoky giant and a sorceress who wants . . .' She hesitated. 'Well, I'm not sure. But according to Pluto, she plans to "rebuild her domain". Whatever that means, it's bad enough that my dad felt like warning me personally.'

Frank grunted. 'And, if we survive all that, we still have to find out where the giants are waking Gaia and get there before the first of August. Besides, the longer Percy and Annabeth are in Tartarus –'

'I know,' Jason said. 'We won't take long in Split. But looking for the sceptre is worth a try. While we're at the palace, I can leave a message for Reyna, letting her know the route we're taking for Epirus.'

Nico nodded. 'The sceptre of Diocletian could make a huge difference. You'll need my help.'

Jason tried not to show his discomfort, but his skin prickled at the thought of going anywhere with Nico di Angelo.

Percy had shared some disturbing stories about Nico. His loyalties weren't always clear. He spent more time with the dead than the living. Once, he'd lured Percy into a trap in the palace of Hades. Maybe Nico had made up for that by helping the Greeks against the Titans, but still . . .

Piper squeezed his hand. 'Hey, sounds fun. I'll go, too.'

Jason wanted to yell: *Thank the gods!*

But Nico shook his head. 'You can't, Piper. It should only be Jason and me. Diocletian's ghost might appear for a son of Jupiter, but any other demigods would most likely . . . ah, *spook* him. And I'm the only one who can talk to his spirit. Even Hazel won't be able to do that.'

Nico's eyes held a gleam of challenge. He seemed curious as to whether or not Jason would protest.

The ship's bell sounded. Festus creaked and whirred over the loudspeaker.

'We've arrived,' Leo announced. 'Time to Split.'

Frank groaned. 'Can we leave Valdez in Croatia?'

Jason stood. 'Frank, you're in charge of defending the ship. Leo, you've got repairs to do. The rest of you, help out wherever you can. Nico and I . . .' He faced the son of Hades. 'We have a ghost to find.'

XXXV

JASON

JASON FIRST SAW THE ANGEL AT THE ICE-CREAM CART.

The *Argo II* had anchored in the bay along with six or seven cruise ships. As usual, the mortals didn't pay the trireme any attention, but, just to be safe, Jason and Nico hopped on a skiff from one of the tourist boats so they would look like part of the crowd when they came ashore.

At first glance, Split seemed like a cool place. Curving around the harbour was a long esplanade lined with palm trees. At the sidewalk cafés, European teenagers were hanging out, speaking a dozen different languages and enjoying the sunny afternoon. The air smelled of grilled meat and fresh-cut flowers.

Beyond the main boulevard, the city was a hodgepodge of mediaeval castle towers, Roman walls, limestone town houses with red-tiled roofs and modern office buildings all crammed together. In the distance, grey-green hills marched towards a mountain ridge, which made Jason a little nervous. He kept glancing at that rocky escarpment, expecting the face of Gaia to appear in its shadows.

Nico and he were wandering along the esplanade when Jason spotted a guy with wings buying an ice-cream bar from a street cart. The vendor lady looked bored as she counted the guy's change. Tourists navigated around the angel's huge wings without a second glance.

Jason nudged Nico. 'Are you seeing this?'

'Yeah,' Nico agreed. 'Maybe we should buy some ice cream.'

As they made their way towards the street cart, Jason worried that this winged dude might be a son of Boreas the North Wind. At his side, the angel carried the same kind of jagged bronze sword the Boreads had, and Jason's last encounter with them hadn't gone so well.

But this guy seemed more *chill* than chilly. He wore a red tank top, Bermuda shorts and huarache sandals. His wings were a combination of russet colours, like a bantam rooster or a lazy sunset. He had a deep tan and black hair almost as curly as Leo's.

'He's not a returned spirit,' Nico murmured. 'Or a creature of the Underworld.'

'No,' Jason agreed. 'I doubt they would eat chocolate-covered ice-cream bars.'

'So what is he?' Nico wondered.

They got within thirty feet, and the winged dude looked directly at them. He smiled, gestured over his shoulder with his ice-cream bar and dissolved into the air.

Jason couldn't exactly *see* him, but he'd had enough experience controlling the wind that he could track the angel's path – a warm wisp of red and gold zipping across the street, spiralling down the sidewalk and blowing postcards from the carousels in front of the tourist shops. The wind headed towards the end of the promenade, where a big fortress-like structure loomed.

'I'm betting that's the palace,' Jason said. 'Come on.'

Even after two millennia, Diocletian's Palace was still impressive. The outer wall was only a pink granite shell, with crumbling columns and arched windows open to the sky, but it was mostly intact, a quarter of a mile long and seventy or eighty feet tall, dwarfing the modern shops and houses that huddled beneath it. Jason imagined what the palace must have looked like when it was newly built, with Imperial guards walking the ramparts and the golden eagles of Rome glinting on the parapets.

The wind angel – or whatever he was – whisked in and out of the pink granite windows, then disappeared on the other side. Jason scanned the palace's facade for an entrance. The only one he saw was several blocks away, with tourists lined up to buy tickets. No time for that.

'We've got to catch him,' Jason said. 'Hold on.'

'But –'

Jason grabbed Nico and lifted them both into the air.

Nico made a muffled sound of protest as they soared over the walls and into a courtyard where more tourists were milling around, taking pictures.

A little kid did a double take when they landed. Then his eyes glazed over and he shook his head, like he was dismissing a juice-box-induced hallucination. No one else paid them any attention.

On the left side of the courtyard stood a line of columns holding up weathered grey arches. On the right side was a white marble building with rows of tall windows.

'The peristyle,' Nico said. 'This was the entrance to Diocletian's private residence.' He scowled at Jason. 'And, please, I don't like being touched. Don't ever grab me again.'

Jason's shoulder blades tensed. He thought he heard the undertone of a threat, like: *unless you want to get a Stygian sword up your nose.* 'Uh, okay. Sorry. How do you know what this place is called?'

Nico scanned the atrium. He focused on some steps in the far corner, leading down.

'I've been here before.' His eyes were as dark as his blade. 'With my mother and Bianca. A weekend trip from Venice. I was maybe . . . six?'

'That was when . . . the 1930s?'

''Thirty-eight or so,' Nico said absently. 'Why do you care? Do you see that winged guy anywhere?'

'No . . .' Jason was still trying to wrap his mind around Nico's past.

Jason always tried to build a good relationship with the people on his team. He'd learned the hard way that if somebody was going to have your back in a fight it was better if you found some common ground and trusted each other. But

Nico wasn't easy to figure out. 'I just . . . I can't imagine how weird that must be, coming from another time.'

'No, you *can't*.' Nico stared at the stone floor. He took a deep breath.

'Look . . . I don't like talking about it. Honestly, I think Hazel has it worse. She remembers more about when she was young. She had to come back from the dead and adjust to the modern world. Me . . . me and Bianca, we were stuck at the Lotus Hotel. Time passed so quickly. In a weird way, that made the transition easier.'

'Percy told me about that place,' Jason said. 'Seventy years, but it only felt like a month?'

Nico clenched his fist until his fingers turned white. 'Yeah. I'm sure Percy told you all about me.'

His voice was heavy with bitterness – more than Jason could understand. He knew that Nico had blamed Percy for getting his sister Bianca killed, but they'd supposedly got past that, at least according to Percy. Piper had also mentioned a rumour that Nico had a crush on Annabeth. Maybe that was part of it.

Still . . . Jason didn't get why Nico pushed people away, why he never spent much time at either camp, why he preferred the dead to the living. He *really* didn't get why Nico had promised to lead the *Argo II* to Epirus if he hated Percy Jackson so much.

Nico's eyes swept the windows above them. 'Roman dead are everywhere here . . . Lares. *Lemures*. They're watching. They're angry.'

'At us?' Jason's hand went to his sword.

'At everything.' Nico pointed to a small stone building on the west end of the courtyard. 'That used to be a temple to Jupiter. The Christians changed it to a baptistery. The Roman ghosts don't like that.'

Jason stared at the dark doorway.

He'd never met Jupiter, but he thought of his father as a living person – the guy who'd fallen in love with his mom. Of course he knew his dad was immortal, but somehow the full meaning of that had never really sunk in until now as he stared at a doorway Romans had walked through, thousands of years ago, to worship *his* dad. The idea gave Jason a splitting headache.

'And over there . . .' Nico pointed east to a hexagonal building ringed with freestanding columns. 'That was the mausoleum of the emperor.'

'But his tomb isn't there any more,' Jason guessed.

'Not for centuries,' Nico said. 'When the empire collapsed, the building was turned into a Christian cathedral.'

Jason swallowed. 'So if Diocletian's ghost is still around here –'

'He's probably not happy.'

The wind rustled, pushing leaves and food wrappers across the peristyle. In the corner of his eye, Jason caught a glimpse of movement – a blur of red and gold.

When he turned, a single rust-coloured feather was settling on the steps that led down.

'That way.' Jason pointed. 'The winged guy. Where do you think those stairs lead?'

Nico drew his sword. His smile was even more unsettling than his scowl. 'Underground,' he said. 'My favourite place.'

Underground was *not* Jason's favourite place.

Ever since his trip beneath Rome with Piper and Percy, fighting those twin giants in the hypogeum under the Colosseum, most of his nightmares had been about basements, trapdoors and large hamster-wheels.

Having Nico along was not reassuring. His Stygian iron blade seemed to make the shadows even gloomier, as if the infernal metal were drawing the light and heat out of the air.

They crept through a vast cellar with thick support columns holding up a vaulted ceiling. The limestone blocks were so old they had fused together from centuries of moisture, making the place look almost like a naturally formed cave.

None of the tourists had ventured down here. Obviously, they were smarter than demigods.

Jason drew his *gladius*. They made their way under the low archways, their steps echoing on the stone floor. Barred windows lined the top of one wall, facing the street level, but that just made the cellar feel more claustrophobic. The shafts of sunlight looked like slanted prison bars, swirling with ancient dust.

Jason passed a support beam, looked to his left and almost had a heart attack. Staring right at him was a marble bust of Diocletian, his limestone face glowering with disapproval.

Jason steadied his breathing. This seemed like a good place to leave the note he'd written for Reyna, telling her of their route to Epirus. It was away from the crowds, but he trusted

Reyna would find it. She had the instincts of a hunter. He slipped the note between the bust and its pedestal and stepped back.

Diocletian's marble eyes made him jumpy. Jason couldn't help thinking of Terminus, the talking statue-god back at New Rome. He hoped Diocletian wouldn't bark at him or suddenly burst into song.

'Hello!'

Before Jason could register that the voice had come from somewhere else, he sliced off the emperor's head. The bust toppled and shattered against the floor.

'That wasn't very nice,' said the voice behind them.

Jason turned. The winged man from the ice-cream stand was leaning against a nearby column, casually tossing a small bronze hoop in the air. At his feet sat a wicker picnic basket full of fruit.

'I mean,' the man said, 'what did Diocletian ever do to you?'

The air swirled around Jason's feet. The shards of marble gathered into a miniature tornado, spiralled back to the pedestal and reassembled into a complete bust, the note still tucked underneath.

'Uh –' Jason lowered his sword. 'It was an accident. You startled me.'

The winged dude chuckled. 'Jason Grace, the West Wind has been called many things . . . warm, gentle, life-giving and devilishly handsome. But I have never been called *startling*. I leave that crass behaviour to my gusty brethren in the north.'

Nico inched backwards. 'The West Wind? You mean you're –'

'Favonius,' Jason realized. 'God of the West Wind.'

Favonius smiled and bowed, obviously pleased to be recognized. 'You can call me by my Roman name, certainly, or Zephyros, if you're Greek. I'm not hung up about it.'

Nico looked pretty hung up about it. 'Why aren't your Greek and Roman sides in conflict, like the other gods?'

'Oh, I have the occasional headache.' Favonius shrugged. 'Some mornings I'll wake up in a Greek *chiton* when I'm sure I went to sleep in my SPQR pyjamas. But mostly the war doesn't bother me. I'm a minor god, you know – never really been much in the limelight. The to-and-fro battles among you demigods don't affect me as greatly.'

'So . . .' Jason wasn't quite sure whether to sheathe his sword. 'What are you doing here?'

'Several things!' Favonius said. 'Hanging out with my basket of fruit. I always carry a basket of fruit. Would you like a pear?'

'I'm good. Thanks.'

'Let's see . . . earlier I was eating ice cream. Right now I'm tossing this quoit ring.' Favonius spun the bronze hoop on his index finger.

Jason had no idea what a *quoit* was, but he tried to stay focused. 'I mean why did you appear to us? Why did you lead us to this cellar?'

'Oh!' Favonius nodded. 'The sarcophagus of Diocletian. Yes. This was its final resting place. The Christians moved it out of the mausoleum. Then some barbarians destroyed the coffin. I just wanted to show you –' he spread his hands sadly – 'that what you're looking for isn't here. My master has taken it.'

'Your master?' Jason had a flashback to a floating palace above Pike's Peak in Colorado, where he'd visited (and barely survived) the studio of a crazy weatherman who claimed he was the god of all the winds. 'Please tell me your master isn't Aeolus.'

'*That* airhead?' Favonius snorted. 'No, of course not.'

'He means Eros.' Nico's voice turned edgy. 'Cupid, in Latin.'

Favonius smiled. 'Very good, Nico di Angelo. I'm glad to see you again, by the way. It's been a long time.'

Nico knitted his eyebrows. 'I've never met you.'

'You've never *seen* me,' the god corrected. 'But I've been watching you. When you came here as a small boy, and several times since. I knew eventually you would return to look upon my master's face.'

Nico turned even paler than usual. His eyes darted around the cavernous room as if he was starting to feel trapped.

'Nico?' Jason said. 'What's he talking about?'

'I don't know. Nothing.'

'Nothing?' Favonius cried. 'The one you care for most . . . plunged into Tartarus, and still you will not allow the truth?'

Suddenly Jason felt like he was eavesdropping.

The one you care for most.

He remembered what Piper had told him about Nico's

crush on Annabeth. Apparently Nico's feelings went *way* deeper than a simple crush.

'We've only come for Diocletian's sceptre,' Nico said, clearly anxious to change the subject. 'Where is it?'

'Ah . . .' Favonius nodded sadly. 'You thought it would be as easy as facing Diocletian's ghost? I'm afraid not, Nico. Your trials will be *much* more difficult. You know, long before this was Diocletian's Palace, it was the gateway to my master's court. I've dwelt here for aeons, bringing those who sought love into the presence of Cupid.'

Jason didn't like the mention of difficult trials. He didn't trust this weird god with the hoop and the wings and the basket of fruit. But an old story surfaced in his mind – something he'd heard at Camp Jupiter. 'Like Psyche, Cupid's wife. You carried her to his palace.'

Favonius's eyes twinkled. 'Very good, Jason Grace. From this exact spot, I carried Psyche on the winds and brought her to the chambers of my master. In fact, that is why Diocletian built *his* palace here. This place has always been graced by the gentle West Wind.' He spread his arms. 'It is a spot of tranquillity and love in a turbulent world. When Diocletian's Palace was ransacked –'

'You took the sceptre,' Jason guessed.

'For safekeeping,' Favonius agreed. 'It is one of Cupid's many treasures, a reminder of better times. If you want it . . .' Favonius turned to Nico. 'You must face the god of love.'

Nico stared at the sunlight coming through the windows, as if wishing he could escape through those narrow openings.

Jason wasn't sure what Favonius wanted, but if *facing the god of love* meant forcing Nico into some sort of confession about which girl he liked, that didn't seem so bad.

'Nico, you can do this,' Jason said. 'It might be embarrassing, but it's for the sceptre.'

Nico didn't look convinced. In fact he looked like he was going to be sick. But he squared his shoulders and nodded. 'You're right. I – I'm not afraid of a love god.'

Favonius beamed. 'Excellent! Would you like a snack before you go?' He plucked a green apple from his basket and frowned at it. 'Oh, bluster. I keep forgetting my symbol is a basket of *unripe* fruit. Why doesn't the spring wind get more credit? Summer has *all* the fun.'

'That's okay,' Nico said quickly. 'Just take us to Cupid.'

Favonius spun the hoop on his finger, and Jason's body dissolved into air.

XXXVI

JASON

JASON HAD RIDDEN THE WIND MANY TIMES. *Being* the wind was not the same.

He felt out of control, his thoughts scattered, no boundaries between his body and the rest of the world. He wondered if this was how monsters felt when they were defeated – bursting into dust, helpless and formless.

Jason could sense Nico's presence nearby. The West Wind carried them into the sky above Split. Together they raced over the hills, past Roman aqueducts, highways and vineyards. As they approached the mountains, Jason saw the ruins of a Roman town spread out in a valley below – crumbling walls, square foundations and cracked roads, all overgrown with grass – so it looked like a giant, mossy game board.

Favonius set them down in the middle of the ruins, next to a broken column the size of a redwood.

Jason's body re-formed. For a moment it felt even worse

than being the wind, like he'd suddenly been wrapped in a lead overcoat.

'Yes, mortal bodies are *terribly* bulky,' Favonius said, as if reading his thoughts. The wind god settled on a nearby wall with his basket of fruit and spread his russet wings in the sun. 'Honestly, I don't know how you stand it, day in and day out.'

Jason scanned their surroundings. The town must have been huge once. He could make out the shells of temples and bathhouses, a half-buried amphitheatre and empty pedestals that must have once held statues. Rows of columns marched off to nowhere. The old city walls weaved in and out of the hillside like stone thread through a green cloth.

Some areas looked like they'd been excavated, but most of the city just seemed abandoned, as if it had been left to the elements for the last two thousand years.

'Welcome to Salona,' Favonius said. 'Capital of Dalmatia! Birthplace of Diocletian! But before that, *long* before that, it was the home of Cupid.'

The name echoed, as if voices were whispering it through the ruins.

Something about this place seemed even creepier than the palace basement in Split. Jason had never thought much about Cupid. He'd certainly never thought of Cupid as *scary*. Even for Roman demigods, the name conjured up an image of a silly winged baby with a toy bow and arrow, flying around in his diapers on Valentine's Day.

'Oh, he's not like that,' said Favonius.

Jason flinched. 'You can read my mind?'

'I don't need to.' Favonius tossed his bronze hoop in the air. '*Everyone* has the wrong impression of Cupid . . . until they meet him.'

Nico braced himself against a column, his legs trembling visibly.

'Hey, man . . .' Jason stepped towards him, but Nico waved him off.

At Nico's feet, the grass turned brown and wilted. The dead patch spread outwards, as if poison were seeping from the soles of his shoes.

'Ah . . .' Favonius nodded sympathetically. 'I don't blame you for being nervous, Nico di Angelo. Do you know how *I* ended up serving Cupid?'

'I don't serve anyone,' Nico muttered. 'Especially not Cupid.'

Favonius continued as if he hadn't heard. 'I fell in love with a mortal named Hyacinthus. He was *quite* extraordinary.'

'He . . . ?' Jason's brain was still fuzzy from his wind trip, so it took him a second to process that. 'Oh . . .'

'Yes, Jason Grace.' Favonius arched an eyebrow. 'I fell in love with a *dude*. Does that shock you?'

Honestly, Jason wasn't sure. He tried not to think about the details of godly love lives, no matter *who* they fell in love with. After all, his dad, Jupiter, wasn't exactly a model of good behaviour. Compared to some of the Olympian love scandals he'd heard about, the West Wind falling in love with a mortal guy didn't seem very shocking. 'I guess not. So . . . Cupid struck you with his arrow, and you fell in love.'

Favonius snorted. 'You make it sound so simple. Alas, love is never simple. You see, the god Apollo also liked Hyacinthus. He claimed they were just friends. I don't know. But one day I came across them together, playing a game of quoits –'

There was that weird word again. 'Quoits?'

'A game with those hoops,' Nico explained, though his voice was brittle. 'Like horseshoes.'

'Sort of,' Favonius said. 'At any rate, I was jealous. Instead of confronting them and finding out the truth, I shifted the wind and sent a heavy metal ring right at Hyacinthus's head and . . . well.' The wind god sighed. 'As Hyacinthus died, Apollo turned him into a flower, the hyacinth. I'm sure Apollo would've taken horrible vengeance on me, but Cupid offered me his protection. I'd done a terrible thing, but I'd been driven mad by love, so he spared me, on the condition that I work for him forever.'

CUPID.

The name echoed through the ruins again.

'That would be my cue.' Favonius stood. 'Think long and hard about how you proceed, Nico di Angelo. You cannot lie to Cupid. If you let your anger rule you . . . well, your fate will be even sadder than mine.'

Jason felt like his brain was turning back into wind. He didn't understand what Favonius was talking about or why Nico seemed so shaken, but he had no time to think about it. The wind god disappeared in a swirl of red and gold. The summer air suddenly felt oppressive. The ground shook, and Jason and Nico drew their swords.

• • •

So.

The voice rushed past Jason's ear like a bullet. When he turned, no one was there.

You come to claim the sceptre.

Nico stood at his back, and for once Jason was glad to have the guy's company.

'Cupid,' Jason called, 'where are you?'

The voice laughed. It definitely didn't *sound* like a cute baby angel's. It sounded deep and rich, but also threatening – like a tremor before a major earthquake.

Where you least expect me, Cupid answered. *As Love always is.*

Something slammed into Jason and hurled him across the street. He toppled down a set of steps and sprawled on the floor of an excavated Roman basement.

I would think you'd know better, Jason Grace. Cupid's voice whirled around him. *You've found true love, after all. Or do you still doubt yourself?*

Nico scrambled down the steps. 'You okay?'

Jason accepted his hand and got to his feet. 'Yeah. Just sucker punched.'

Oh, did you expect me to play fair? Cupid laughed. *I am the god of love. I am* never *fair.*

This time, Jason's senses were on high alert. He felt the air ripple just as an arrow materialized, racing towards Nico's chest.

Jason intercepted it with his sword and deflected it sideways. The arrow exploded against the nearest wall, peppering them with limestone shrapnel.

They ran up the steps. Jason pulled Nico to one side as

another gust of wind toppled a column that would have crushed him flat.

'Is this guy Love or Death?' Jason growled.

Ask your friends, Cupid said. *Frank, Hazel and Percy met my counterpart, Thanatos. We are not so different. Except Death is sometimes kinder.*

'We just want the sceptre!' Nico shouted. 'We're trying to stop Gaia. Are you on the gods' side or not?'

A second arrow hit the ground between Nico's feet and glowed white-hot. Nico stumbled back as the arrow burst into a geyser of flame.

Love is on every side, Cupid said. *And no one's side. Don't ask what Love can do for you.*

'Great,' Jason said. 'Now he's spouting greeting card messages.'

Movement behind him: Jason spun, slicing his sword through the air. His blade bit into something solid. He heard a grunt and he swung again, but the invisible god was gone. On the paving stones, a trail of golden ichor shimmered – the blood of the gods.

Very good, Jason, Cupid said. *At least you can sense my presence. Even a glancing hit at true love is more than most heroes manage.*

'So now I get the sceptre?' Jason asked.

Cupid laughed. *Unfortunately, you could not wield it. Only a child of the Underworld can summon the dead legions. And only an officer of Rome can lead them.*

'But . . .' Jason wavered. He *was* an officer. He was praetor. Then he remembered all his second thoughts about where he belonged. In New Rome, he'd offered to give up his position to

Percy Jackson. Did that make him unworthy to lead a legion of Roman ghosts?

He decided to face that problem when the time came.

'Just leave that to us,' he said. 'Nico can summon –'

The third arrow zipped by Jason's shoulder. He couldn't stop it in time. Nico gasped as it sank into his sword arm.

'Nico!'

The son of Hades stumbled. The arrow dissolved, leaving no blood and no visible wound, but Nico's face was tight with rage and pain.

'Enough games!' Nico shouted. 'Show yourself!'

It is a costly thing, Cupid said, *looking on the true face of Love.*

Another column toppled. Jason scrambled out of its way.

My wife Psyche learned that lesson, Cupid said. *She was brought here aeons ago, when this was the site of my palace. We met only in the dark. She was warned never to look upon me, and yet she could not stand the mystery. She feared I was a monster. One night, she lit a candle, and beheld my face as I slept.*

'Were you *that* ugly?' Jason thought he had zeroed in on Cupid's voice – at the edge of the amphitheatre about twenty yards away – but he wanted to make sure.

The god laughed. *I was too handsome, I'm afraid. A mortal cannot gaze upon the true appearance of a god without suffering consequences. My mother, Aphrodite, cursed Psyche for her distrust. My poor lover was tormented, forced into exile, given horrible tasks to prove her worth. She was even sent to the Underworld on a quest to show her dedication. She earned her way back to my side, but she suffered greatly.*

Now I've got you, Jason thought.

He thrust his sword in the sky and thunder shook the valley. Lightning blasted a crater where the voice had been speaking.

Silence. Jason was just thinking, *Dang, it actually worked*, when an invisible force knocked him to the ground. His sword skittered across the road.

A good try, Cupid said, his voice already distant. *But Love cannot be pinned down so easily.*

Next to him, a wall collapsed. Jason barely managed to roll aside.

'Stop it!' Nico yelled. 'It's me you want. Leave him alone!'

Jason's ears rang. He was dizzy from getting smacked around. His mouth tasted like limestone dust. He didn't understand why Nico would think of himself as the main target, but Cupid seemed to agree.

Poor Nico di Angelo. The god's voice was tinged with disappointment. *Do you know what* you *want, much less what I want? My beloved Psyche risked everything in the name of Love. It was the only way to atone for her lack of faith. And you — what have you risked in my name?*

'I've been to Tartarus and back,' Nico snarled. 'You don't scare me.'

I scare you very, very much. Face me. Be honest.

Jason pulled himself up.

All around Nico, the ground shifted. The grass withered, and the stones cracked as if something was moving in the earth beneath, trying to push its way through.

'Give us Diocletian's sceptre,' Nico said. 'We don't have time for games.'

Games? Cupid struck, slapping Nico sideways into a granite pedestal. *Love is no game! It is no flowery softness! It is hard work – a quest that never ends. It demands everything from you – especially the truth. Only then does it yield rewards.*

Jason retrieved his sword. If this invisible guy was Love, Jason was beginning to think Love was overrated. He liked Piper's version better – considerate, kind and beautiful. Aphrodite he could understand. Cupid seemed more like a thug, an enforcer.

'Nico,' he called, 'what does this guy *want* from you?'

Tell him, Nico di Angelo, Cupid said. *Tell him you are a coward, afraid of yourself and your feelings. Tell him the real reason you ran from Camp Half-Blood, and why you are always alone.*

Nico let loose a guttural scream. The ground at his feet split open and skeletons crawled forth – dead Romans with missing hands and caved-in skulls, cracked ribs and jaws unhinged. Some were dressed in the remnants of togas. Others had glinting pieces of armour hanging off their chests.

Will you hide among the dead, as you always do? Cupid taunted.

Waves of darkness rolled off the son of Hades. When they hit Jason, he almost lost consciousness – overwhelmed by hatred and fear and shame . . .

Images flashed through his mind. He saw Nico and his sister on a snowy cliff in Maine, Percy Jackson protecting them from a manticore. Percy's sword gleamed in the dark. He'd been the first demigod Nico had ever seen in action.

Later, at Camp Half-Blood, Percy took Nico by the arm,

promising to keep his sister Bianca safe. Nico had believed him. Nico had looked into his sea-green eyes and thought, *How can he possibly fail? This is a real hero.* He was Nico's favourite game, Mythomagic, brought to life.

Jason saw the moment when Percy returned and told Nico that Bianca was dead. Nico had screamed and called him a liar. He'd felt betrayed, but still . . . when the skeleton warriors attacked, he couldn't let them harm Percy. Nico had called on the earth to swallow them up, and then he'd run away – terrified of his own powers, and his own emotions.

Jason saw a dozen more scenes like this from Nico's point of view . . . And they left him stunned, unable to move or speak.

Meanwhile, Nico's Roman skeletons surged forward and grappled with something invisible. The god struggled, flinging the dead aside, breaking off ribs and skulls, but the skeletons kept coming, pinning the god's arms.

Interesting! Cupid said. *Do you have the strength, after all?*

'I left Camp Half-Blood because of love,' Nico said. 'Annabeth . . . she –'

Still hiding, Cupid said, smashing another skeleton to pieces. *You do not have the strength.*

'Nico,' Jason managed to say, 'it's okay. I get it.'

Nico glanced over, pain and misery washing across his face.

'No, you don't,' he said. 'There's no way you can understand.'

And so you run away again, Cupid chided. *From your friends, from yourself.*

'I don't have friends!' Nico yelled. 'I left Camp Half-Blood because I don't belong! I'll never belong!'

The skeletons had Cupid pinned now, but the invisible god laughed so cruelly that Jason wanted to summon another bolt of lightning. Unfortunately, he doubted he had the strength.

'Leave him alone, Cupid,' Jason croaked. 'This isn't . . .'

His voice failed. He wanted to say it wasn't Cupid's business, but he realized this was *exactly* Cupid's business. Something Favonius said kept buzzing in his ears: *Are you shocked?*

The story of Psyche finally made sense to him – why a mortal girl would be so afraid. Why she would risk breaking the rules to look the god of love in the face, because she feared he might be a monster.

Psyche had been right. Cupid *was* a monster. Love was the most savage monster of all.

Nico's voice was like broken glass. 'I – I wasn't in love with Annabeth.'

'You were jealous of her,' Jason said. 'That's why you didn't want to be around her. Especially why you didn't want to be around . . . him. It makes total sense.'

All the fight and denial seemed to go out of Nico at once. The darkness subsided. The Roman dead collapsed into bones and crumbled to dust.

'I hated myself,' Nico said. 'I hated Percy Jackson.'

Cupid became visible – a lean, muscular young man with snowy white wings, straight black hair, a simple white frock and jeans. The bow and quiver slung over his shoulder were no toys – they were weapons of war. His eyes were as red as blood, as if every valentine in the world had been squeezed dry, distilled into one poisonous mixture. His face was handsome, but also harsh – as difficult to look at as a spotlight. He watched Nico with satisfaction, as if he'd identified the exact spot for his next arrow to make a clean kill.

'I had a crush on Percy,' Nico spat. 'That's the truth. That's the big secret.'

He glared at Cupid. 'Happy now?'

For the first time, Cupid's gaze seemed sympathetic. 'Oh, I wouldn't say Love always makes you happy.' His voice sounded smaller, much more human. 'Sometimes it makes you incredibly sad. But at least you've *faced* it now. That's the only way to conquer me.'

Cupid dissolved into the wind.

On the ground where he'd stood lay an ivory staff three feet long, topped with a dark globe of polished marble about the size of a baseball, nestled on the backs of three gold Roman eagles. The sceptre of Diocletian.

Nico knelt and picked it up. He regarded Jason, as if waiting for an attack. 'If the others found out –'

'If the others found out,' Jason said, 'you'd have that many more people to back you up and to unleash the fury of the gods on anybody who gives you trouble.'

Nico scowled. Jason still felt the resentment and anger rippling off him.

'But it's your call,' Jason added. 'Your decision to share or not. I can only tell you –'

'I don't feel that way any more,' Nico muttered. 'I mean . . .

I gave up on Percy. I was young and impressionable, and I – I don't . . .'

His voice cracked, and Jason could tell the guy was about to get teary-eyed. Whether Nico had really given up on Percy or not, Jason couldn't imagine what it had been like for Nico all those years, keeping a secret that would've been unthinkable to share in the 1940s, denying who he was, feeling completely alone – even more isolated than other demigods.

'Nico,' he said gently, 'I've seen a lot of brave things. But what you just did? That was maybe the bravest.'

Nico looked up uncertainly. 'We should get back to the ship.'

'Yeah. I can fly us –'

'No,' Nico announced. 'This time we're shadow-travelling. I've had enough of the winds for a while.'

XXXVII

ANNABETH

LOSING HER SIGHT HAD BEEN BAD ENOUGH. Being isolated from Percy had been horrible.

But now that she could see again, watching him die slowly from gorgon's blood poison and being unable to do anything about it – that was the worst curse of all.

Bob slung Percy over his shoulder like a bag of sports equipment while the skeleton kitten Small Bob curled up on Percy's back and purred. Bob lumbered along at a fast pace, even for a Titan, which made it almost impossible for Annabeth to keep up.

Her lungs rattled. Her skin had started to blister again. She probably needed another drink of firewater, but they'd left the River Phlegethon behind. Her body was so sore and battered that she'd forgotten what it was like *not* to be in pain.

'How much longer?' she wheezed.

'Almost too long,' Bob called back. 'But maybe not.'

Very helpful, Annabeth thought, but she was too winded to say it.

The landscape changed again. They were still going downhill, which should have made travelling easier, but the ground sloped at just the wrong angle – too steep to jog, too treacherous to let her guard down even for a moment. The surface was sometimes loose gravel, sometimes patches of slime. Annabeth stepped around random bristles sharp enough to impale her foot, and clusters of . . . well, not rocks exactly. More like warts the size of watermelons. If Annabeth had to guess (and she didn't want to) she supposed Bob was leading her down the length of Tartarus's large intestine.

The air got thicker and stank of sewage. The darkness maybe wasn't quite as intense, but she could only see Bob because of the glint of his white hair and the point of his spear. She noticed he hadn't retracted the spearhead on his broom since their fight with the *arai*. That didn't reassure her.

Percy flopped around, causing the kitten to readjust his nest in the small of Percy's back. Occasionally Percy would groan in pain, and Annabeth felt like a fist was squeezing her heart.

She flashed back to her tea party with Piper, Hazel and Aphrodite in Charleston. Gods, that seemed so long ago. Aphrodite had sighed and waxed nostalgic about the good old days of the Civil War – how love and war always went hand in hand.

Aphrodite had gestured proudly to Annabeth, using her

as an example for the other girls: *I once promised to make* her *love life interesting. And didn't I?*

Annabeth had wanted to throttle the goddess of love. She'd had more than her share of *interesting*. Now Annabeth was holding out for a happy ending. Surely that was possible, no matter what the legends said about tragic heroes. There had to be exceptions, right? If suffering led to reward, then Percy and she deserved the grand prize.

She thought about Percy's daydream of New Rome – the two of them settling down there, going to college together. At first, the idea of living among the Romans had appalled her. She had resented them for taking Percy away from her.

Now she would accept that offer gladly.

If only they survived this. If only Reyna had got her message. If only a million other long shots paid off.

Stop it, she chided herself.

She had to concentrate on the present, putting one foot in front of the other, taking this downhill intestinal hike one giant wart at a time.

Her knees felt warm and wobbly, like wire hangers bent to the point of snapping. Percy groaned and muttered something she couldn't make out.

Bob stopped suddenly. 'Look.'

Ahead in the gloom, the terrain levelled out into a black swamp. Sulphur-yellow mist hung in the air. Even without sunlight, there were actual plants – clumps of reeds, scrawny leafless trees, even a few sickly-looking flowers blooming in the muck. Mossy trails wound between bubbling tar pits.

Directly in front of Annabeth, sunk into the bog, were footprints the size of trashcan lids, with long, pointed toes.

Sadly, Annabeth was pretty sure she knew what had made them. 'Drakon?'

'Yes.' Bob grinned at her. 'That is good!'

'Uh . . . why?'

'Because we are close.'

Bob marched into the swamp.

Annabeth wanted to scream. She hated being at the mercy of a Titan – especially one who was slowly recovering his memory and bringing them to see a 'good' giant. She hated forging through a swamp that was obviously the stomping ground of a drakon.

But Bob had Percy. If she hesitated, she would lose them in the dark. She hurried after him, hopping from moss patch to moss patch and praying to Athena that she didn't fall in a sinkhole.

At least the terrain forced Bob to go more slowly. Once Annabeth caught up, she could walk right behind him and keep an eye on Percy, who was muttering deliriously, his forehead dangerously hot. Several times he mumbled *Annabeth* and she fought back a sob. The kitten just purred louder and snuggled up.

Finally the yellow mist parted, revealing a muddy clearing like an island in the muck. The ground was dotted with stunted trees and wart mounds. In the centre loomed a large, domed hut made of bones and greenish leather. Smoke rose from a hole in the top. The entrance was covered with curtains of scaly reptile skin and, flanking the entrance, two torches made from colossal femur bones burned bright yellow.

What really caught Annabeth's attention was the drakon skull. Fifty yards into the clearing, about halfway to the hut, a massive oak tree jutted from the ground at a forty-five-degree angle. The jaws of a drakon skull encircled the trunk, as if the oak tree were the dead monster's tongue.

'Yes,' Bob murmured. 'This is very good.'

Nothing about this place felt good to Annabeth.

Before she could protest, Small Bob arched his back and hissed. Behind them, a mighty roar echoed through the swamp – a sound Annabeth had last heard in the Battle of Manhattan.

She turned and saw the drakon charging towards them.

XXXVIII

ANNABETH

THE MOST INSULTING PART?

The drakon was easily the most beautiful thing Annabeth had seen since she had fallen into Tartarus. Its hide was dappled green and yellow, like sunlight through a forest canopy. Its reptilian eyes were Annabeth's favourite shade of sea green (just like Percy's). When its frills unfurled around its head, Annabeth couldn't help but think what a regal and amazing monster it was that was about to kill her.

It was easily as long as a subway train. Its massive talons dug into the mud as it pulled itself forward, its tail whipping from side to side. The drakon hissed, spitting jets of green poison that smoked on the mossy ground and set tar pits on fire, filling the air with the scent of fresh pine and ginger. The monster even *smelled* good. Like most drakons, it was wingless, longer and more snake-like than a dragon, and it looked hungry.

'Bob,' Annabeth said, 'what are we facing here?'

'Maeonian drakon,' Bob said. 'From Maeonia.'

More helpful information. Annabeth would've smacked Bob upside the head with his own broom if she could lift it. 'Any way we can kill it?'

'Us?' Bob said. 'No.'

The drakon roared as if to accentuate the point, filling the air with more pine-ginger poison, which would have made an excellent car-freshener scent. 'Get Percy to safety,' Annabeth said. 'I'll distract it.'

She had no idea how she would do that, but it was her only choice. She couldn't let Percy die – not if she still had the strength to stand.

'You don't have to,' Bob said. 'Any minute –'

'ROOOOOAAAR!'

Annabeth turned as the giant emerged from his hut.

He was about twenty feet tall – typical giant height – with a humanoid upper body and scaly reptilian legs, like a bipedal dinosaur. He held no weapon. Instead of armour, he wore only a shirt stitched together from sheep hides and green-spotted leather. His skin was cherry-red; his beard and hair the colour of iron rust, braided with tufts of grass, leaves and swamp flowers.

He shouted in challenge, but thankfully he wasn't looking at Annabeth. Bob pulled her out of the way as the giant stormed towards the drakon.

They clashed like some sort of weird Christmas combat scene – the red versus the green. The drakon spewed poison. The giant lunged to one side. He grabbed the oak tree and pulled it from the ground, roots and all. The old skull crumbled to dust as the giant hefted the tree like a baseball bat.

The drakon's tail lashed around the giant's waist, dragging him closer to its gnashing teeth. But as soon as the giant was in range he shoved the tree straight down the monster's throat.

Annabeth hoped she never had to see such a gruesome scene again. The tree pierced the drakon's gullet and impaled it on the ground. The roots began to move, digging deeper as they touched the earth, anchoring the oak until it looked like it had stood in that spot for centuries. The drakon shook and thrashed, but it was pinned fast.

The giant brought his fist down on the drakon's neck. *CRACK*. The monster went limp. It began to dissolve, leaving only scraps of bone, meat, hide and a new drakon skull whose open jaws ringed the oak tree.

Bob grunted. 'Good one.'

The kitten purred in agreement and started cleaning his paws.

The giant kicked at the drakon's remains, examining them critically. 'No good bones,' he complained. 'I wanted a new walking stick. Hmpf. Some good skin for the outhouse, though.'

He ripped some soft hide from the dragon's frills and tucked it in his belt.

'Uh . . .' Annabeth wanted to ask if the giant really used drakon hide for toilet paper, but she decided against it. 'Bob, do you want to introduce us?'

'Annabeth . . .' Bob patted Percy's legs. 'This is Percy.'

Annabeth hoped the Titan was just messing with her, though Bob's face revealed nothing.

She gritted her teeth. 'I meant the giant. You promised he could help.'

'Promise?' The giant glanced over from his work. His eyes narrowed under his bushy red brows. 'A big thing, a promise. Why would Bob promise my help?'

Bob shifted his weight. Titans were scary, but Annabeth had never seen one next to a giant before. Compared to the drakon-killer, Bob looked downright runty.

'Damasen is a good giant,' Bob said. 'He is peaceful. He can cure poisons.'

Annabeth watched the giant Damasen, who was now ripping chunks of bloody meat from the drakon carcass with his bare hands.

'Peaceful,' she said. 'Yes, I can see that.'

'Good meat for dinner.' Damasen stood up straight and studied Annabeth, as if she were another potential source of protein. 'Come inside. We will have stew. Then we will see about this promise.'

XXXIX

ANNABETH

Cosy.

Annabeth never thought she would describe anything in Tartarus that way, but, despite the fact that the giant's hut was as big as a planetarium and constructed of bones, mud and drakon skin, it definitely felt cosy.

In the centre blazed a bonfire made of pitch and bone; yet the smoke was white and odourless, rising through the hole in the middle of the ceiling. The floor was covered with dry marsh grass and grey wool rugs. At one end lay a massive bed of sheepskins and drakon leather. At the other end, free-standing racks were hung with drying plants, cured leather and what looked like strips of drakon jerky. The whole place smelled of stew, smoke, basil and thyme.

The only thing that worried Annabeth was the flock of sheep huddled in a pen at the back of the hut.

Annabeth remembered the cave of Polyphemus the

Cyclops, who ate demigods and sheep indiscriminately. She wondered if giants had similar tastes.

Part of her was tempted to run, but Bob had already placed Percy in the giant's bed, where he nearly disappeared in the wool and leather. Small Bob hopped off Percy and kneaded the blankets, purring so strongly the bed rattled like a Thousand Finger Massage.

Damasen plodded to the bonfire. He tossed his drakon meat into a hanging pot that seemed to be made from an old monster skull, then picked up a ladle and began to stir.

Annabeth didn't want to be the next ingredient in his stew, but she'd come here for a reason. She took a deep breath and marched up to Damasen. 'My friend is dying. Can you cure him or not?'

Her voice caught on the word *friend*. Percy was a lot more than that. Even *boyfriend* really didn't cover it. They'd been through so much together, at this point Percy was *part* of her – a sometimes annoying part, sure, but definitely a part she could not live without.

Damasen looked down at her, glowering under his bushy red eyebrows. Annabeth had met large scary humanoids before, but Damasen unsettled her in a different way. He didn't seem hostile. He radiated sorrow and bitterness, as if he were so wrapped up in his own misery that he resented Annabeth for trying to make him focus on anything else.

'I don't hear words like those in Tartarus,' the giant grumbled. '*Friend. Promise.*'

Annabeth crossed her arms. 'How about *gorgon's blood*? Can you cure that, or did Bob overstate your talents?'

Angering a twenty-foot-tall drakon-slayer probably wasn't a wise strategy, but Percy was dying. She didn't have time for diplomacy.

Damasen scowled at her. 'You question my talents? A half-dead mortal straggles into my swamp and questions my talents?'

'Yep,' she said.

'Hmph.' Damasen handed Bob the ladle. 'Stir.'

As Bob tended the stew, Damasen perused his drying racks, plucking various leaves and roots. He popped a fistful of plant material into his mouth, chewed it up then spat it into a clump of wool.

'Cup of broth,' Damasen ordered.

Bob ladled some stew juice into a hollow gourd. He handed it to Damasen, who dunked the chewed-up gunk ball and stirred it with his finger.

'Gorgon's blood,' he muttered. 'Hardly a challenge for *my* talents.'

He lumbered to the bedside and propped up Percy with one hand. Small Bob the kitten sniffed the broth and hissed. He scratched the sheets with his paws like he wanted to bury it.

'You're going to feed him *that*?' Annabeth asked.

The giant glared at her. 'Who is the healer here? You?'

Annabeth shut her mouth. She watched as the giant made Percy sip the broth. Damasen handled him with surprising gentleness, murmuring words of encouragement that she couldn't quite catch.

With each sip, Percy's colour improved. He drained the cup, and his eyes fluttered open. He looked around with a dazed expression, spotted Annabeth and gave her a drunken grin. 'Feel great.'

His eyes rolled up in his head. He fell back in the bed and began to snore.

'A few hours of sleep,' Damasen pronounced. 'He'll be good as new.'

Annabeth sobbed with relief.

'Thank you,' she said.

Damasen stared at her mournfully. 'Oh, don't thank me. You're still doomed. And I require payment for my services.'

Annabeth mouth went dry. 'Uh . . . what sort of payment?'

'A story.' The giant's eyes glittered. 'It gets boring in Tartarus. You can tell me your story while we eat, eh?'

Annabeth felt uneasy telling a giant about their plans.

Still, Damasen was a good host. He'd saved Percy. His drakon-meat stew was excellent (especially compared to firewater). His hut was warm and comfortable, and for the first time since plunging into Tartarus Annabeth felt like she could relax. Which was ironic, since she was having dinner with a Titan and a giant.

She told Damasen about her life and her adventures with Percy. She explained how Percy had met Bob, wiped his memory in the River Lethe and left him in the care of Hades.

'Percy was trying to do something good,' she promised Bob. 'He didn't know Hades would be such a creep.'

Even to her, it didn't sound convincing. Hades was *always* a creep.

She thought about what the *arai* had said – how Nico di Angelo had been the only person to visit Bob in the palace of the Underworld. Nico was one of the least outgoing, least friendly demigods Annabeth knew. Yet he'd been kind to Bob. By convincing Bob that Percy was a friend, Nico had inadvertently saved their lives. Annabeth wondered if she would *ever* figure that guy out.

Bob washed his bowl with his squirt bottle and rag.

Damasen made a rolling gesture with his spoon. 'Continue your story, Annabeth Chase.'

She explained about their quest in the *Argo II*. When she got to the part about stopping Gaia from waking, she faltered. 'She's, um . . . she's your mom, right?'

Damasen scraped his bowl. His face was covered with old poison burns, gouges and scar tissue, so it looked like the surface of an asteroid.

'Yes,' he said. 'And Tartarus is my father.' He gestured around the hut. 'As you can see, I was a disappointment to my parents. They expected . . . *more* from me.'

Annabeth couldn't quite wrap her mind around the fact that she was sharing soup with a twenty-foot-tall lizard-legged man whose parents were Earth and the Pit of Darkness.

Olympian gods were hard enough to imagine as parents, but at least they resembled humans. The old primordial gods like Gaia and Tartarus . . . How could you leave home and ever be independent of your parents, when they literally encompassed the entire world?

'So . . .' she said. 'You don't mind us fighting your mom?'

Damasen snorted like a bull. 'Best of luck. At present, it's my father you should worry about. With him opposing you, you have no chance to survive.'

Suddenly Annabeth didn't feel so hungry. She put her bowl on the floor. Small Bob came over the check it out.

'Opposing us how?' she asked.

'*All* of this.' Damasen cracked a drakon bone and used a splinter as a toothpick. 'All that you see is the body of Tartarus, or at least one manifestation of it. He knows you are here. He tries to thwart your progress at every step. My brethren hunt you. It is remarkable you have lived this long, even with the help of Iapetus.'

Bob scowled when he heard his name. 'The defeated ones hunt us, yes. They will be close behind now.'

Damasen spat out his toothpick. 'I can obscure your path for a while, long enough for you to rest. I have power in this swamp. But eventually they will catch you.'

'My friends must reach the Doors of Death,' Bob said. 'That is the way out.'

'Impossible,' Damasen muttered. 'The Doors are too well guarded.'

Annabeth sat forward. 'But you know where they are?'

'Of course. All of Tartarus flows down to one place: his heart. The Doors of Death are there. But you cannot make it there alive with only Iapetus.'

'Then come with us,' Annabeth said. 'Help us.'

'HA!'

Annabeth jumped. In the bed, Percy muttered deliriously in his sleep, 'Ha, ha, ha.'

'Child of Athena,' the giant said, 'I am not your friend.

I helped mortals once, and you see where it got me.'

'You helped mortals?' Annabeth knew a lot about Greek legends, but she drew a total blank on the name Damasen. 'I – I don't understand.'

'Bad story,' Bob explained. 'Good giants have bad stories. Damasen was created to oppose Ares.'

'Yes,' the giant agreed. 'Like all my brethren, I was born to answer a certain god. My foe was Ares. But Ares was the god of war. And so when I was born –'

'You were his opposite,' Annabeth guessed. 'You were peaceful.'

'Peaceful for a giant, at least.' Damasen sighed. 'I wandered the fields of Maeonia, in the land you now call Turkey. I tended my sheep and collected my herbs. It was a good life. But I would not fight the gods. My mother and father cursed me for that. The final insult: one day the Maeonian drakon killed a human shepherd, a friend of mine, so I hunted the creature down and slew it, thrusting a tree straight through its mouth. I used the power of the earth to regrow the tree's roots, planting the drakon firmly in the ground. I made sure it would terrorize mortals no more. That was a deed Gaia could not forgive.'

'Because you helped someone?'

'Yes.' Damasen looked ashamed. 'Gaia opened the earth, and I was consumed, exiled here in the belly of my father Tartarus, where all the useless flotsam collects – all the bits of creation he does not care for.' The giant plucked a flower out of his hair and regarded it absently. 'They let me live, tending my sheep, collecting my herbs, so I might know the uselessness of the life I chose. Every day – or what passes for day in this lightless place – the Maeonian drakon re-forms and attacks me. Killing it is my endless task.'

Annabeth gazed around the hut, trying to imagine how many aeons Damasen had been exiled here – slaying the drakon, collecting its bones and hide and meat, knowing it would attack again the next day. She could barely imagine surviving a *week* in Tartarus. Exiling your own son here for centuries – that was beyond cruel.

'Break the curse,' she blurted out. 'Come with us.'

Damasen chuckled sourly. 'As simple as that. Don't you think I have tried to leave this place? It is impossible. No matter which direction I travel, I end up here again. The swamp is the only thing I know – the only destination I can imagine. No, little demigod. My curse has overtaken me. I have no hope left.'

'No hope,' Bob echoed.

'There must be a way.' Annabeth couldn't stand the expression on the giant's face. It reminded her of her own father, the few times he'd confessed to her that he still loved Athena. He had looked so sad and defeated, wishing for something he knew was impossible.

'Bob has a plan to reach the Doors of Death,' she insisted. 'He said we could hide in some sort of Death Mist.'

'Death Mist?' Damasen scowled at Bob. 'You would take them to *Akhlys*?'

'It is the only way,' Bob said.

'You will die,' Damasen said. 'Painfully. In darkness. Akhlys trusts no one and helps no one.'

Bob looked like he wanted to argue, but he pressed his lips together and remained silent.

'Is there another way?' Annabeth asked.

'No,' Damasen said. 'The Death Mist . . . that is the best plan. Unfortunately, it is a terrible plan.'

Annabeth felt like she was hanging over the pit again, unable to pull herself up, unable to maintain her grip – left with no good options.

'But isn't it worth trying?' she asked. 'You could return to the mortal world. You could see the sun again.'

Damasen's eyes were like the sockets of the drakon's skull – dark and hollow, devoid of hope. He flicked a broken bone into the fire and rose to his full height – a massive red warrior in sheepskin and drakon leather, with dried flowers and herbs in his hair. Annabeth could see how he was the *anti*-Ares. Ares was the worst god, blustery and violent. Damasen was the best giant, kind and helpful . . . and for that he'd been cursed to eternal torment.

'Get some sleep,' the giant said. 'I will prepare supplies for your journey. I am sorry, but I cannot do more.'

Annabeth wanted to argue, but, as soon as he said *sleep*, her body betrayed her, despite her resolution never to sleep in Tartarus again. Her belly was full. The fire made a pleasant crackling sound. The herbs in the air reminded her of the hills around Camp Half-Blood in the summer, when the satyrs and naiads gathered wild plants in the lazy afternoons.

'Maybe a little sleep,' she agreed.

Bob scooped her up like a rag doll. She didn't protest. He set her next to Percy on the giant's bed, and she closed her eyes.

ANNABETH

ANNABETH WOKE STARING at the shadows dancing across the hut's ceiling. She hadn't had a single dream. That was so unusual, she wasn't sure if she'd actually woken up.

As she lay there, Percy snoring next to her and Small Bob purring on her belly, she heard Bob and Damasen deep in conversation.

'You haven't told her,' Damasen said.

'No,' Bob admitted. 'She is already scared.'

The giant grumbled. 'She *should* be. And if you cannot guide them past Night?'

Damasen said *Night* like it was a proper name – an *evil* name.

'I have to,' Bob said.

'Why?' Damasen wondered. 'What have the demigods given you? They have erased your old self, everything you were. Titans and giants . . . we are meant to be the foes of the gods and their children. Are we not?'

'Then why did you heal the boy?'

Damasen exhaled. 'I have been wondering that myself. Perhaps because the girl goaded me, or perhaps . . . I find these two demigods intriguing. They are resilient to have made it so far. That is admirable. Still, how can we help them any further? It is not our fate.'

'Perhaps,' Bob said uncomfortably. 'But . . . do you like our fate?'

'What a question. Does anyone like his fate?'

'I liked being Bob,' Bob murmured. 'Before I started to remember . . .'

'Huh.' There was a shuffling sound, as if Damasen was stuffing a leather bag.

'Damasen,' the Titan asked, 'do you remember the sun?'

The shuffling stopped. Annabeth heard the giant exhale through his nostrils. 'Yes. It was yellow. When it touched the horizon, it turned the sky beautiful colours.'

'I miss the sun,' Bob said. 'The stars, too. I would like to say hello to the stars again.'

'Stars . . .' Damasen said the word as if he'd forgotten its meaning. 'Yes. They made silver patterns in the night sky.' He threw something to the floor with a thump. 'Bah. This is useless talk. We cannot –'

In the distance, the Maeonian drakon roared.

Percy sat bolt upright. 'What? What – where – what?'

'It's okay.' Annabeth took his arm.

When he registered that they were together in a giant's bed with a skeleton cat, he looked more confused than ever. 'That noise . . . where are we?'

'How much do you remember?' she asked.

Percy frowned. His eyes seemed alert. All his wounds had vanished. Except for his tattered clothes and a few layers of dirt and grime, he looked as if he'd never fallen into Tartarus.

'I – the demon grandmothers – and then . . . not much.'

Damasen loomed over the bed. 'There is no time, little mortals. The drakon is returning. I fear its roar will draw the others – my brethren, hunting you. They will be here within minutes.'

Annabeth's pulse quickened. 'What will you tell them when they get here?'

Damasen's mouth twitched. 'What is there to tell? Nothing of significance, as long as you are gone.'

He tossed them two drakon-leather satchels. 'Clothes, food, drink.'

Bob was wearing a similar but larger pack. He leaned on his broom, gazing at Annabeth as if still pondering Damasen's words: *What have the demigods given you? We are meant to be the foes of the gods and their children.*

Suddenly Annabeth was struck by a thought so sharp and clear, it was like a blade from Athena herself.

'The Prophecy of Seven,' she said.

Percy had already climbed out of the bed and was shouldering his pack. He frowned at her. 'What about it?'

Annabeth grabbed Damasen's hand, startling the giant. His brow furrowed. His skin was as rough as sandstone.

'You *have* to come with us,' she pleaded. 'The prophecy says *foes bear arms to the Doors of Death*. I thought it meant Romans and Greeks, but that's not it. The line means *us* – demigods, a Titan, a giant. We *need* you to close the Doors!'

The drakon roared outside, closer this time. Damasen gently pulled his hand away.

'No, child,' he murmured. 'My curse is here. I cannot escape it.'

'Yes, you can,' Annabeth said. 'Don't fight the drakon. Figure out a way to break the cycle! Find *another* fate.'

Damasen shook his head. 'Even if I could, I cannot leave this swamp. It is the only destination I can picture.'

Annabeth's mind raced. 'There *is* another destination. Look at me! Remember my face. When you're ready, come find me. We'll take you to the mortal world with us. You can see the sunlight and stars.'

The ground shook. The drakon was close now, stomping through the marsh, blasting trees and moss with its poison spray. Further away, Annabeth heard the voice of the giant Polybotes, urging his followers forward. 'THE SEA GOD'S SON! HE IS CLOSE!'

'Annabeth,' Percy said urgently, 'that's our cue to leave.'

Damasen took something from his belt. In his massive hand, the white shard looked like another toothpick, but when he offered it to Annabeth she realized it was a sword – a blade of drakon bone, honed to a deadly edge, with a simple grip of leather.

'One last gift for the child of Athena,' rumbled the giant. 'I cannot have you walking to your death unarmed. Now, go! Before it is too late.'

Annabeth wanted to sob. She took the sword, but she

couldn't even make herself say thank you. She knew the giant was meant to fight at their side. That was the answer – but Damasen turned away.

'We must leave,' Bob urged as his kitten climbed onto his shoulder.

'He's right, Annabeth,' Percy said.

They ran for the entrance. Annabeth didn't look back as she followed Percy and Bob into the swamp, but she heard Damasen behind them, shouting his battle cry at the advancing drakon, his voice cracking with despair as he faced his old enemy yet again.

XLI

PIPER

PIPER DIDN'T KNOW MUCH about the Mediterranean, but she was pretty sure it wasn't supposed to freeze in July.

Two days out to sea from Split, grey clouds swallowed the sky. The waves turned choppy. Cold drizzle sprayed across the deck, forming ice on the rails and the ropes.

'It's the sceptre,' Nico murmured, hefting the ancient staff. 'It has to be.'

Piper wondered. Ever since Jason and Nico had returned from Diocletian's Palace, they'd been acting nervous and cagey. Something major had happened there – something Jason wouldn't share with her.

It made sense that the sceptre might have caused this weather change. The black orb on top seemed to leach the colour right out of the air. The golden eagles at its base glinted coldly. The sceptre could supposedly control the dead, and it *definitely* gave off bad vibes. Coach Hedge had taken one look at the thing, turned pale and announced that he was going to his room to console himself with Chuck Norris videos. (Although Piper suspected that he was actually making Iris-messages back home to his girlfriend Mellie; the coach had been acting very agitated about her lately, though he wouldn't tell Piper what was going on.)

So, yes . . . *maybe* the sceptre could cause a freak ice storm. But Piper didn't think that was it. She feared something else was happening – something even worse.

'We can't talk up here,' Jason decided. 'Let's postpone the meeting.'

They'd all gathered on the quarterdeck to discuss strategy as they got closer to Epirus. Now it was clearly not a good place to hang out. Wind swept frost across the deck. The sea churned beneath them.

Piper didn't mind the waves so much. The rocking and pitching reminded her of surfing with her dad off the California coast. But she could tell Hazel wasn't doing well. The poor girl got seasick even in calm waters. She looked like she was trying to swallow a billiard ball.

'Need to –' Hazel gagged and pointed below.

'Yeah, go.' Nico kissed her cheek, which Piper found surprising. He hardly ever made gestures of affection, even to his sister. He seemed to hate physical contact. Kissing Hazel . . . it was almost like he was saying goodbye.

'I'll walk you down.' Frank put his arm around Hazel's waist and helped her to the stairs.

Piper hoped Hazel would be okay. The last few nights, since that fight with Sciron, they'd had some good talks together. Being the only two girls on board was kind of rough.

They'd shared stories, complained about the guys' gross habits and shed some tears together about Annabeth. Hazel had told her what it was like to control the Mist, and Piper had been surprised by how much it sounded like using charm-speak. Piper had offered to help her if she could. In return, Hazel had promised to coach her in sword fighting – a skill at which Piper epically sucked. Piper felt like she had a new friend, which was great . . . assuming they lived long enough to enjoy the friendship.

Nico brushed some ice from his hair. He frowned at the sceptre of Diocletian. 'I should put this thing away. If it's really causing the weather, maybe taking it below deck will help . . .'

'Sure,' Jason said.

Nico glanced at Piper and Leo, as if worried what they might say when he was gone. Piper felt his defences going up, like he was curling into a psychological ball, the way he'd gone into a death trance in that bronze jar.

Once he'd headed below, Piper studied Jason's face. His eyes were full of concern. What had *happened* in Croatia?

Leo pulled a screwdriver from his belt. 'So much for the big team meeting. Looks like it's just us again.'

Just us again.

Piper remembered a wintry day in Chicago last December, when the three of them had landed in Millennial Park on their first quest.

Leo hadn't changed much since then, except he seemed more comfortable in his role as a child of Hephaestus. He'd always had too much nervous energy. Now he knew how to use it. His hands were constantly in motion, pulling tools from his belt, working controls, tinkering with his beloved Archimedes sphere. Today he'd removed it from the control panel and shut down Festus the figurehead for maintenance – something about rewiring his processor for a motor-control upgrade with the sphere, whatever the heck that meant.

As for Jason, he looked thinner, taller and more careworn. His hair had gone from close-cropped Roman style to longer and shaggier. The groove Sciron had shot across the left side of his scalp was interesting, too – almost like a rebellious streak. His icy blue eyes looked older, somehow – full of worry and responsibility.

Piper knew what her friends whispered about Jason – he was *too* perfect, too straitlaced. If that had ever been true, it wasn't any more. He'd been battered on this journey, and not just physically. His hardships hadn't weakened him, but he'd been weathered and softened like leather – as if he were becoming a more comfortable version of himself.

And Piper? She could only imagine what Leo and Jason thought when they looked at her. She definitely didn't feel like the same person she'd been last winter.

That first quest to rescue Hera seemed like centuries ago. So much had changed in seven months . . . she wondered how the gods could stand being alive for thousands of years. How much change had *they* seen? Maybe it wasn't surprising that the Olympians seemed a little crazy. If Piper had lived through three millennia, she would have gone loopy.

She gazed into the cold rain. She would have given anything to be back at Camp Half-Blood, where the weather was controlled even in the winter. The images she'd seen in her knife recently . . . well, they didn't give her much to look forward to.

Jason squeezed her shoulder. 'Hey, it'll be fine. We're close to Epirus now. Another day or so, if Nico's directions are right.'

'Yep.' Leo tinkered with his sphere, tapping and nudging one of the jewels on its surface. 'By tomorrow morning, we'll reach the western coast of Greece. Then another hour inland, and bang – House of Hades! I'ma get me the T-shirt!'

'Yay,' Piper muttered.

She wasn't anxious to plunge into the darkness again. She still had nightmares about the nymphaeum and the hypogeum under Rome. In the blade of Katoptris, she'd seen images similar to what Leo and Hazel had described from their dreams – a pale sorceress in a gold dress, her hands weaving golden light in the air like silk on a loom; a giant wrapped in shadows, marching down a long corridor lined with torches. As he passed each one, the flames died. She saw a huge cavern filled with monsters – Cyclopes, Earthborn and stranger things – surrounding her and her friends, hopelessly outnumbering them.

Every time she saw those images, a voice in her head kept repeating one line over and over.

'Guys,' she said, 'I've been thinking about the Prophecy of Seven.'

It took a lot to get Leo's attention away from his work, but that did the trick.

'What about it?' he asked. 'Like . . . good stuff, I hope?'

She readjusted her cornucopia's shoulder strap. Sometimes the horn of plenty seemed so light she forgot about it. Other times it felt like an anvil, as if the river god Achelous were sending out bad thoughts, trying to punish her for taking his horn.

'In Katoptris,' she started, 'I keep seeing that giant Clytius – the guy who's wrapped in shadows. I know his weakness is fire, but in my visions he snuffs out flames wherever he goes. Any kind of light just gets sucked into his cloud of darkness.'

'Sounds like Nico,' Leo said. 'You think they're related?'

Jason scowled. 'Hey, man, cut Nico some slack. So, Piper, what about this giant? What are you thinking?'

She and Leo exchanged a quizzical look, like: *Since when does Jason defend Nico di Angelo?* She decided not to comment.

'I keep thinking about fire,' Piper said. 'How we expect Leo to beat this giant because he's . . .'

'Hot?' Leo suggested with a grin.

'Um, let's go with *flammable*. Anyway, that line from the prophecy bothers me: *To storm or fire the world must fall.*'

'Yeah, we know all about it,' Leo promised. 'You're gonna say I'm fire. And Jason here is storm.'

Piper nodded reluctantly. She knew that none of them liked talking about this, but they all must have *felt* it was the truth.

The ship pitched to starboard. Jason grabbed the icy railing. 'So you're worried one of us will endanger the quest, maybe accidentally destroy the world?'

'No,' Piper said. 'I think we've been reading that line the

wrong way. The *world* . . . the earth. In Greek, the word for that would be . . .'

She hesitated, not wanting to say the name aloud, even at sea.

'Gaia.' Jason's eyes gleamed with sudden interest. 'You mean, *to storm or fire Gaia must fall*?'

'Oh . . .' Leo grinned even wider. 'You know, I like your version a lot better. 'Cause if Gaia falls to me, Mr Fire, that is absolutely copacetic.'

'Or to me . . . storm.' Jason kissed her. 'Piper, that's brilliant! If you're right, this is great news. We just have to figure out which of us destroys Gaia.'

'Maybe.' She felt uneasy getting their hopes up. 'But, see, it's storm *or* fire . . .'

She unsheathed Katoptris and set it on the console. Immediately, the blade flickered, showing the dark shape of the giant Clytius moving through a corridor, snuffing out torches.

'I'm worried about Leo and this fight with Clytius,' she said. 'That line in the prophecy makes it sound like only *one* of you can succeed. And if the *storm or fire* part is connected to the third line, *an oath to keep with a final breath* . . .'

She didn't finish the thought, but from Jason's and Leo's expressions she saw that they understood. If she was reading the prophecy right, either Leo or Jason would defeat Gaia. The other one would die.

XLII

PIPER

LEO STARED AT THE DAGGER. 'Okay . . . so I don't like your idea as much as I thought. You think one of us defeats Gaia and the other one dies? Or maybe one of us dies *while* defeating her? Or –'

'Guys,' Jason said, 'we'll drive ourselves crazy overthinking it. You know how prophecies are. Heroes always get into trouble trying to thwart them.'

'Yeah,' Leo muttered. 'We'd *hate* to get into trouble. We've got it so good right now.'

'You know what I mean,' Jason said. 'The *final breath* line might not be connected to the *storm and fire* part. For all we know, the two of us aren't even storm and fire. Percy can raise hurricanes.'

'And I could always set Coach Hedge on fire,' Leo volunteered. 'Then *he* can be fire.'

The thought of a blazing satyr screaming, 'Die, scumbag!'

as he attacked Gaia was almost enough to make Piper laugh – almost.

'I hope I'm wrong,' she said cautiously. 'But the whole quest started with us finding Hera and waking that giant king Porphyrion. I have a feeling the war will end with us too. For better or worse.'

'Hey,' Jason said, 'personally, I *like* us.'

'Agreed,' Leo said. '*Us* is my favourite people.'

Piper managed a smile. She really did love these guys. She wished she could use her charmspeak on the Fates, describe a happy ending and force them to make it come true.

Unfortunately, it was hard to imagine a happy ending with all the dark thoughts in her head. She worried that the giant Clytius had been put in their path to eliminate Leo as a threat. If so, that meant Gaia would also try to eliminate Jason. Without storm or fire, their quest couldn't succeed.

And this wintry weather bothered her too . . . She felt certain it was being caused by something more than just Diocletian's sceptre. The cold wind, the mix of ice and rain seemed actively hostile and somehow familiar.

That smell in the air, the thick smell of . . .

Piper should have understood what was happening sooner, but she'd spent most of her life in southern California with no major changes of season. She hadn't grown up with that smell . . . the smell of impending snow.

Every muscle in her body tensed. 'Leo, sound the alarm.'

Piper hadn't realized she was charmspeaking, but Leo

immediately dropped his screwdriver and punched the alarm button. He frowned when nothing happened.

'Uh, it's disconnected,' he remembered. 'Festus is shut down. Gimme a minute to get the system back online.'

'We don't have a minute! Fires – we need vials of Greek fire. Jason, call the winds. Warm, southerly winds.'

'Wait, what?' Jason stared at her in confusion. 'Piper, what's wrong?'

'It's her!' Piper snatched up her dagger. 'She's back! We have to –'

Before she could finish, the boat listed to port. The temperature dropped so fast that the sails crackled with ice. The bronze shields along the rails popped like over-pressurized soda cans.

Jason drew his sword, but it was too late. A wave of ice particles swept over him, coating him like a glazed doughnut and freezing him in place. Under a layer of ice, his eyes were wide with amazement.

'Leo! Flames! Now!' Piper yelled.

Leo's right hand blazed, but the wind swirled around him and doused the fire. Leo clutched his Archimedes sphere as a funnel cloud of sleet lifted him off his feet.

'Hey!' he yelled. 'Hey! Let me go!'

Piper ran towards him, but a voice in the storm said, 'Oh, yes, Leo Valdez. I will let you go *permanently*.'

Leo shot skywards, like he'd been launched from a catapult. He disappeared into the clouds.

'No!' Piper raised her knife, but there was nothing to attack. She looked desperately at the stairwell, hoping to see her friends charging to the rescue, but a block of ice had sealed the hatch. The whole lower deck might have been frozen solid.

She needed a better weapon to fight with – something more than her voice, a stupid fortune-telling dagger and a cornucopia that shot ham and fresh fruit.

She wondered whether she could make it to the ballista.

Then her enemies appeared, and she realized that no weapon would be enough.

Standing amidships was a girl in a flowing dress of white silk, her mane of black hair pinned back with a circlet of diamonds. Her eyes were the colour of coffee, but without the warmth.

Behind her stood her brothers – two young men with purple-feathered wings, stark white hair and jagged swords of Celestial bronze.

'So good to see you again, *ma chère*,' said Khione, the goddess of snow. 'It's time we had a very cold reunion.'

XLIII

PIPER

PIPER DIDN'T PLAN TO SHOOT BLUEBERRY MUFFINS. The cornucopia must have sensed her distress and thought she and her visitors could use some warm baked goods.

Half a dozen steamy muffins flew from the horn of plenty like buckshot. It wasn't the most effective opening attack.

Khione simply leaned to one side. Most of the muffins sailed past her over the rail. Her brothers, the Boreads, each caught one and began to eat.

'Muffins,' said the bigger one. Cal, Piper remembered: short for *Calais*. He was dressed exactly as he had been in Quebec – in cleats, sweatpants and a red hockey jersey – and had two black eyes and several broken teeth. 'Muffins are good.'

'Ah, *merci*,' said the scrawny brother – Zethes, she recalled – who stood on the catapult platform, his purple wings spread. His white hair was still feathered in a horrible Disco Age mullet. The collar of his silk shirt stuck out over his breastplate. His chartreuse polyester trousers were grotesquely tight, and his acne had only got worse. Despite that, he wriggled his eyebrows and smiled like he was the demigod of pickup artists.

'I knew the pretty girl would miss me.' He spoke Québécois French, which Piper translated effortlessly. Thanks to her mom, Aphrodite, the language of love was hardwired into her, though she didn't want to speak it with Zethes.

'What are you doing?' Piper demanded. Then, in charm-speak: 'Let my friends go.'

Zethes blinked. 'We should let your friends go.'

'Yes,' Cal agreed.

'No, you idiots!' Khione snapped. 'She is charmspeaking. Use your wits.'

'Wits . . .' Cal frowned as if he wasn't sure what wits were. 'Muffins are better.'

He stuffed the whole thing in his mouth and began to chew.

Zethes picked a blueberry off the top of his and nibbled it delicately. 'Ah, my beautiful Piper . . . so long I have waited to see you again. Sadly, my sister is right. We cannot let your friends go. In fact we must take them to Quebec, where they shall be laughed at eternally. I am so sorry, but these are our orders.'

'Orders . . . ?'

Ever since last winter, Piper had expected Khione to show her frosty face sooner or later. When they'd defeated her at the Wolf House in Sonoma, the snow goddess had vowed revenge. But why were Zethes and Cal here? In Quebec, the

Boreads had seemed almost friendly – at least compared to their sub-zero sister.

'Guys, listen,' Piper said. 'Your sister disobeyed Boreas. She's working with the giants, trying to raise Gaia. She's planning to take over your father's throne.'

Khione laughed, soft and cold. 'Dear Piper McLean. You would manipulate my weak-willed brothers with your charms, like a true daughter of the love goddess. Such a skilful liar.'

'*Liar?*' Piper cried. 'You tried to kill us! Zethes, she's working for Gaia!'

Zethes winced. 'Alas, beautiful girl. We all are working for Gaia now. I fear these orders are from our father, Boreas himself.'

'What?' Piper didn't want to believe it, but Khione's smug smile told her it was true.

'At last my father saw the wisdom of my counsel,' Khione purred, 'or at least he *did* before his Roman side began warring with his Greek side. I fear he is quite incapacitated now, but he left me in charge. He has ordered that the forces of the North Wind be used in the service of King Porphyrion and of course . . . the Earth Mother.'

Piper gulped. 'How are you even here?' She gestured at the ice all over the ship. 'It's summer!'

Khione shrugged. 'Our powers grow. The rules of nature are turned upside down. Once the Earth Mother wakes, we shall remake the world as we choose!'

'With hockey,' Cal said, his mouth still full. 'And pizza. And muffins.'

'Yes, yes,' Khione sneered. 'I had to promise a few things to the big simpleton. And to Zethes –'

'Oh, my needs are simple.' Zethes slicked back his hair and winked at Piper. 'I should have kept you at our palace when we first met, my dear Piper. But soon we will go there again, together, and I shall romance you most incredibly.'

'Thanks, but no thanks,' Piper said. 'Now, *let Jason go*.'

She put all her power into the words, and Zethes obeyed. He snapped his fingers. Jason instantly defrosted. He crumpled to the floor, gasping and steaming, but at least he was alive.

'You imbecile!' Khione thrust out her hand, and Jason refroze, now flat on the deck like a bearskin rug. She wheeled on Zethes. 'If you wish the girl as your prize, you must prove you can control her. Not the other way around!'

'Yes, of course.' Zethes looked chagrined.

'As for Jason Grace . . .' Khione's brown eyes gleamed. 'He and the rest of your friends will join our court of ice statues in Quebec. Jason will *grace* my throne room.'

'Clever,' Piper muttered. 'Take you all day to think up that line?'

At least she knew Jason was still alive, which made Piper a little less panicky. The deep freeze could be reversed. That meant her other friends were probably still alive below deck. She just needed a plan to free them.

Unfortunately, she wasn't Annabeth. She wasn't so good at devising plans on the fly. She needed time to think.

'What about Leo?' she blurted. 'Where did you send him?'

The snow goddess stepped lightly around Jason, examining him as if he were sidewalk art.

'Leo Valdez deserved a special punishment,' she said. 'I have sent him to a place from which he can never return.'

Piper couldn't breathe. Poor Leo. The idea of never seeing him again almost destroyed her. Khione must've seen it in her face.

'Alas, my dear Piper!' She smiled in triumph. 'But it is for the best. Leo could not be tolerated, even as an ice statue . . . not after he insulted me. The fool refused to rule at my side! And his power over fire . . .' She shook her head. 'He could not be allowed to reach the House of Hades. I'm afraid Lord Clytius likes fire even less than I do.'

Piper gripped her dagger.

Fire, she thought. *Thanks for reminding me, you witch.*

She scanned the deck. How to make fire? A box of Greek fire vials was secured by the forward ballista, but that was too far away. Even if she made it without getting frozen, Greek fire would burn everything, including the ship and all her friends. There had to be another way. Her eyes strayed to the prow.

Oh.

Festus the figurehead could blow some serious flames. Unfortunately, Leo had switched him off. Piper had no idea how to reactivate him. She would never have time to figure out the right controls at the ship's console. She had vague memories of Leo tinkering around inside the dragon's bronze skull, mumbling about a control disk, but even if Piper could make it to the prow she would have no idea what she was doing.

Still, some instinct told her Festus was her best chance, if only she could figure out how to convince her captors to let her get close enough . . .

'Well!' Khione interrupted her thoughts. 'I fear our time together is at a close. Zethes, if you would –'

'Wait!' Piper said.

A simple command, and it worked. The Boreads and Khione frowned at her, waiting.

Piper was fairly sure she could control the brothers with charmspeak, but Khione was a problem. Charmspeak worked poorly if the person wasn't attracted to you. It worked poorly on a powerful being like a god. And it worked poorly when your victim *knew* about charmspeak and was actively on guard against it. All of the above applied to Khione.

What would Annabeth do?

Delay, Piper thought. When in doubt, talk some more.

'You're afraid of my friends,' she said. 'So why not just kill them?'

Khione laughed. 'You are not a god, or you would understand. Death is so short, so . . . unsatisfying. Your puny mortal souls flit off to the Underworld, and what happens then? The *best* I can hope for is that you go to the Fields of Punishment or Asphodel, but you demigods are insufferably noble. More likely you will go to Elysium – or get reborn in a new life. Why would I want to reward your friends that way? Why . . . when I can punish them eternally?'

'And me?' Piper hated to ask. 'Why am I still alive and unfrozen?'

Khione glanced at her brothers with annoyance. 'Zethes has claimed you, for one thing.'

'I kiss magnificently,' Zethes promised. 'You will see, beautiful one.'

The idea made Piper's stomach churn.

'But that is not the only reason,' Khione said. 'It is because I *hate* you, Piper. Deeply and truly. Without you, Jason would have stayed with me in Quebec.'

'Delusional, much?'

Khione's eyes turned as hard as the diamonds in her circlet. 'You are a meddler, the daughter of a useless goddess. What can you do alone? Nothing. Of all the seven demigods, you have no purpose, no power. I wish you to stay on this ship, adrift and helpless, while Gaia rises and the world ends. And just to be sure you are well out of the way . . .'

She gestured to Zethes, who plucked something from the air — a frozen sphere the size of a softball, covered in icy spikes.

'A bomb,' Zethes explained, 'especially for you, my love.'

'Bombs!' Cal laughed. 'A good day! Bombs and muffins!'

'Uh . . .' Piper lowered her dagger, which seemed even more useless than usual. 'Flowers would've been fine.'

'Oh, it will not kill the pretty girl.' Zethes frowned. 'Well . . . I am *fairly* sure of this. But when the fragile container cracks, in . . . ah, roughly not very long . . . it will unleash the full force of the northern winds. This ship will be blown very far off course. Very, very far.'

'Indeed.' Khione's voice prickled with false sympathy. 'We will take your friends for our statue collection, then unleash the winds and bid you goodbye! You can watch the end of the world from . . . well, the end of the world! Perhaps you can charmspeak the fish, and feed yourself with your silly cornucopia. You can pace the deck of this empty ship and watch our victory in the blade of your dagger. When Gaia has arisen and the world you knew is dead, *then* Zethes can come back and retrieve you for his bride. What will you do to stop us, Piper? A hero? Ha! You are a joke.'

Her words stung like sleet, mostly because Piper had had the same thoughts herself. What could she do? How could she save her friends with what she had?

She came close to snapping – flying at her enemies in a rage and getting herself killed.

She looked at Khione's smug expression and she realized the goddess was *hoping* for that. She wanted Piper to break. She wanted entertainment.

Piper's spine turned to steel. She remembered the girls who used to make fun of her at the Wilderness School. She remembered Drew, the cruel head counsellor she had replaced in Aphrodite's cabin; and Medea, who had charmed Jason and Leo in Chicago; and Jessica, her dad's old assistant, who had always treated her like a useless brat. All her life, Piper had been looked down upon, told she was useless.

It has never been true, another voice whispered – a voice that sounded like her mother's. *Each of them berated you because they feared you and envied you. So does Khione. Use that!*

Piper didn't feel like it, but she managed a laugh. She tried it again, and the laughter came more easily. Soon she was doubled over, giggling and snorting.

Calais joined in, until Zethes elbowed him.

Khione's smile wavered. 'What? What is so funny? I have doomed you!'

'Doomed me!' Piper laughed again. 'Oh, gods . . . sorry.' She took a shaky breath and tried to stop giggling. 'Oh, boy . . . okay. You really think I'm powerless? You *really* think I'm useless? Gods of Olympus, your brain must have freezer burn. You don't know my secret, do you?'

Khione's eyes narrowed.

'You have no secret,' she said. 'You are lying.'

'Okay, whatever,' Piper said. 'Yeah, go ahead and take my friends. Leave me here . . . *useless*.' She snorted. 'Yeah. Gaia will be *really* pleased with you.'

Snow swirled around the goddess. Zethes and Calais glanced at each other nervously.

'Sister,' Zethes said, 'if she really has some secret –'

'Pizza?' Cal speculated. 'Hockey?'

'– then we must know,' Zethes continued.

Khione obviously didn't buy it. Piper tried to keep a straight face, but she made her eyes dance with mischief and humour.

Go ahead, she dared. *Call my bluff.*

'What secret?' Khione demanded. 'Reveal it to us!'

Piper shrugged. 'Suit yourself.' She pointed casually towards the prow. 'Follow me, ice people.'

XLIV

PIPER

SHE PUSHED BETWEEN THE BOREADS, which was like walking through a meat freezer. The air around them was so cold it burned her face. She felt like she was breathing pure snow.

Piper tried not to look down at Jason's frozen body as she passed. She tried not to think about her friends below, or Leo shot into the sky to a place of no return. She *definitely* tried not to think about the Boreads and the snow goddess, who were following her.

She fixed her eyes on the figurehead.

The ship rocked under her feet. A single gust of summer air made it through the chill, and Piper breathed it in, taking it as a good omen. It was still summer out there. Khione and her brothers did *not* belong here.

Piper knew she couldn't win a straight fight against Khione and two winged guys with swords. She wasn't as clever as

Annabeth, or as good at problem solving as Leo. But she *did* have power. And she intended to use it.

Last night, during her talk with Hazel, Piper had realized that the secret of charmspeak was a lot like using the Mist. In the past, Piper had had a lot of trouble making her charms work, because she always ordered her enemies do what *she* wanted. She would yell *Don't kill us* when the monster's fondest wish was to kill them. She would put all her power into her voice and hope it was enough to overwhelm her enemy's will.

Sometimes it worked, but it was exhausting and unreliable. Aphrodite wasn't about head-on confrontation. Aphrodite was about subtlety and guile and charm. Piper decided she shouldn't focus on making people do what she wanted. She needed to push them to do the things *they* wanted.

A great theory, if she could make it work . . .

She stopped at the foremast and faced Khione. 'Wow, I just realized why you hate us so much,' she said, filling her voice with pity. 'We humiliated you pretty badly in Sonoma.'

Khione's eyes glinted like iced espresso. She shot an uneasy look at her brothers.

Piper laughed. 'Oh, you didn't tell them!' she guessed. 'I don't blame you. You had a giant king on your side, plus an army of wolves and Earthborn, and you still couldn't beat us.'

'Silence!' the goddess hissed.

The air turned misty. Piper felt frost gathering on her eyebrows and freezing her ear canals, but she feigned a smile.

'Whatever.' She winked at Zethes. 'But it *was* pretty funny.'

'The beautiful girl must be lying,' Zethes said. 'Khione was not *beaten* at the Wolf House. She said it was a . . . ah, what is the term? A tactical retreat.'

'Treats?' Cal asked. 'Treats are good.'

Piper pushed the big guy's chest playfully. 'No, Cal. He means that your sister ran away.'

'I did not!' Khione shrieked.

'What did Hera call you?' Piper mused. 'Right – a D-list goddess!'

She burst out laughing again, and her amusement was so genuine that Zethes and Cal started laughing, too.

'That is *très bon!*' Zethes said. 'A D-list goddess. Ha!'

'Ha!' Cal said. 'Sister ran away! Ha!'

Khione's white dress began to steam. Ice formed over Zethes's and Cal's mouths, plugging them up.

'Show us this secret of yours, Piper McLean,' Khione growled. 'Then *pray* I leave you on this ship intact. If you are toying with us, I will show you the horrors of frostbite. I doubt Zethes will still want you if you have no fingers or toes . . . perhaps no nose or ears.'

Zethes and Cal spat the ice plugs out of their mouths.

'The pretty girl would look less pretty without a nose,' Zethes admitted.

Piper had seen pictures of frostbite victims. The threat terrified her, but she didn't let it show.

'Come on, then.' She led the way to the prow, humming one of her dad's favourite songs – 'Summertime'.

When she got to the figurehead, she put her hand on Festus's neck. His bronze scales were cold. There was no hum of machinery. His ruby eyes were dull and dark.

'You remember our dragon?' Piper asked.

Khione scoffed. 'This cannot be your secret. The dragon is broken. Its fire is gone.'

'Well, yes . . .' Piper stroked the dragon's snout.

She didn't have Leo's power to make gears turn or circuits spark. She couldn't sense anything about the workings of a machine. All she could do was speak her heart and tell the dragon what he *most* wanted to hear. 'But Festus is more than a machine. He's a living creature.'

'Ridiculous,' the goddess spat. 'Zethes, Cal – gather the frozen demigods from below. Then we shall break open the sphere of winds.'

'You could do that, boys,' Piper agreed. 'But then you wouldn't see Khione humiliated. I know you'd like that.'

The Boreads hesitated.

'Hockey?' Cal asked.

'Almost as good,' Piper promised. 'You fought at the side of Jason and the Argonauts, didn't you? On a ship like this, the first *Argo.*'

'Yes,' Zethes agreed. 'The *Argo.* Much like this, but we did not have a dragon.'

'Don't listen to her!' Khione snapped.

Piper felt ice forming on her lips.

'You could shut me up,' she said quickly. 'But you want to know my secret power – how I will destroy you, and Gaia, and the giants.'

Hatred seethed in Khione's eyes, but she withheld her frost.

'You – have – no – power,' she insisted.

'Spoken like a D-list goddess,' Piper said. 'One who never gets taken seriously, who *always* wants more power.'

She turned to Festus and ran her hand behind his metal ears. 'You're a good friend, Festus. No one can truly deactivate you. You're more than a machine. Khione doesn't understand that.'

She turned to the Boreads. 'She doesn't value you, either, you know. She thinks she can boss you around because you're demigods, not full-fledged gods. She doesn't understand that you're a powerful team.'

'A team,' Cal grunted. 'Like the Ca-na-di-ens.'

He had to struggle with the word since it was more than two syllables. He grinned and looked very pleased with himself.

'Exactly,' Piper said. 'Just like a hockey team. The whole is greater than the parts.'

'Like a pizza,' Cal added.

Piper laughed. 'You *are* smart, Cal! Even I underestimated you.'

'Wait, now,' Zethes protested. 'I am smart also. And good-looking.'

'Very smart,' Piper agreed, ignoring the *good-looking* part. 'So put down the wind bomb and watch Khione get humiliated.'

Zethes grinned. He crouched and rolled the ice sphere across the deck.

'You fool!' Khione yelled.

Before the goddess could go after the sphere, Piper cried, 'Our secret weapon, Khione! We're not just a bunch of demigods. We're a team. Just like Festus isn't only a collection of parts. He's *alive*. He's *my friend*. And when his friends are in trouble, especially Leo, he can wake up *on his own*.'

She willed all her confidence into her voice – all her love for the metal dragon and everything he'd done for them.

The rational part of her knew this was hopeless. How could you start a machine with emotions?

But Aphrodite wasn't rational. She ruled through emotions. She was the oldest and most primordial of the Olympians, born from the blood of Ouranos churning in the sea. Her power was more ancient than that of Hephaestus or Athena or even Zeus.

For a terrible moment, nothing happened. Khione glared at her. The Boreads began to come out of their daze, looking disappointed.

'Never mind our plan,' Khione snarled. 'Kill her!'

As the Boreads raised their swords, the dragon's metal skin grew warm under Piper's hand. She dived out of the way, tackling the snow goddess, as Festus turned his head one hundred and eighty degrees and blasted the Boreads, vaporizing them on the spot. For some reason, Zethes's sword was spared. It clunked to the deck, still steaming.

Piper scrambled to her feet. She spotted the sphere of winds at the base of the foremast. She ran for it, but before she could get close Khione materialized in front of her in a swirl of frost. Her skin glowed bright enough to cause snow blindness.

'You *miserable* girl,' she hissed. 'You think you can defeat me – a *goddess*?'

At Piper's back, Festus roared and blew steam, but Piper knew he couldn't breathe fire again without hitting her, too.

About twenty feet behind the goddess, the ice sphere began to crack and hiss.

Piper was out of time for subtlety. She yelled and raised her dagger, charging the goddess.

Khione grabbed her wrist. Ice spread over Piper's arm. The blade of Katoptris turned white.

The goddess's face was only six inches from hers. Khione smiled, knowing she had won.

'A child of Aphrodite,' she chided. 'You are *nothing*.'

Festus creaked again. Piper could swear he was trying to shout encouragement.

Suddenly her chest grew warm – not with anger or fear but with love for that dragon; and Jason, who was depending on her; and her friends trapped below; and Leo, who was lost and would need her help.

Maybe love was no match for ice . . . but Piper had used it to wake a metal dragon. Mortals did superhuman feats in the name of love all the time. Mothers lifted cars to save their children. And Piper was more than just mortal. She was a demigod. A hero.

The ice melted on her blade. Her arm steamed under Khione's grip.

'Still underestimating me,' Piper told the goddess. 'You really need to work on that.'

Khione's smug expression faltered as Piper drove her dagger straight down.

The blade touched Khione's chest, and the goddess

exploded in a miniature blizzard. Piper collapsed, dazed from the cold. She heard Festus clacking and whirring, the reactivated alarm bells ringing.

The bomb.

Piper struggled to rise. The sphere was ten feet away, hissing and spinning as the winds inside began to stir.

Piper dived for it.

Her fingers closed around the bomb just as the ice shattered and the winds exploded.

PERCY

PERCY FELT HOMESICK FOR THE SWAMP.

He never thought he'd miss sleeping in a giant's leather bed in a drakon-bone hut in a festering cesspool, but right now that sounded like Elysium.

He and Annabeth and Bob stumbled along in the darkness, the air thick and cold, the ground alternating patches of pointy rocks and pools of muck. The terrain seemed to be designed so that Percy could never let his guard down. Even walking ten feet was exhausting.

Percy had started out from the giant's hut feeling strong again, his head clear, his belly full of drakon jerky from their packs of provisions. Now his legs were sore. Every muscle ached. He pulled a makeshift tunic of drakon leather over his shredded T-shirt, but it did nothing to keep out the chill.

His focus narrowed to the ground in front of him. Nothing existed except for that and Annabeth at his side.

Whenever he felt like giving up, plopping himself down,

and dying (which was, like, every ten minutes), he reached over and took her hand, just to remember there was warmth in the world.

After Annabeth's talk with Damasen, Percy was worried about her. Annabeth didn't give in to despair easily, but as they walked she wiped tears from her eyes, trying not to let Percy see. He knew she hated it when her plans didn't work out. She was convinced they needed Damasen's help, but the giant had turned them down.

Part of Percy was relieved. He was concerned enough about Bob staying on their side once they reached the Doors of Death. He wasn't sure he wanted a giant as his wingman, even if that giant could cook a mean bowl of stew.

He wondered what had happened after they left Damasen's hut. He hadn't heard their pursuers in hours, but he could sense their hatred . . . especially Polybotes's. That giant was back there somewhere, following, pushing them deeper into Tartarus.

Percy tried to think of good things to keep his spirits up – the lake at Camp Half-Blood; the time he'd kissed Annabeth underwater. He tried to imagine the two of them at New Rome together, walking through the hills and holding hands. But Camp Jupiter and Camp Half-Blood both seemed like dreams. He felt as if only Tartarus existed. This was the real world – death, darkness, cold, pain. He'd been imagining all the rest.

He shivered. No. That was the pit speaking to him, sapping his resolve. He wondered how Nico had survived down here alone without going insane. That kid had more strength than Percy had given him credit for. The deeper they travelled, the harder it became to stay focused.

'This place is worse than the River Cocytus,' he muttered.

'Yes,' Bob called back happily. 'Much worse! It means we are close.'

Close to what? Percy wondered. But he didn't have the strength to ask. He noticed Small Bob the cat had hidden himself in Bob's coveralls again, which reinforced Percy's opinion that the kitten was the smartest one in their group.

Annabeth laced her fingers through his. In the light of his bronze sword, her face was beautiful.

'We're together,' she reminded him. 'We'll get through this.'

He'd been so worried about lifting her spirits, and here she was reassuring *him*.

'Yeah,' he agreed. 'Piece of cake.'

'But next time,' she said, 'I want to go somewhere different on a date.'

'Paris was nice,' he recalled.

She managed a smile. Months ago, before Percy got amnesia, they'd had dinner in Paris one night, compliments of Hermes. That seemed like another lifetime.

'I'd settle for New Rome,' she offered. 'As long as you're there with me.'

Man, Annabeth was awesome. For a moment, Percy actually remembered what it was like to feel happy. He had an amazing girlfriend. They could have a future together.

Then the darkness dispersed with a massive sigh, like the last breath of a dying god. In front of them was a clearing – a barren field of dust and stones. In the centre, about twenty yards away, knelt the gruesome figure of a woman, her clothes tattered, her limbs emaciated, her skin leathery green. Her head was bent as she sobbed quietly, and the sound shattered all Percy's hopes.

He realized that life was pointless. His struggles were for nothing. This woman cried as if mourning the death of the entire world.

'We're here,' Bob announced. 'Akhlys can help.'

PERCY

IF THE SOBBING GHOUL WAS BOB'S IDEA OF HELP, Percy was pretty sure he didn't want it.

Nevertheless, Bob trudged forward. Percy felt obliged to follow. If nothing else, this area was less dark – not exactly light, but with more of a soupy white fog.

'Akhlys!' Bob called.

The creature raised her head, and Percy's stomach screamed, *Help me!*

Her body was bad enough. She looked like the victim of a famine – limbs like sticks, swollen knees and knobby elbows, rags for clothes, broken fingernails and toenails. Dust was caked on her skin and piled on her shoulders as if she'd taken a shower at the bottom of an hourglass.

Her face was utter desolation. Her eyes were sunken and rheumy, pouring out tears. Her nose dripped like a water-fall. Her stringy grey hair was matted to her skull in greasy tufts, and her cheeks were raked and bleeding as if she'd been clawing herself.

Percy couldn't stand to meet her eyes, so he lowered his gaze. Across her knees lay an ancient shield – a battered circle of wood and bronze, painted with the likeness of Akhlys herself holding a shield, so the image seemed to go on forever, smaller and smaller.

'That shield,' Annabeth murmured. 'That's *his*. I thought it was just a story.'

'Oh, no,' the old hag wailed. 'The shield of Hercules. He painted me on its surface, so his enemies would see me in their final moments – the goddess of misery.' She coughed so hard it made Percy's chest hurt. 'As if Hercules knew true misery. It's not even a good likeness!'

Percy gulped. When he and his friends had encountered Hercules at the Straits of Gibraltar, it hadn't gone well. The exchange had involved a lot of yelling, death threats and high-velocity pineapples.

'What's his shield doing here?' Percy asked.

The goddess stared at him with her wet milky eyes. Her cheeks dripped blood, making red polka dots on her tattered dress. 'He doesn't need it any more, does he? It came here when his mortal body was burned. A reminder, I suppose, that no shield is sufficient. In the end, misery overtakes all of you. Even Hercules.'

Percy inched closer to Annabeth. He tried to remember why they were here, but the sense of despair made it difficult to think. Hearing Akhlys speak, he no longer found it strange that she had clawed her own cheeks. The goddess radiated pure pain.

'Bob,' Percy said, 'we shouldn't have come here.'

From somewhere inside Bob's uniform, the skeleton kitten mewled in agreement.

The Titan shifted and winced as if Small Bob was clawing his armpit. 'Akhlys controls the Death Mist,' he insisted. 'She can hide you.'

'*Hide* them?' Akhlys made a gurgling sound. She was either laughing or choking to death. 'Why would I do that?'

'They must reach the Doors of Death,' Bob said. 'To return to the mortal world.'

'Impossible!' Akhlys said. 'The armies of Tartarus will find you. They will kill you.'

Annabeth turned the blade of her drakon-bone sword, which Percy had to admit made her look pretty intimidating and hot in a 'Barbarian Princess' kind of way. 'So I guess your Death Mist is pretty useless, then,' she said.

The goddess bared her broken yellow teeth. '*Useless?* Who are you?'

'A daughter of Athena.' Annabeth's voice sounded brave – though how she did it, Percy didn't know. 'I didn't walk halfway across Tartarus to be told what's impossible by some minor goddess.'

The dust quivered at their feet. Fog swirled around them with a sound like agonized wailing.

'Minor goddess?' Akhlys's gnarled fingernails dug into Hercules's shield, gouging the metal. 'I was old before the

Titans were born, you ignorant girl. I was old when Gaia first woke. Misery is *eternal*. Existence is misery. I was born of the eldest ones – of Chaos and Night. I was –'

'Yes, yes,' Annabeth said. 'Sadness and misery, blah blah blah. But you still don't have enough power to hide two demigods with your Death Mist. Like I said: useless.'

Percy cleared his throat. 'Uh, Annabeth –'

She flashed him a warning look: *Work with me*. He realized how terrified she was, but she had no choice. This was their best shot at stirring the goddess into action.

'I mean . . . Annabeth is right!' Percy volunteered. 'Bob brought us all this way because he thought you could help. But I guess you're too busy staring at that shield and crying. I can't blame you. It looks just like you.'

Akhlys wailed and glared at the Titan. 'Why did you inflict these annoying children on me?'

Bob made a sound somewhere between a rumble and a whimper. 'I thought – I thought –'

'The Death Mist is not for *helping*!' Akhlys shrieked. 'It shrouds mortals in misery as their souls pass into the Underworld. It is the very breath of Tartarus, of death, of despair!'

'Awesome,' Percy said. 'Could we get two orders of that to go?'

Akhlys hissed. 'Ask me for a more sensible gift. I am also the goddess of poisons. I could give you death – thousands of ways to die less painful than the one you have chosen by marching into the heart of the pit.'

Around the goddess, flowers bloomed in the dust – dark

purple, orange and red blossoms that smelled sickly sweet. Percy's head swam.

'Nightshade,' Akhlys offered. 'Hemlock. Belladonna, henbane or strychnine. I can dissolve your innards, boil your blood.'

'That's very nice of you,' Percy said. 'But I've had enough poison for one trip. Now, can you hide us in your Death Mist, or not?'

'Yeah, it'll be fun,' Annabeth said.

The goddess's eyes narrowed. '*Fun?*'

'Sure,' Annabeth promised. 'If we fail, think how great it will be for you, gloating over our spirits when we die in agony. You'll get to say *I told you so* for eternity.'

'Or, if we succeed,' Percy added, 'think of all the suffering you'll bring to the monsters down here. We intend to seal the Doors of Death. That's going to cause a lot of wailing and moaning.'

Akhlys considered. 'I enjoy suffering. Wailing is also good.'

'Then it's settled,' Percy said. 'Make us invisible.'

Akhlys struggled to her feet. The shield of Hercules rolled away and wobbled to a stop in a patch of poison flowers. 'It is not so simple,' the goddess said. 'The Death Mist comes at the moment you are closest to your end. Your eyes will be clouded only then. The world will fade.'

Percy's mouth felt dry. 'Okay. But . . . we'll be shrouded from the monsters?'

'Oh, yes,' Akhlys said. 'If you survive the process, you will be able to pass unnoticed among the armies of Tartarus. It is hopeless, of course, but if you are determined, then come. I will show you the way.'

'The way to where, exactly?' Annabeth asked.

The goddess was already shuffling into the gloom.

Percy turned to look at Bob, but the Titan was gone. How does a ten-foot-tall silver dude with a very loud kitten disappear?

'Hey!' Percy yelled to Akhlys. 'Where's our friend?'

'He cannot take this path,' the goddess called back. 'He is not mortal. Come, little fools. Come, experience the Death Mist.'

Annabeth exhaled and grabbed his hand. 'Well . . . how bad can it be?'

The question was so ridiculous Percy laughed, even though it hurt his lungs. 'Yeah. Next date, though – dinner in New Rome.'

They followed the goddess's dusty footprints through the poison flowers, deeper into the fog.

XLVII

PERCY

PERCY MISSED BOB.

He'd got used to having the Titan on his side, lighting their way with his silver hair and his fearsome war broom.

Now their only guide was an emaciated corpse lady with serious self-esteem issues.

As they struggled across the dusty plain, the fog became so thick that Percy had to resist the urge to swat it away with his hands. The only reason he was able to follow Akhlys's path was because poisonous plants sprang up wherever she walked.

If they were still on the body of Tartarus, Percy figured they must be on the bottom of his foot – a rough, calloused expanse where only the most disgusting plant life grew.

Finally they arrived at the end of the big toe. At least that's what it looked like to Percy. The fog dissipated, and they found themselves on a peninsula that jutted out over a pitch-black void.

'Here we are.' Akhlys turned and leered at them. Blood

from her cheeks dripped on her dress. Her sickly eyes looked moist and swollen but somehow excited. Can Misery look excited?

'Uh . . . great,' Percy asked. 'Where is *here*?'

'The verge of final death,' Akhlys said. 'Where Night meets the void below Tartarus.'

Annabeth inched forward and peered over the cliff. 'I thought there was nothing below Tartarus.'

'Oh, certainly there is . . .' Akhlys coughed. 'Even Tartarus had to rise from somewhere. This is the edge of the earliest darkness, which was my mother. Below lies the realm of Chaos, my father. Here, you are closer to nothingness than any mortal has ever been. Can you not feel it?'

Percy knew what she meant. The void seemed to be pulling at him, leaching the breath from his lungs and the oxygen from his blood. He looked at Annabeth and saw that her lips were tinged blue.

'We can't stay here,' he said.

'No, indeed!' Akhlys said. 'Don't you feel the Death Mist? Even now, you pass between. Look!'

White smoke gathered around Percy's feet. As it coiled up his legs, he realized the smoke wasn't surrounding him. It was coming *from* him. His whole body was dissolving. He held up his hands and found they were fuzzy and indistinct. He couldn't even tell how many fingers he had. Hopefully still ten.

He turned to Annabeth and stifled a yelp. 'You're – uh –' He couldn't say it. She looked *dead*.

Her skin was sallow, her eye sockets dark and sunken. Her beautiful hair had dried into a skein of cobwebs. She looked like she'd been stuck in a cool, dark mausoleum for decades, slowly withering into a desiccated husk. When she turned to look at him, her features momentarily blurred into mist.

Percy's blood moved like sap in his veins.

For years, he had worried about Annabeth dying. When you're a demigod, that goes with the territory. Most half-bloods don't live long. You always knew that the next monster you fought could be your last. But seeing Annabeth like this was too painful. He'd rather stand in the River Phlegethon, or get attacked by *arai*, or be trampled by giants.

'Oh, gods,' Annabeth sobbed. 'Percy, the way you look . . .'

Percy studied his arms. All he saw were blobs of white mist, but he guessed that to Annabeth he looked like a corpse. He took a few steps, though it was difficult. His body felt insubstantial, like he was made of helium and cotton candy.

'I've looked better,' he decided. 'I can't move very well. But I'm all right.'

Akhlys clucked. 'Oh, you're definitely *not* all right.'

Percy frowned. 'But we'll pass unseen now? We can get to the Doors of Death?'

'Well, perhaps you could,' the goddess said, 'if you lived that long, which you won't.'

Akhlys spread her gnarled fingers. More plants bloomed along the edge of the pit – hemlock, nightshade and oleander spreading towards Percy's feet like a deadly carpet. 'The Death Mist is not simply a disguise, you see. It is a state of being. I could not bring you this gift unless death followed – true death.'

'It's a trap,' Annabeth said.

The goddess cackled. 'Didn't you *expect* me to betray you?'

'Yes,' Annabeth and Percy said together.

'Well, then, it was hardly a trap! More of an inevitability. Misery is inevitable. Pain is –'

'Yeah, yeah,' Percy growled. 'Let's get to the fighting.'

He drew Riptide, but the blade was made of smoke. When he slashed at Akhlys, the sword just floated across her like a gentle breeze.

The goddess's ruined mouth split into a grin. 'Did I forget to mention? You are only mist now – a shadow before death. Perhaps if you had time, you could learn to control your new form. But you do *not* have time. Since you cannot touch me, I fear any fight with Misery will be quite one-sided.'

Her fingernails grew into talons. Her jaw unhinged, and her yellow teeth elongated into fangs.

XLVIII

PERCY

AKHLYS LUNGED AT PERCY, and for a split second he thought: *Well, hey, I'm just smoke. She can't touch me, right?*

He imagined the Fates up in Olympus, laughing at his wishful thinking: *LOL, NOOB!*

The goddess's claws raked across his chest and stung like boiling water.

Percy stumbled backwards, but he wasn't used to being smoky. His legs moved too slowly. His arms felt like tissue paper. In desperation, he threw his backpack at her, thinking maybe it would turn solid when it left his hand, but no such luck. It fell with a soft thud.

Akhlys snarled, crouching to spring. She would have bitten Percy's face off if Annabeth hadn't charged and screamed *HEY!* right in the goddess's ear.

Akhlys flinched, turning towards the sound.

She lashed out at Annabeth, but Annabeth was better at moving than Percy. Maybe she wasn't feeling as smoky, or maybe she'd just had more combat training. She'd been at Camp Half-Blood since she was seven. Probably she'd had classes Percy never got, like How to Fight While Partially Made of Smoke.

Annabeth dived straight between the goddess's legs and somersaulted to her feet. Akhlys turned and attacked, but Annabeth dodged again, like a matador.

Percy was so stunned he lost a few precious seconds. He stared at corpse Annabeth, shrouded in mist but moving as fast and confidently as ever. Then it occurred to him why she was doing this: to buy them time. Which meant Percy needed to help.

He thought furiously, trying to come up with a way to defeat Misery. How could he fight when he couldn't touch anything?

On Akhlys's third attack, Annabeth wasn't so lucky. She tried to veer aside, but the goddess grabbed Annabeth's wrist and pulled her hard, sending her sprawling.

Before the goddess could pounce, Percy advanced, yelling and waving his sword. He still felt about as solid as a Kleenex, but his anger seemed to help him move faster.

'Hey, Happy!' he yelled.

Akhlys spun, dropping Annabeth's arm. 'Happy?' she demanded.

'Yeah!' He ducked as she swiped at his head. 'You're downright cheerful!'

'Arggh!' She lunged again, but she was off-balance. Percy sidestepped and backed away, leading the goddess further from Annabeth.

'Pleasant!' he called. 'Delightful!'

The goddess snarled and winced. She stumbled after Percy. Each compliment seemed to hit her like sand in the face.

'I will kill you slowly!' she growled, her eyes and nose watering, blood dripping from her cheeks. 'I will cut you into pieces as a sacrifice to Night!'

Annabeth struggled to her feet. She started rifling through her pack, no doubt looking for something that might help.

Percy wanted to give her more time. She was the brains. Better for him to get attacked while she came up with a brilliant plan.

'Cuddly!' Percy yelled. 'Fuzzy, warm and huggable!'

Akhlys made a growling, choking noise, like a cat having a seizure.

'A slow death!' she screamed. 'A death from a thousand poisons!'

All around her, poisonous plants grew and burst like over-filled balloons. Green-and-white sap trickled out, collecting into pools, and began flowing across the ground towards Percy. The sweet-smelling fumes made his head feel wobbly.

'Percy!' Annabeth's voice sounded far away. 'Uh, hey, Miss Wonderful! Cheerful! Grins! Over here!'

But the goddess of misery was now fixated on Percy. He tried to retreat again. Unfortunately the poison ichor was flowing all around him now, making the ground steam and the air burn. Percy found himself stuck on an island of dust not much bigger than a shield. A few yards away, his backpack smoked and dissolved into a puddle of goo. Percy had nowhere to go.

He fell to one knee. He wanted to tell Annabeth to run, but he couldn't speak. His throat was as dry as dead leaves.

He wished there were water in Tartarus – some nice pool he could jump into to heal himself, or maybe a river he could control. He'd settle for a bottle of Evian.

'You will feed the eternal darkness,' Akhlys said. 'You will die in the arms of Night!'

He was dimly aware of Annabeth shouting, throwing random pieces of drakon jerky at the goddess. The white-green poison kept pooling, little streams trickling from the plants as the venomous lake around him got wider and wider.

Lake, he thought. Streams. Water.

Probably it was just his brain getting fried from poison fumes, but he croaked out a laugh. Poison was liquid. If it moved like water, it must be partially water.

He remembered some science lecture about the human body being mostly water. He remembered extracting water from Jason's lungs back in Rome . . . If he could control *that*, then why not other liquids?

It was a crazy idea. Poseidon was the god of the sea, not of every liquid everywhere.

Then again, Tartarus had its own rules. Fire was drinkable. The ground was the body of a dark god. The air was acid, and demigods could be turned into smoky corpses.

So why not try? He had nothing left to lose.

He glared at the poison flood encroaching from all sides. He concentrated so hard that something inside him cracked – as if a crystal ball had shattered in his stomach.

Warmth flowed through him. The poison tide stopped.

The fumes blew away from him – back towards the goddess. The lake of poison rolled towards her in tiny waves and rivulets.

Akhlys shrieked. 'What is this?'

'Poison,' Percy said. 'That's your speciality, right?'

He stood, his anger growing hotter in his gut. As the flood of venom rolled towards the goddess, the fumes began to make her cough. Her eyes watered even more.

Oh, good, Percy thought. More water.

Percy imagined her nose and throat filling with her own tears.

Akhlys gagged. 'I –' The tide of venom reached her feet, sizzling like droplets on a hot iron. She wailed and stumbled back.

'Percy!' Annabeth called.

She'd retreated to the edge of the cliff, even though the poison wasn't after her. She sounded terrified. It took Percy a moment to realize she was terrified of *him*.

'Stop . . .' she pleaded, her voice hoarse.

He didn't want to stop. He wanted to choke this goddess. He wanted to watch her drown in her own poison. He wanted to see just how much misery Misery could take.

'Percy, please . . .' Annabeth's face was still pale and corpse-like, but her eyes were the same as always. The anguish in them made Percy's anger fade.

He turned to the goddess. He willed the poison to recede, creating a small path of retreat along the edge of the cliff.

'Leave!' he bellowed.

For an emaciated ghoul, Akhlys could run pretty fast when

she wanted to. She scrambled along the path, fell on her face and got up again, wailing as she sped into the dark.

As soon as she was gone, the pools of poison evaporated. The plants withered to dust and blew away.

Annabeth stumbled towards him. She looked like a corpse wreathed in smoke, but she felt solid enough when she gripped his arms.

'Percy, please don't ever . . .' Her voice broke in a sob. 'Some things aren't meant to be controlled. Please.'

His whole body tingled with power, but the anger was subsiding. The broken glass inside him was beginning to smooth at the edges.

'Yeah,' he said. 'Yeah, okay.'

'We have to get away from this cliff,' Annabeth said. 'If Akhlys brought us here as some kind of sacrifice . . .'

Percy tried to think. He was getting used to moving with the Death Mist around him. He felt more solid, more like himself. But his mind still felt stuffed with cotton wool.

'She said something about feeding us to the night,' he remembered. 'What was that about?'

The temperature dropped. The abyss before them seemed to exhale.

Percy grabbed Annabeth and backed away from the edge as a presence emerged from the void – a form so vast and shadowy he felt like he understood the concept of *dark* for the first time.

'I imagine,' said the darkness, in a feminine voice as soft as coffin lining, 'that she meant Night, with a capital N. After all, I am the only one.'

XLIX

LEO

THE WAY LEO FIGURED IT, he spent more time crashing than he did flying.

If there were a rewards card for frequent crashers, he'd be, like, double platinum level.

He regained consciousness as he was free-falling through the clouds. He had a hazy memory of Khione taunting him right before he got shot into the sky. He hadn't actually seen her, but he could never forget that snow witch's voice. He had no idea how long he'd been gaining altitude, but at some point he must have passed out from the cold and the lack of oxygen. Now he was on his way down, heading for his biggest crash ever.

The clouds parted around him. He saw the glittering sea far, *far* below. No sign of the *Argo II*. No sign of any coastline, familiar or otherwise, except for one tiny island at the horizon.

Leo couldn't fly. He had a couple of minutes at most before he'd hit the water and go *ker-splat*.

He decided he didn't like that ending to the Epic Ballad of Leo.

He was still clutching the Archimedes sphere, which didn't surprise him. Unconscious or not, he would never let go of his most valuable possession. With a little manoeuvring, he managed to pull some duct tape from his tool belt and strap the sphere to his chest. That made him look like a low-budget Iron Man, but at least he had both hands free. He started to work, furiously tinkering with the sphere, pulling out anything he thought would help from his magic tool belt: a drop cloth, metal extenders, some string and grommets.

Working while falling was almost impossible. The wind roared in his ears. It kept ripping tools, screws and canvas out of his hands, but finally he constructed a makeshift frame. He popped open a hatch on the sphere, teased out two wires and connected them to his crossbar.

How long until he hit the water? Maybe a minute?

He turned the sphere's control dial, and it whirred into action. More bronze wires shot from the orb, intuitively sensing what Leo needed. Cords laced up the canvas drop cloth. The frame began to expand on its own. Leo pulled out a can of kerosene and a rubber tube and lashed them to the thirsty new engine that the orb was helping him assemble.

Finally he made himself a rope halter and shifted so that the X-frame was attached to his back. The sea got closer and closer – a glittering expanse of slap-you-in-the-face death.

He yelled in defiance and punched the sphere's override switch.

The engine coughed to life. The makeshift rotor turned.

The canvas blades spun, but much too slowly. Leo's head was pointed straight down at the sea – maybe thirty seconds to impact.

At least nobody's around, he thought bitterly, or I'd be a demigod joke forever. *What was the last thing to go through Leo's mind? The Mediterranean.*

Suddenly the orb got warm against his chest. The blades turned faster. The engine coughed, and Leo tilted sideways, slicing through the air.

'YES!' he yelled.

He had successfully created the world's most dangerous personal helicopter.

He shot towards the island in the distance, but he was still falling much too fast. The blades shuddered. The canvas screamed.

The beach was only a few hundred yards away when the sphere turned lava-hot and the helicopter exploded, shooting flames in every direction. If he hadn't been immune to fire, Leo would have been charcoal. As it was, the midair explosion probably saved his life. The blast flung Leo sideways while the bulk of his flaming contraption smashed into the shore at full speed with a massive *KA-BOOM!*

Leo opened his eyes, amazed to be alive. He was sitting in a bathtub-sized crater in the sand. A few yards away, a column of thick black smoke roiled into the sky from a much larger crater. The surrounding beach was peppered with smaller pieces of burning wreckage.

'My sphere.' Leo patted his chest. The sphere wasn't there. His duct tape and rope halter had disintegrated.

He struggled to his feet. None of his bones seemed broken, which was good, but mostly he was worried about his Archimedes sphere. If he'd destroyed his priceless artefact to make a flaming thirty-second helicopter, he was going to track down that stupid snow goddess Khione and smack her with a monkey wrench.

He staggered across the beach, wondering why there weren't any tourists or hotels or boats in sight. The island seemed perfect for a resort, with blue water and soft white sand. Maybe it was uncharted. Did they still *have* uncharted islands in the world? Maybe Khione had blasted him out of the Mediterranean altogether. For all he knew, he was in Bora Bora.

The larger crater was about eight feet deep. At the bottom, the helicopter blades were still trying to turn. The engine belched smoke. The rotor croaked like a stepped-on frog, but *dang* – pretty impressive for a rush job.

The helicopter had apparently crashed *onto* something. The crater was littered with broken wooden furniture, shattered china plates, some half-melted pewter goblets and burning linen napkins. Leo wasn't sure why all that fancy stuff had been on the beach, but at least it meant that this place was inhabited, after all.

Finally he spotted the Archimedes sphere – steaming and charred but still intact, making unhappy clicking noises in the centre of the wreckage.

'Sphere!' he yelled. 'Come to Papa!'

He skidded to the bottom of the crater and snatched up the sphere. He collapsed, sat cross-legged and cradled the device in his hands. The bronze surface was searing hot, but Leo didn't care. It was still in one piece, which meant he could use it.

Now, if he could just figure out where he was and how to get back to his friends . . .

He was making a mental list of tools he might need when a girl's voice interrupted him: 'What are you *doing*? You blew up my dining table!'

Immediately Leo thought: *Uh-oh.*

He'd met a lot of goddesses, but the girl glaring down at him from the edge of the crater actually *looked* like a goddess.

She wore a sleeveless white Greek-style dress with a gold braided belt. Her hair was long, straight and golden brown – almost the same cinnamon-toast colour as Hazel's, but the similarity to Hazel ended there. The girl's face was milky pale, with dark almond-shaped eyes and pouty lips. She looked maybe fifteen, about Leo's age, and sure she was pretty, but with that angry expression on her face she reminded Leo of every popular girl in every school he'd ever attended – the ones who made fun of him, gossiped a lot, thought they were *so* superior and basically did everything they could to make his life miserable.

Leo disliked her instantly.

'Oh, I'm sorry!' he said. 'I just fell out of the sky. I constructed a helicopter in midair, burst into flames halfway down, crash-landed and barely survived. But by all means – let's talk about your dining table!'

He snatched up a half-melted goblet. 'Who puts a dining

table on the beach where innocent demigods can crash into it? Who *does* that?'

The girl clenched her fists. Leo was pretty sure she was going to march down the crater and punch him in the face. Instead she looked up at the sky.

'REALLY?' she screamed at the empty blue. 'You want to make my curse even *worse*? Zeus! Hephaestus! Hermes! Have you no shame?'

'Uh . . .' Leo noticed that she'd just picked three gods to blame, and one of them was his dad. He figured that wasn't a good sign. 'I doubt they're listening. You know, the whole split-personality thing –'

'Show yourself!' the girl yelled at the sky, completely ignoring Leo. 'It's not bad enough I am exiled? It's not bad enough you take away the few *good* heroes I'm allowed to meet? You think it's funny to send me this – this charbroiled runt of a boy to ruin my tranquillity? This is NOT FUNNY! Take him back!'

'Hey, Sunshine,' Leo said. 'I'm right here, you know.'

She growled like a cornered animal. 'Do *not* call me Sunshine! Get out of that hole and come with me *now* so I can get you off my island!'

'Well, since you asked so nicely . . .'

Leo didn't know what the crazy girl was so worked up about, but he didn't really care. If she could help him leave this island, that was totally fine by him. He clutched his charred sphere and climbed out of the crater. When he reached the top, the girl was already marching down the shoreline. He jogged to catch up.

She gestured in disgust at the burning wreckage. 'This was a pristine beach! Look at it now.'

'Yeah, my bad,' Leo muttered. 'I should've crashed on one of the other islands. Oh, wait – there aren't any!'

She snarled and kept walking along the edge of the water. Leo caught a whiff of cinnamon – maybe her perfume? Not that he cared. Her hair swayed down her back in a mesmerizing kind of way, which of course he didn't care about either.

He scanned the sea. Just like he'd seen during his fall, there were no landmasses or ships all the way to the horizon. Looking inland, he saw grassy hills dotted with trees. A footpath wound through a grove of cedars. Leo wondered where it led: probably to the girl's secret lair, where she roasted her enemies so she could eat them at her dining table on the beach.

He was so busy thinking about that he didn't notice when the girl stopped. He ran into her.

'Gah!' She turned and grabbed his arms to keep from falling in the surf. Her hands were strong, as though she worked with them for a living. Back at camp, the girls in the Hephaestus cabin had had strong hands like that, but she didn't look like a Hephaestus kid.

She glared at him, her dark almond eyes only a few inches from his. Her cinnamon smell reminded him of his *abuela*'s apartment. Man, he hadn't thought about that place in years.

The girl pushed him away. 'All right. This spot is good. Now tell me you want to leave.'

'What?' Leo's brain was still kind of muddled from the crash-landing. He wasn't sure he had heard her right.

'Do you want to *leave*?' she demanded. 'Surely you've got somewhere to go!'

'Uh . . . yeah. My friends are in trouble. I need to get back to my ship and –'

'Fine,' she snapped. 'Just say, *I want to leave Ogygia.*'

'Uh, okay.' Leo wasn't sure why, but her tone kind of hurt . . . which was stupid, since he didn't care what this girl thought. 'I want to leave – whatever you said.'

'Oh-gee-gee-ah.' The girl pronounced it slowly, as if Leo were five years old.

'I want to leave Oh-gee-gee-ah,' he said.

She exhaled, clearly relieved. 'Good. In a moment, a magical raft will appear. It will take you wherever you want to go.'

'Who *are* you?'

She looked like she was about to answer but stopped herself. 'It doesn't matter. You'll be gone soon. You're obviously a mistake.'

That was harsh, Leo thought.

He'd spent enough time thinking he was a mistake – as a demigod, on this quest, in life in general. He didn't need a random crazy goddess reinforcing the idea.

He remembered a Greek legend about a girl on an island . . . Maybe one of his friends had mentioned it? It didn't matter. As long as she let him leave.

'Any moment now . . .' The girl stared out at the water.

No magical raft appeared.

'Maybe it got stuck in traffic,' Leo said.

'This is wrong.' She glared at the sky. 'This is completely wrong!'

'So . . . plan B?' Leo asked. 'You got a phone, or –'

'Agh!' The girl turned and stormed inland. When she got to the footpath, she sprinted into the grove of trees and disappeared.

'Okay,' Leo said. 'Or you could just run away.'

From his tool-belt pouches he pulled some rope and a snap hook, then fastened the Archimedes sphere to his belt.

He looked out to sea. Still no magic raft.

He could stand here and wait, but he was hungry, thirsty and tired. He was banged up pretty bad from his fall.

He didn't want to follow that crazy girl, no matter how good she smelled.

On the other hand, he had no place else to go. The girl had a dining table, so she probably had food. And she seemed to find Leo's presence annoying.

'Annoying her is a plus,' he decided.

He followed her into the hills.

LEO

'HOLY HEPHAESTUS,' LEO SAID.

The path opened into the nicest garden Leo had ever seen. Not that he had spent a lot of time in gardens, but *dang*. On the left was an orchard and a vineyard – peach trees with red-golden fruit that smelled awesome in the warm sun, carefully pruned vines bursting with grapes, bowers of flowering jasmine and a bunch of other plants Leo couldn't name.

On the right were neat beds of vegetables and herbs, arranged like spokes around a big sparkling fountain where bronze satyrs spewed water into a central bowl.

At the back of the garden, where the footpath ended, a cave opened in the side of a grassy hill. Compared to Bunker Nine back at camp, the entrance was tiny, but it was impressive in its own way. On either side, crystalline rock had been carved into glittering Grecian columns. The tops were fitted with a bronze rod that held silky white curtains.

Leo's nose was assaulted by good smells – cedar, juniper, jasmine, peaches and fresh herbs. The aroma from the cave really caught his attention – like beef stew cooking.

He started towards the entrance. Seriously, how could he not? He stopped when he noticed the girl. She was kneeling in her vegetable garden, her back to Leo. She muttered to herself as she dug furiously with a trowel.

Leo approached her from one side so she could see him. He didn't feel like surprising her when she was armed with a sharp gardening implement.

She kept cursing in Ancient Greek and stabbing at the dirt. She had flecks of soil all over her arms, her face and her white dress, but she didn't seem to care.

Leo could appreciate that. She looked better with a little mud – less like a beauty queen and more like an actual get-your-hands-dirty kind of person.

'I think you've punished that dirt enough,' he offered.

She scowled at him, her eyes red and watery. 'Just go away.'

'You're crying,' he said, which was stupidly obvious, but seeing her that way took the wind out of his helicopter blades, so to speak. It was hard to stay mad at someone who was crying.

'None of your business,' she muttered. 'It's a big island. Just . . . find your own place. Leave me alone.' She waved vaguely towards the south. 'Go that way, maybe.'

'So, no magic raft,' Leo said. 'No other way off the island?'

'Apparently not!'

'What am I supposed to do, then? Sit in the sand dunes until I die?'

'That would be fine . . .' The girl threw down her trowel and cursed at the sky. 'Except I suppose he *can't* die here, can he? Zeus! This is not funny!'

Can't *die here*?

'Hold up.' Leo's head spun like a crankshaft. He couldn't quite translate what this girl was saying – like when he heard Spaniards or South Americans speaking Spanish. Yeah, he could understand it, sort of, but it sounded so different that it was almost another language.

'I'm going to need some more information here,' he said. 'You don't want me in your face, that's cool. I don't want to be here either. But I'm not going to go die and in a corner. I have to get off this island. There's *got* to be a way. Every problem has a fix.'

She laughed bitterly. 'You haven't lived very long, if you still believe that.'

The way she said it sent a shiver up his back. She looked the same age as him, but he wondered how old she really was.

'You said something about a curse,' he prompted.

She flexed her fingers, like she was practising her throat-strangling technique. 'Yes. I cannot leave Ogygia. My father, Atlas, fought against the gods, and I supported him.'

'Atlas,' Leo said. 'As in the *Titan* Atlas?'

The girl rolled her eyes. 'Yes, you impossible little . . .' Whatever she was going to say, she bit it back. 'I was imprisoned here, where I could cause the Olympians no trouble. About a year ago, after the Second Titan War, the gods vowed to forgive their enemies and offer amnesty. Supposedly Percy made them promise –'

'Percy,' Leo said. 'Percy Jackson?'

She squeezed her eyes shut. A tear trickled down her cheek.

Oh, Leo thought.

'Percy came here,' he said.

She dug her fingers into the soil. 'I – I thought I would be released. I dared to hope . . . but I am still here.'

Leo remembered now. The story was supposed to be a secret, but of course that meant it had spread like wildfire across the camp. Percy had told Annabeth. Months later, when Percy had gone missing, Annabeth told Piper. Piper told Jason . . .

Percy had talked about visiting this island. He had met a goddess who'd developed a major crush on him and wanted him to stay, but eventually she let him go.

'You're that lady,' Leo said. 'The one who was named after Caribbean music.'

Her eyes glinted murderously. 'Caribbean music.'

'Yeah. Reggae?' Leo shook his head. 'Merengue? Hold on, I'll get it.'

He snapped his fingers. 'Calypso! But Percy said you were awesome. He said you were all sweet and helpful, not, um . . .'

She shot to her feet. 'Yes?'

'Uh, nothing,' Leo said.

'Would you be *sweet*,' she demanded, 'if the gods forgot their promise to let you go? Would you be sweet if they *laughed* at you by sending another hero, but a hero who looked like – like *you*?'

'Is that a trick question?'

'*Di Immortales!*' She turned and marched into her cave.

'Hey!' Leo ran after her.

When he got inside, he lost his train of thought. The walls were made from multicoloured chunks of crystal. White curtains divided the cave into different rooms with comfy pillows and woven rugs and platters of fresh fruit. He spotted a harp in one corner, a loom in another and a big cooking pot where the stew was bubbling, filling the cavern with luscious smells.

The strangest thing? The chores were doing themselves. Towels floated through the air, folding and stacking into neat piles. Spoons washed themselves in a copper sink. The scene reminded Leo of the invisible wind spirits that had served him lunch at Camp Jupiter.

Calypso stood at a washbasin, cleaning the dirt off her arms.

She scowled at Leo, but she didn't yell at him to leave. She seemed to be running out of energy for her anger.

Leo cleared his throat. If he was going to get any help from this lady, he needed to be nice. 'So . . . I get why you're angry. You probably never want to see another demigod again. I guess that didn't sit right when, uh, Percy left you –'

'He was only the latest,' she growled. 'Before him, it was that pirate Drake. And before him, Odysseus. They were all the same! The gods send me the greatest heroes, the ones I cannot help but . . .'

'You fall in love with them,' Leo guessed. 'And then they leave you.'

Her chin trembled. 'That is my curse. I had hoped to be

free of it by now, but here I am, still stuck on Ogygia after three thousand years.'

'Three thousand.' Leo's mouth felt tingly, like he'd just eaten Pop Rocks. 'Uh, you look good for three thousand.'

'And now . . . the worst insult of all. The gods mock me by sending *you*.'

Anger bubbled in Leo's stomach.

Yeah, typical. If Jason were here, Calypso would fall all over him. She'd beg him to stay, but he'd be all noble about returning to his duties, and he'd leave Calypso brokenhearted. That magic raft would *totally* arrive for him.

But Leo? He was the annoying guest she couldn't get rid of. She'd never fall for him, because she was totally out of his league. Not that he cared. She wasn't his type anyway. She was way too annoying and beautiful and – well, it didn't matter.

'Fine,' he said. 'I'll leave you alone. I'll build something myself and get off this stupid island without your help.'

She shook her head sadly. 'You don't understand, do you? The gods are laughing at both of us. If the raft will not appear, that means they've closed Ogygia. You're stuck here the same as me. You can never leave.'

LI

LEO

THE FIRST FEW DAYS WERE THE WORST.

Leo slept outside on a bed of drop cloths under the stars.
It got cold at night, even on the beach in the summer, so he
built fires with the remains of Calypso's dining table. That
cheered him up a little.

During the days, he walked the circumference of the island
and found nothing of interest – unless you liked beaches
and endless sea in every direction. He tried to send an Iris-
message in the rainbows that formed in the sea spray, but he
had no luck. He didn't have any drachmas for an offering, and
apparently the goddess Iris wasn't interested in nuts and bolts.

He didn't even dream, which was unusual for him – or for
any demigod – so he had no idea what was going on in the
outside world. Had his friends got rid of Khione? Were they
looking for him, or had they sailed on to Epirus to complete
the quest?

He wasn't even sure what to hope for.

The dream he'd had back on the *Argo II* finally made sense to him – when the evil sorceress lady had told him to either jump off a cliff into the clouds, or descend into a dark tunnel where ghostly voices whispered. That tunnel must have represented the House of Hades, which Leo would never see now. He'd taken the cliff instead – falling through the sky to this stupid island. But in the dream Leo had been given a choice. In real life he'd had none. Khione had simply plucked him off his ship and shot him into orbit. Totally unfair.

The worst part of being stuck here? He was losing track of the days. He woke up one morning and couldn't remember if he'd been on Ogygia for three nights or four.

Calypso wasn't much help. Leo confronted her in the garden, but she just shook her head. 'Time is difficult here.'

Great. For all Leo knew, a century had passed in the real world and the war with Gaia was over for better or worse. Or maybe he'd only been on Ogygia for five minutes. His whole life might pass here in the time it took his friends on the *Argo II* to have breakfast.

Either way, he needed to get off this island.

Calypso took pity on him in some ways. She sent her invisible servants to leave bowls of stew and goblets of lemonade at the edge of the garden. She even sent him a few new sets of clothes – simple undyed cotton trousers and shirts that she must have made on her loom. They fitted him so well, Leo wondered how she'd got his measurements. Maybe she just used her generic pattern for SCRAWNY MALE.

Anyway, he was glad to have new threads, since his old ones were pretty smelly and burnt. Usually Leo could keep his clothes from burning when he caught fire, but it took concentration. Sometimes back at camp, if he wasn't thinking about it, he'd be working on some metal project at the hot forge, look down and realize his clothes had burned away, except for his magic tool belt and a smoking pair of underpants. Kind of embarrassing.

Despite the gifts, Calypso obviously didn't want to see him. One time he poked his head inside the cave and she freaked out, yelling and throwing pots at his head.

Yeah, she was *definitely* on Team Leo.

He ended up pitching a more permanent camp near the footpath, where the beach met the hills. That way he was close enough to pick up his meals, but Calypso didn't have to see him and go into a pot-throwing rage.

He made himself a lean-to with sticks and canvas. He dug a campfire pit. He even managed to build himself a bench and a worktable from some driftwood and dead cedar branches. He spent hours fixing the Archimedes sphere, cleaning it and repairing its circuits. He made himself a compass, but the needle would spin all crazy no matter what he tried. Leo guessed a GPS would have been useless, too. This island was designed to be off the charts, impossible to leave.

He remembered the old bronze astrolabe he'd picked up in Bologna – the one the dwarfs told him Odysseus had made. He had a sneaking suspicion Odysseus had been thinking about this island when he constructed it, but unfortunately

Leo had left it back on the ship with Buford the Wonder Table. Besides, the dwarfs had told him the astrolabe didn't work. Something about a missing crystal . . .

He walked the beach, wondering why Khione had sent him here – assuming his landing here wasn't an accident. Why not just kill him instead? Maybe Khione wanted him to be in limbo forever. Perhaps she knew the gods were too incapacitated to pay attention to Ogygia, and so the island's magic was broken. That could be why Calypso was still stuck here and why the magic raft wouldn't appear for Leo.

Or maybe the magic of this place was working just fine. The gods had punished Calypso by sending her buff courageous dudes who left as soon as she fell for them. Maybe that was the problem. Calypso would *never* fall for Leo. She *wanted* him to leave. So they were stuck in a vicious circle. If that was Khione's plan . . . wow. Major-league devious.

Then one morning he made a discovery, and things got even more complicated.

Leo was walking in the hills, following a little brook that ran between two big cedar trees. He liked this area – it was the only place on Ogygia where he couldn't see the sea, so he could pretend he wasn't stuck on an island. In the shade of the trees, he almost felt like he was back at Camp Half-Blood, heading through the woods towards Bunker Nine.

He jumped over the creek. Instead of landing on soft earth, his feet hit something much harder.

CLANG.

Metal.

Excited, Leo dug through the mulch until he saw the glint of bronze.

'Oh, man.' He giggled like a crazy person as he excavated the scraps.

He had no idea why the stuff was here. Hephaestus was always tossing broken parts out of his godly workshop and littering the earth with scrap metal, but what were the chances some of it would hit Ogygia?

Leo found a handful of wires, a few bent gears, a piston that might still work and several hammered sheets of Celestial bronze – the smallest the size of a drink coaster, the largest the size of a war shield.

It wasn't a lot – not compared to Bunker Nine or even to his supplies aboard the *Argo II*. But it was more than sand and rocks.

He looked up at the sunlight winking through the cedar branches. 'Dad? If you sent this here for me – thanks. If you didn't . . . well, thanks, anyway.'

He gathered up his treasure trove and lugged it back to his campsite.

After that, the days passed more quickly, and with a lot more noise.

First Leo made himself a forge out of mud bricks, each one baked with his own fiery hands. He found a large rock he could use as an anvil base, and he pulled nails from his tool belt until he had enough to melt into a plate for a hammering surface.

Once that was done, he began to recast the Celestial bronze scraps. Each day his hammer rang on bronze until his rock anvil broke, or his tongs bent, or he ran out of firewood.

Each evening he collapsed, drenched in sweat and covered in soot, but he felt great. At least he was working, trying to solve his problem.

The first time Calypso came to check on him, it was to complain about the noise.

'Smoke and fire,' she said. 'Clanging on metal all day long. You're scaring away the birds!'

'Oh, no, not the birds!' Leo grumbled.

'What do you hope to accomplish?'

He glanced up and almost smashed his thumb with his hammer. He'd been staring at metal and fire so long he'd forgotten how beautiful Calypso was. *Annoyingly* beautiful. She stood there with the sunlight in her hair, her white skirt fluttering around her legs, a basket of grapes and fresh-baked bread tucked under one arm.

Leo tried to ignore his rumbling stomach.

'I'm *hoping* to get off this island,' he said. 'That is what you want, right?'

Calypso scowled. She set the basket near his bedroll. 'You haven't eaten in two days. Take a break and *eat*.'

'Two days?' Leo hadn't even noticed, which surprised him, since he liked food. He was even more surprised that Calypso *had* noticed.

'Thanks,' he muttered. 'I'll, uh, try to hammer more quietly.'

'Huh.' She sounded unimpressed.

After that, she didn't complain about the noise or the smoke.

The next time she visited, Leo was putting the final touches to his first project. He didn't see her approach until she spoke right behind him.

'I brought you –'

Leo jumped, dropping his wires. 'Bronze bulls, girl! Don't sneak up on me like that!'

She was wearing red today – Leo's favourite colour. That was completely irrelevant. She looked really good in red. Also irrelevant.

'I wasn't *sneaking*,' she said. 'I was bringing you these.'

She showed him the clothes that were folded over her arm: a new pair of jeans, a white T-shirt, an army fatigue jacket . . . wait, those were *his* clothes, except that they couldn't be. His original army jacket had burned up months ago. He hadn't been *wearing* it when he landed on Ogygia. But the clothes Calypso held looked exactly like the clothes he'd been wearing the first day he'd arrived at Camp Half-Blood – except these looked bigger, resized to fit him better.

'How?' he asked.

Calypso set the clothes at his feet and backed away as if he were a dangerous beast. 'I do have a little magic, you know. You keep burning through the clothes I give you, so I thought I would weave something less flammable.'

'These won't burn?' He picked up the jeans, but they felt just like normal denim.

'They are completely fireproof,' Calypso promised. 'They'll

stay clean and expand to fit you, should you ever become less scrawny.'

'Thanks.' He meant it to sound sarcastic, but he was honestly impressed. Leo could make a lot of things, but an inflammable, self-cleaning outfit wasn't one of them. 'So . . . you made an exact replica of my favourite outfit. Did you, like, google me or something?'

She frowned. 'I don't know that word.'

'You looked me up,' he said. 'Almost like you had some interest in me.'

She wrinkled her nose. 'I have an interest in not making you a new set of clothes every other day. I have an interest in you not smelling so bad and walking around my island in smouldering rags.'

'Oh, yeah.' Leo grinned. 'You're really warming up to me.'

Her face got even redder. 'You are the most insufferable person I have ever met! I was only returning a favour. You fixed my fountain.'

'That?' Leo laughed. The problem had been so simple he'd almost forgotten about it. One of the bronze satyrs had been turned sideways and the water pressure was off, so it started making an annoying ticking sound, jiggling up and down and spewing water over the rim of the pool. He'd pulled out a couple of tools and fixed it in about two minutes. 'That was no big deal. I don't like it when things don't work right.'

'And the curtains across the cave entrance?'

'The rod wasn't level.'

'And my gardening tools?'

'Look, I just sharpened the shears. Cutting vines with a

dull blade is dangerous. And the pruners needed to be oiled at the hinge, and –'

'Oh, yeah,' Calypso said, in a pretty good imitation of his voice. 'You're really warming up to me.'

For once, Leo was speechless. Calypso's eyes glittered. He knew she was making fun of him, but somehow it didn't feel mean.

She pointed at his worktable. 'What are you building?'

'Oh.' He looked at the bronze mirror, which he'd just finished wiring up to the Archimedes sphere. In the screen's polished surface, his own reflection surprised him. His hair had grown out longer and curlier. His face was thinner and more chiselled, maybe because he hadn't been eating. His eyes were dark and a little ferocious when he wasn't smiling – kind of a Tarzan look, if Tarzan came in extra-small Latino. He couldn't blame Calypso for backing away from him.

'Uh, it's a seeing device,' he said. 'We found one like this in Rome, in the workshop of Archimedes. If I can make it work, maybe I can find out what's going on with my friends.'

Calypso shook her head. 'That's impossible. This island is hidden, cut off from the world by strong magic. Time doesn't even flow the same here.'

'Well, you've got to have some kind of outside contact. How did you find out that I used to wear an army jacket?'

She twisted her hair as if the question made her uncomfortable. 'Seeing the past is simple magic. Seeing the present or the future – that is not.'

'Yeah, well,' Leo said. 'Watch and learn, Sunshine. I just connect these last two wires, and –'

The bronze plate sparked. Smoke billowed from the sphere. A flash fire raced up Leo's sleeve. He pulled off his shirt, threw it down and stomped on it.

He could tell Calypso was trying not to laugh, but she was shaking with the effort.

'Not a word,' Leo warned.

She glanced at his bare chest, which was sweaty, bony and streaked with old scars from weapon-making accidents.

'Nothing worth commenting on,' she assured him. 'If you want that device to work, perhaps you should try a musical invocation.'

'Right,' he said. 'Whenever an engine malfunctions, I like to tap-dance around it. Works every time.'

She took a deep breath and began to sing.

Her voice hit him like a cool breeze – like that first cold front in Texas when the summer heat finally breaks and you start to believe things might get better. Leo couldn't understand the words, but the song was plaintive and bittersweet, as if she were describing a home she could never return to.

Her singing was magic, no doubt. But it wasn't like Medea's trance-inducing voice, or even Piper's charmspeak. The music didn't want anything from him. It simply reminded him of his best memories – building things with his mom in her workshop; sitting in the sunshine with his friends at camp. It made him miss home.

Calypso stopped singing. Leo realized he was staring like an idiot.

'Any luck?' she asked.

'Uh . . .' He forced his eyes back to the bronze mirror. 'Nothing. Wait . . .'

The screen glowed. In the air above it, holographic pictures shimmered to life.

Leo recognized the commons at Camp Half-Blood.

There was no sound, but Clarisse La Rue from the Ares cabin was yelling orders at the campers, forming them into lines. Leo's brethren from Cabin Nine hurried around, fitting everyone with armour and passing out weapons.

Even Chiron the centaur was dressed for war. He trotted up and down the ranks, his plumed helmet gleaming, his legs decked in bronze greaves. His usual friendly smile was gone, replaced with a look of grim determination.

In the distance, Greek triremes floated on Long Island Sound, prepped for war. Along the hills, catapults were being primed. Satyrs patrolled the fields, and riders on pegasi circled overhead, alert for aerial attacks.

'Your friends?' Calypso asked.

Leo nodded. His face felt numb. 'They're preparing for war.'

'Against whom?'

'Look,' Leo said.

The scene changed. A phalanx of Roman demigods marched through a moonlit vineyard. An illuminated sign in the distance read: GOLDSMITH WINERY.

'I've seen that sign before,' Leo said. 'That's not far from Camp Half-Blood.'

Suddenly the Roman ranks deteriorated into chaos.

Demigods scattered. Shields fell. Javelins swung wildly, like the whole group had stepped in fire ants.

Darting through the moonlight were two small hairy shapes dressed in mismatched clothes and garish hats. They seemed to be everywhere at once – whacking Romans on the head, stealing their weapons, cutting their belts so their trousers fell around their ankles.

Leo couldn't help grinning. 'Those beautiful little trouble-makers! They kept their promise.'

Calypso leaned in, watching the Kerkopes. 'Cousins of yours?'

'Ha, ha, ha, no,' Leo said. 'Couple of dwarfs I met in Bologna. I sent them to slow down the Romans, and they're doing it.'

'But for how long?' Calypso wondered.

Good question. The scene shifted again. Leo saw Octavian – that no-good blond scarecrow of an augur. He stood in a gas-station parking lot, surrounded by black SUVs and Roman demigods. He held up a long pole wrapped in canvas. When he uncovered it, a golden eagle glimmered at the top.

'Oh, that's not good,' Leo said.

'A Roman standard,' Calypso noted.

'Yeah. And this one shoots lightning, according to Percy.'

As soon as he said Percy's name, Leo regretted it. He glanced at Calypso. He could see in her eyes how much she was struggling, trying to marshal her emotions into neat orderly rows like strands on her loom. What surprised Leo most was the surge of anger he felt. It wasn't just annoyance or jealousy. He was *mad* at Percy for hurting this girl.

He refocused on the holographic images. Now he saw a single rider – Reyna, the praetor from Camp Jupiter – flying through a storm on the back of a light-brown pegasus. Reyna's dark hair flew in the wind. Her purple cloak fluttered, revealing the glimmer of her armour. She was bleeding from cuts on her arms and face. Her pegasus's eyes were wild, his mouth slathering from hard riding, but Reyna peered steadfastly forward into the storm.

As Leo watched, a wild gryphon dived out of the clouds. It raked its claws across the horse's ribs, almost throwing Reyna. She drew her sword and slashed the monster down. Seconds later, three *venti* appeared – dark air spirits swirling like miniature tornadoes laced with lightning. Reyna charged them, yelling defiantly.

Then the bronze mirror went dark.

'No!' Leo yelled. 'No, not now. Show me what happens!' He banged on the mirror. 'Calypso, can you sing again or something?'

She glared at him. 'I suppose that is your girlfriend? Your Penelope? Your Elizabeth? Your Annabeth?'

'What?' Leo couldn't figure this girl out. Half the stuff she said made no sense. 'That's Reyna. She's not my girlfriend! I need to see more! I need –'

NEED, a voice rumbled in the ground beneath his feet. Leo staggered, suddenly feeling like he was standing on the surface of a trampoline.

NEED is an overused word. A swirling human figure erupted from the sand – Leo's least favourite goddess, the Mistress of Mud, the Princess of Potty Sludge, Gaia herself.

Leo threw a pair of pliers at her. Unfortunately she wasn't solid and they passed right through. Her eyes were closed, but she didn't look asleep, exactly. She had a smile on her dust-devil face, as if she was intently listening to her favourite song. Her sandy robes shifted and folded, reminding Leo of the undulating fins on that stupid shrimpzilla monster they'd fought in the Atlantic. For his money, though, Gaia was uglier.

You want to live, Gaia said. *You want to join your friends. But you do not need this, my poor boy. It would make no difference. Your friends will die, regardless.*

Leo's legs shook. He hated it, but whenever this witch appeared he felt like he was eight years old again, trapped in the lobby of his mom's machine shop, listening to Gaia's soothing evil voice while his mother was locked inside the burning warehouse, dying from heat and smoke.

'What I *don't* need,' he growled, 'is more lies from you, Dirt Face. You told me my great-granddad died in the 1960s. Wrong! You told me I couldn't save my friends in Rome. Wrong! You told me a lot of things.'

Gaia's laughter was a soft rustling sound, like gravel trickling down a hill in the first moments of an avalanche.

I tried to help you make better choices. You could have saved yourself. But you defied me at every step. You built your ship. You joined that foolish quest. Now you are trapped here, helpless, while the mortal world dies.

Leo's hands burst into flame. He wanted to melt Gaia's sandy face to glass. Then he felt Calypso's hand on his shoulder.

'Gaia.' Her voice was stern and steady. 'You are not welcome.'

Leo wished he could sound as confident as Calypso. Then he remembered that this annoying fifteen-year-old girl was actually the immortal daughter of a Titan.

Ah, Calypso. Gaia raised her arms as if for a hug. *Still here, I see, despite the gods' promises. Why do you think that is, my dear grandchild? Are the Olympians being spiteful, leaving you with no company except this undergrown fool? Or have they simply forgotten you, because you are not worth their time?*

Calypso stared straight through the swirling face of Gaia, all the way to the horizon.

Yes, Gaia murmured sympathetically. *The Olympians are faithless. They do not give second chances. Why do you hold out hope? You supported your father, Atlas, in his great war. You knew that the gods must be destroyed. Why do you hesitate now? I offer you a chance that Zeus would never give you.*

'Where were you these last three thousand years?' Calypso asked. 'If you are so concerned with my fate, why do you visit me only now?'

Gaia turned up her palms. *The earth is slow to wake. War comes in its own time. But do not think it will pass you by on Ogygia. When I remake the world, this prison will be destroyed as well.*

'Ogygia destroyed?' Calypso shook her head, as if she couldn't imagine those two words going together.

You do not have to be here when that happens, Gaia promised. *Join me now. Kill this boy. Spill his blood upon the earth, and help me to wake. I will free you and grant you any wish. Freedom.*

Revenge against the gods. Even a prize. Would you still have the demigod Percy Jackson? I will spare him for you. I will raise him from Tartarus. He will be yours to punish or to love, as you choose. Only kill this trespassing boy. Show your loyalty.

Several scenarios went through Leo's head – none of them good. He was positive Calypso would strangle him on the spot, or order her invisible wind servants to chop him into a Leo purée.

Why wouldn't she? Gaia was making her the ultimate deal – kill one annoying guy, get a handsome one free!

Calypso thrust her hand towards Gaia in a three-fingered gesture Leo recognized from Camp Half-Blood: the Ancient Greek ward against evil. 'This is not just my prison, Grandmother. It is my home. And *you* are the trespasser.'

The wind ripped Gaia's form into nothingness, scattering the sand into the blue sky.

Leo swallowed. 'Uh, don't take this the wrong way, but you didn't kill me. Are you crazy?'

Calypso's eyes smouldered with anger, but for once Leo didn't think the anger was aimed at him. 'Your friends must need you, or else Gaia would not ask for your death.'

'I – uh, yeah. I guess.'

'Then we have work to do,' she said. 'We must get you back to your ship.'

LII

LEO

LEO THOUGHT HE'D BEEN BUSY BEFORE. When Calypso set her mind to something, she was a machine.

Within a day, she'd gathered enough supplies for a week-long voyage – food, flasks of water, herbal medicines from her garden. She wove a sail big enough for a small yacht and made enough rope for all the rigging.

She got so much done that by the second day she asked Leo if he needed any help with his own project.

He looked up from the circuit board that was slowly coming together. 'If I didn't know better, I'd think you were anxious to get rid of me.'

'That's a bonus,' she admitted. She was dressed for work in a pair of jeans and a grubby white T-shirt. When he asked her about the wardrobe change, she claimed she had realized how practical these clothes were after making some for Leo.

In the blue jeans, she didn't look much like a goddess. Her T-shirt was covered with grass and dirt stains, like she'd just run through a swirling Gaia. Her feet were bare. Her cinnamon-toast hair was tied back, which made her almond eyes look even larger and more startling. Her hands were calloused and blistered from working with rope.

Looking at her, Leo felt a tugging in his stomach that he couldn't quite explain.

'So?' she prompted.

'So . . . what?'

She nodded at the circuitry. 'So can I help? How is it coming on?'

'Oh, uh, I'm good here. I guess. If I can wire this thing up to the boat, I should be able to navigate back to the world.'

'Now all you need is a boat.'

He tried to read her expression. He wasn't sure if she was annoyed that he was still here or wistful that she wasn't leaving too. Then he looked at all the supplies she'd stacked up – easily enough for two people for several days.

'What Gaia said . . .' He hesitated. 'About you getting off this island. Would you want to try it?'

She scowled. 'What do you mean?'

'Well . . . I'm not saying it would be fun having you along, always complaining and glaring at me and stuff. But I suppose I could stand it, if you wanted to try.'

Her expression softened just a little.

'How noble,' she muttered. 'But no, Leo. If I tried to come with you, your tiny chance of escape would be no chance at all. The gods have placed ancient magic on this island to keep me here. A hero can leave. I cannot. The most important thing is getting you free so you can stop Gaia. Not that I care what happens to you,' she added quickly. 'But the world's fate is at stake.'

'Why would you care about that?' he asked. 'I mean, after being away from the world for so long?'

She arched her eyebrows, as if surprised that he'd asked a sensible question. 'I suppose I don't like being told what to do – by Gaia or anyone else. As much as I hate the gods sometimes, over the past three millennia I've come to see that they're better than the Titans. They're *definitely* better than the giants. At least the gods kept in touch. Hermes has always been kind to me. And your father, Hephaestus, has often visited. He is a good person.'

Leo wasn't sure what to make of her faraway tone. She almost sounded like she was pondering *his* worth, not his dad's.

She reached out and closed his mouth. He hadn't realized it was hanging open.

'Now,' Calypso said, 'how can I help?'

'Oh.' He stared down at his project, but when he spoke he blurted out an idea that had been forming ever since Calypso had made his new clothes. 'You know that flameproof cloth? You think you could make me a little bag of that fabric?'

He described the dimensions. Calypso waved her hand impatiently. 'That will only take minutes. Will it help on your quest?'

'Yeah. It might save a life. And, um, could you chip off a little piece of crystal from your cave? I don't need much.'

She frowned. 'That's an odd request.'

'Humour me.'

'All right. Consider it done. I'll make the fireproof pouch tonight at the loom, when I've cleaned up. But what can I do now, while my hands are dirty?'

She held up her calloused, grimy fingers. Leo couldn't help thinking there was *nothing* hotter than a girl who didn't mind getting her hands dirty. But of course that was just a general comment. Didn't apply to Calypso. Obviously.

'Well,' he said, 'you could twist some more bronze coils. But that's kind of specialized –'

She pushed in next to him on the bench and began to work, her hands braiding the bronze wiring faster than he could have. 'Just like weaving,' she said. 'This isn't so hard.'

'Huh,' Leo said. 'Well, if you ever get off this island and want a job, let me know. You're not a total klutz.'

She smirked. 'A job, eh? Making things in your forge?'

'Nah, we could start our own shop,' Leo said, surprising himself. Starting a machine shop had always been one of his dreams, but he'd never told anyone about it. 'Leo and Calypso's Garage: Auto Repair and Mechanical Monsters.'

'Fresh fruits and vegetables,' Calypso offered.

'Lemonade and stew,' Leo added. 'We could even provide entertainment. You could sing and I could, like, randomly burst into flames.'

Calypso laughed – a clear, happy sound that made Leo's heart go *ka-bump*.

'See,' he said, 'I'm funny.'

She managed to kill her smile. 'You are *not* funny. Now, get back to work, or no lemonade and stew.'

'Yes, ma'am,' he said. They worked in silence, side by side, for the rest of the afternoon.

Two nights later, the guidance console was finished.

Leo and Calypso sat on the beach, near the spot where Leo had destroyed the dining table, and they ate a picnic dinner together. The full moon turned the waves to silver. Their campfire sent orange sparks into the sky. Calypso wore a fresh white shirt and her jeans, which she'd apparently decided to live in.

Behind them in the dunes, the supplies were carefully packed and ready to go.

'All we need now is a boat,' Calypso said.

Leo nodded. He tried not to linger on the word *we*. Calypso had made it clear she wasn't going.

'I can start chopping wood into boards tomorrow,' Leo said. 'Few days, we'll have enough for a small hull.'

'You've made a ship before,' Calypso remembered. 'Your *Argo II*.'

Leo nodded. He thought about all those months he'd spent creating the *Argo II*. Somehow, making a boat to sail from Ogygia seemed like a more daunting task.

'So how long until you sail?' Calypso's tone was light, but she didn't meet his eyes.

'Uh, not sure. Another week?' For some reason, saying that made Leo feel less agitated. When he had got here, he couldn't wait to leave. Now, he was glad he had a few more days. Weird.

Calypso ran her fingers across the completed circuit board. 'This took so long to make.'

'You can't rush perfection.'

A smile tugged at the edge of her mouth. 'Yes, but will it work?'

'Getting out, no problem,' Leo said. 'But to get back I'll need Festus and –'

'*What?*'

Leo blinked. 'Festus. My bronze dragon. Once I figure out how to rebuild him, I'll –'

'You told me about Festus,' Calypso said. 'But what do you mean *get back?*'

Leo grinned nervously. 'Well . . . to get back here, duh. I'm sure I said that.'

'You most definitely did not.'

'I'm not gonna leave you here! After you helped me and everything? Of course I'm coming back. Once I rebuild Festus, he'll be able to handle an improved guidance system. There's this astrolabe that I, uh . . .' He stopped, deciding it was best not to mention that it had been built by one of Calypso's old flames. '. . . that I found in Bologna. Anyway, I think with that crystal you gave me –'

'You can't come back,' Calypso insisted.

Leo's heart went *clunk*. 'Because I'm not welcome?'

'Because you *can't*. It's impossible. No man finds Ogygia twice. That is the rule.'

Leo rolled his eyes. 'Yeah, well, you might've noticed I'm not good at following rules. I'm coming back here with my dragon, and we'll spring you. Take you wherever you want to go. It's only fair.'

'Fair . . .' Calypso's voice was barely audible.

In the firelight, her eyes looked so sad, Leo couldn't stand it. Did she think he was lying to her just to make her feel better? He considered it a given that he would come back and free her from this island. How could he not?

'You didn't really think I could start Leo and Calypso's Auto Repair without Calypso, did you?' he asked. 'I can't make lemonade and stew, and I *sure* can't sing.'

She stared at the sand.

'Well, anyway,' Leo said, 'tomorrow I'll start on the lumber. And in a few days . . .'

He looked out over the water. Something was bobbing on the waves. Leo watched in disbelief as a large wooden raft floated in on the tide and slid to a stop on the beach.

Leo was too dazed to move, but Calypso sprang to her feet.

'Hurry!' She sprinted across the beach, grabbed some supply bags and ran them to the raft. 'I don't know how long it will stay!'

'But . . .' Leo stood. His legs felt like they'd turned to rock. He had just convinced himself he had another week on Ogygia. Now he didn't have time to finish dinner. 'That's the magic raft?'

'Duh!' Calypso yelled. 'It *might* work like it's supposed to and take you where you want to go. But we can't be sure. The island's magic is obviously unstable. You must rig up your guidance device to navigate.'

She snatched up the console and ran towards the raft, which got Leo moving. He helped her fasten it to the raft and run wires to the small rudder in the back. The raft was already fitted with a mast, so Leo and Calypso hauled their sail aboard and started on the rigging.

They worked side by side in perfect harmony. Even among the Hephaestus campers, Leo had never worked with anyone as intuitive as this immortal gardener girl. In no time, they had the sail in place and all the supplies aboard. Leo hit the buttons on the Archimedes sphere, muttered a prayer to his dad, Hephaestus, and the Celestial bronze console hummed to life.

The rigging tightened. The sail turned. The raft began scraping against the sand, straining to reach the waves.

'Go,' Calypso said.

Leo turned. She was so close he couldn't stand it. She smelled like cinnamon and wood smoke, and he thought he'd never smell anything that good again.

'The raft finally got here,' he said.

Calypso snorted. Her eyes might have been red, but it was hard to tell in the moonlight. 'You just noticed?'

'But if it only shows up for guys you like –'

'Don't push your luck, Leo Valdez,' she said. 'I *still* hate you.'

'Okay.'

'And you are *not* coming back here,' she insisted. 'So don't give me any empty promises.'

'How about a *full* promise?' he said. 'Because I'm definitely –'

She grabbed his face and pulled him into a kiss, which effectively shut him up.

For all his joking and flirting, Leo had never kissed a girl before. Well, sisterly pecks on the cheek from Piper, but that didn't count. This was a real, full-contact kiss. If Leo had had gears and wires in his brain, they would've short-circuited.

Calypso pushed him away. 'That didn't happen.'

'Okay.' His voice sounded an octave higher than usual.

'Get out of here.'

'Okay.'

She turned, wiping her eyes furiously, and stormed up the beach, the breeze tousling her hair.

Leo wanted to call to her, but the sail caught the full force of the wind and the raft cleared the beach. He struggled to align the guidance console. By the time Leo looked back, the island of Ogygia was a dark line in the distance, their campfire pulsing like a tiny orange heart.

His lips still tingled from the kiss.

That didn't happen, he told himself. *I can't be in love with an immortal girl. She definitely can't be in love with me. Not possible.*

As his raft skimmed over the water, taking him back to the mortal world, he understood a line from the Prophecy better – *an oath to keep with a final breath.*

He understood how dangerous oaths could be. But Leo didn't care.

'I'm coming back for you, Calypso,' he said to the night wind. 'I swear it on the River Styx.'

LIII

ANNABETH

ANNABETH HAD NEVER BEEN SCARED OF THE DARK.

But normally the dark wasn't forty feet tall. It didn't have black wings, a whip made out of stars and a shadowy chariot pulled by vampire horses.

Nyx was almost too much to take in. Looming over the chasm, she was a churning figure of ash and smoke, as big as the Athena Parthenos statue, but very much alive. Her dress was void black, mixed with the colours of a space nebula, as if galaxies were being born in her bodice. Her face was hard to see except for the pinpoints of her eyes, which shone like quasars. When her wings beat, waves of darkness rolled over the cliffs, making Annabeth feel heavy and sleepy, her eyesight dim.

The goddess's chariot was made of the same material as Nico di Angelo's sword – Stygian iron – pulled by two massive horses, all black except for their pointed silver fangs. The beasts' legs floated in the abyss, turning from solid to smoke as they moved.

The horses snarled and bared their fangs at Annabeth. The goddess lashed her whip – a thin streak of stars like diamond barbs – and the horses reared back.

'No, Shade,' the goddess said. 'Down, Shadow. These little prizes are not for you.'

Percy eyed the horses as they nickered. He was still shrouded in Death Mist, so he looked like an out-of-focus corpse – which broke Annabeth's heart every time she saw him. It also must not have been very good camouflage, since Nyx could obviously see them.

Annabeth couldn't read the expression on Percy's ghoulish face very well. Apparently he didn't like whatever the horses were saying.

'Uh, so you won't let them eat us?' he asked the goddess. 'They really want to eat us.'

Nyx's quasar eyes burned. 'Of course not. I would not let my horses eat you, any more than I would let Akhlys kill you. Such fine prizes, I will kill myself!'

Annabeth didn't feel particularly witty or courageous, but her instincts told her to take the initiative or this would be a very short conversation.

'Oh, don't kill yourself!' she cried. 'We're not *that* scary.'

The goddess lowered her whip. 'What? No, I didn't mean –'

'Well, I'd hope not!' Annabeth looked at Percy and forced a laugh. 'We wouldn't want to scare her, would we?'

'Ha, ha,' Percy said weakly. 'No, we wouldn't.'

The vampire horses looked confused. They reared and snorted and knocked their dark heads together. Nyx pulled back on the reins.

'Do you know who I am?' she demanded.

'Well, you're Night, I suppose,' said Annabeth. 'I mean, I can tell because you're *dark* and everything, though the brochure didn't say much about you.'

Nyx's eyes winked out for a moment. 'What brochure?'

Annabeth patted her pockets. 'We had one, didn't we?'

Percy licked his lips. 'Uh-huh.' He was still watching the horses, his hand tight on his sword hilt, but he was smart enough to follow Annabeth's lead. Now she just had to hope she wasn't making things worse . . . though, honestly, she didn't see how things *could* be worse.

'Anyway,' she said, 'I guess the brochure didn't say much because you weren't spotlighted on the tour. We got to see the River Phlegethon, the Cocytus, the *arai*, the poison glade of Akhlys, even some random Titans and giants, but Nyx . . . hmm, no, you weren't really featured.'

'*Featured? Spotlighted?*'

'Yeah,' Percy said, warming up to the idea. 'We came down here for the Tartarus tour – like, exotic destinations, you know? The Underworld is overdone. Mount Olympus is a tourist trap –'

'Gods, totally!' Annabeth agreed. 'So we booked the Tartarus excursion, but no one even mentioned we'd run into Nyx. Huh. Oh, well. Guess they didn't think you were important.'

'Not important!' Nyx cracked her whip. Her horses bucked and snapped their silvery fangs. Waves of darkness rolled out of the chasm, turning Annabeth's insides to jelly, but she couldn't show her fear.

She pushed down Percy's sword arm, forcing him to lower his weapon. This was a goddess beyond anything they had ever faced. Nyx was older than any Olympian or Titan or giant, older even than Gaia. She couldn't be defeated by two demigods – at least not two demigods using *force*.

Annabeth made herself look at the goddess's massive dark face.

'Well, how many other demigods have come to see you on the tour?' she asked innocently.

Nyx's hand went slack on the reins. 'None. Not one. This is unacceptable!'

Annabeth shrugged. 'Maybe it's because you haven't really *done* anything to get in the news. I mean, I can understand Tartarus being important! This whole place is named after him. Or if we could meet Day –'

'Oh, yeah,' Percy chimed in. 'Day? She would be impressive. I'd totally want to meet her. Maybe get her autograph.'

'Day!' Nyx gripped the rail of her black chariot. The whole vehicle shuddered. 'You mean Hemera? She is my daughter! Night is much more powerful than Day!'

'Eh,' said Annabeth. 'I liked the *arai*, or even Akhlys better.'

'They are my children as well!'

Percy stifled a yawn. 'Got a lot of children, huh?'

'I am the mother of all terrors!' Nyx cried. 'The Fates themselves! Hecate! Old Age! Pain! Sleep! Death! And all of the curses! Behold how newsworthy I am!'

LIV

ANNABETH

NYX LASHED HER WHIP AGAIN. The darkness congealed around her. On either side, an army of shadows appeared – more dark-winged *arai*, which Annabeth was not thrilled to see; a withered crone who must have been Geras, the goddess of old age; and a younger woman in a black toga, her eyes gleaming and her smile like a serial killer's – no doubt Eris, the goddess of strife. More kept appearing: dozens of demons and minor gods, each one the spawn of Night.

Annabeth wanted to run. She was facing a brood of horrors that could snap anyone's sanity. But if she ran she would die.

Next to her, Percy's breathing turned shallow. Even through his misty ghoul disguise, Annabeth could tell he was on the verge of panic. She had to stand her ground for both of them.

I am a daughter of Athena, she thought. I control my own mind.

She imagined a mental frame around what she was seeing.

She told herself it was just a movie – a scary movie, sure, but it could not hurt her. She was in control.

'Yeah, not bad,' she admitted. 'I guess we could get one picture for the scrapbook, but I don't know. You guys are so . . . *dark*. Even if I used a flash, I'm not sure it would come out.'

'Y-yeah,' Percy managed. 'You guys aren't photogenic.'

'You – miserable – tourists!' Nyx hissed. 'How dare you not tremble before me! How dare you not whimper and beg for my autograph and a picture for your scrapbook! You want *news-worthy*? My son Hypnos once put Zeus to sleep! When Zeus pursued him across the earth, bent on vengeance, Hypnos hid in *my* palace for safety, and Zeus did not follow. Even the king of Olympus fears me!'

'Uh-huh.' Annabeth turned to Percy. 'Well, it's getting late. We should probably get lunch at one of those restaurants the tour guide recommended. Then we can find the Doors of Death.'

'Aha!' Nyx cried in triumph. Her brood of shadows stirred and echoed: 'Aha! Aha!'

'You wish to see the Doors of Death?' Nyx asked. 'They lie at the very heart of Tartarus. Mortals such as you could never reach them, except through the halls of my palace – the Mansion of Night!'

She gestured behind her. Floating in the abyss, maybe three hundred feet below, was a doorway of black marble, leading into some sort of large room.

Annabeth's heart pounded so strongly she felt it in her toes. That was the way forward – but it was so far down, an impossible jump. If they missed, they would fall into Chaos and be scattered into nothingness – a final death with no do-over. Even if they could make the jump, the goddess of Night and her most fearsome children stood in their way.

With a jolt, Annabeth realized what needed to happen. Like everything she'd ever done, it was a long shot. In a way, that calmed her down. A crazy idea in the face of death?

Okay, her body seemed to say, relaxing. *This is familiar territory.*

She managed a bored sigh. 'I suppose we could do one picture, but a group shot won't work. Nyx, how about one of you with your favourite child? Which one is that?'

The brood rustled. Dozens of horrible glowing eyes turned towards Nyx.

The goddess shifted uncomfortably, as if her chariot were heating up under her feet. Her shadow horses huffed and pawed at the void.

'My favourite child?' she asked. '*All* my children are terrifying!'

Percy snorted. 'Seriously? I've met the Fates. I've met Thanatos. They weren't so scary. You've got to have somebody in this crowd who's worse than that.'

'The darkest,' Annabeth said. 'The most like you.'

'I am the darkest,' hissed Eris. 'Wars and strife! I have caused all manner of death!'

'I am darker still!' snarled Geras. 'I dim the eyes and addle the brain. Every mortal fears old age!'

'Yeah, yeah,' Annabeth said, trying to ignore her chattering teeth. 'I'm not seeing enough dark. I mean, you're the children of Night! Show me dark!'

The horde of *arai* wailed, flapping their leathery wings and stirring up clouds of blackness. Geras spread her withered hands and dimmed the entire abyss. Eris breathed a shadowy spray of buckshot across the void.

'I am the darkest!' hissed one of the demons.

'No, I!'

'No! Behold my darkness!'

If a thousand giant octopuses had squirted ink at the same time, at the bottom of the deepest, most sunless ocean trench, it could not have been blacker. Annabeth might as well have been blind. She gripped Percy's hand and steeled her nerves.

'Wait!' Nyx called, suddenly panicked. 'I can't see anything.'

'Yes!' shouted one of her children proudly. 'I did that!'

'No, I did!'

'Fool, it was me!'

Dozens of voices argued in the darkness.

The horses whinnied in alarm.

'Stop it!' Nyx yelled. 'Whose foot is that?'

'Eris is hitting me!' cried someone. 'Mother, tell her to stop hitting me!'

'I did *not!*' yelled Eris. 'Ouch!'

The sounds of scuffling got louder. If possible, the darkness became even deeper. Annabeth's eyes dilated so much, they felt like they were being pulled out of their sockets.

She squeezed Percy's hand. 'Ready?'

'For what?' After a pause, he grunted unhappily. 'Poseidon's underpants, you can't be serious.'

'Somebody give me light!' Nyx screamed. 'Gah! I can't believe I just said that!'

'It's a trick!' Eris yelled. 'The demigods are escaping!'

'I've got them,' screamed an *arai*.

'No, that's my neck!' Geras gagged.

'Jump!' Annabeth told Percy.

They leaped into the darkness, aiming for the doorway far, far below.

LV

ANNABETH

AFTER THEIR FALL INTO TARTARUS, jumping three hundred feet to the Mansion of Night should have felt quick.

Instead, Annabeth's heart seemed to slow down. Between the beats she had ample time to write her own obituary.

Annabeth Chase, died age 17.

BA-BOOM.

(Assuming her birthday, July 12, had passed while she was in Tartarus, but, honestly, she had no idea.)

BA-BOOM.

Died of massive injuries while leaping like an idiot into the abyss of Chaos and splattering on the entry hall floor of Nyx's mansion.

BA-BOOM.

Survived by her father, stepmother and two stepbrothers who barely knew her.

BA-BOOM.

In lieu of flowers, please send donations to Camp Half-Blood, assuming Gaia hasn't already destroyed it.

Her feet hit solid floor. Pain shot up her legs, but she stumbled forward and broke into a run, hauling Percy after her.

Above them in the dark, Nyx and her children scuffled and yelled, 'I've got them! My foot! Stop it!'

Annabeth kept running. She couldn't see anyway, so she closed her eyes. She used her other senses – listening for the echo of open spaces, feeling for cross-breezes against her face, sniffing for any scent of danger – smoke or poison or the stench of demons.

It wasn't the first time she'd plunged through darkness. She imagined she was back in the tunnels under Rome, searching out the Athena Parthenos. In retrospect, her journey to Arachne's cavern seemed like a trip to Disneyland.

The squabbling sounds of Nyx's children got further away. That was good. Percy was still running at her side, holding her hand. Also good.

In the distance ahead of them, Annabeth began to hear a throbbing sound, like her own heartbeat echoing back, amplified so powerfully the floor vibrated underfoot. The sound filled her with dread, so she figured it must be the right way to go. She ran towards it.

As the beat got louder, she smelled smoke and heard the flickering of torches on either side. She guessed there would be light, but a crawling sensation across her neck warned her it would be a mistake to open her eyes.

'Don't look,' she told Percy.

'Wasn't planning on it,' he said. 'You can feel that, right? We're still in the Mansion of Night. I do *not* want to see it.'

Smart boy, Annabeth thought. She used to tease Percy for being dumb, but in truth his instincts were usually right on target.

Whatever horrors lay in the Mansion of Night, they weren't meant for mortal eyes. Seeing them would be worse than staring at the face of Medusa. Better to run in darkness.

The throbbing got louder still, sending vibrations straight up Annabeth's spine. It felt like someone was knocking on the bottom of the world, demanding to be let in. She sensed the walls opening up on either side of them. The air smelled fresher – or at least not quite as sulphurous. There was another sound, too, closer than the deep pulsing . . . the sound of flowing water.

Annabeth's heart raced. She knew the exit was close. If they could make it out of the Mansion of Night, maybe they could leave the dark brood of demons behind.

She began to run faster, which would have led to her death if Percy hadn't stopped her.

LVI

ANNABETH

'ANNABETH!' PERCY PULLED HER BACK just as her foot hit the edge of a drop. She almost pitched forward into who-knew-what, but Percy grabbed her and wrapped her in his arms.

'It's okay,' he promised.

She pressed her face into his shirt and kept her eyes closed tight. She was trembling, but not just from fear. Percy's embrace was so warm and comforting she wanted to stay there forever, safe and protected . . . but that wasn't reality. She couldn't afford to relax. She couldn't lean on Percy any more than she had to. He needed *her*, too.

'Thanks . . .' She gently disentangled herself from his arms. 'Can you tell what's in front us?'

'Water,' he said. 'I'm still not looking. I don't think it's safe yet.'

'Agreed.'

'I can sense a river . . . or maybe it's a moat. It's blocking our path, flowing left to right through a channel cut in the rock. The opposite side is about twenty feet away.'

Annabeth mentally scolded herself. She'd heard the flowing water, but she had never considered she might be running headlong into it.

'Is there a bridge, or –'

'I don't think so,' Percy said. 'And there's something wrong with the water. Listen.'

Annabeth concentrated. Within the roaring current, thousands of voices cried out – shrieking in agony, pleading for mercy.

Help! they groaned. *It was an accident!*

The pain! their voices wailed. *Make it stop!*

Annabeth didn't need her eyes to imagine the river – a black briny current filled with tortured souls being swept deeper and deeper into Tartarus.

'The River Acheron,' she guessed. 'The fifth river of the Underworld.'

'I liked the Phlegethon better than this,' Percy muttered.

'It's the River of Pain. The ultimate punishment for the souls of the damned – murderers, especially.'

Murderers! the river wailed. *Yes, like you!*

Join us, another voice whispered. *You are no better than we are.*

Annabeth's head was flooded with images of all the monsters she'd killed over the years.

That wasn't murder, she protested. *I was defending myself!*

The river changed course through her mind – showing her Zoë Nightshade, who had been slain on Mount Tamalpais because she'd come to rescue Annabeth from the Titans.

She saw Nico's sister, Bianca di Angelo, dying in the collapse of the metal giant Talos because she also had tried to save Annabeth.

Michael Yew and Silena Beauregard . . . who had died in the Battle of Manhattan.

You could have prevented it, the river told Annabeth. *You should have seen a better way.*

Most painful of all: Luke Castellan. Annabeth remembered Luke's blood on her dagger after he'd sacrificed himself to stop Kronos from destroying Olympus.

His blood is on your hands! the river wailed. *There should have been another way!*

Annabeth had wrestled with the same thought many times. She'd tried to convince herself Luke's death wasn't her fault. Luke had chosen his fate. Still . . . she didn't know if his soul had found peace in the Underworld, or if he'd been reborn, or if he'd been washed into Tartarus because of his crimes. He might be one of the tortured voices flowing past right now.

You murdered him! the river cried. *Jump in and share his punishment!*

Percy gripped her arm. 'Don't listen.'

'But –'

'I know.' His voice sounded as brittle as ice. 'They're telling me the same stuff. I think . . . I think this moat must be the border of Night's territory. If we get across, we should be okay. We'll have to jump.'

'You said it was twenty feet!'

'Yeah. You'll have to trust me. Put your arms around my neck and hang on.'

'How can you possibly –'

'There!' cried a voice behind them. 'Kill the ungrateful tourists!'

The children of Nyx had found them. Annabeth wrapped her arms around Percy's neck. 'Go!'

With her eyes closed, she could only guess how he managed it. Maybe he used the force of the river somehow. Maybe he was just scared out of his mind and charged with adrenalin. Percy leaped with more strength than she would have thought possible. They sailed through the air as the river churned and wailed below them, splashing Annabeth's bare ankles with stinging brine.

Then – *CLUMP*. They were on solid ground again.

'You can open your eyes,' Percy said, breathing hard. 'But you won't like what you see.'

Annabeth blinked. After the darkness of Nyx, even the dim red glow of Tartarus seemed blinding.

Before them stretched a valley big enough to hold the San Francisco Bay. The booming noise came from the entire landscape, as if thunder were echoing from beneath the ground. Under poisonous clouds, the rolling terrain glistened purple with dark red and blue scar lines.

'It looks like . . .' Annabeth fought down her revulsion. 'Like a giant heart.'

'The heart of Tartarus,' Percy murmured.

The centre of the valley was covered with a fine black fuzz

of peppery dots. They were so far away, it took Annabeth a moment to realize she was looking at an army – thousands, maybe tens of thousands of monsters, gathered around a central pinpoint of darkness. It was too far to see any details, but Annabeth had no doubt what the pinpoint was. Even from the edge of the valley, Annabeth could feel its power tugging at her soul.

'The Doors of Death.'

'Yeah.' Percy's voice was hoarse. He still had the pale, wasted complexion of a corpse . . . which meant he looked about as good as Annabeth felt.

She realized she'd forgotten all about their pursuers. 'What happened to Nyx . . . ?'

She turned. Somehow they'd landed several hundred yards from the banks of Acheron, which flowed through a channel cut into black volcanic hills. Beyond that was nothing but darkness.

No sign of anyone coming after them. Apparently even the minions of Night didn't like to cross the Acheron.

She was about to ask Percy how he had jumped so far when she heard the skittering of a rockslide in the hills to their left. She drew her drakon-bone sword. Percy raised Riptide.

A patch of glowing white hair appeared over the ridge, then a familiar grinning face with pure silver eyes.

'Bob?' Annabeth was so happy she actually jumped. 'Oh my gods!'

'Friends!' The Titan lumbered towards them. The bristles of his broom had been burned off. His janitor's uniform was slashed with new claw marks, but he looked delighted. On his shoulder, Small Bob the kitten purred almost as loudly as the pulsing heart of Tartarus.

'I found you!' Bob gathered them both in a rib-crushing hug. 'You look like smoking dead people. That is good!'

'Urf,' Percy said. 'How did you get here? Through the Mansion of Night?'

'No, no.' Bob shook his head adamantly. 'That place is too scary. Another way – only good for Titans and such.'

'Let me guess,' Annabeth said. 'You went sideways.'

Bob scratched his chin, evidently at a loss for words. 'Hmm. No. More . . . *diagonal.*'

Annabeth laughed. Here they were at the heart of Tartarus, facing an impossible army – she would take any comfort she could get. She was ridiculously glad to have Bob the Titan with them again.

She kissed his immortal nose, which made him blink.

'We stay together now?' he asked.

'Yes,' Annabeth agreed. 'Time to see if this Death Mist works.'

'And if it doesn't . . .' Percy stopped himself.

There was no point in wondering about that. They were about to march into the middle of an enemy army. If they were spotted, they were dead.

Despite that, Annabeth managed a smile. Their goal was in sight. They had a Titan with a broom and a very loud kitten on their side. That had to count for something.

'Doors of Death,' she said, 'here we come.'

LVII

JASON

JASON WASN'T SURE WHAT TO HOPE FOR: storm or fire.

As he waited for his daily audience with the lord of the South Wind, he tried to decide which of the god's personalities, Roman or Greek, was worse. But after five days in the palace he was only certain about one thing: he and his crew were unlikely to get out of here alive.

He leaned against the balcony rail. The air was so hot and dry it sucked the moisture right out of his lungs. Over the last week, his skin had got darker. His hair had turned as white as corn silk. Whenever he glanced in the mirror, he was startled by the wild, empty look in his eyes, as if he'd gone blind wandering in the desert.

A hundred feet below, the bay glittered against a crescent of red sand beach. They were somewhere on the northern coast of Africa. That's as much as the wind spirits would tell him.

The palace itself stretched out on either side of him – a

honeycomb of halls and tunnels, balconies, colonnades and cavernous rooms carved into the sandstone cliffs, all designed for the wind to blow through and make as much noise as possible. The constant pipe-organ sounds reminded Jason of the floating lair of Aeolus, back in Colorado, except here the winds seemed in no hurry.

Which was part of the problem.

On their best days, the southern *venti* were slow and lazy. On their worst days, they were gusty and angry. They'd initially welcomed the *Argo II*, since any enemy of Boreas was a friend of the South Wind, but they seemed to have forgotten that the demigods were their guests. The *venti* had quickly lost interest in helping to repair the ship. Their king's mood got worse every day.

Down at the dock, Jason's friends were working on the *Argo II*. The main sail had been repaired, the rigging replaced. Now they were mending the oars. Without Leo, none of them knew how to repair the more complicated parts of the ship, even with the help of Buford the table and Festus (who was now permanently activated thanks to Piper's charmspeak – and *none* of them understood that). But they kept trying.

Hazel and Frank stood at the helm, tinkering with the controls. Piper relayed their commands to Coach Hedge, who was hanging over the side of the ship, banging out dents in the oars. Hedge was well suited for banging on things.

They didn't seem to be making much progress, but, considering what they'd been through, it was a miracle the ship was in one piece.

Jason shivered when he thought about Khione's attack.

He'd been rendered helpless – frozen solid not once but twice, while Leo was blasted into the sky and Piper was forced to save them all single-handedly.

Thank the gods for Piper. She considered herself a failure for not having stopped the wind bomb from exploding, but the truth was she'd saved the entire crew from becoming ice sculptures in Quebec.

She'd also managed to direct the explosion of the icy sphere so, even though the ship had been pushed halfway across the Mediterranean, it had sustained relatively minor damage.

Down at the dock, Hedge yelled, 'Try it now!'

Hazel and Frank pulled some the levers. The port oars went crazy, chopping up and down and doing the wave. Coach Hedge tried to dodge, but one smacked him in the rear and launched him into the air. He came down screaming and splashed into the bay.

Jason sighed. At this rate, they'd never be able to sail, even if the southern *venti* allowed them to. Somewhere in the north, Reyna was flying towards Epirus, assuming she'd got his note at Diocletian's Palace. Leo was lost and in trouble. Percy and Annabeth . . . well, best-case scenario they were still alive, making their way to the Doors of Death. Jason couldn't let them down.

A rustling sound made him turn. Nico di Angelo stood in the shadow of the nearest column. He'd shed his jacket. Now he just wore his black T-shirt and black jeans. His sword and the sceptre of Diocletian hung on either side of his belt.

Days in the hot sun hadn't tanned *his* skin. If anything, he looked paler. His dark hair fell over his eyes. His face was still gaunt, but he was definitely in better shape than when they'd left Croatia. He had regained enough weight not to look starved. His arms were surprisingly taut with muscles, as if he'd spent the past week sword fighting. For all Jason knew, he'd been slipping off to practise raising spirits with Diocletian's sceptre, then sparring with them. After their expedition in Split, nothing would surprise him.

'Any word from the king?' Nico asked.

Jason shook his head. 'Every day, he calls for me later and later.'

'We need to leave,' Nico said. 'Soon.'

Jason had been having the same feeling, but hearing Nico say it made him even edgier. 'You sense something?'

'Percy is close to the Doors,' Nico said. 'He'll need us if he's going to make it through alive.'

Jason noticed that he didn't mention Annabeth. He decided not to bring that up.

'All right,' Jason said. 'But if we can't repair the ship –'

'I promised I'd lead you to the House of Hades,' Nico said. 'One way or another, I will.'

'You can't shadow-travel with all of us. And it *will* take all of us to reach the Doors of Death.'

The orb at the end of Diocletian's sceptre glowed purple. Over the past week, it seemed to have aligned itself to Nico di Angelo's moods. Jason wasn't sure that was a good thing.

'Then you've *got* to convince the king of the South Wind to help.' Nico's voice seethed with anger. 'I didn't come all this way, suffer so many humiliations . . .'

Jason had to make a conscious effort not to reach for his

sword. Whenever Nico got angry, all of Jason's instincts screamed *Danger!*

'Look, Nico,' he said, 'I'm here if you want to talk about, you know, what happened in Croatia. I get how difficult –'

'You don't get anything.'

'Nobody's going to judge you.'

Nico's mouth twisted in a sneer. 'Really? That would be a first. I'm the son of *Hades*, Jason. I might as well be covered in blood or sewage, the way people treat me. I don't belong anywhere. I'm not even from this *century*. But even that's not enough to set me apart. I've got to be – to be –'

'Dude! It's not like you've got a choice. It's just who you are.'

'Just who I am . . .' The balcony trembled. Patterns shifted in the stone floor, like bones coming to the surface. 'Easy for you to say. You're everybody's golden boy, the son of *Jupiter*. The only person who ever accepted *me* was Bianca, and she *died*! I didn't choose any of this. My father, my feelings . . .'

Jason tried to think of something to say. He wanted to be Nico's friend. He knew that was the only way to help. But Nico wasn't making it easy.

He raised his hands in submission. 'Yeah, okay. But, Nico, you *do* choose how to live your life. You want to trust somebody? Maybe take a risk that I'm really your friend and I'll accept you. It's better than hiding.'

The floor cracked between them. The crevice hissed. The air around Nico shimmered with spectral light.

'Hiding?' Nico's voice was deadly quiet.

Jason's fingers itched to draw his sword. He'd met plenty of scary demigods, but he was starting to realize that Nico di Angelo – as pale and gaunt as he looked – might be more than he could handle.

Nevertheless, he held Nico's gaze. 'Yes, hiding. You've run away from both camps. You're so afraid you'll get rejected that you won't even try. Maybe it's time you came out of the shadows.'

Just when the tension became unbearable, Nico dropped his eyes. The fissure closed in the balcony floor. The ghostly light faded.

'I'm going to honour my promise,' Nico said, not much louder than a whisper. 'I'll take you to Epirus. I'll help you close the Doors of Death. Then that's it. I'm leaving – forever.'

Behind them, the doors of the throne room blasted open with a gust of scorching air.

A disembodied voice said: *Lord Auster will see you now.*

As much as he dreaded this meeting, Jason felt relieved. At the moment, arguing with a crazy wind god seemed safer than befriending an angry son of Hades. He turned to tell Nico goodbye, but Nico had disappeared – melting back into the darkness.

LVIII

JASON

So it was a *storm* day. Auster, the Roman version of the South Wind, was holding court.

The two previous days, Jason had dealt with Notus. While the god's Greek version was fiery and quick to anger, at least he was *quick*. Auster . . . well, not so much.

White and red marble columns lined the throne room. The rough sandstone floor smoked under Jason's shoes. Steam hung in the air, like the bathhouse back at Camp Jupiter, except bathhouses usually didn't have thunderstorms crackling across the ceiling, lighting the room in disorienting flashes.

Southern *venti* swirled through the hall in clouds of red dust and superheated air. Jason was careful to stay away from them. On his first day here, he'd accidentally brushed his hand through one. He'd got so many blisters his fingers looked like tentacles.

At the end of the room was the strangest throne Jason had

ever seen – made of equal parts fire and water. The dais was a bonfire. Flames and smoke curled up to form a seat. The back of the chair was a churning storm cloud. The armrests sizzled where moisture met fire. It didn't look very comfortable, but the god Auster lounged on it like he was ready for an easy afternoon of watching football.

Standing up, he would have been about ten feet tall. A crown of steam wreathed his shaggy white hair. His beard was made of clouds, constantly popping with lightning and raining down on the god's chest, soaking his sand-coloured toga. Jason wondered if you could shave a thundercloud beard. He thought it might be annoying to rain on yourself all the time, but Auster didn't seem to care. He reminded Jason of a soggy Santa Claus, but more lazy than jolly.

'So . . .' The god's voice rumbled like an oncoming front. 'The son of Jupiter returns.'

Auster made it sound like Jason was late. Jason was tempted to remind the stupid wind god that he had spent hours outside every day waiting to be called, but he just bowed.

'My lord,' he said. 'Have you received any news of my friend?'

'Friend?'

'Leo Valdez.' Jason tried to stay patient. 'The one who was taken by the winds.'

'Oh . . . yes. Or rather, no. We have had no word. He was not taken by *my* winds. No doubt this was the work of Boreas or his spawn.'

'Uh, yes. We knew that.'

'That is the only reason I took you in, of course.' Auster's eyebrows rose into his wreath of steam. 'Boreas must be opposed! The north winds must be driven back!'

'Yes, my lord. But to oppose Boreas we really need to get our ship out of the harbour.'

'Ship in the harbour!' The god leaned back and chuckled, rain pouring out of his beard. 'You know the *last* time mortal ships came into my harbour? A king of Libya . . . Psyollos was his name. He blamed *me* for the scorching winds that burned his crops. Can you believe it?'

Jason gritted his teeth. He'd learned that Auster couldn't be rushed. In his rainy form, he was sluggish and warm and random.

'And did you burn those crops, my lord?'

'Of course!' Auster smiled good-naturedly. 'But what did Psyollos expect, planting crops at the edge of the Sahara? The fool launched his entire fleet against me. He intended to destroy my stronghold so the south wind could never blow again. I destroyed his fleet, of course.'

'Of course.'

Auster narrowed his eyes. 'You aren't with Psyollos, are you?'

'No, Lord Auster. I'm Jason Grace, son of –'

'Jupiter! Yes, of course. I like sons of Jupiter. But why are you still in my harbour?'

Jason suppressed a sigh. 'We don't have your permission to leave, my lord. Also, our ship is damaged. We need our mechanic, Leo Valdez, to repair the engine, unless you know of another way.'

'Hmm.' Auster held up his fingers and let a dust devil

swirl between them like a baton. 'You know, people accuse me of being fickle. Some days I am the scorching wind, the destroyer of crops, the sirocco from Africa! Other days I am gentle, heralding the warm summer rains and cooling fogs of the southern Mediterranean. And in the off-season I have a lovely place in Cancun! At any rate, in ancient times, mortals both feared me and loved me. For a god, unpredictability can be a strength.'

'Then you are truly strong,' Jason said.

'Thank you! Yes! But the same is not true of demigods.' Auster leaned forward, close enough so that Jason could smell rain-soaked fields and hot sandy beaches. 'You remind me of my own children, Jason Grace. You have blown from place to place. You are undecided. You change day to day. If you could turn the wind sock, which way would it blow?'

Sweat trickled between Jason's shoulder blades. 'Excuse me?'

'You say you need a navigator. You need my permission. I say you need neither. It is time to choose a direction. A wind that blows aimlessly is of no use to anyone.'

'I don't . . . I don't understand.'

Even as he said it, he *did* understand. Nico had talked about not belonging anywhere. At least Nico was free of attachments. He could go wherever he chose.

For months, Jason had been wrestling with the question of where he belonged. He'd always chafed against the traditions of Camp Jupiter, the power plays, the infighting. But Reyna was a good person. She needed his help. If he turned his back on her . . . someone like Octavian could take over and ruin everything Jason *did* love about New Rome. Could he be so selfish as to leave? The very idea crushed him with guilt.

But in his heart he *wanted* to be at Camp Half-Blood. The months he'd spent there with Piper and Leo had felt more satisfying, more *right* than all his years at Camp Jupiter. Besides, at Camp Half-Blood, there was at least a *chance* he might meet his father some day. The gods hardly ever stopped by Camp Jupiter to say hello.

Jason took a shaky breath. 'Yes. I know the direction I want to take.'

'Good! And?'

'Uh, we still need a way to fix the ship. Is there –'

Auster raised an index finger. 'Still expecting guidance from the wind lords? A son of Jupiter should know better.'

Jason hesitated. 'We're leaving, Lord Auster. Today.'

The wind god grinned and spread his hands. 'At last, you announce your purpose! Then you have my permission to go, though you do not need it. And how will you sail without your engineer, without your engines fixed?'

Jason felt the south winds zipping around him, whinnying in challenge like headstrong mustangs, testing his will.

All week he had been waiting, hoping Auster would decide to help. For months he had worried about his obligations to Camp Jupiter, hoping his path would become clear. Now, he realized, he simply had to take what he wanted. He had to control the winds, not the other way around.

'You're going to help us,' Jason said. 'Your *venti* can take the form of horses. You'll give us a team to pull the *Argo II*. They'll lead us to wherever Leo is.'

'Wonderful!' Auster beamed, his beard flashing with electricity. 'Now . . . can you make good on those bold words? Can you control what you ask for, or will you be torn apart?'

The god clapped his hands. Winds swirled around his throne and took the form of horses. These weren't dark and cold like Jason's friend Tempest. The South Wind horses were made of fire, sand and hot thunderstorm. Four of them raced past, their heat singeing the hair off Jason's arms. They galloped around the marble columns, spitting flames, neighing with a sound like sandblasters. The more they ran, they wilder they became. They started to eye Jason.

Auster stroked his rainy beard. 'Do you know why the *venti* can appear as horses, my boy? Every so often, we wind gods travel the earth in equine form. On occasion, we've been known to sire the fastest of all horses.'

'Thanks,' Jason muttered, though his teeth were chattering with fear. 'Too much information.'

One of the *venti* charged at Jason. He ducked aside, his clothes smoking from the close call.

'Sometimes,' Auster continued cheerfully, 'mortals recognize our divine blood. They will say, *That horse runs like the wind.* And for good reason. Like the fastest stallions, the *venti* are our children!'

The wind horses began to circle Jason.

'Like my friend Tempest,' he ventured.

'Oh, well . . .' Auster scowled. 'I fear that one is a child of Boreas. How you tamed him, I will never know. These are my own offspring, a fine team of southern winds. Control them, Jason Grace, and they will pull your ship from the harbour.'

Control them, Jason thought. Yeah, right.

They ran back and forth, working up a frenzy. Like their master the South Wind, they were conflicted – half hot, dry sirocco, half stormy thunderhead.

I need speed, Jason thought. I need purpose.

He envisioned Notus, the Greek version of the South Wind – blistering hot, but very fast.

In that moment, he *chose* Greek. He threw in his lot with Camp Half-Blood – and the horses changed. The storm clouds inside burned away, leaving nothing but red dust and shimmering heat, like mirages on the Sahara.

'Well done,' said the god.

On the throne now sat Notus – a bronze-skinned old man in a fiery Greek *chiton*, his head crowned with a wreath of withered, smoking barley.

'What are you waiting for?' the god prompted.

Jason turned towards the fiery wind steeds. Suddenly he wasn't afraid of them.

He thrust out his hand. A swirl of dust shot towards the nearest horse. A lasso – a rope of wind, more tightly wound than any tornado – wrapped around the horse's neck. The wind formed a halter and brought the beast to a stop.

Jason summoned another wind rope. He lashed a second horse, binding it to his will. In less than a minute, he had tethered all four *venti*. He reined them in, still whinnying and bucking, but they couldn't break Jason's ropes. It felt like flying four kites in a strong wind – hard, yes, but not impossible.

'Very good, Jason Grace,' Notus said. 'You are a son of

Jupiter, yet you have chosen your own path – as all the greatest demigods have done before you. You cannot control your parentage, but you *can* choose your legacy. Now, go. Lash your team to the prow and direct them towards Malta.'

'Malta?' Jason tried to focus, but the heat from the horses was making him light-headed. He knew nothing about Malta, except for some vague story about a Maltese falcon. Were malts invented there?

'Once you arrive in the city of Valletta,' Notus said, 'you will no longer need these horses.'

'You mean . . . we'll find Leo there?'

The god shimmered, slowly fading into waves of heat. 'Your destiny grows clearer, Jason Grace. When the choice comes again – storm or fire – remember me. And do not despair.'

The doors of the throne room burst open. The horses, smelling freedom, bolted for the exit.

LIX

JASON

AT SIXTEEN, MOST KIDS WOULD STRESS about parallel parking tests, getting a driver's licence and affording a car.

Jason stressed about controlling a team of fiery horses with wind ropes.

After making sure his friends were aboard and safely below deck, he lashed the *venti* to the prow of the *Argo II* (which Festus was *not* happy about), straddled the figurehead and yelled, 'Giddyup!'

The *venti* tore across the waves. They weren't quite as fast as Hazel's horse, Arion, but they had a lot more heat. They kicked up a rooster tail of steam that made it almost impossible for Jason to see where they were going. The ship shot out of the bay. In no time Africa was a hazy line on the horizon behind them.

Maintaining the wind ropes took all of Jason's concentration. The horses strained to break free. Only his willpower kept them in check.

Malta, he ordered. *Straight to Malta.*

By the time land finally appeared in the distance – a hilly island carpeted with low stone buildings – Jason was soaked in sweat. His arms felt rubbery, like he'd been holding a barbell straight out in front of him.

He hoped they'd reached the right place, because he couldn't keep the horses together any longer. He released the wind reins. The *venti* scattered into particles of sand and steam.

Exhausted, Jason climbed down from the prow. He leaned against Festus's neck. The dragon turned and gave him a chin hug.

'Thanks, man,' Jason said. 'Rough day, huh?'

Behind him, the deck boards creaked.

'Jason?' Piper called. 'Oh, gods, your arms . . .'

He hadn't noticed, but his skin was dotted with blisters.

Piper unwrapped a square of ambrosia. 'Eat this.'

He chewed. His mouth was filled with the taste of fresh brownies – his favourite treat from the bakeries in New Rome. The blisters faded on his arms. His strength returned, but the brownie ambrosia tasted more bitter than usual, as if it somehow knew that Jason was turning his back on Camp Jupiter. This was no longer the taste of home.

'Thanks, Pipes,' he murmured. 'How long was I –'

'About six hours.'

Wow, Jason thought. No wonder he felt sore and hungry. 'The others?'

'All fine. Tired of being cooped up. Should I tell them it's safe to come above deck?'

Jason licked his dry lips. Despite the ambrosia, he felt shaky. He didn't want to others to see him like this.

'Give me a second,' he said. '. . . catch my breath.'

Piper leaned next to him. In her green tank top, her beige shorts and her hiking boots, she looked like she was ready to climb a mountain – and then fight an army at the top. Her dagger was strapped to her belt. Her cornucopia was slung over one shoulder. She'd taken to wearing the jagged bronze sword she'd recovered from Zethes the Boread, which was only slightly less intimidating than an assault rifle.

During their time at Auster's palace, Jason had watched Piper and Hazel spend hours sword-fighting – something Piper had never been interested in before. Since her encounter with Khione, Piper seemed more wired, tensed up inside like a primed catapult, as if she were determined never to be caught off guard again.

Jason understood the feeling, but he worried she was being too hard on herself. Nobody could be ready for anything all the time. He should know. He'd spent the last fight as a freeze-dried throw rug.

He must have been staring, because she gave him a knowing smirk. 'Hey, I'm fine. *We're* fine.'

She perched on her tiptoes and kissed him, which felt as good as the ambrosia. Her eyes were flecked with so many colours Jason could've stared into them all day, studying the changing patterns, the way people watched the northern lights.

'I'm lucky to have you,' he said.

'Yeah, you are.' She pushed his chest gently. 'Now, how do we get this ship to the docks?'

Jason frowned across the water. They were still half a mile from the island. He had no idea whether they could get the engines working, or the sails . . .

Fortunately, Festus had been listening. He faced front and blew a plume of fire. The ship's engine clattered and hummed. It sounded like a massive bike with a busted chain – but they lurched forward. Slowly, the *Argo II* headed towards the shore.

'Good dragon.' Piper patted Festus's neck.

The dragon's ruby eyes glinted as if he was pleased with himself.

'He seems different since you woke him,' Jason said. 'More . . . alive.'

'The way he *should* be.' Piper smiled. 'I guess once in a while we all need a wake-up call from somebody who loves us.'

Standing next to her, Jason felt so good, he could almost imagine their future together at Camp Half-Blood, once the war was over – assuming they lived, assuming there was still a camp left to return to.

When the choice comes again, Notus had said, *storm or fire – remember me. And do not despair.*

The closer they got to Greece, the more dread settled in Jason's chest. He was starting to think Piper was right about the *storm or fire* line in the prophecy – one of them, Jason or Leo, would not come back from this voyage alive.

Which was why they *had* to find Leo. As much as Jason

loved his life, he couldn't let his friend die for his sake. He could never live with the guilt.

Of course he hoped he was wrong. He hoped they both came out this quest okay. But, if not, Jason had to be prepared. He would protect his friends and stop Gaia – whatever it took.

Do not despair.

Yeah. Easy for an immortal wind god to say.

As the island got closer, Jason saw docks bristling with sails. From the rocky shoreline rose fortress-like seawalls – fifty or sixty feet tall. Above that sprawled a mediaeval-looking city of church spires, domes and tightly wedged buildings, all made of the same golden stone. From where Jason stood, it looked as if the city covered every inch of the island.

He scanned the boats in the harbour. A hundred yards ahead, tied to the end of the longest dock, was a makeshift raft with a simple mast and a square canvas sail. On the back, the rudder was wired to some sort of machine. Even from this distance, Jason could see the glint of Celestial bronze.

Jason grinned. Only one demigod would make a boat like that, and he'd moored it as far out in the harbour as possible, where the *Argo II* couldn't fail to spot it.

'Get the others,' Jason told Piper. 'Leo is here.'

LX

JASON

THEY FOUND LEO AT THE TOP of the city fortifications. He was sitting at an open-air café, overlooking the sea, drinking a cup of coffee and dressed in . . . wow. Time warp. Leo's outfit was identical to the one he'd worn the day they first arrived at Camp Half-Blood – jeans, a white shirt and an old army jacket. Except that jacket had burned up months ago.

Piper nearly knocked him out of his chair with a hug. 'Leo! Gods, where have you been?'

'Valdez!' Coach Hedge grinned. Then he seemed to remember he had a reputation to protect and he forced a scowl. 'You ever disappear like that again, you little punk, I'll knock you into next month!'

Frank patted Leo on the back so hard it made him wince. Even Nico shook his hand.

Hazel kissed Leo on the cheek. 'We thought you were dead!'

Leo mustered a faint smile. 'Hey, guys. Nah, nah, I'm good.'

Jason could tell he *wasn't* good. Leo wouldn't meet their eyes. His hands were perfectly still on the table. Leo's hands were *never* still. All the nervous energy had drained right out of him, replaced by a kind of wistful sadness.

Jason wondered why his expression seemed familiar. Then he realized Nico di Angelo had looked the same way after facing Cupid in the ruins of Salona.

Leo was heartsick.

As the others grabbed chairs from the nearby tables, Jason leaned in and squeezed his friend's shoulder.

'Hey, man,' he said, 'what happened?'

Leo's eyes swept around the group. The message was clear: *Not here. Not in front of everyone.*

'I got marooned,' Leo said. 'Long story. How about you guys? What happened with Khione?'

Coach Hedge snorted. 'What happened? *Piper* happened! I'm telling you, this girl has skills!'

'Coach . . .' Piper protested.

Hedge began retelling the story, but in his version Piper was a kung fu assassin and there were a lot more Boreads.

As the coach talked, Jason studied Leo with concern. This café had a perfect view of the harbour. Leo must have seen the *Argo II* sail in. Yet he'd sat here drinking coffee – which he didn't even *like* – waiting for them to find him. That wasn't like Leo at all. The ship was the most important thing in his life. When he saw it coming to rescue him, Leo should have run down to the docks, whooping at the top of his lungs.

Coach Hedge was just describing how Piper had defeated Khione with a roundhouse kick when Piper interrupted.

'Coach!' she said. 'It didn't happen like that at all. I couldn't have done *anything* without Festus.'

Leo raised his eyebrows. 'But Festus was deactivated.'

'Um, about that,' Piper said. 'I sort of woke him up.'

Piper explained her version of events – how she'd rebooted the metal dragon with charmspeak.

Leo tapped his fingers on the table, like some of his old energy was coming back.

'Shouldn't be possible,' he murmured. 'Unless the upgrades let him respond to voice commands. But if he's permanently activated, that means the navigation system and the crystal . . .'

'Crystal?' Jason asked.

Leo flinched. 'Um, nothing. Anyway, what happened after the wind bomb went off?'

Hazel took up the story. A waitress came over and offered them menus. In no time they were chowing down on sandwiches and sodas, enjoying the sunny day almost like a group of regular teenagers.

Frank grabbed a tourist brochure stuck under the napkin dispenser. He began to read it. Piper patted Leo's arm, like she couldn't believe he was really here. Nico stood at the edge of the group, eyeing the passing pedestrians as if they might be enemies. Coach Hedge munched on the salt and pepper shakers.

Despite the happy reunion, everybody seemed more subdued than usual – like they were picking up on Leo's mood.

Jason had never really considered how important Leo's sense of humour was to the group. Even when things were super serious, they could always depend on Leo to lighten things up. Now, it felt like the whole team had dropped anchor.

'So then Jason harnessed the *venti*,' Hazel finished. 'And here we are.'

Leo whistled. 'Hot-air horses? Dang, Jason. So, basically, you held a bunch of gas together all the way to Malta and then you let it loose.'

Jason frowned. 'You know, it doesn't sound so heroic when you put it that way.'

'Yeah, well. I'm an expert on hot air. I'm still wondering, why Malta? I just kind of ended up here on the raft, but was that a random thing, or –'

'Maybe because of this.' Frank tapped his brochure. 'Says here Malta was where Calypso lived.'

A pint of blood drained from Leo's face. 'W-what, now?'

Frank shrugged. 'According to this, her original home was an island called Gozo just north of here. Calypso's a Greek myth thingie, right?'

'Ah, a Greek myth thingie!' Coach Hedge rubbed his hands together. 'Maybe we get to fight her! Do we get to fight her? 'Cause I'm ready.'

'No,' Leo murmured. 'No, we don't have to fight her, Coach.'

Piper frowned. 'Leo, what's wrong? You look –'

'Nothing's wrong!' Leo shot to his feet. 'Hey, we should get going. We've got work to do!'

'But . . . where did you go?' Hazel asked. 'Where did you get those clothes? How –'

'Jeez, ladies!' Leo said. 'I appreciate the concern, but I don't need two extra moms!'

Piper smiled uncertainly. 'Okay, but –'

'Ships to fix!' Leo said. 'Festus to check! Earth goddesses to punch in the face! What are we waiting for? Leo's back!'

He spread his arms and grinned.

He was making a brave attempt, but Jason could see the sadness lingering in his eyes. Something had happened to him . . . something to do with Calypso.

Jason tried to remember the story about her. She was a sorceress of some sort, maybe like Medea or Circe. But, if Leo had escaped from an evil sorceress's lair, why did he seem so sad? Jason would have to talk to him later, make sure his buddy was okay. For now Leo clearly didn't want to be interrogated.

Jason got up and clapped him on the shoulder. 'Leo's right. We should get going.'

Everybody took the cue. They started wrapping up their food and finishing their drinks.

Suddenly, Hazel gasped. 'Guys . . .'

She pointed to the northeast horizon. At first, Jason saw nothing but the sea. Then a streak of darkness shot into the air like black lightning – as if pure night had torn through the daytime.

'I don't see anything,' Coach Hedge grumbled.

'Me neither,' Piper said.

Jason scanned his friends' faces. Most of them just looked

confused. Nico was the only other one who seemed to have noticed the black lightning.

'That can't be . . .' Nico muttered. 'Greece is still hundreds of miles away.'

The darkness flashed again, momentarily leaching the colour from the horizon.

'You think it's Epirus?' Jason's whole skeleton tingled, the way he felt when he got hit by a thousand volts. He didn't know why he could see the dark flashes. He wasn't a child of the Underworld. But it gave him a very bad feeling.

Nico nodded. 'The House of Hades is open for business.'

A few seconds later, a rumbling sound washed over them like distant artillery.

'It's begun,' Hazel said.

'What has?' Leo asked.

When the next flash happened, Hazel's gold eyes darkened like foil in fire. 'Gaia's final push,' she said. 'The Doors of Death are working overtime. Her forces are entering the mortal world en masse.'

'We'll never make it,' Nico said. 'By the time we arrive, there'll be too many monsters to fight.'

Jason set his jaw. 'We'll defeat them. And we'll make it there fast. We've got Leo back. He'll give us the speed we need.'

He turned to his friend. 'Or is that just hot air?'

Leo managed a crooked grin. His eyes seemed to say: *Thanks.*

'Time to fly, boys and girls,' he said. 'Uncle Leo's still got a few tricks up his sleeves!'

LXI

PERCY

PERCY WASN'T DEAD YET, but he was already tired of being a corpse.

As they trudged towards the heart of Tartarus, he kept glancing down at his body, wondering how it could belong to him. His arms looked like bleached leather pulled over sticks. His skeletal legs seemed to dissolve into smoke with every step. He'd learned to move normally within the Death Mist, more or less, but the magical shroud still made him feel like he was wrapped in a coat of helium.

He worried that the Death Mist might cling to him forever, even if they somehow managed to survive Tartarus. He didn't want to spend the rest of his life looking like an extra from *The Walking Dead*.

Percy tried to focus on something else, but there was no safe direction to look.

Under his feet, the ground glistened a nauseating purple, pulsing with webs of veins. In the dim red light of the blood clouds, Death Mist Annabeth looked like a freshly risen zombie.

Ahead of them was the most depressing view of all.

Spread to the horizon was an army of monsters – flocks of winged *arai*, tribes of lumbering Cyclopes, clusters of floating evil spirits. Thousands of baddies, maybe *tens* of thousands, all milling restlessly, pressing against one another, growling and fighting for space – like the locker area of an overcrowded school between classes, if all the students were 'roid-raging mutants who smelled *really* bad.

Bob led them towards the edge of the army. He made no effort to hide, not that it would have done any good. Being ten feet tall and glowing silver, Bob didn't do stealth very well.

About thirty yards from the nearest monsters, Bob turned to face Percy.

'Stay quiet and stay behind me,' he advised. 'They will not notice you.'

'We hope,' Percy muttered.

On the Titan's shoulder, Small Bob woke up from a nap. He purred seismically and arched his back, turning skeletal then back to calico. At least *he* didn't seem nervous.

Annabeth examined her own zombie hands. 'Bob, if we're invisible . . . how can *you* see us? I mean, you're technically, you know . . .'

'Yes,' Bob said. 'But we are friends.'

'Nyx and her children could see us,' Annabeth said.

Bob shrugged. 'That was in Nyx's realm. That is different.'

'Uh . . . right.' Annabeth didn't sound reassured, but they were here now. They didn't have any choice but to try.

Percy stared at the swarm of vicious monsters. 'Well, at least we won't have to worry about bumping into any other *friends* in this crowd.'

Bob grinned. 'Yes, that is good news! Now, let's go. Death is close.'

'The *Doors* of Death are close,' Annabeth corrected. 'Let's watch the phrasing.'

They plunged into the crowd. Percy trembled so badly he was afraid the Death Mist would shake right off him. He'd seen large groups of monsters before. He'd fought an army of them during the Battle of Manhattan. But this was different.

Whenever he'd fought monsters in the mortal world, Percy at least knew he was defending his home. That gave him courage, no matter how bad the odds were. Here, *Percy* was the invader. He didn't belong in this multitude of monsters any more than the Minotaur belonged in Penn Station at rush hour.

A few feet away, a group of *empousai* tore into the carcass of a gryphon while other gryphons flew around them, squawking in outrage. A six-armed Earthborn and a Laistrygonian giant pummelled each other with rocks, though Percy wasn't sure if they were fighting or just messing around. A dark wisp of smoke – Percy guessed it must be an eidolon – seeped into a Cyclops, made the monster hit himself in the face, then drifted off to possess another victim.

Annabeth whispered, 'Percy, look.'

A stone's throw away, a guy in a cowboy outfit was cracking a whip at some fire-breathing horses. The wrangler wore a Stetson hat on his greasy hair, an extra-large set of jeans and a pair of black leather boots. From the side, he might have passed for human – until he turned, and Percy saw that his upper body was split into three different chests, each one dressed in a different colour Western shirt.

It was definitely Geryon, who had tried to kill Percy two years ago in Texas. Apparently the evil rancher was anxious to break in a new herd. The idea of that guy riding out of the Doors of Death made Percy's sides hurt all over again. His ribs throbbed where the *arai* had unleashed Geryon's dying curse back in the forest. He wanted to march up to the three-bodied rancher, smack him in the face and yell, *Thanks a lot, Tex!*

Sadly, he couldn't.

How many other old enemies were in this crowd? Percy began to realize that every battle he'd ever won had only been a temporary victory. No matter how strong or lucky he was, no matter how many monsters he destroyed, Percy would eventually fail. He was only one mortal. He would get too old, too weak, or too slow. He would die. And these monsters . . . they lasted *forever*. They just kept coming back. Maybe it would take them months or years to re-form, maybe even centuries. But they *would* be reborn.

Seeing them assembled in Tartarus, Percy felt as hopeless as the spirits in the River Cocytus. So what if he was a hero? So what if he did something brave? Evil was always here, regenerating, bubbling under the surface. Percy was no more than a minor annoyance to these immortal beings. They just had to outwait him. Some day, Percy's sons or daughters might have to face them all over again.

Sons and daughters.

The thought jarred him. As quickly as hopelessness had overtaken him, it disappeared. He glanced at Annabeth. She still looked like a misty corpse, but he imagined her true appearance – her grey eyes full of determination, her blonde hair pulled back in a bandanna, her face weary and streaked with grime, but as beautiful as ever.

Okay, maybe monsters kept coming back forever. But so did demigods. Generation after generation, Camp Half-Blood had endured. And Camp Jupiter. Even separately, the two camps had survived. Now, if the Greeks and Romans could come together, they would be even stronger.

There was still hope. He and Annabeth come this far. The Doors of Death were almost within reach.

Sons and daughters. A ridiculous thought. An awesome thought. Right there in the middle of Tartarus, Percy grinned.

'What's wrong?' Annabeth whispered.

With his zombie Death Mist disguise, Percy probably looked like he was grimacing in pain.

'Nothing,' he said. 'I was just –'

Somewhere in front of them, a deep voice bellowed: 'IAPETUS!'

LXII

PERCY

A Titan strode towards them, casually kicking lesser monsters out of his way. He was roughly the same height as Bob, with elaborate Stygian iron armour, a single diamond blazing in the centre of his breastplate. His eyes were blue-white, like core samples from a glacier and just as cold. His hair was the same colour, cut military style. A battle helmet shaped like a bear's head was tucked under his arm. From his belt hung a sword the size of a surfboard.

Despite his battle scars, the Titan's face was handsome and strangely familiar. Percy was pretty sure he'd never seen the guy before, but his eyes and his smile reminded Percy of someone . . .

The Titan stopped in front of Bob. He clapped him on the shoulder. 'Iapetus! Don't tell me you don't recognize your own brother!'

'No!' Bob agreed nervously. 'I won't tell you that.'

The other Titan threw back his head and laughed. 'I heard

you were thrown into the Lethe. Must've been terrible! We all knew you would heal eventually. It's Koios! Koios!'

'Of course,' Bob said. 'Koios, Titan of . . .'

'The North!' Koios said.

'I know!' Bob shouted.

They laughed together and took turns hitting each other in the arm.

Apparently miffed by all the jostling, Small Bob crawled onto Bob's head and began making a nest in the Titan's silver hair.

'Poor old Iapetus,' said Koios. 'They must have laid you low indeed. Look at you! A broom? A servant's uniform? A cat in your hair? Truly, Hades must pay for these insults. Who was that demigod who took your memory? Bah! We must rip him to pieces, you and I, eh?'

'Ha-ha.' Bob swallowed. 'Yes, indeed. Rip him to pieces.'

Percy's fingers closed around his pen. He didn't think much of Bob's brother, even without the *rip him to pieces* threat. Compared to Bob's simple way of speaking, Koios sounded like he was reciting Shakespeare. That alone was enough to make Percy irritated.

He was ready to uncap Riptide if he had to, but so far Koios didn't seem to have noticed him. And Bob hadn't betrayed them yet, though he'd had plenty of opportunities.

'Ah, it's good to see you . . .' Koios drummed his fingers on his bear's-head helmet. 'You remember what fun we had in the old days?'

'Of course!' Bob chirped. 'When we, uh . . .'

'Holding down our father Ouranos,' Koios said.

'Yes! We loved wrestling with Dad . . .'

'We restrained him.'

'That's what I meant!'

'While Kronos cut him to pieces with his scythe.'

'Yes, ha-ha.' Bob looked mildly ill. 'What fun.'

'You grabbed Father's right foot, as I recall,' Koios said. 'And Ouranos kicked you in the face as he struggled. How we used to tease you about that!'

'Silly me,' Bob agreed.

'Sadly, our brother Kronos was dissolved by those impudent demigods.' Koios heaved a sigh. 'Bits and pieces of his essence remain, but nothing you could put together again. I suppose some injuries even Tartarus cannot heal.'

'Alas!'

'But the rest of us have another chance to shine, eh?' He leaned forward conspiratorially. 'These giants may *think* they will rule. Let them be our shock troops and destroy the Olympians – all well and good. But once the Earth Mother is awake she will remember that *we* are her eldest children. Mark my words. The Titans will yet rule the cosmos.'

'Hmm,' Bob said. 'The giants may not like that.'

'Spit on what *they* like,' Koios said. 'They've already passed through the Doors of Death, anyway, back to the mortal world. Polybotes was the last one, not half an hour ago, still grumbling about missing his prey. Apparently some demigods he was after got swallowed by Nyx. Never see *them* again, I wager!'

Annabeth gripped Percy's wrist. Through the Death Mist,

he couldn't read her expression very well, but he saw the alarm in her eyes.

If the giants had already passed through the Doors, then at least they wouldn't be hunting through Tartarus for Percy and Annabeth. Unfortunately, that also meant their friends in the mortal world were in even greater danger. All of the earlier fights with the giants had been in vain. Their enemies would be reborn as strong as ever.

'Well!' Koios drew his massive sword. The blade radiated a cold deeper than the Hubbard Glacier. 'I must be off. Leto should have regenerated by now. I will convince her to fight.'

'Of course,' Bob murmured. 'Leto.'

Koios laughed. 'You've forgotten my daughter, as well? I suppose it's been too long since you've seen her. The peaceful ones like her always take the longest to re-form. This time, though, I'm sure Leto will fight for vengeance. The way Zeus treated her, after she bore him those fine twins? Outrageous!'

Percy almost grunted out loud.

The twins.

He remembered the name Leto: the mother of Apollo and Artemis. This guy Koios looked vaguely familiar because he had Artemis's cold eyes and Apollo's smile. The Titan was their grandfather, Leto's father. The idea gave Percy a migraine.

'Well! I'll see you in the mortal world!' Koios chestbumped Bob, almost knocking the cat off his head. 'Oh, and our two *other* brothers are guarding this side of the Doors, so you'll see them soon enough!'

'I will?'

'Count on it!' Koios lumbered off, almost knocking over Percy and Annabeth as they scrambled out of his way.

Before the crowd of monsters could fill the empty space, Percy motioned for Bob to lean in.

'You okay, big guy?' Percy whispered.

Bob frowned. 'I do not know. In all this –' he gestured around them – 'what is the meaning of *okay*?'

Fair point, Percy thought.

Annabeth peered towards the Doors of Death, though the crowd of monsters blocked them from view. 'Did I hear correctly? Two more Titans guarding our exit? That's not good.'

Percy looked at Bob. The Titan's distant expression worried him.

'Do you remember Koios?' he asked gently. 'All that stuff he was talking about?'

Bob gripped his broom. 'When he told it, I remembered. He handed me my past like . . . like a spear. But I do not know if I should take it. Is it still mine, if I do not want it?'

'No,' Annabeth said firmly. 'Bob, you're different now. You're *better*.'

The kitten jumped off Bob's head. He circled the Titan's feet, bumping his head against the Titan's trouser cuffs. Bob didn't seem to notice.

Percy wished he could be as certain as Annabeth. He wished he could tell Bob with absolute confidence that he should forget about his past.

But Percy understood Bob's confusion. He remembered

the day he'd opened his eyes at the Wolf House in California, his memory wiped clean by Hera. If somebody had been waiting for Percy when he first woke up, if they'd convinced Percy that his name was Bob and he was a friend of the Titans and the giants . . . would Percy have believed it? Would he have felt betrayed once he found out his true identity?

This is different, he told himself. *We're the good guys.*

But were they? Percy had left Bob in Hades's palace, at the mercy of a new master who hated him. Percy didn't feel like he had much right to tell Bob what to do now – even if their lives depended on it.

'I think you can choose, Bob,' Percy ventured. 'Take the parts of Iapetus's past that you want to keep. Leave the rest. Your future is what matters.'

'Future . . .' Bob mused. 'That is a mortal concept. I am not meant to change, Percy Friend.' He gazed around him at the horde of monsters. 'We are the same . . . forever.'

'If you were the same,' Percy said, 'Annabeth and I would be dead already. Maybe we weren't meant to be friends, but we *are*. You've been the best friend we could ask for.'

Bob's silver eyes looked darker than usual. He held out his hand, and Small Bob the kitten jumped into it. The Titan rose to his full height. 'Let us go, then, friends. Not much further.'

Stomping on Tartarus's heart wasn't nearly as much fun as it sounded.

The purplish ground was slippery and constantly pulsing. It looked flat from a distance, but up close it was made of folds and ridges that got harder to navigate the further they walked. Gnarled lumps of red arteries and blue veins gave Percy some footholds when he had to climb, but the going was slow.

And, of course, the monsters were everywhere. Packs of hellhounds prowled the plains, baying and snarling and attacking any monster that dropped its guard. *Arai* wheeled overhead on leathery wings, making ghastly dark silhouettes in the poison clouds.

Percy stumbled. His hand touched a red artery, and a tingling sensation went up his arm. 'There's water in here,' he said. 'Actual water.'

Bob grunted. 'One of the five rivers. His blood.'

'His blood?' Annabeth stepped away from the nearest clump of veins. 'I knew the Underworld rivers all emptied into Tartarus, but –'

'Yes,' Bob agreed. 'They all flow through his heart.'

Percy traced his hand across a web of capillaries. Was the water of the Styx flowing beneath his fingers, or maybe the Lethe? If one of those veins popped when he stepped on it . . . Percy shuddered. He realized he was taking a stroll across the most dangerous circulatory system in the universe.

'We should hurry,' Annabeth said. 'If we can't . . .'

Her voice trailed off.

Ahead of them, jagged streaks of darkness tore through the air – like lightning, except pure black.

'The Doors,' Bob said. 'Must be a large group going through.'

Percy's mouth tasted like gorgon's blood. Even if his friends from the *Argo II* managed to find the other side of the Doors of Death, how could they possibly fight the waves of monsters that were coming through, especially if all the giants were already waiting for them?

'Do all the monsters go through the House of Hades?' he asked. 'How big *is* that place?'

Bob shrugged. 'Perhaps they are sent elsewhere when they step through. The House of Hades is in the earth, yes? That is Gaia's realm. She could send her minions wherever she wishes.'

Percy's spirits sank. Monsters coming through the Doors of Death to threaten his friends at Epirus – that was bad enough. Now he imagined the ground on the mortal side as one big subway system, depositing giants and other nasties anywhere Gaia wanted them to go – Camp Half-Blood, Camp Jupiter or in the path of the *Argo II* before it could even reach Epirus.

'If Gaia has that much power,' Annabeth asked, 'couldn't she control where *we* end up?'

Percy really hated that question. Sometimes he wished Annabeth weren't so smart.

Bob scratched his chin. 'You are not monsters. It may be different for you.'

Great, Percy thought.

He didn't relish the idea of Gaia waiting for them on the other side, ready to teleport them into the middle of a mountain, but at least the Doors were a chance to get out of Tartarus. It wasn't like they had a better option.

Bob helped them over the top of another ridge. Suddenly the Doors of Death were in plain view – a freestanding rectangle of darkness at the top of the next heart-muscle hill, about a quarter of a mile away, surrounding by a horde of monsters so thick Percy could've walked on their heads all the way across.

The Doors were still too far away to make out much detail, but the Titans flanking either side were familiar enough. The one on the left wore shining golden armour that shimmered with heat.

'Hyperion,' Percy muttered. 'That guy just won't stay dead.'

The one on the right wore dark-blue armour, with ram horns curling from the sides of his helmet. Percy had only seen him in dreams before, but it was definitely Krios, the Titan that Jason had killed in the battle for Mount Tam.

'Bob's other brothers,' Annabeth said. The Death Mist shimmered around her, temporarily turning her face into a grinning skull. 'Bob, if you have to fight them, can you?'

Bob hefted his broom, like he was ready for a messy cleaning job. 'We must hurry,' he said, which Percy noticed wasn't really an answer. 'Follow me.'

LXIII

PERCY

SO FAR, THEIR DEATH MIST camouflage plan seemed to be working. So, naturally, Percy expected a massive last-minute fail.

Fifty feet from the Doors of Death, he and Annabeth froze.

'Oh, gods,' Annabeth murmured. 'They're the *same*.'

Percy knew what she meant. Framed in Stygian iron, the magical portal was a set of elevator doors – two panels of silver and black etched with art deco designs. Except for the fact that the colours were inverted, they looked exactly like the elevators in the Empire State Building, the entrance to Olympus.

Seeing them, Percy felt so homesick he couldn't breathe. He didn't just miss Mount Olympus. He missed everything he'd left behind: New York City, Camp Half-Blood, his mom and stepdad. His eyes stung. He didn't trust himself to talk.

The Doors of Death seemed like a personal insult, designed to remind him of everything he couldn't have.

As he got over his initial shock, he noticed other details: the frost spreading from the base of the Doors, the purplish glow in the air around them and the chains that held them fast.

Cords of black iron ran down either side of the frame, like rigging lines on a suspension bridge. They were tethered to hooks embedded in the fleshy ground. The two Titans, Krios and Hyperion, stood guard at the anchor points.

As Percy watched, the entire frame shuddered. Black lightning flashed into the sky. The chains shook, and the Titans planted their feet on the hooks to keep them secure. The Doors slid open, revealing the gilded interior of an elevator car.

Percy tensed, ready to charge forward, but Bob planted a hand on his shoulder. 'Wait,' he cautioned.

Hyperion yelled to the surrounding crowd: 'Group A-22! Hurry up, you sluggards!'

A dozen Cyclopes rushed forward, waving little red tickets and shouting excitedly. They shouldn't have been able to fit inside those human-sized doors, but as the Cyclopes got close their bodies distorted and shrank, the Doors of Death sucking them inside.

The Titan Krios jabbed his thumb against the UP button on the elevator's right side. The Doors slid closed.

The frame shuddered again. Dark lightning faded.

'You must understand how it works,' Bob muttered. He addressed the kitten in his palm, maybe so the other monsters wouldn't wonder who he was talking to. 'Each time the Doors open, they try to teleport to a new location. Thanatos made them this way, so only he could find them. But now they are chained. The Doors cannot relocate.'

'Then we cut the chains,' Annabeth whispered.

Percy looked at the blazing form of Hyperion. The last time he'd fought the Titan, it had taken every ounce of his strength. Even then Percy had almost died. Now there were *two* Titans, with several thousand monsters for backup.

'Our camouflage,' he said. 'Will it disappear if we do something aggressive, like cutting the chains?'

'I do not know,' Bob told his kitten.

'Mrow,' said Small Bob.

'Bob, you'll have to distract them,' Annabeth said. 'Percy and I will sneak around the two Titans and cut the chains from behind.'

'Yes, fine,' Bob said. 'But that is only one problem. Once you are inside the Doors, someone must stay outside to push the button and defend it.'

Percy tried to swallow. 'Uh . . . defend the button?'

Bob nodded, scratching his kitten under the chin. 'Someone must keep pressing the UP button for twelve minutes, or the journey will not finish.'

Percy glanced at the Doors. Sure enough, Krios still had his thumb jammed on the UP button. Twelve minutes . . . Somehow, they would have to get the Titans away from those doors. Then Bob, Percy or Annabeth would have to keep that button pushed for twelve long minutes, in the middle of an army of monsters in the heart of Tartarus, while the other two rode to the mortal world. It was impossible.

'Why twelve minutes?' Percy asked.

'I do not know,' Bob said. 'Why twelve Olympians or twelve Titans?'

'Fair enough,' Percy said, though he had a bitter taste in his mouth.

'What do you mean the journey won't finish?' Annabeth asked. 'What happens to the passengers?'

Bob didn't answer. Judging from his pained expression, Percy decided he didn't want to be in that elevator if the car stalled between Tartarus and the mortal world.

'If we *do* push the button for twelve minutes,' Percy said, 'and the chains are cut –'

'The Doors should reset,' Bob said. 'That is what they are supposed to do. They will disappear from Tartarus. They will appear somewhere else, where Gaia cannot use them.'

'Thanatos can reclaim them,' Annabeth said. 'Death goes back to normal, and the monsters lose their shortcut to the mortal world.'

Percy exhaled. 'Easy-peasy. Except for . . . well, everything.'

Small Bob purred.

'I will push the button,' Bob volunteered.

A mix of feelings churned in Percy's gut – grief, sadness, gratitude and guilt thickening into emotional cement. 'Bob, we can't ask you to do that. You want to go through the Doors, too. You want to see the sky again and the stars and –'

'I would like that,' Bob agreed. 'But someone must push the button. And once the chains are cut . . . my brethren will fight to stop your passage. They will not want the Doors to disappear.'

Percy gazed at the endless horde of monsters. Even if he let Bob make this sacrifice, how could one Titan defend himself against so many for twelve minutes, all the while keeping his finger on a button?

The cement settled in Percy's stomach. He had always suspected how this would end. He would have to stay behind. While Bob fended off the army, Percy would hold the elevator button and make sure Annabeth got to safety.

Somehow, he had to convince her to go without him. As long as she was safe and the Doors disappeared, he could die knowing he'd done something right.

'Percy . . . ?' Annabeth stared at him, a suspicious edge to her voice.

She was too smart. If he met her eyes, she would see exactly what he was thinking.

'First things first,' he said. 'Let's cut those chains.'

LXIV

PERCY

'Iapetus!' Hyperion bellowed. 'Well, well. I thought you were hiding under a cleaning bucket somewhere.'

Bob lumbered forward, scowling. 'I was not hiding.'

Percy crept towards the right side of the Doors. Annabeth sneaked towards the left. The Titans gave no sign of noticing them, but Percy took no chances. He kept Riptide in pen form. He crouched low, stepping as quietly as possible. The lesser monsters kept a respectful distance from the Titans, so there was enough empty space to manoeuvre around the Doors, but Percy was keenly aware of the snarling mob at his back.

Annabeth had decided to take the side Hyperion was guarding, on the theory that Hyperion was more likely to sense Percy. After all, Percy was the last one to have killed him in the mortal world. That was fine with Percy. After being in Tartarus for so long, he could barely look at Hyperion's burning golden armour without getting spots in his eyes.

On Percy's side of the Doors, Krios stood dark and silent,

his ram-horned helmet covering his face. He kept one foot planted on the chain's anchor and his thumb on the UP button.

Bob faced his brethren. He planted his spear and tried to look as fierce as possible with a kitten on his shoulder. 'Hyperion and Krios. I remember you both.'

'Do you, Iapetus?' The golden Titan laughed, glancing at Krios to share the joke. 'Well, that's good to know! I heard Percy Jackson turned you into a brainwashed scullery maid. What did he rename you . . . Betty?'

'Bob,' snarled Bob.

'Well, it's about time you showed up, *Bob*. Krios and I have been stuck here for *weeks* –'

'Hours,' Krios corrected, his voice a deep rumble inside his helmet.

'Whatever!' Hyperion said. 'It's boring work, guarding these doors, shuffling monsters through at Gaia's orders. Krios, what's our next group, anyway?'

'Double Red,' said Krios.

Hyperion sighed. The flames glowed hotter across his shoulders. 'Double Red. Why do we go from A-22 to Double Red? What kind of system is that?' He glared at Bob. 'This is no job for me – the Lord of Light! Titan of the East! Master of Dawn! Why am I forced to wait in the darkness while the *giants* go into battle and get all the glory? Now, *Krios* I can understand –'

'I get all the worst assignments,' Krios muttered, his thumb still on the button.

'But *me*?' Hyperion said. 'Ridiculous! This should be your job, Iapetus. Here, take my place for a while.'

Bob stared at the Doors, but his gaze was distant – lost in the past. 'The four of us held down our father, Ouranos,' he remembered. 'Koios and me and the two of you. Kronos promised us mastery of the four corners of the earth for helping with the murder.'

'Indeed,' Hyperion said. 'And I was happy to do it! I would've wielded the scythe myself if I'd had the chance! But you, *Bob* . . . you were always conflicted about that killing, weren't you? The *soft* Titan of the West, soft as the sunset! Why our parents named you the *Piercer,* I will never know. More like the *Whimper.*'

Percy reached the anchor hook. He uncapped his pen and Riptide grew to full length. Krios didn't react. His attention was firmly fixed on Bob, who had just levelled the point of his spear at Hyperion's chest.

'I can still pierce,' Bob said, his voice low and even. 'You brag too much, Hyperion. You are bright and fiery, but Percy Jackson defeated you anyway. I hear you became a nice tree in Central Park.'

Hyperion's eyes smouldered. 'Careful, brother.'

'At least a janitor's work is honest,' Bob said. 'I clean up after others. I leave the palace better than I found it. But you . . . you do not care what messes you make. You followed Kronos blindly. Now you take orders from Gaia.'

'She is our *mother!*' Hyperion bellowed.

'She did not wake for *our* war on Olympus,' Bob recalled. 'She favours her second brood, the giants.'

Krios grunted. 'That's true enough. The children of the pit.'

'Both of you hold your tongues!' Hyperion's voice was tinged with fear. 'You never know when he is listening.'

The elevator dinged. All three Titans jumped.

Had it been twelve minutes? Percy had lost track of time. Krios took his finger off the button and called out, 'Double Red! Where is Double Red?'

Hordes of monsters stirred and jostled one another, but none of them came forward.

Krios heaved a sigh. 'I *told* them to hang on to their tickets. Double Red! You'll lose your place in the queue!'

Annabeth was in position, right behind Hyperion. She raised her drakon-bone sword over the base of the chains. In the fiery light of the Titan's armour, her Death Mist disguise made her look like a burning ghoul.

She held up three fingers, ready to count down. They had to cut the chains before the next group tried to take the elevator, but they also had to make sure the Titans were as distracted as possible.

Hyperion muttered a curse. 'Just *wonderful*. This will completely mess up our schedule.' He sneered at Bob. 'Make your choice, brother. Fight us or help us. I don't have time for your lectures.'

Bob glanced at Annabeth and Percy. Percy thought he might start a fight, but instead he raised the point of his spear. 'Very well. I will take guard duty. Which of you wants a break first?'

'Me, of course,' Hyperion said.

'Me!' Krios snapped. 'I've been holding that button so long my thumb is going to fall off.'

'I've been standing here longer,' Hyperion grumbled. 'You two guard the Doors while *I* go up to the mortal world. I have some Greek heroes to wreak vengeance upon!'

'Oh, no!' Krios complained. 'That Roman boy is on his way to Epirus – the one who killed me on Mount Othrys. Got lucky, he did. Now it's my turn.'

'Bah!' Hyperion drew his sword. 'I'll gut you first, Ram-head!'

Krios raised his own blade. 'You can try, but I won't be stuck in this stinking pit any longer!'

Annabeth caught Percy's eyes. She mouthed: *One, two* –

Before he could strike the chains, a high-pitched whine pierced his ears, like the sound of an incoming rocket. Percy just had time to think: *Uh-oh*. Then an explosion rocked the hillside. A wave of heat knocked Percy backwards. Dark shrapnel ripped through Krios and Hyperion, shredding them as easily as wood in a chipper.

STINKING PIT. A hollow voice rolled across the plains, shaking the warm fleshy ground.

Bob staggered to his feet. Somehow the explosion hadn't touched him. He swept his spear in front of him, trying to locate the source of the voice. Small Bob the kitten crawled into his coveralls.

Annabeth had landed about twenty feet from the Doors. When she stood, Percy was so relieved she was alive it took him a moment to realize she looked like herself. The Death Mist had evaporated.

He looked at his own hands. His disguise was gone too.

TITANS, said the voice disdainfully. *LESSER BEINGS. IMPERFECT AND WEAK.*

In front of the Doors of Death, the air darkened and solidified. The being who appeared was so massive, radiating such pure malevolence, that Percy wanted to crawl away and hide.

Instead, he forced his eyes to trace the god's form, starting with his black iron boots, each one as large as a coffin. His legs were covered in dark greaves; his flesh all thick purple muscle, like the ground. His armoured skirt was made from thousands of blackened, twisted bones, woven together like chain links and clasped in place by a belt of interlocking monstrous arms.

On the surface of the warrior's breastplate, murky faces appeared and submerged – giants, Cyclopes, gorgons and drakons – all pressing against the armour as if trying to get out.

The warrior's arms were bare – muscular, purple and glistening – his hands as large as crane scoops.

Worst of all was his head: a helmet of twisted rock and metal with no particular shape – just jagged spikes and pulsing patches of magma. His entire face was a whirlpool – an inward spiral of darkness. As Percy watched, the last particles of Titan essence from Hyperion and Krios were vacuumed into the warrior's maw.

Somehow Percy found his voice. 'Tartarus.'

The warrior made a sound like a mountain cracking in half: a roar or a laugh, Percy couldn't be sure.

This form is only a small manifestation of my power, said the god. *But it is enough to deal with you. I do not interfere lightly, little demigod. It is beneath me to deal with gnats such as yourself.*

'Uh . . .' Percy's legs threatened to collapse under him. 'Don't . . . you know . . . go to any trouble.'

You have proven surprisingly resilient, Tartarus said. *You have come too far. I can no longer stand by and watch your progress.*

Tartarus spread his arms. Throughout the valley, thousands of monsters wailed and roared, clashing their weapons and bellowing in triumph. The Doors of Death shuddered in their chains.

Be honoured, little demigods, said the god of the pit. *Even the Olympians were never worthy of my personal attention. But you will be destroyed by Tartarus himself!*

LXV

FRANK

FRANK WAS HOPING FOR FIREWORKS.

Or at least a big sign that read: WELCOME HOME!

More than three thousand years ago, his Greek ancestor – good old Periclymenus the shape-shifter – had sailed east with the Argonauts. Centuries later, Periclymenus's descendants had served in the eastern Roman legions. Then, through a series of misadventures, the family had ended up in China, finally emigrating to Canada in the twentieth century. Now Frank was back in Greece, which meant that the Zhang family had completely circled the globe.

That seemed like cause for celebration, but the only welcoming committee was a flock of wild, hungry harpies who attacked the ship. Frank felt kind of bad as he shot them down with his bow. He kept thinking of Ella, their freakishly smart harpy friend from Portland. But these harpies weren't Ella. They gladly would have chewed Frank's face off. So he blasted them into clouds of dust and feathers.

The Greek landscape below was just as inhospitable. The hills were strewn with boulders and stunted cedars, all shimmering in the hazy air. The sun beat down as if trying to hammer the countryside into a Celestial bronze shield. Even from a hundred feet up, Frank could hear the drone of cicadas buzzing in the trees – a sleepy, otherworldly sound that made his eyes heavy. Even the duelling voices of the war gods inside his head seemed to have dozed off. They had hardly bothered Frank at all since the crew had crossed into Greece.

Sweat trickled down his neck. After being frozen below deck by that crazy snow goddess, Frank had thought he would never feel warm again, but now the back of his shirt was soaked.

'Hot and steamy!' Leo grinned at the helm. 'Makes me homesick for Houston! What do you say, Hazel? All we need now are some giant mosquitoes, and it'll feel just like the Gulf Coast!'

'Thanks a lot, Leo,' Hazel grumbled. 'We'll probably get attacked by Ancient Greek mosquito monsters now.'

Frank studied the two of them, quietly marvelling how the tension between them had disappeared. Whatever had happened to Leo during his five days of exile, it had changed him. He still joked around, but Frank sensed something different about him – like a ship with a new keel. Maybe you couldn't *see* the keel, but you could tell it was there by the way the ship cut through the waves.

Leo didn't seem so intent on teasing Frank. He chatted more easily with Hazel – not stealing those wistful, mooning glances that had always made Frank uncomfortable.

Hazel had diagnosed the problem privately to Frank: 'He met someone.'

Frank was incredulous. 'How? Where? How could you possibly know?'

Hazel smiled. 'I just do.'

As if she were a child of Venus rather than Pluto. Frank didn't get it.

Of course he was relieved that Leo wasn't hitting on his girl, but Frank was also kind of worried about Leo. Sure, they'd had their differences, but after all they'd been through together Frank didn't want to see Leo get his heart broken.

'There!' Nico's voice shook Frank out of his thoughts. As usual, di Angelo was perched atop the foremast. He pointed towards a glittering green river snaking through the hills a kilometre away. 'Manoeuvre us that way. We're close to the temple. *Very* close.'

As if to prove his point, black lightning ripped through the sky, leaving dark spots before Frank's eyes and making the hairs on his arms stand up.

Jason strapped on his sword belt. 'Everyone, arm yourself. Leo, get us close, but don't land – no more contact with the ground than necessary. Piper, Hazel, get the mooring ropes.'

'On it!' Piper said.

Hazel gave Frank a peck on the cheek and ran to help.

'Frank,' Jason called, 'get below and find Coach Hedge.'

'Yep!'

He climbed downstairs and headed for Hedge's cabin. As he neared the door, he slowed down. He didn't want to surprise the satyr with any loud noises. Coach Hedge had a habit of jumping into the gangway with his baseball bat if he thought attackers were on board. Frank had almost got his head taken off a couple of times on his way to the bathroom.

He raised his hand to knock. Then he realized the door was cracked open. He heard Coach Hedge talking inside.

'Come on, babe!' the satyr said. 'You know it's not like that!'

Frank froze. He didn't mean to eavesdrop, but he wasn't sure what to do. Hazel had mentioned being worried about the coach. She'd insisted something was bothering him, but Frank hadn't thought much of it until now.

He'd never heard the coach talk so *gently*. Usually the only sounds Frank heard from the coach's cabin were sporting events on the TV, or the coach yelling, 'Yeah! Get 'em!' as he watched his favourite martial arts movies. Frank was pretty sure the coach wouldn't be calling Chuck Norris *babe*.

Another voice spoke – female, but barely audible, like it was coming from a long way away.

'I will,' Coach Hedge promised. 'But, uh, we're going into battle –' he cleared his throat – 'and it may get ugly. You just *stay safe*. I'll get back. Honest.'

Frank couldn't stand it any more. He knocked loudly. 'Hey, Coach?'

The talking stopped.

Frank counted to six. The door flew open.

Coach Hedge stood there scowling, his eyes bloodshot, like he'd been watching too much TV. He wore his usual baseball cap and gym shorts, with a leather cuirass over his shirt and a whistle hanging from his neck, maybe in case he wanted to call a foul against the monster armies.

'Zhang. What do you want?'

'Uh, we're getting ready for battle. We need you above deck.'

The coach's goatee quivered. 'Yeah. Course you do.' He sounded strangely unexcited about the prospect of a fight.

'I didn't mean to – I mean, I heard you talking,' Frank stammered. 'Were you sending an Iris-message?'

Hedge looked like he might smack Frank in the face or at least blow the whistle really loud. Then his shoulders slumped. He heaved a sigh and turned inside, leaving Frank standing awkwardly in the doorway.

The coach plopped down on his berth. His cupped his chin in his hand and stared glumly around his cabin. The place looked like a college dorm room after a hurricane – the floor strewn with laundry (maybe for wearing, maybe for snacks; it was hard to tell with satyrs), DVDs and dirty dishes scattered around the TV on the dresser. Every time the ship tilted, a mismatched herd of sports equipment rolled across the floor – footballs, basketballs, baseballs and, for some reason, a single billiard ball. Tufts of goat hair floated through the air and collected under the furniture in clumps. Dust goats? Goat bunnies?

On the coach's nightstand sat a bowl of water, a stack of golden drachmas, a flashlight and glass prism for making rainbows. The coach had obviously come prepared to make a lot of Iris-messages.

Frank remembered what Piper had told him about the coach's cloud nymph girlfriend who worked for Piper's dad. What was the girlfriend's name . . . Melinda? Millicent? No, Mellie.

'Uh, is your girlfriend Mellie all right?' Frank ventured.

'None of your business!' the coach snapped.

'Okay.'

Hedge rolled his eyes. 'Fine! If you must know – yes, I was talking to Mellie. But she's not my girlfriend any more.'

'Oh . . .' Frank's heart sank. 'You broke up?'

'No, you dolt! We got married! She's my wife!'

Frank would've been less stunned if the coach had smacked him. 'Coach, that's – that's great! When – how –?'

'None of your business!' he yelled again.

'Um . . . all right.'

'End of May,' the coach said. 'Just before the *Argo II* sailed. We didn't want to make a big deal out of it.'

Frank felt like the ship was tilting again, but it must have been just him. The herd of wild sports equipment stayed put against the far wall.

All this time the coach had been *married*? In spite of being a newlywed, he'd agreed to come on this quest. No wonder Hedge made so many calls back home. No wonder he was so cranky and belligerent.

Still . . . Frank sensed there was more going on. The coach's tone during the Iris-message made it sound like they were discussing a problem.

'I didn't mean to eavesdrop,' Frank said. 'But . . . is she okay?'

'It was a private conversation!'

'Yeah. You're right.'

'Fine! I'll tell you.' Hedge plucked some fur off his thigh and let it float through the air. 'She took a break from her job in L.A., went to Camp Half-Blood for the summer, because we figured –' His voice cracked. 'We figured it would be safer. Now she's stuck there, with the Romans about to attack. She's . . . she's pretty scared.'

Frank became very aware of the centurion badge on his shirt, the SPQR tattoo on his forearm.

'Sorry,' he murmured. 'But, if she's a cloud spirit, couldn't she just . . . you know, float away?'

The coach curled his fingers around the grip of his baseball bat. 'Normally, yeah. But see . . . she's in a delicate condition. It wouldn't be safe.'

'A delicate . . .' Frank's eyes widened. 'She's going to have a *baby*? You're going to be a *dad*?'

'Shout it a little louder,' Hedge grumbled. 'I don't think they heard you in Croatia.'

Frank couldn't help grinning. 'But, Coach, that's awesome! A little baby satyr? Or maybe a nymph? You'll be a fantastic dad.'

Frank wasn't sure why he felt that way, considering the coach's love of baseball bats and roundhouse kicks, but he *was* sure.

Coach Hedge scowled even deeper. 'The war's coming, Zhang. Nowhere is safe. I should be there for Mellie. If I gotta die somewhere –'

'Hey, nobody's going to die,' Frank said.

Hedge met his eyes. Frank could tell the coach didn't believe it.

'Always had a soft spot for children of Ares,' Hedge muttered. 'Or Mars – whichever. Maybe that's why I'm not pulverizing you for asking so many questions.'

'But I wasn't –'

'Fine, I'll tell you!' Hedge sighed again. 'Back when I was on my first assignment as a seeker, I was way out in Arizona. Brought in this kid named Clarisse.'

'Clarisse?'

'Sibling of yours,' Hedge said. 'Ares kid. Violent. Rude. Lots of potential. Anyway, while I was out, I had this dream about my mom. She – she was a cloud nymph like Mellie. I dreamed she was in trouble and needed my help right away. But I said to myself, *Nah, it's just a dream. Who would hurt a sweet old cloud nymph? Besides, I gotta get this half-blood to safety.* So I finished my mission, brought Clarisse to Camp Half-Blood. Afterwards, I went looking for my mom. I was too late.'

Frank watched the tuft of goat hair settle on top of a basketball. 'What happened to her?'

Hedge shrugged. 'No idea. Never saw her again. Maybe if I'd been there for her, if I'd got back sooner . . .'

Frank wanted to say something comforting, but he wasn't sure what. He had lost his mom in the war in Afghanistan, and he knew how empty the words *I'm sorry* could sound.

'You were doing your job,' Frank offered. 'You saved a demigod's life.'

Hedge grunted. 'Now my wife and my unborn kid are in

danger, halfway across the world, and I can't do anything to help.'

'You *are* doing something,' Frank said. 'We're over here to stop the giants from waking Gaia. That's the best way we can keep our friends safe.'

'Yeah. Yeah, I suppose.'

Frank wished he could do more to lift Hedge's spirits, but this talk was making *him* worry about everyone he'd left behind. He wondered who was defending Camp Jupiter now that the legion had marched east, especially with all the monsters Gaia was unleashing from the Doors of Death. He worried about his friends in the Fifth Cohort and how they must be feeling as Octavian ordered them to march on Camp Half-Blood. Frank wanted to be back there, if only to stuff a teddy bear down the throat of that slimeball augur.

The ship listed forward. The herd of sports equipment rolled under the coach's berth.

'We're descending,' said Hedge. 'We'd better get above.'

'Yeah,' Frank said, his voice hoarse.

'You're a nosy Roman, Zhang.'

'But –'

'Come on,' Hedge said. 'And not a word about this to the others, you blabbermouth.'

As the others made fast the aerial moorings, Leo grabbed Frank and Hazel by the arms. He dragged them to the aft ballista. 'Okay, here's the plan.'

Hazel narrowed her eyes. 'I *hate* your plans.'

'I need that piece of magic firewood,' Leo said. 'Snappy!'

Frank nearly choked on his own tongue. Hazel backed away, instinctively covering her coat pocket. 'Leo, you can't –'

'I found a solution.' Leo turned to Frank. 'It's your call, big guy, but I can protect you.'

Frank thought about how many times he'd seen Leo's fingers burst into flame. One false move, and Leo could incinerate the piece of tinder that controlled Frank's life.

But for some reason Frank wasn't terrified. Since facing down the cow monsters in Venice, Frank had barely thought about his fragile lifeline. Yes, the smallest bit of fire might kill him. But he'd also survived some impossible things and made his dad proud. Frank had decided that whatever his fate was, he wouldn't worry about it. He would just do the best he could to help his friends.

Besides, Leo sounded serious. His eyes were still full of that weird melancholy, like he was in two places at once, but nothing about his expression indicated any kind of joke.

'Go ahead, Hazel,' Frank said.

'But . . .' Hazel took a deep breath. 'Okay.' She took out the piece of firewood and handed it to Leo.

In Leo's hands, it wasn't much bigger than a screwdriver. The tinder was still charred on one side from where Frank had used it to burn through the icy chains that had imprisoned the god Thanatos in Alaska.

From a pocket of his tool belt, Leo produced a piece of white cloth. 'Behold!'

Frank scowled. 'A handkerchief?'

'A surrender flag?' Hazel guessed.

'No, unbelievers!' Leo said. 'This is a pouch woven from seriously cool fabric – a gift from a friend of mine.'

Leo slipped the firewood into the pouch and pulled it closed with a tie of bronze thread.

'The drawstring was my idea,' Leo said proudly. 'It took some work, lacing that into the fabric, but the pouch won't open unless you want it to. The fabric breathes just like regular cloth, so the firewood isn't any more sealed up than it would be in Hazel's coat pocket.'

'Uh . . .' Hazel said. 'How is that an improvement, then?'

'Hold this so I don't give you a heart attack.' Leo tossed the pouch to Frank, who almost fumbled it.

Leo summoned a white-hot ball of fire into his right hand. He held his left forearm over the flames, grinning as they licked the sleeve of his jacket.

'See?' he said. 'It doesn't burn!'

Frank didn't like to argue with a guy who was holding a ball of fire, but he said, 'Uh . . . you're *immune* to flames.'

Leo rolled his eyes. 'Yeah, but I have to *concentrate* if I don't want my clothes to burn. And I'm not concentrating, see? This is totally fireproof cloth. Which means your firewood won't burn in that pouch.'

Hazel looked unconvinced. 'How can you be sure?'

'Sheesh, tough audience.' Leo shut off the fire. 'Guess there's only one way to persuade you.' He held out his hand to Frank.

'Uh, no, no.' Frank backed off. Suddenly all those brave thoughts about accepting his fate seemed far away. 'That's okay, Leo. Thanks, but I – I can't –'

'Man, you gotta trust me.'

Frank's heart raced. Did he trust Leo? Well, sure . . . with an engine. With a practical joke. But with his life?

He remembered the day they had got stuck in the underground workshop in Rome. Gaia had promised they would die in that room. Leo had promised he would get Hazel and Frank out of the trap. And he'd done it.

Now Leo spoke with the same kind of confidence.

'Okay.' Frank handed Leo the pouch. 'Try not to kill me.'

Leo's hand blazed. The pouch didn't blacken or burn.

Frank waited for something to go horribly wrong. He counted to twenty, but he was still alive. He felt as if a block of ice was melting just behind his sternum – a frozen chunk of fear he'd got so used to he didn't even think about it until it was gone.

Leo extinguished his fire. He wriggled his eyebrows at Frank. 'Who's your best buddy?'

'Don't answer that,' Hazel said. 'But, Leo, that *was* amazing.'

'It was, wasn't it?' Leo agreed. 'So who wants to take this newly ultra-safe piece of firewood?'

'I'll keep it,' Frank said.

Hazel pursed her lips. She looked down, maybe so Frank wouldn't see the hurt in her eyes. She'd protected that firewood for him through a lot of hard battles. It was a sign of trust between them, a symbol of their relationship.

'Hazel, it's not about you,' Frank said, as gently as he could. 'I can't explain, but I – I have a feeling I'm going to need to step up when we're in the House of Hades. I need to carry my own burden.'

Hazel's golden eyes were full of concern. 'I understand. I just . . . I worry.'

Leo tossed Frank the pouch. Frank tied it around his belt. He felt strange carrying his fatal weakness so openly, after months of keeping it hidden.

'And, Leo,' he said, 'thanks.'

It seemed inadequate for the gift Leo had given him, but Leo grinned. 'What are genius friends for?'

'Hey, guys!' Piper called from the bow. 'Better get over here. You need to see this.'

They'd found the source of the dark lightning.

The *Argo II* hovered directly over the river. A few hundred metres away at the top of the nearest hill stood a cluster of ruins. They didn't look like much – just some crumbling walls encircling the limestone shells of a few buildings – but, from somewhere within the ruins, tendrils of black ether curled into the sky, like a smoky squid peeking from its cave. As Frank watched, a bolt of dark energy ripped through the air, rocking the ship and sending a cold shockwave across the landscape.

'The Necromanteion,' Nico said. 'The House of Hades.'

Frank steadied himself at the rail. He supposed it was too late to suggest turning back. He was starting to feel nostalgic about the monsters he'd fought in Rome. Heck, chasing poison cows through Venice had been more appealing than this place.

Piper hugged her arms. 'I feel vulnerable floating up here like this. Couldn't we set down in the river?'

'I wouldn't,' Hazel said. 'That's the River Acheron.'

Jason squinted in the sunlight. 'I thought the Acheron was in the Underworld.'

'It is,' Hazel said. 'But its headwaters are in the mortal world. That river below us? Eventually it flows underground, straight into the realm of Pluto – er, Hades. Landing a demi-god ship on those waters –'

'Yeah, let's stay up here,' Leo decided. 'I don't want any zombie water on my hull.'

Half a kilometre downstream, some fishing boats were puttering along. Frank guessed they didn't know or care about the history of this river. Must be nice, being a regular mortal.

Next to Frank, Nico di Angelo raised the sceptre of Diocletian. Its orb glowed with purple light, as if in sympathy with the dark storm. Roman relic or not, the sceptre troubled Frank. If it really had the power to summon a legion of the dead . . . well, Frank wasn't sure that was such a great idea.

Jason had once told him that the children of Mars had a similar ability. Supposedly, Frank could call on ghostly soldiers from the losing side of any war to serve him. He'd never had much luck with that power, probably because it freaked him out too much. He was worried he might *become* one of those ghosts if they lost this war – eternally doomed to pay for his failures, assuming there was anyone left to summon him.

'So, uh, Nico . . .' Frank gestured at the sceptre. 'Have you learned to use that thing?'

'We'll find out.' Nico stared at the tendrils of darkness undulating from the ruins. 'I don't intend to try until I have to. The Doors of Death are already working overtime bringing in Gaia's monsters. Any more activity raising the dead and the Doors might shatter permanently, leaving a rip in the mortal world that can't be closed.'

Coach Hedge grunted. 'I hate rips in the world. Let's go bust some monster heads.'

Frank looked at the satyr's grim expression. Suddenly he had an idea. 'Coach, you should stay on board, cover us with the ballistae.'

Hedge frowned. 'Stay behind? Me? I'm your best soldier!'

'We might need air support,' Frank said. 'Like we did in Rome. You saved our *braccae*.'

He didn't add: *Plus, I'd like you to get back to your wife and baby alive.*

Hedge apparently got the message. His scowl relaxed. Relief showed in his eyes.

'Well . . .' he grumbled, 'I suppose somebody's got to save your *braccae*.'

Jason clapped the coach on the shoulder. Then he gave Frank an appreciative nod. 'So that's settled. Everybody else – let's get to the ruins. Time to crash Gaia's party.'

LXVI

FRANK

DESPITE THE MIDDAY HEAT and the raging storm of death energy, a group of tourists was climbing over the ruins. Fortunately there weren't many and they didn't give the demigods a second look.

After the crowds in Rome, Frank had stopped worrying too much about getting noticed. If they could fly their warship into the Roman Colosseum with ballistae blazing and not even cause a traffic slowdown, he figured they could get away with anything.

Nico led the way. At the top of the hill, they climbed over an old retaining wall and down into an excavated trench. Finally they arrived at a stone doorway leading straight into the side of the hill. The death storm seemed to originate right above their heads. Looking up at the swirling tentacles of darkness, Frank felt like he was trapped at the bottom of a flushing toilet bowl. That *really* didn't calm his nerves.

Nico faced the group. 'From here, it gets tough.'

'Sweet,' Leo said. "Cause so far I've totally been pulling my punches.'

Nico glared at him. 'We'll see how long you keep your sense of humour. Remember, this is where pilgrims came to commune with dead ancestors. Underground, you may see things that are hard to look at, or hear voices trying to lead you astray in the tunnels. Frank, do you have the barley cakes?'

'What?' Frank had been thinking about his grandmother and his mom, wondering if they might appear to him. For the first time in days, the voices of Ares and Mars had started to argue again in the back of Frank's mind, debating their favourite forms of violent death.

'I've got the cakes,' Hazel said. She pulled out the magical barley crackers they'd made from the grain Triptolemus had given them in Venice.

'Eat up,' Nico advised.

Frank chewed his cracker of death and tried not to gag. It reminded him of a cookie made with sawdust instead of sugar.

'Yum,' Piper said. Even the daughter of Aphrodite couldn't avoid making a face.

'Okay.' Nico choked down the last of his barley. 'That should protect us from the poison.'

'Poison?' Leo asked. 'Did I miss the poison? 'Cause I love poison.'

'Soon enough,' Nico promised. 'Just stick close together, and maybe we can avoid getting lost or going insane.'

On that happy note, Nico led them underground.

The tunnel spiralled gently downwards, the ceiling supported by white stone arches that reminded Frank of a whale's rib cage.

As they walked, Hazel ran her hands along the masonry. 'This wasn't part of a temple,' she whispered. 'This was . . . the basement for a manor house, built in later Greek times.'

Frank found it eerie how Hazel could tell so much about an underground place just by being there. He'd never known her to be mistaken.

'A manor house?' he asked. 'Please don't tell me we're in the wrong place.'

'The House of Hades is below us,' Nico assured him. 'But Hazel's right, these upper levels are much newer. When the archaeologists first excavated this site, they thought they'd found the Necromanteion. Then they realized the ruins were too recent, so they decided it was the wrong spot. They were right the first time. They just didn't dig deep enough.'

They turned a corner and stopped. In front of them, the tunnel ended in a huge block of stone.

'A cave-in?' Jason asked.

'A test,' Nico said. 'Hazel, would you do the honours?'

Hazel stepped forward. She placed her hand on the rock, and the entire boulder crumbled to dust.

The tunnel shuddered. Cracks spread across the ceiling. For a terrifying moment, Frank imagined they'd all be crushed under tons of earth – a disappointing way to die, after all they'd been through. Then the rumbling stopped. The dust settled.

A set of stairs curved deeper into the earth, the barrelled ceiling held up by more repeating arches, closer together and carved from polished black stone. The descending arches made Frank feel dizzy, as if he were looking into an endlessly reflecting mirror. Painted on the walls were crude pictures of black cattle marching downwards.

'I really don't like cows,' Piper muttered.

'Agreed,' Frank said.

'Those are the cattle of Hades,' Nico said. 'It's just a symbol of –'

'Look.' Frank pointed.

On the first step of the stairwell, a golden chalice gleamed. Frank was pretty sure it hadn't been there a moment before. The cup was full of dark-green liquid.

'Hooray,' Leo said halfheartedly. 'I suppose that's our poison.'

Nico picked up the chalice. 'We're standing at the ancient entrance of the Necromanteion. Odysseus came here, and dozens of other heroes, seeking advice from the dead.'

'Did the dead advise them to leave immediately?' Leo asked.

'I would be fine with that,' Piper admitted.

Nico drank from the chalice, then offered it to Jason. 'You asked me about trust, and taking a risk? Well, here you go, son of Jupiter. How much do you trust me?'

Frank wasn't sure what Nico was talking about, but Jason didn't hesitate. He took the cup and drank.

They passed it around, each taking a sip of poison. As he

waited his turn, Frank tried to keep his legs from shaking and his gut from churning. He wondered what his grandmother would say if she could see him.

Stupid, Fai Zhang! she would probably scold. *If all your friends were drinking poison, would you do it too?*

Frank went last. The taste of the green liquid reminded him of spoiled apple juice. He drained the chalice. It turned to smoke in his hands.

Nico nodded, apparently satisfied. 'Congratulations. Assuming the poison doesn't kill us, we should be able to find our way through the Necromanteion's first level.'

'Just the *first* level?' Piper asked.

Nico turned to Hazel and gestured at the stairs. 'After you, sister.'

In no time, Frank felt completely lost. The stairs split in three different directions. As soon as Hazel chose a path, the stairs split again. They wound their way through interconnecting tunnels and rough-hewn burial chambers that all looked the same – the walls carved with dusty niches that might once have held bodies. The arches over the doors were painted with black cows, white poplar trees and owls.

'I thought the owl was Minerva's symbol,' Jason murmured.

'The screech owl is one of Hades's sacred animals,' Nico said. 'Its cry is a bad omen.'

'This way.' Hazel pointed to a doorway that looked the same as all the others. 'It's the only one that won't collapse on us.'

'Good choice, then,' Leo said.

Frank began to feel like he was leaving the world of the living. His skin tingled, and he wondered if it was a side effect of the poison. The pouch with his firewood seemed heavier on his belt. In the eerie glow of their magic weapons, his friends looked like flickering ghosts.

Cold air brushed against his face. In his mind, Ares and Mars had gone silent, but Frank thought he heard other voices whispering in the side corridors, beckoning him to veer off course, to come closer and listen to them speak.

Finally they reached an archway carved in the shape of human skulls – or maybe they *were* human skulls embedded in the rock. In the purple light of Diocletian's sceptre, the hollow eye sockets seemed to blink.

Frank almost hit the ceiling when Hazel put a hand on his arm.

'This is the entrance to the second level,' she said. 'I'd better take a look.'

Frank hadn't even realized that he'd moved in front of the doorway.

'Uh, yeah . . .' He made way for her.

Hazel traced her fingers across the carved skulls. 'No traps on the doorway, but . . . something is strange here. My underground sense is – is fuzzy, like someone is working against me, hiding what's ahead of us.'

'The sorceress that Hecate warned you about?' Jason guessed. 'The one Leo saw in his dream? What was her name?'

Hazel chewed her lip. 'It would be safer not to say her name. But stay alert. One thing I'm sure of: from this point on, the dead are stronger than the living.'

Frank wasn't sure how she knew that, but he believed her. The voices in the darkness seemed to whisper louder. He caught glimpses of movement in the shadows. From the way his friends' eyes darted around, he guessed they were seeing things too.

'Where are the monsters?' he wondered aloud. 'I thought Gaia had an army guarding the Doors.'

'Don't know,' Jason said. His pale skin looked as green as the poison from the chalice. 'At this point I'd almost prefer a straight-up fight.'

'Careful what you wish for, man.' Leo summoned a ball of fire to his hand, and for once Frank was glad to see the flames. 'Personally, I'm hoping nobody's home. We walk in, find Percy and Annabeth, destroy the Doors of Death and walk out. Maybe stop at the gift shop.'

'Yeah,' Frank said. 'That'll happen.'

The tunnel shook. Rubble rained down from the ceiling.

Hazel grabbed Frank's hand. 'That was close,' she muttered. 'These passageways won't take much more.'

'The Doors of Death just opened again,' Nico said.

'It's happening like every fifteen minutes,' Piper noted.

'Every twelve,' Nico corrected, though he didn't explain how he knew. 'We'd better hurry. Percy and Annabeth are close. They're in danger. I can sense it.'

As they travelled deeper, the corridors widened. The

ceilings rose to six metres high, decorated with elaborate paintings of owls in the branches of white poplars. The extra space should have made Frank feel better, but all he could think about was the tactical situation. The tunnels were big enough to accommodate large monsters, even giants. There were blind corners everywhere, perfect for ambushes. Their group could be flanked or surrounded easily. They would have no good options for retreat.

All of Frank's instincts told him to get out of these tunnels. If no monsters were visible, that just meant they were hiding, waiting to spring a trap. Even though Frank knew that, there wasn't much he could do about it. They *had* to find the Doors of Death.

Leo held his fire close to the walls. Frank saw Ancient Greek graffiti scratched into the stone. He couldn't read Ancient Greek, but he guessed they were prayers or supplications to the dead, written by pilgrims thousands of years ago. The tunnel floor was littered with ceramic shards and silver coins.

'Offerings?' Piper guessed.

'Yes,' Nico said. 'If you wanted your ancestors to appear, you had to make an offering.'

'Let's not make an offering,' Jason suggested.

Nobody argued.

'The tunnel from here is unstable,' Hazel warned. 'The floor might . . . well, just follow me. Step *exactly* where I step.'

She made her way forward. Frank walked right behind her – not because he felt particularly brave but because he wanted to be close if Hazel needed his help. The voices of the war gods were arguing again in his ears. He could sense danger – very close now.

Fai Zhang.

He stopped cold. That voice . . . it wasn't Ares or Mars. It seemed to come from right next to him, like someone whispering in his ear.

'Frank?' Jason whispered behind him. 'Hazel, hold up a second. Frank, what's wrong?'

'Nothing,' Frank murmured. 'I just –'

Pylos, the voice said. *I await you in Pylos.*

Frank felt like the poison was bubbling back up his throat. He'd been scared plenty of times before. He'd even faced the god of death.

But this voice terrified him in a different way. It resonated right down to his bones, as if it knew everything about him – his curse, his history, his future.

His grandmother had always been big on honouring the ancestors. It was a Chinese thing. You had to appease ghosts. You had to take them seriously.

Frank had always thought his grandmother's superstitions were silly. Now he changed his mind. He had no doubt . . . the voice that spoke to him was one of his ancestors.

'Frank, don't move.' Hazel sounded alarmed.

He looked down and realized he'd been about to step out of line.

To survive, you must lead, the voice said. *At the break, you must take charge.*

'Lead where?' he asked aloud.

Then the voice was gone. Frank could feel its absence, as if the humidity had suddenly dropped.

'Uh, big guy?' Leo said. 'Could you not freak out on us? Please and thank you.'

Frank's friends were all looking at him with concern.

'I'm okay,' he managed. 'Just . . . a voice.'

Nico nodded. 'I *did* warn you. It'll only get worse. We should –'

Hazel held up her hand for silence. 'Wait here, everybody.'

Frank didn't like it, but she forged ahead alone. He counted to twenty-three before she came back, her face drawn and pensive.

'Scary room ahead,' she warned. 'Don't panic.'

'Those two things don't go together,' Leo murmured. But they followed Hazel into the cavern.

The place was like a circular cathedral, with a ceiling so high it was lost in the gloom. Dozens of other tunnels led off in different directions, each echoing with ghostly voices. The thing that made Frank nervous was the floor. It was a gruesome mosaic of bones and gems – human femurs, hip bones and ribs twisted and fused together into a smooth surface, dotted with diamonds and rubies. The bones formed patterns, like skeletal contortionists tumbling together, curling to protect the precious stones – a dance of death and riches.

'Touch nothing,' Hazel said.

'Wasn't planning on it,' Leo muttered.

Jason scanned the exits. 'Which way now?'

For once, Nico looked uncertain. 'This should be the room where the priests invoked the most powerful spirits. One of these passages leads deeper into the temple, to the third level and the altar of Hades himself. But which –?'

'That one.' Frank pointed. In a doorway at the opposite end of the room, a ghostly Roman legionnaire beckoned to them. His face was misty and indistinct, but Frank got the feeling the ghost was looking directly at him.

Hazel frowned. 'Why that one?'

'You don't see the ghost?' Frank asked.

'Ghost?' Nico asked.

Okay . . . if Frank was seeing a ghost that the Underworld kids couldn't see, something was definitely wrong. He felt like the floor was vibrating underneath him. Then he realized it *was* vibrating.

'We need to get to that exit,' he said. 'Now!'

Hazel almost had to tackle him to restrain him. 'Wait, Frank! This floor is *not* stable, and underneath . . . well, I'm not sure *what's* underneath. I need to scout a safe path.'

'Hurry, then,' he urged.

He drew his bow and herded Hazel along as fast as he dared. Leo scrambled behind him to provide light. The others guarded the rear. Frank could tell he was scaring his friends, but he couldn't help it. He knew in his gut they had only seconds before . . .

In front of them, the legionnaire ghost vaporized. The cavern reverberated with monstrous roars – dozens, maybe hundreds of enemies coming from every direction. Frank recognized the throaty bellow of the Earthborn, the screech of gryphons, the guttural war cries of Cyclopes – all sounds he remembered from the Battle of New Rome, amplified underground, echoing in his head even louder than the war god's voices.

'Hazel, don't stop!' Nico ordered. He pulled the sceptre of Diocletian from his belt. Piper and Jason drew their swords as the monsters spilled into the cavern.

A vanguard of six-armed Earthborn threw a volley of stones that shattered the bone-and-jewel floor like ice. A fissure spread across the centre of the room, coming straight towards Leo and Hazel.

No time for caution. Frank tackled his friends, and the three of them skidded across the cavern, landing at the edge of the ghost's tunnel as rocks and spears flew overhead.

'Go!' Frank yelled. 'Go, go!'

Hazel and Leo scrambled into the tunnel, which seemed to be the only one free of monsters. Frank wasn't sure that was a good sign.

Two metres in, Leo turned. 'The others!'

The entire cavern shuddered. Frank looked back and his courage crumbled to dust. Dividing the cavern was a new fifteen-metre-wide chasm, spanned only by two rickety stretches of bone flooring. The bulk of the monster army was on the opposite side, howling in frustration and throwing whatever they could find, including each other. Some attempted to cross the bridges, which creaked and crackled under their weight.

Jason, Piper and Nico stood on the near side of the chasm, which was good, but they were surrounded by a ring of

Cyclopes and hellhounds. More monsters kept pouring in from the side corridors, while gryphons wheeled overhead, undeterred by the crumbling floor.

The three demigods would never make it to the tunnel. Even if Jason tried to fly them, they'd be shot out of the air.

Frank remembered the voice of his ancestor: *At the break, you must take charge.*

'We have to help them,' Hazel said.

Frank's mind raced, doing battle calculations. He saw exactly what would happen – where and when his friends would be overwhelmed, how all six of them would die here in this cavern . . . unless Frank changed the equation.

'Nico!' he yelled. 'The sceptre.'

Nico raised Diocletian's sceptre, and the cavern air shimmered purple. Ghosts climbed from the fissure and seeped from the walls – an entire Roman legion in full battle gear. They began taking on physical form, like walking corpses, but they seemed confused. Jason yelled in Latin, ordering them to form ranks and attack. The undead just shuffled among the monsters, causing momentary confusion, but that wouldn't last.

Frank turned to Hazel and Leo. 'You two keep going.'

Hazel's eyes widened. 'What? No!'

'You have to.' It was the hardest thing Frank had ever done, but he knew it was the only choice. 'Find the Doors. Save Annabeth and Percy.'

'But –' Leo glanced over Frank's shoulder. 'Hit the deck!'

Frank dived for cover as a volley of rocks slammed overhead. When he managed to get up, coughing and covered in dust, the entrance to the tunnel was gone. An entire section of wall had collapsed, leaving a slope of smoking rubble.

'Hazel . . .' Frank's voice broke. He had to hope she and Leo were alive on the other side. He couldn't afford to think otherwise.

Anger swelled in his chest. He turned and charged towards the monster army.

LXVII

FRANK

FRANK WAS NO EXPERT ON GHOSTS, but the dead legionnaires must have all been demigods, because they were totally ADHD.

They clawed their way out of the pit, then milled about aimlessly, chest-bumping each other for no apparent reason, pushing one another back into the chasm, shooting arrows into the air as if trying to kill flies and occasionally, out of sheer luck, throwing a javelin, a sword or an ally in the direction of the enemy.

Meanwhile, the army of monsters got thicker and angrier. Earthborn threw volleys of stones that ploughed into the zombie legionnaires, crushing them like paper. Female demons with mismatched legs and fiery hair (Frank guessed they were *empousai*) gnashed their fangs and shouted orders at the other monsters. A dozen Cyclopes advanced on the crumbling bridges, while seal-shaped humanoids – telkhines, like Frank had seen in Atlanta – lobbed vials of Greek fire across the chasm. There were even some wild centaurs in the mix, shooting flaming arrows and trampling their smaller allies under hoof. In fact, most of the enemy seemed to be armed with some kind of fiery weapon. Despite his new fireproof pouch, Frank found that extremely uncool.

He pushed through the crowd of dead Romans, shooting down monsters until his arrows were spent, slowly making his way towards his friends.

A little late, he realized – *duh* – he should turn into something big and powerful, like a bear or a dragon. As soon as the thought occurred, pain flared in his arm. He stumbled, looked down and was astonished to find an arrow shaft protruding from his left biceps. His sleeve was soaked with blood.

The sight made him dizzy. Mostly it made him angry. He tried to turn into a dragon, with no luck. The pain made it too hard to focus. Maybe he couldn't change shape while wounded.

Great, he thought. Now I find out.

He dropped his bow and picked up a sword from a fallen . . . well, he actually wasn't sure *what* it was – some sort of reptilian lady warrior with snake trunks instead of legs. He slashed his way forward, trying to ignore the pain and the blood dripping down his arm.

About five metres ahead, Nico was swinging his black sword with one hand, holding the sceptre of Diocletian aloft with the other. He kept shouting orders at the legionnaires, but they paid him no attention.

Of course not, Frank thought. He's *Greek*.

Jason and Piper stood at Nico's back. Jason summoned gusts of wind to blast aside javelins and arrows. He deflected a vial of Greek fire right up the throat of a gryphon, which burst into flames and spiralled into the pit. Piper put her new sword to good use, while spraying food from the cornucopia in her other hand – using hams, chickens, apples and oranges as interceptor missiles. The air above the chasm turned into a fireworks show of flaming projectiles, exploding rocks and fresh produce.

Still, Frank's friends couldn't hold out forever. Jason's face was already beaded with sweat. He kept shouting in Latin: 'Form ranks!' But the dead legionnaires wouldn't listen to him, either. Some of the zombies were helpful just by standing in the way, blocking monsters and taking fire. If they kept getting mowed down, though, there wouldn't be enough of them left to organize.

'Make way!' Frank shouted. To his surprise, the dead legionnaires parted for him. The closest ones turned and stared at him with blank eyes, as if waiting for further orders.

'Oh, great . . .' Frank mumbled.

In Venice, Mars had warned him that his true test of leadership was coming. Frank's ghostly ancestor had urged him to take charge. But, if these dead Romans wouldn't listen to Jason, why should they listen to him? Because he was a child of Mars, or maybe because . . .

The truth hit him. Jason wasn't quite Roman any more. His time at Camp Half-Blood had changed him. Reyna had recognized that. Apparently, so did the undead legionnaires.

If Jason no longer gave off the right sort of vibe or aura of a Roman leader . . .

Frank made it to his friends as a wave of Cyclopes crashed into them. He lifted his sword to parry a Cyclops's club, then stabbed the monster in the leg, sending him backwards into the pit. Another one charged. Frank managed to impale him, but blood loss was making him weak. His vision blurred. His ears rang.

He was dimly aware of Jason on his left flank, deflecting the incoming missiles with wind; Piper on his right, yelling charmspeak commands – encouraging the monsters to attack each other or take a refreshing jump into the chasm.

'It'll be fun!' she promised.

A few listened, but across the pit the *empousai* were countering her orders. Apparently they had charmspeak too. The monsters crowded so thickly around Frank that he could barely use his sword. The stench of their breath and body odour was almost enough to knock him out, even without the arrow throbbing in his arm.

What was Frank supposed to do? He'd had a plan, but his thoughts were getting fuzzy.

'Stupid ghosts!' Nico shouted.

'They won't listen!' Jason agreed.

That was it. Frank had to make the ghosts listen.

He summoned all his strength and yelled, 'Cohorts – lock shields!'

The zombies around him stirred. They lined up in front of Frank, putting their shields together in a ragged defensive formation. But they were moving too slowly, like sleepwalkers, and only a few had responded to his voice.

'Frank, how did you do that?' Jason yelled.

Frank's head swam with pain. He forced himself not to pass out. 'I'm the ranking Roman officer,' he said. 'They – uh, they don't recognize you. Sorry.'

Jason grimaced, but he didn't look particularly surprised. 'How can we help?'

Frank wished he had an answer. A gryphon soared overhead, almost decapitating him with its talons. Nico smacked it with the sceptre of Diocletian, and the monster veered into a wall.

'*Orbem formate!*' Frank ordered.

About two dozen zombies obeyed, struggling to form a defensive ring around Frank and his friends. It was enough to give the demigods a little respite, but there were too many enemies pressing forward. Most of the ghostly legionnaires were still wandering around in a daze.

'My rank,' Frank realized.

'*All* these monsters are rank!' Piper yelled, stabbing a wild centaur.

'No,' Frank said. 'I'm only a centurion.'

Jason cursed in Latin. 'He means he can't control a whole legion. He's not of high enough rank.'

Nico swung his black sword at another gryphon. 'Well, then, promote him!'

Frank's mind was sluggish. He didn't understand what Nico was saying. *Promote* him? How?

Jason shouted in his best drill-sergeant voice: 'Frank Zhang! I, Jason Grace, praetor of the Twelfth Legion Fulminata, give you my final order: I resign my post and give you emergency field promotion to praetor, with the full powers of that rank. Take command of this legion!'

Frank felt as if a door had opened somewhere in the House of Hades, letting in a blast of fresh air that swept through the tunnels. The arrow in his arm suddenly didn't matter. His thoughts cleared. His eyesight sharpened. The voices of Mars and Ares spoke in his mind, strong and unified: *Break them!*

Frank hardly recognized his own voice when he yelled, 'Legion, *agmen formate!*'

Instantly, every dead legionnaire in the cavern drew his sword and raised his shield. They scrambled towards Frank's position, pushing and hacking monsters out of their way until they stood shoulder to shoulder with the comrades, arranging themselves in a square formation. Stones, javelins and fire rained down, but now Frank had a disciplined defensive line sheltering them behind a wall of bronze and leather.

'Archers!' Frank yelled. '*Eiaculare flammas!*'

He didn't hold out much hope the command would work. The zombies' bows couldn't be in good shape. But, to his surprise, several dozen ghostly skirmishers nocked arrows in unison. Their arrowheads caught fire spontaneously and a flaming wave of death arced over the legion's line, straight into the enemy. Cyclopes fell. Centaurs stumbled. A telkhine shrieked and ran in circles with a burning arrow impaled in his forehead.

Frank heard a laugh behind him. He glanced back and couldn't believe what he saw. Nico di Angelo was actually smiling.

'That's more like it,' Nico said. 'Let's turn this tide!'

'*Cuneum formate!*' Frank yelled. 'Advance with *pila*!'

The zombie line thickened in the centre, forming a wedge designed to break through the enemy host. They lowered their spears in a bristling row and pushed forward.

Earthborn wailed and threw boulders. Cyclopes smashed their fists and clubs against the locked shields, but the zombie legionnaires were no longer paper targets. They had inhuman strength, hardly wavering under the fiercest attacks. Soon the floor was covered with monster dust. The line of javelins chewed through the enemy like a set of giant teeth, felling ogres and snake women and hellhounds. Frank's archers shot gryphons out of the air and caused chaos in the main body of the monster army across the chasm.

Frank's forces began to take control of their side of the cavern. One of the stone bridges collapsed, but more monsters kept pouring over the other one. Frank would have to stop that.

'Jason,' he called, 'can you fly a few legionnaires across the pit? The enemy's left flank is weak – see? Take it!'

Jason smiled. 'With pleasure.'

Three dead Romans rose into the air and flew across the chasm. Then three more joined them. Finally Jason flew himself across and his squad began cutting through some very surprised-looking telkhines, spreading fear through the enemy's ranks.

'Nico,' Frank said, 'keep trying to raise the dead. We need more numbers.'

'On it.' Nico lifted the sceptre of Diocletian, which glowed even darker purple. More ghostly Romans seeped from the walls to join the fight.

Across the chasm, *empousai* shouted commands in a language Frank didn't know, but the gist was obvious. They were trying to shore up their allies and keep them charging across the bridge.

'Piper!' Frank yelled. 'Counter those *empousai*! We need some chaos.'

'Thought you'd never ask.' She started catcalling at the female demons: 'Your makeup is smeared! Your friend called you ugly! That one is making a face behind your back!' Soon the vampire ladies were too busy fighting one another to shout any commands.

The legionnaires moved forward, keeping up the pressure. They had to take the bridge before Jason got overwhelmed.

'Time to lead from the front,' Frank decided. He raised his borrowed sword and called for a charge.

LXVIII

FRANK

FRANK DIDN'T NOTICE THAT HE WAS GLOWING. Later Jason told him that the blessing of Mars had shrouded him in red light, like it had in Venice. Javelins couldn't touch him. Rocks somehow got deflected. Even with an arrow sticking out of his left biceps, Frank had never felt so full of energy.

The first Cyclops he met went down so quickly it was almost a joke. Frank sliced him in half from shoulder to waist. The big guy exploded into dust. The next Cyclops backed up nervously, so Frank cut his legs out from under him and sent him into the pit.

The remaining monsters on their side of the chasm tried to retreat, but the legion cut them down.

'Testudo formation!' Frank shouted. 'Single file, advance!'

Frank was the first one across the bridge. The dead followed, their shields locked on either side and over their heads, deflecting all attacks. As the last of the zombies crossed, the stone bridge crumbled into the darkness, but by then it didn't matter.

Nico kept summoning more legionnaires to join the fight. Over the history of the empire, thousands of Romans had served and died in Greece. Now they were back, answering the call of Diocletian's sceptre.

Frank waded forward, destroying everything in his path.

'I will burn you!' a telkhine squeaked, desperately waving a vial of Greek fire. 'I have fire!'

Frank took him down. As the vial dropped towards the ground, Frank kicked it over the cliff before it could explode.

An *empousa* raked her claws across Frank's chest, but Frank felt nothing. He sliced the demon into dust and kept moving. Pain was unimportant. Failure was unthinkable.

He was a leader of the legion now, doing what he was born to do – fighting the enemies of Rome, upholding its legacy, protecting the lives of his friends and comrades. He was Praetor Frank Zhang.

His forces swept the enemy away, breaking their every attempt to regroup. Jason and Piper fought at his side, yelling defiantly. Nico waded through the last group of Earthborn, slashing them into mounds of wet clay with his black Stygian sword.

Before Frank knew it, the battle was over. Piper chopped through the last *empousa*, who vaporized with an anguished wail.

'Frank,' Jason said, 'you're on fire.'

He looked down. A few drops of oil must have splattered

on his trousers, because they were starting to smoulder. Frank batted at them until they stopped smoking, but he wasn't particularly worried. Thanks to Leo, he no longer had to fear fire.

Nico cleared his throat. 'Uh . . . you also have an arrow sticking through your arm.'

'I know.' Frank snapped off the point of the arrow and pulled out the shaft by the tail. He felt only a warm tugging sensation. 'I'll be fine.'

Piper made him eat a piece of ambrosia. As she bandaged his wound, she said, 'Frank, you were amazing. Completely terrifying, but amazing.'

Frank had trouble processing her words. *Terrifying* couldn't apply to him. He was just Frank.

His adrenalin drained away. He looked around him, wondering where all the enemies had gone. The only monsters left were his own undead Romans, standing in a stupor with their weapons lowered.

Nico held up his sceptre, its orb dark and dormant. 'The dead won't stay much longer, now that the battle is over.'

Frank faced his troops. 'Legion!'

The zombie soldiers snapped to attention.

'You fought well,' Frank told them. 'Now you may rest. Dismissed.'

They crumbled into piles of bones, armour, shields and weapons. Then even those disintegrated.

Frank felt as if he might crumble too. Despite the ambrosia, his wounded arm began to throb. His eyes were heavy with exhaustion. The blessing of Mars faded, leaving him depleted. But his work wasn't done yet.

'Hazel and Leo,' he said. 'We need to find them.'

His friends peered across the chasm. At the other end of the cavern, the tunnel Hazel and Leo had entered was buried under tons of rubble.

'We can't go that way,' Nico said. 'Maybe . . .'

Suddenly he staggered. He would have fallen if Jason hadn't caught him.

'Nico!' Piper said. 'What is it?'

'The Doors,' Nico said. 'Something's happening. Percy and Annabeth . . . we need to go *now*.'

'But how?' Jason said. 'That tunnel is *gone*.'

Frank clenched his jaw. He hadn't come this far to stand around helplessly while his friends were in trouble. 'It won't be fun,' he said, 'but there's another way.'

LXIX

ANNABETH

GETTING KILLED BY TARTARUS didn't seem like much of an honour.

As Annabeth stared up at his dark whirlpool face, she decided she'd rather die in some less memorable way – maybe falling down the stairs, or going peacefully in her sleep at age eighty, after a nice quiet life with Percy. Yes, that sounded good.

It wasn't the first time Annabeth had faced an enemy she couldn't defeat by force. Normally, this would've been her cue to stall for time with some clever Athena-like chitchat.

Except her voice wouldn't work. She couldn't even close her mouth. For all she knew, she was drooling as badly as Percy did when he slept.

She was dimly aware of the army of monsters swirling around her, but after their initial roar of triumph the horde had fallen silent. Annabeth and Percy should have been ripped to pieces by now. Instead, the monsters kept their distance, waiting for Tartarus to act.

The god of the pit flexed his fingers, examining his

own polished black talons. He had no expression, but he straightened his shoulders as if he were pleased.

It is good to have form, he intoned. *With these hands, I can eviscerate you.*

His voice sounded like a backwards recording – as if the words were being sucked into the vortex of his face rather than projected. In fact, *everything* seemed to be drawn towards the face of this god – the dim light, the poisonous clouds, the essence of the monsters, even Annabeth's own fragile life force. She looked around and realized that every object on this vast plain had grown a vaporous comet's tail – all pointing towards Tartarus.

Annabeth knew she should say something, but her instincts told her to hide, to avoid doing anything that would draw the god's attention.

Besides, what could she say? *You won't get away with this!*

That wasn't true. She and Percy had only survived this long because Tartarus was savouring his new form. He wanted the pleasure of physically ripping them to pieces. If Tartarus wished, Annabeth had no doubt he could devour her existence with a single thought, as easily as he'd vaporized Hyperion and Krios. Would there be any rebirth from that? Annabeth didn't want to find out.

Next to her, Percy did something she'd never seen him do. He dropped his sword. It just fell out of his hand and hit the ground with a thud. Death Mist no longer shrouded his face, but he still had the complexion of a corpse.

Tartarus hissed again – possibly laughing.

Your fear smells wonderful, said the god. *I see the appeal of*

having a physical body with so many senses. Perhaps my beloved
Gaia is right, wishing to wake from her slumber.

He stretched out his massive purple hand and might have
plucked up Percy like a weed, but Bob interrupted.

'Begone!' The Titan levelled his spear at the god. 'You
have no right to meddle!'

Meddle? Tartarus turned. *I am the lord of all creatures of the*
darkness, puny Iapetus. I can do as I please.

His black cyclone face spun faster. The howling sound
was so horrible that Annabeth fell to her knees and clutched
her ears. Bob stumbled, the wispy comet tail of his life force
growing longer as it was sucked towards the face of the god.

Bob roared in defiance. He charged and thrust his spear at
Tartarus's chest. Before it could connect, Tartarus swatted Bob
aside like he was a pesky insect. The Titan went sprawling.

Why do you not disintegrate? Tartarus mused. *You are*
nothing. You are even weaker than Krios and Hyperion.

'I am Bob,' said Bob.

Tartarus hissed. *What is that? What is Bob?*

'I choose to be more than Iapetus,' said the Titan. 'You do
not control me. I am not like my brothers.'

The collar of his coveralls bulged. Small Bob leaped out.
The kitten landed on the ground in front of his master, then
arched his back and hissed at the lord of the abyss.

As Annabeth watched, Small Bob began to grow, his
form flickering until the little kitten had become a full-sized,
translucent skeletal sabre-toothed tiger.

'Also,' Bob announced, 'I have a good cat.'

No-Longer-Small Bob sprang at Tartarus, sinking his

claws into Tartarus's thigh. The tiger scrambled up his leg, straight under the god's chain-link skirt. Tartarus stomped and howled, apparently no longer enamoured with having a physical form. Meanwhile, Bob thrust his spear into the god's side, right below his breastplate.

Tartarus roared. He swatted at Bob, but the Titan backed out of reach. Bob thrust out his fingers. His spear yanked itself free of the god's flesh and flew back to Bob's hand, which made Annabeth gulp in amazement. She'd never imagined a broom could have so many useful features. Small Bob dropped out of Tartarus's skirt. He ran to his master's side, his sabre-toothed fangs dripping with golden ichor.

You will die first, Iapetus, Tartarus decided. *Afterwards, I will add your soul to my armour, where it will slowly dissolve, over and over, in eternal agony.*

Tartarus pounded his fist against his breastplate. Milky faces swirled in the metal, silently screaming to get out.

Bob turned towards Percy and Annabeth. The Titan grinned, which probably would not have been Annabeth's reaction to a threat of eternal agony.

'Take the Doors,' Bob said. 'I will deal with Tartarus.'

Tartarus threw back his head and bellowed – creating a vacuum so strong that the nearest flying demons were pulled into his vortex face and shredded.

Deal with me? the god mocked. *You are only a Titan, a lesser child of Gaia! I will make you suffer for your arrogance. And as for your tiny mortal friends . . .*

Tartarus swept his hand towards the monster army, beckoning them forward. *DESTROY THEM!*

LXX

ANNABETH

DESTROY THEM.

Annabeth had heard those words often enough that they shocked her out of her paralysis. She raised her sword and yelled, 'Percy!'

He snatched up Riptide.

Annabeth dived for the chains holding the Doors of Death. Her drakon-bone blade cut through the left-side moorings in a single swipe. Meanwhile, Percy drove back the first wave of monsters. He stabbed an *arai* and yelped, 'Gah! Stupid curses!' Then he scythed down a half-dozen telkhines. Annabeth lunged behind him and sliced through the chains on the other side.

The Doors shuddered, then opened with a pleasant *Ding!*

Bob and his sabre-toothed sidekick continued to weave around Tartarus's legs, attacking and dodging to stay out of his clutches. They didn't seem to be doing much damage, but

Tartarus lurched around, obviously not used to fighting in a humanoid body. He swiped and missed, swiped and missed.

More monsters surged towards the Doors. A spear flew past Annabeth's head. She turned and stabbed an *empousa* through the gut, then dived for the Doors as they started to close.

She kept them open with her foot as she fought. At least with her back to the elevator car, she didn't have to worry about attacks from behind.

'Percy, get over here!' she yelled.

He joined her in the doorway, his face dripping with sweat and blood from several cuts.

'You okay?' she asked.

He nodded. 'Got some kind of *pain* curse from that *arai*.' He hacked a gryphon out of the air. 'Hurts, but it won't kill me. Get in the elevator. I'll hold the button.'

'Yeah, right!' She smacked a carnivorous horse in the snout with the butt of her sword and sent the monster stampeding through the crowd. 'You promised, Seaweed Brain. We would *not* get separated! Ever again!'

'You're impossible!'

'Love you too!'

An entire phalanx of Cyclopes charged forward, knocking smaller monsters out of the way. Annabeth figured she was about to die. 'It had to be Cyclopes,' she grumbled.

Percy gave a battle cry. At the Cyclopes' feet, a red vein in the ground burst open, spraying the monsters with liquid fire from the Phlegethon. The firewater might have healed mortals, but it didn't do the Cyclopes any favours. They combusted in a tidal wave of heat. The burst vein sealed itself, but nothing remained of the monsters except a row of scorch marks.

'Annabeth, you *have* to go!' Percy said. 'We can't both stay!'

'No!' she cried. 'Duck!'

He didn't ask why. He crouched, and Annabeth vaulted over him, bringing her sword down on the head of a heavily tattooed ogre.

She and Percy stood shoulder to shoulder in the doorway, waiting for the next wave. The exploding vein had given the monsters pause, but it wouldn't be long before they remembered: *Hey, wait, there's seventy-five gazillion of us, and only two of them.*

'Well, then,' Percy said, 'you have a better idea?'

Annabeth wished she did.

The Doors of Death stood right behind them – their exit from this nightmarish world. But they couldn't use the Doors without someone manning the controls for twelve long minutes. If they stepped inside and let the Doors close without someone holding the button, Annabeth didn't think the results would be healthy. And if they stepped away from the Doors for any reason she imagined the elevator would close and disappear without them.

The situation was so pathetically sad it was almost funny.

The crowd of monsters inched forward, snarling and gathering their courage.

Meanwhile, Bob's attacks were getting slower. Tartarus was learning to control his new body. Sabre-toothed Small

Bob lunged at the god, but Tartarus smacked the cat sideways. Bob charged, bellowing with rage, but Tartarus grabbed his spear and yanked it out of his hands. He kicked Bob downhill, knocking over a row of telkhines like sea-mammal bowling pins.

YIELD! Tartarus thundered.

'I will not,' Bob said. 'You are not my master.'

Die in defiance, then, said the god of the pit. *You Titans are nothing to me. My children the giants were always better, stronger and more vicious. They will make the upper world as dark as my realm!*

Tartarus snapped the spear in half. Bob wailed in agony. Sabre-toothed Small Bob leaped to his aid, snarling at Tartarus and baring his fangs. The Titan struggled to rise, but Annabeth knew it was over. Even the monsters turned to watch, as if sensing that their master Tartarus was about to take the spotlight. The death of a Titan was worth seeing.

Percy gripped Annabeth's hand. 'Stay here. I've got to help him.'

'Percy, you can't,' she croaked. 'Tartarus *can't* be fought. Not by us.'

She knew she was right. Tartarus was in a class by himself. He was more powerful than the gods or Titans. Demigods were nothing to him. If Percy charged to help Bob, he would get squashed like an ant.

But Annabeth also knew that Percy wouldn't listen. He couldn't leave Bob to die alone. That just wasn't him – and that was one of the many reasons she loved him, even if he was an Olympian-sized pain in the *podex*.

'We'll go together,' Annabeth decided, knowing this would be their final battle. If they stepped away from the Doors, they would never leave Tartarus. At least they would die fighting side by side.

She was about to say: *Now.*

A ripple of alarm passed through the army. In the distance, Annabeth heard shrieks, screams and a persistent *boom, boom, boom* that was too fast to be the heartbeat in the ground – more like something large and heavy, running at full speed. An Earthborn spun into the air as if he'd been tossed. A plume of bright-green gas billowed across the top of the monstrous horde like the spray from a poison riot hose. Everything in its path dissolved.

Across the swath of sizzling, newly empty ground, Annabeth saw the cause of the commotion. She started to grin.

The Maeonian drakon spread its frilled collar and hissed, its poison breath filling the battlefield with the smell of pine and ginger. It shifted its hundred-foot-long body, flicking its dappled green tail and wiping out a battalion of ogres.

Riding on its back was a red-skinned giant with flowers in his rust-coloured braids, a jerkin of green leather and a drakon-rib lance in his hand.

'Damasen!' Annabeth cried.

The giant inclined his head. 'Annabeth Chase, I took your advice. I chose myself a new fate.'

LXXI

ANNABETH

WHAT IS THIS? THE GOD OF THE PIT HISSED. *Why have you come, my disgraced son?*

Damasen glanced at Annabeth, a clear message in his eyes: *Go. Now.*

He turned towards Tartarus. The Maeonian drakon stamped its feet and snarled.

'Father, you wished for a more worthy opponent?' Damasen asked calmly. 'I am one of the giants you are so proud of. You wished me to be more war-like? Perhaps I will start by destroying you!'

Damasen levelled his lance and charged.

The monstrous army swarmed him, but the Maeonian drakon flattened everything in its path, sweeping its tail and spraying poison while Damasen jabbed at Tartarus, forcing the god to retreat like a cornered lion.

Bob stumbled away from the battle, his sabre-toothed cat at his side. Percy gave them as much cover as he could – causing blood vessels in the ground to burst one after the other. Some monsters were vaporized in Styx water. Others got a Cocytus shower and collapsed, weeping hopelessly. Others were doused with liquid Lethe and stared blankly around them, no longer sure where they were or even *who* they were.

Bob limped to the Doors. Golden ichor flowed from the wounds on his arms and chest. His janitor's outfit hung in tatters. His posture was twisted and hunched, as if Tartarus breaking the spear had broken something inside him. Despite all that, he was grinning, his silver eyes bright with satisfaction.

'Go,' he ordered. 'I will hold the button.'

Percy gawked at him. 'Bob, you're in no condition –'

'Percy.' Annabeth's voice threatened to break. She hated herself for letting Bob do this, but she knew it was the only way. 'We have to.'

'We can't just leave them!'

'You must, friend.' Bob clapped Percy on the arm, nearly knocking him over. 'I can still press a button. And I have a good cat to guard me.'

Small Bob the sabre-toothed growled in agreement.

'Besides,' Bob said, 'it is your destiny to return to the world. Put an end to this madness of Gaia.'

A screaming Cyclops, sizzling from poison spray, sailed over their heads.

Fifty yards away, the Maeonian drakon trampled through monsters, its feet making sickening *squish squish* noises as if stomping grapes. On its back, Damasen yelled insults and jabbed at the god of the pit, taunting Tartarus further away from the Doors.

Tartarus lumbered after him, his iron boots making craters in the ground.

You cannot kill me! he bellowed. *I am the pit itself. You might as well try to kill the earth. Gaia and I – we are eternal. We own you, flesh and spirit!*

He brought down his massive fist, but Damasen side-stepped, impaling his javelin in the side of Tartarus's neck.

Tartarus growled, apparently more annoyed than hurt. He turned his swirling vacuum face towards the giant, but Damasen got out of the way in time. A dozen monsters were sucked into the vortex and disintegrated.

'Bob, don't!' Percy said, his eyes pleading. 'He'll destroy you permanently. No coming back. No regeneration.'

Bob shrugged. 'Who knows what will be? You must go now. Tartarus is right about one thing. We cannot defeat him. We can only buy you time.'

The Doors tried to close on Annabeth's foot.

'Twelve minutes,' said the Titan. 'I can give you that.'

'Percy . . . hold the Doors.' Annabeth jumped and threw her arms around the Titan's neck. She kissed his cheek, her eyes so full of tears she couldn't see straight. Bob's stubbly face smelled of cleaning supplies – fresh lemony furniture polish and Murphy Oil wood soap.

'Monsters are eternal,' she told him, trying to keep herself from sobbing. 'We will remember you and Damasen as heroes, as the *best* Titan and the *best* giant. We'll tell our children. We'll keep the story alive. Some day, you will regenerate.'

Bob ruffled her hair. Smile lines crinkled around his eyes. 'That is good. Until then, my friends, tell the sun and the stars hello for me. And be strong. This may not be the last sacrifice you must make to stop Gaia.'

He pushed her away gently. 'No more time. Go.'

Annabeth grabbed Percy's arm. She dragged him into the elevator car. She had one last glimpse of the Maeonian drakon shaking an ogre like a sock puppet, Damasen jabbing at Tartarus's legs.

The god of the pit pointed at the Doors of Death and yelled: *Monsters, stop them!*

Small Bob the sabre-toothed cat crouched and snarled, ready for action.

Bob winked at Annabeth. 'Hold the Doors closed on your side,' he said. 'They will resist your passage. Hold them –'

The panels slid shut.

LXXII

ANNABETH

'PERCY, HELP ME!' ANNABETH YELPED.

She shoved her entire body against the left door, pressing it towards the centre. Percy did the same on the right. There were no handles, or anything else to hold on to. As the elevator car ascended, the Doors shook and tried to open, threatening to spill them into whatever was between life and death.

Annabeth's shoulders ached. The elevator's easy-listening music didn't help. If all monsters had to hear that song about liking piña coladas and getting caught in the rain, no wonder they were in the mood for carnage when they reached the mortal world.

'We left Bob and Damasen,' Percy croaked. 'They'll die for us, and we just –'

'I know,' she murmured. 'Gods of Olympus, Percy, I know.'

Annabeth was almost glad of the job of keeping the Doors closed. The terror racing through her heart at least kept her from dissolving into misery. Abandoning Damasen and Bob had been the hardest thing she'd ever done.

For years at Camp Half-Blood, she had chafed as other campers went on quests while she stayed behind. She'd watched as others gained glory . . . or failed and didn't come back. Since she was seven years old, she had thought: *Why don't I get to prove my skills? Why can't I lead a quest?*

Now, she realized that the hardest test for a child of Athena wasn't leading a quest or facing death in combat. It was making the strategic decision to step back, to let someone else take the brunt of the danger – especially when that person was your friend. She had to face the fact that she couldn't protect everyone she loved. She couldn't solve every problem.

She hated it, but she didn't have time for self-pity. She blinked away her tears.

'Percy, the Doors,' she warned.

The panels had started to slide apart, letting in a whiff of . . . ozone? Sulphur?

Percy pushed on his side furiously and the crack closed. His eyes blazed with anger. She hoped he wasn't mad at her, but if he was she couldn't blame him.

If it keeps him going, she thought, then let him be angry.

'I will kill Gaia,' he muttered. 'I will tear her apart with my bare hands.'

Annabeth nodded, but she was thinking about Tartarus's boast. He could not be killed. Neither could Gaia. Against such power, even Titans and giants were hopelessly outmatched. Demigods stood no chance.

She also remembered Bob's warning: *This may not be the last sacrifice you must make to stop Gaia.*

She felt that truth deep in her bones.

'Twelve minutes,' she murmured. 'Just twelve minutes.'

She prayed to Athena that Bob could hold the UP button that long. She prayed for strength and wisdom. She wondered what they would find once they reached the top of this elevator ride.

If their friends weren't there, controlling the other side . . .

'We can do this,' Percy said. 'We *have* to.'

'Yeah,' Annabeth said. 'Yeah, we do.'

They held the Doors shut as the elevator shuddered and the music played, while somewhere below them a Titan and a giant sacrificed their lives for their escape.

LXXIII

HAZEL

HAZEL WASN'T PROUD OF CRYING.

After the tunnel collapsed, she wept and screamed like a two-year-old throwing a tantrum. She couldn't move the debris that separated her and Leo from the others. If the earth shifted any more, the entire complex might collapse on their heads. Still, she pounded her fists against the stones and yelled curses that would've earned her a mouth-washing with lye soap back at St Agnes Academy.

Leo stared at her, wide-eyed and speechless.

She wasn't being fair to him.

The last time the two of them had been together, she'd zapped him into her past and shown him Sammy, his great-grandfather – Hazel's first boyfriend. She'd burdened him with emotional baggage he didn't need and left him so dazed they had almost been killed by a giant shrimp monster.

Now here they were, alone again, while their friends

might be dying at the hands of a monster army, and she was throwing a fit.

'Sorry.' She wiped her face.

'Hey, you know . . .' Leo shrugged. 'I've attacked a few rocks in my day.'

She swallowed with difficulty. 'Frank is . . . he's –'

'Listen,' Leo said. 'Frank Zhang has *moves*. He's probably gonna turn into a kangaroo and do some marsupial jujitsu on their ugly faces.'

He helped her to her feet. Despite the panic simmering inside her, she knew Leo was right. Frank and the others weren't helpless. They would find a way to survive. The best thing she and Leo could do was carry on.

She studied Leo. His hair had grown out longer and shaggier, and his face was leaner, so he looked less like an imp and more like one of those willowy elves in the fairy tales. The biggest difference was his eyes. They constantly drifted, as if Leo was trying to spot something over the horizon.

'Leo, I'm sorry,' she said.

He raised an eyebrow. 'Okay. For what?'

'For . . .' She gestured around her helplessly. 'Everything. For thinking you were Sammy, for leading you on. I mean, I didn't mean to, but if I did –'

'Hey.' He squeezed her hand, though Hazel sensed nothing romantic in the gesture. 'Machines are designed to work.'

'Uh, what?'

'I figure the universe is basically like a machine. I don't know who made it, if it was the Fates or the gods or capital-G

God or whatever. But it chugs along the way it's supposed to most of the time. Sure, little pieces break and stuff goes haywire once in a while, but mostly . . . things happen for a reason. Like you and me meeting.'

'Leo Valdez,' Hazel marvelled, 'you're a philosopher.'

'Nah,' he said. 'I'm just a mechanic. But I figure my *bisabuelo* Sammy knew what was what. He let you go, Hazel. My job is to tell you that it's okay. You and Frank – you're good together. We're all going to get through this. I hope you guys get a chance to be happy. Besides, Zhang couldn't tie his shoes without your help.'

'That's mean,' Hazel chided, but she felt like something was untangling inside her – a knot of tension she'd been carrying for weeks.

Leo really *had* changed. Hazel was starting to think she'd found a good friend.

'What happened to you when you were on your own?' she asked. 'Who did you meet?'

Leo's eye twitched. 'Long story. I'll tell you sometime, but I'm still waiting to see how it shakes out.'

'The universe is a machine,' Hazel said, 'so it'll be fine.'

'Hopefully.'

'As long as it's not one of *your* machines,' Hazel added. 'Because your machines *never* do what they're supposed to.'

'Yeah, ha-ha.' Leo summoned fire into his hand. 'Now, which way, Miss Underground?'

Hazel scanned the path in front of them. About thirty feet down, the tunnel split into four smaller arteries, each one identical, but the one on the left radiated cold.

'That way,' she decided. 'It feels the most dangerous.'

'I'm sold,' said Leo.

They began their descent.

As soon as they reached the first archway, the polecat Gale found them.

She scurried up Hazel's side and curled around her neck, chittering crossly as if to say: *Where have you been? You're late.*

'Not the farting weasel again,' Leo complained. 'If that thing lets loose in close quarters like this, with my fire and all, we're gonna explode.'

Gale barked a polecat insult at Leo.

Hazel hushed them both. She could sense the tunnel ahead, sloping gently down for about three hundred feet, then opening into a large chamber. In that chamber was a presence . . . cold, heavy and powerful. Hazel hadn't felt anything like it since the cave in Alaska where Gaia had forced her to resurrect Porphyrion the giant king. Hazel had thwarted Gaia's plans that time, but she'd had to pull down the cavern, sacrificing her life and her mother's. She wasn't anxious to have a similar experience.

'Leo, be ready,' she whispered. 'We're getting close.'

'Close to what?'

A woman's voice echoed down the corridor: 'Close to *me*.'

A wave of nausea hit Hazel so hard her knees buckled. The whole world shifted. Her sense of direction, usually flawless underground, became completely unmoored.

She and Leo didn't seem to move, but suddenly they were

three hundred feet down the corridor, at the entrance of the chamber.

'Welcome,' said the woman's voice. 'I've looked forward to this.'

Hazel's eyes swept the cavern. She couldn't see the speaker.

The room reminded her of the Pantheon in Rome, except this place had been decorated in Hades Modern.

The obsidian walls were carved with scenes of death: plague victims, corpses on the battlefield, torture chambers with skeletons hanging in iron cages – all of it embellished with precious gems that somehow made the scenes even more ghastly.

As in the Pantheon, the domed roof was a waffle pattern of recessed square panels, but here each panel was a stela – a grave marker with Ancient Greek inscriptions. Hazel wondered if actual bodies were buried behind them. With her underground senses out of whack, she couldn't be sure.

She saw no other exits. At the apex of the ceiling, where the Pantheon's skylight would've been, a circle of pure black stone gleamed, as if to reinforce the sense that there was no way out of this place – no sky above, only darkness.

Hazel's eyes drifted to the centre of the room.

'Yep,' Leo muttered. 'Those are doors, all right.'

Fifty feet away was a set of freestanding elevator doors, their panels etched in silver and iron. Rows of chains ran down either side, bolting the frame to large hooks in the floor.

The area around the doors was littered with black rubble. With a tightening sense of anger, Hazel realized that an ancient altar to Hades had once stood there. It had been destroyed to make room for the Doors of Death.

'Where are you?' she shouted.

'Don't you see us?' taunted the woman's voice. 'I thought Hecate chose you for your skill.'

Another bout of queasiness churned through Hazel's gut. On her shoulder, Gale barked and passed gas, which didn't help.

Dark spots floated in Hazel's eyes. She tried to blink them away, but they only turned darker. The spots consolidated into a twenty-foot-tall shadowy figure looming next to the Doors.

The giant Clytius was shrouded in the black smoke, just as she'd seen in her vision at the crossroads, but now Hazel could dimly make out his form – dragon-like legs with ash-coloured scales; a massive humanoid upper body encased in Stygian armour; long, braided hair that seemed to be made from smoke. His complexion was as dark as Death's (Hazel should know, since she had met Death personally). His eyes glinted cold as diamonds. He carried no weapon, but that didn't make him any less terrifying.

Leo whistled. 'You know, Clytius . . . for such a big dude, you've got a beautiful voice.'

'Idiot,' hissed the woman.

Halfway between Hazel and the giant, the air shimmered. The sorceress appeared.

She wore an elegant sleeveless dress of woven gold, her dark hair piled into a cone, encircled with diamonds and emeralds. Around her neck hung a pendant like a miniature maze, on a cord set with rubies that made Hazel think of crystallized blood drops.

The woman was beautiful in a timeless, regal way – like a statue you might admire but could never love. Her eyes sparkled with malice.

'Pasiphaë,' Hazel said.

The woman inclined her head. 'My dear Hazel Levesque.'

Leo coughed. 'You two know each other? Like Underworld chums, or –'

'Silence, fool.' Pasiphaë's voice was soft, but full of venom. 'I have no use for demigod boys – always so full of themselves, so brash and destructive.'

'Hey, lady,' Leo protested. 'I don't destroy things much. I'm a son of Hephaestus.'

'A tinkerer,' snapped Pasiphaë. 'Even worse. I knew Daedalus. His inventions brought me nothing but trouble.'

Leo blinked. 'Daedalus . . . like, *the* Daedalus? Well, then, you should know all about us *tinkerers*. We're more into fixing, building, occasionally sticking wads of oilcloth in the mouths of rude ladies –'

'Leo.' Hazel put her arm across his chest. She had a feeling the sorceress was about to turn him into something unpleasant if he didn't shut up. 'Let me take this, okay?'

'Listen to your friend,' Pasiphaë said. 'Be a good boy and let the women talk.'

Pasiphaë paced in front of them, examining Hazel, her eyes so full of hate it made Hazel's skin tingle. The sorceress's power radiated from her like heat from a furnace. Her expression was unsettling and vaguely familiar . . .

Somehow, though, the giant Clytius unnerved Hazel more.

He stood in the background, silent and motionless except for the dark smoke pouring from his body, pooling around his feet. *He* was the cold presence Hazel had felt earlier – like a vast deposit of obsidian, so heavy that Hazel couldn't possibly move it, powerful and indestructible and completely devoid of emotion.

'Your – your friend doesn't say much,' Hazel noted.

Pasiphaë looked back at the giant and sniffed with disdain. 'Pray he stays silent, my dear. Gaia has given me the pleasure of dealing with you, but Clytius is my, ah, insurance. Just between you and me, as sister sorceresses, I think he's also here to keep my powers in check, in case I forget my new mistress's orders. Gaia is careful that way.'

Hazel was tempted to protest that she wasn't a sorceress. She didn't want to know how Pasiphaë planned to 'deal' with them, or how the giant kept her magic in check. But she straightened her back and tried to look confident.

'Whatever you're planning,' Hazel said, 'it won't work. We've cut through every monster Gaia's put in our path. If you're smart, you'll get out of our way.'

Gale the polecat gnashed her teeth in approval, but Pasiphaë didn't seem impressed.

'You don't look like much,' the sorceress mused. 'But then you demigods never do. My husband, Minos, king of Crete? He was a son of Zeus. You would never have known it by looking at him. He was almost as scrawny as that one.' She flicked a hand towards Leo.

'Wow,' muttered Leo. 'Minos must've done something really horrible to deserve *you*.'

Pasiphaë's nostrils flared. 'Oh . . . you have no *idea*. He was too proud to make the proper sacrifices to Poseidon, so the gods punished *me* for his arrogance.'

'The Minotaur,' Hazel suddenly remembered.

The story was so revolting and grotesque Hazel had always shut her ears when they told it at Camp Jupiter. Pasiphaë had been cursed to fall in love with her husband's prize bull. She'd given birth to the Minotaur – half man, half bull.

Now, as Pasiphaë glared daggers at her, Hazel realized why her expression was so familiar.

The sorceress had the same bitterness and hatred in her eyes that Hazel's mother sometimes had. In her worst moments, Marie Levesque would look at Hazel as if *Hazel* were a monstrous child, a curse from the gods, the source of all Marie's problems. That's why the Minotaur story bothered Hazel – not just the repellent idea of Pasiphaë and the bull but the idea that a child, *any* child, could be considered a monster, a punishment to its parents, to be locked away and hated. To Hazel, the Minotaur had always seemed like a victim in the story.

'Yes,' Pasiphaë said at last. 'My disgrace was unbearable. After my son was born and locked in the Labyrinth, Minos refused to have anything to do with me. He said I had ruined *his* reputation! And do you know what happened to Minos, Hazel Levesque? For his crimes and his pride? He was *rewarded*. He was made a judge of the dead in the

Underworld, as if he had any right to judge others! Hades gave him that position. *Your father.*'

'Pluto, actually.'

Pasiphaë sneered. 'Irrelevant. So you see, I hate demigods as much as I hate the gods. Any of your brethren who survive the war, Gaia has promised to me, so that I may watch them die slowly in my new domain. I only wish I had more time to torture you two properly. Alas –'

In the centre of the room, the Doors of Death made a pleasant chiming sound. The green UP button on the right side of the frame began to glow. The chains shook.

'There, you see?' Pasiphaë shrugged apologetically. 'The Doors are in use. Twelve minutes, and they will open.'

Hazel's gut trembled almost as much as the chains. 'More giants?'

'Thankfully, no,' said the sorceress. 'They are all accounted for – back in the mortal world and in place for the final assault.' Pasiphaë gave her a cold smile. 'No, I would imagine the Doors are being used by someone else . . . someone unauthorized.'

Leo inched forward. Smoke rose from his fists. 'Percy and Annabeth.'

Hazel couldn't speak. She wasn't sure whether the lump in her throat was from joy or frustration. If their friends had made it to the Doors, if they were really going to show up here in twelve minutes . . .

'Oh, not to worry.' Pasiphaë waved her hand dismissively. 'Clytius will handle them. You see, when the chime sounds again, someone on *our* side needs to push the UP button or the

Doors will fail to open and whoever is inside – *poof.* Gone. Or perhaps Clytius will let them out and deal with them in person. That depends on *you* two.'

Hazel's mouth tasted like tin. She didn't want to ask, but she had to. 'How exactly does it depend on us?'

'Well, obviously, we need only one set of demigods alive,' Pasiphaë said. 'The lucky two will be taken to Athens and sacrificed to Gaia at the Feast of Hope.'

'Obviously,' Leo muttered.

'So will it be you two or your friends in the elevator?' The sorceress spread her hands. 'Let's see who is still alive in twelve . . . actually, eleven minutes, now.'

The cavern dissolved into darkness.

LXXIV

HAZEL

HAZEL'S INTERNAL COMPASS SPUN WILDLY.

She remembered when she had been very small, in New Orleans in the late 1930s, her mother had taken her to the dentist to get a bad tooth pulled. It was the first and only time Hazel had ever received ether. The dentist promised it would make her sleepy and relaxed, but Hazel felt like she was floating away from her own body, panicky and out of control. When the ether wore off, she'd been sick for three days.

This felt like a massive dose of ether.

Part of her knew she was still in the cavern. Pasiphaë stood only a few feet in front of them. Clytius waited silently at the Doors of Death.

But layers of Mist enfolded Hazel, twisting her sense of reality. She took one step forward and bumped into a wall that shouldn't have been there.

Leo pressed his hands against the stone. 'What the heck? Where are we?'

A corridor stretched out to their left and right. Torches guttered in iron sconces. The air smelled of mildew, as in an old tomb. On Hazel's shoulder, Gale barked angrily, digging her claws into Hazel's collarbone.

'Yes, I know,' Hazel muttered to the weasel. 'It's an illusion.'

Leo pounded on the wall. 'Pretty solid illusion.'

Pasiphaë laughed. Her voice sounded watery and far away. 'Is it an illusion, Hazel Levesque, or something more? Don't you see what I have created?'

Hazel felt so off-balance she could barely stand, much less think straight. She tried to extend her senses, to see through the Mist and find the cavern again, but all she felt were tunnels splitting off in a dozen directions, going everywhere *except* forward.

Random thoughts glinted in her mind, like gold nuggets coming to the surface: *Daedalus. The Minotaur locked away. Die slowly in my new domain.*

'The Labyrinth,' Hazel said. 'She's remaking the Labyrinth.'

'*What* now?' Leo had been tapping the wall with a ball-peen hammer, but he turned and frowned at her. 'I thought the Labyrinth collapsed during that battle at Camp Half-Blood – like, it was connected to Daedalus's life force or something, and then he died.'

Pasiphaë's voice clucked disapprovingly. 'Ah, but *I* am still alive. You credit Daedalus with all the maze's secrets? *I* breathed magical life into his Labyrinth. Daedalus was nothing compared to me – the immortal sorceress, daughter of Helios, sister of Circe! Now the Labyrinth will be *my* domain.'

'It's an illusion,' Hazel insisted. 'We just have to break through it.'

Even as she said it, the walls seemed to grow more solid, the smell of mildew more intense.

'Too late, too late,' Pasiphaë crooned. 'The maze is already awake. It will spread under the skin of the earth once more while your mortal world is levelled. You demigods . . . you *heroes* . . . will wander its corridors, dying slowly of thirst and fear and misery. Or perhaps, if I am feeling merciful, you will die quickly, in great pain!'

Holes opened in the floor beneath Hazel's feet. She grabbed Leo and pushed him aside as a row of spikes shot upward, impaling the ceiling.

'Run!' she yelled.

Pasiphaë's laughter echoed down the corridor. 'Where are you going, young sorceress? Running from an illusion?'

Hazel didn't answer. She was too busy trying to stay alive. Behind them, row after row of spikes shot towards the ceiling with a persistent *thunk, thunk, thunk.*

She pulled Leo down a side corridor, leaped over a trip wire, then stumbled to a halt in front of a pit twenty feet across.

'How deep is that?' Leo gasped for breath. His trouser leg was ripped where one of the spikes had grazed him.

Hazel's senses told her that the pit was at least fifty feet straight down, with a pool of poison at the bottom. Could she trust her senses? Whether or not Pasiphaë had created a new Labyrinth, Hazel believed they were still in the same cavern, being made to run aimlessly back and forth while Pasiphaë and Clytius watched in amusement. Illusion or not: unless

Hazel could figure out how to get out of this maze, the traps would kill them.

'Eight minutes now,' said the voice of Pasiphaë. 'I'd love to see you survive, truly. That would prove you worthy sacrifices to Gaia in Athens. But then, of course, we wouldn't need your friends in the elevator.'

Hazel's heart pounded. She faced the wall to her left. Despite what her senses told her, that *should* be the direction of the Doors. Pasiphaë should be right in front of her.

Hazel wanted to burst through the wall and throttle the sorceress. In eight minutes, she and Leo needed to be at the Doors of Death to let their friends out.

But Pasiphaë was an immortal sorceress with thousands of years of experience in weaving spells. Hazel couldn't defeat her through sheer willpower. She'd managed to fool the bandit Sciron by showing him what he expected to see. Hazel needed to figure out what Pasiphaë wanted most.

'Seven minutes now,' Pasiphaë lamented. 'If only we had more time! So many indignities I'd like you to suffer.'

That was it, Hazel realized. She had to run the gauntlet. She had to make the maze *more* dangerous, *more* spectacular – make Pasiphaë focus on the traps rather than the direction the Labyrinth was leading.

'Leo, we're going to jump,' Hazel said.

'But –'

'It's not as far as it looks. Go!' She grabbed his hand and they launched themselves across the pit. When they landed, Hazel looked back and saw no pit at all – just a three-inch crack in the floor.

'Come on!' she urged.

They ran as the voice of Pasiphaë droned on. 'Oh, dear, no. You'll never survive *that* way. Six minutes.'

The ceiling above them cracked apart. Gale the weasel squeaked in alarm, but Hazel imagined a new tunnel leading off to the left – a tunnel even more dangerous, going in the wrong direction. The Mist softened under her will. The tunnel appeared, and they dashed to one side.

Pasiphaë sighed with disappointment. 'You really aren't very good at this, my dear.'

But Hazel felt a spark of hope. She'd created a tunnel. She'd driven a small wedge into the magic fabric of the Labyrinth.

The floor collapsed under them. Hazel jumped to one side, dragging Leo with her. She imagined another tunnel, veering back the way they'd come, but full of poisonous gas. The maze obliged.

'Leo, hold your breath,' she warned.

They plunged through the toxic fog. Hazel's eyes felt like they were being rinsed in pepper juice, but she kept running.

'Five minutes,' Pasiphaë said. 'Alas! If only I could watch you suffer longer.'

They burst into a corridor with fresh air. Leo coughed. 'If only she would shut up.'

They ducked under a bronze garrote wire. Hazel imagined the tunnel curving back towards Pasiphaë, ever so slightly. The Mist bent to her will.

The walls of the tunnel began to close in on either side. Hazel didn't try to stop them. She made them close faster, shaking the floor and cracking the ceiling. She and Leo ran for their lives, following the curve as it brought them closer to what she hoped was the centre of the room.

'A pity,' said Pasiphaë. 'I wish I could kill you *and* your friends in the elevator, but Gaia has insisted that two of you must be kept alive until the Feast of Hope, when your blood will be put to good use! Ah, well. I will have to find other victims for my Labyrinth. You two have been second-rate failures.'

Hazel and Leo stumbled to a stop. In front of them stretched a chasm so wide, Hazel couldn't see the other side. From somewhere below in the darkness came the sound of hissing – thousands and thousands of snakes.

Hazel was tempted to retreat, but the tunnel was closing behind them, leaving them stranded on a tiny ledge. Gale the weasel paced across Hazel's shoulders and farted with anxiety.

'Okay, okay,' Leo muttered. 'The walls are moving parts. They gotta be mechanical. Give me a second.'

'No, Leo,' Hazel said. 'There's no way back.'

'But –'

'Hold my hand,' she said. 'On three.'

'But –'

'Three!'

'*What?*'

Hazel leaped into the pit, pulling Leo with her. She tried to ignore his screaming and the flatulent weasel clinging to her neck. She bent all her will into redirecting the magic of the Labyrinth.

Pasiphaë laughed with delight, knowing that any moment they would be crushed or bitten to death in a pit of snakes.

Instead, Hazel imagined a chute in the darkness, just to their left. She twisted in midair and fell towards it. She and Leo hit the chute hard and slid into the cavern, landing right on top of Pasiphaë.

'Ack!' The sorceress's head smacked against the floor as Leo sat down hard on her chest.

For a moment, the three of them and the weasel were a pile of sprawling bodies and flailing limbs. Hazel tried to draw her sword, but Pasiphaë managed to extricate herself first. The sorceress backed away, her hairdo bent sideways like a collapsed cake. Her dress was smeared with grease stains from Leo's tool belt.

'You *miserable* wretches!' she howled.

The maze was gone. A few feet away, Clytius stood with his back to them, watching the Doors of Death. By Hazel's calculation, they had about thirty seconds until their friends arrived. Hazel felt exhausted from her run through the maze while controlling the Mist, but she needed to pull off one more trick.

She had successfully made Pasiphaë see what she most desired. Now Hazel had to make the sorceress see what she most feared.

'You must really hate demigods,' Hazel said, trying to mimic Pasiphaë's cruel smile. 'We always get the better of you, don't we, Pasiphaë?'

'Nonsense!' screamed Pasiphaë. 'I will tear you apart! I will –'

'We're always pulling the rug out from under your feet,' Hazel sympathized. 'Your husband betrayed you. Theseus killed the Minotaur and stole your daughter Ariadne. Now two second-rate failures have turned your own maze against you. But you knew it would come to this, didn't you? You always fall in the end.'

'I am immortal!' Pasiphaë wailed. She took a step back, fingering her necklace. 'You cannot stand against me!'

'You can't stand at all,' Hazel countered. 'Look.'

She pointed at the feet of the sorceress. A trapdoor opened underneath Pasiphaë. She fell, screaming, into a bottomless pit that didn't really exist.

The floor solidified. The sorceress was gone.

Leo stared at Hazel in amazement. 'How did you –'

Just then the elevator dinged. Rather than pushing the UP button, Clytius stepped back from the controls, keeping their friends trapped inside.

'Leo!' Hazel yelled.

They were thirty feet away – much too far to reach the elevator – but Leo pulled out a screwdriver and chucked it like a throwing knife. An impossible shot. The screwdriver spun straight past Clytius and slammed into the UP button.

The Doors of Death opened with a hiss. Black smoke billowed out, and two bodies spilled face-first onto the floor – Percy and Annabeth, limp as corpses.

Hazel sobbed. 'Oh, gods . . .'

She and Leo started forward, but Clytius raised his hand in an unmistakable gesture – *stop*. He lifted his massive reptilian foot over Percy's head.

The giant's smoky shroud poured over the floor, covering Annabeth and Percy in a pool of dark fog.

'Clytius, you've lost,' Hazel snarled. 'Let them go, or you'll end up like Pasiphaë.'

The giant tilted his head. His diamond eyes gleamed. At his feet, Annabeth lurched like she'd hit a power line. She rolled on her back, black smoke coiling from her mouth.

'*I am not Pasiphaë.*' Annabeth spoke in a voice that wasn't hers – the words as deep as a bass guitar. '*You have won nothing.*'

'Stop that!' Even from thirty feet away, Hazel could sense Annabeth's life force waning, her pulse becoming thready. Whatever Clytius was doing, pulling words from her mouth – it was killing her.

Clytius nudged Percy's head with his foot. Percy's face lolled to one side.

'*Not quite dead.*' The giant's words boomed from Percy's mouth. '*A terrible shock to the mortal body, I would imagine, coming back from Tartarus. They'll be out for a while.*'

He turned his attention back to Annabeth. More smoke poured from between her lips. '*I'll tie them up and take them to Porphyrion in Athens. Just the sacrifice we need. Unfortunately, that means I have no further use for you two.*'

'Oh, yeah?' Leo growled. 'Well, maybe you got the smoke, buddy, but I've got the fire.'

His hands blazed. He shot white-hot columns of flame at the giant, but Clytius's smoky aura absorbed them on impact. Tendrils of black haze travelled back up the lines of fire, snuffing out the light and heat and covering Leo in darkness.

Leo fell to his knees, clutching at his throat.

'No!' Hazel ran towards him, but Gale chattered urgently on her shoulder – a clear warning.

'*I would not.*' Clytius's voice reverberated from Leo's mouth. '*You do not understand, Hazel Levesque. I devour magic. I destroy the voice and the soul. You cannot oppose me.*'

Black fog spread further across the room, covering Annabeth and Percy, billowing towards Hazel.

Blood roared in Hazel's ears. She had to act – but how? If that black smoke could incapacitate Leo so quickly, what chance did she have?

'F-fire,' she stammered in a small voice. 'You're supposed to be weak against it.'

The giant chuckled, using Annabeth's vocal cords this time. '*You were counting on that, eh? It is true I do not like fire. But Leo Valdez's flames are not strong enough to trouble me.*'

Somewhere behind Hazel, a soft, lyrical voice said, 'What about *my* flames, old friend?'

Gale squeaked excitedly and jumped from Hazel's shoulder, scampering to the entrance of the cavern where a blonde woman stood in a black dress, the Mist swirling around her.

The giant stumbled backwards, bumping into the Doors of Death.

'*You,*' he said from Percy's mouth.

'Me,' Hecate agreed. She spread her arms. Blazing torches appeared in her hands. 'It has been millennia since I fought at the side of a demigod, but Hazel Levesque has proven herself worthy. What do you say, Clytius? Shall we play with fire?'

LXXV

HAZEL

IF THE GIANT HAD RUN AWAY SCREAMING, Hazel would've been grateful. Then they all could have taken the rest of the day off.

Clytius disappointed her.

When he saw the goddess's torches blazing, the giant seemed to recover his wits. He stomped his foot, shaking the floor and almost stepping on Annabeth's arm. Dark smoke billowed around him until Annabeth and Percy were totally hidden. Hazel could see nothing but the giant's gleaming eyes.

'*Bold words.*' Clytius spoke from Leo's mouth. '*You forget, goddess. When we last met, you had the help of Hercules and Dionysus – the most powerful heroes in the world, both of them destined to become gods. Now you bring . . . these?*'

Leo's unconscious body contorted in pain.

'Stop it!' Hazel yelled.

She didn't plan what happened next. She simply knew she had to protect her friends. She imagined them behind her, the same way she'd imagined new tunnels appearing in Pasiphaë's Labyrinth. Leo dissolved. He reappeared at Hazel's feet, along with Percy and Annabeth. The Mist whirled around her, spilling over the stones and enveloping her friends. Where the white Mist met the dark smoke of Clytius, it steamed and sizzled, like lava rolling into the sea.

Leo opened his eyes and gasped. 'Wh-what . . . ?'

Annabeth and Percy remained motionless, but Hazel could sense their heartbeats getting stronger, their breath coming more evenly.

On Hecate's shoulder, Gale the polecat barked with admiration.

The goddess stepped forward, her dark eyes glittering in the torchlight. 'You're right, Clytius. Hazel Levesque is not Hercules or Dionysus, but I think you will her find just as formidable.'

Through the smoky shroud, Hazel saw the giant open his mouth. No words came out. Clytius sneered in frustration.

Leo tried to sit up. 'What's going on? What can I –'

'Watch Percy and Annabeth.' Hazel drew her *spatha*. 'Stay behind me. Stay in the Mist.'

'But –'

The look Hazel gave him must have been more severe than she realized.

Leo gulped. 'Yeah, got it. White Mist good. Black smoke bad.'

Hazel advanced. The giant spread his arms. The domed ceiling shook, and the giant's voice echoed through the room, magnified a hundred times.

Formidable? the giant demanded. It sounded as if he were speaking through a chorus of the dead, using all the unfortunate souls who'd been buried behind the dome's stelae. *Because the girl has learned your magic tricks, Hecate? Because you allow these weaklings to hide in your Mist?*

A sword appeared in the giant's hand – a Stygian iron blade much like Nico's, except five times the size. *I do not understand why Gaia would find any of these demigods worthy of sacrifice. I will crush them like empty nutshells.*

Hazel's fear turned to rage. She screamed. The walls of the chamber made a crackling sound like ice in warm water, and dozens of gems streaked towards the giant, punching through his armour like buckshot.

Clytius staggered backwards. His disembodied voice bellowed with pain. His iron breastplate was peppered with holes.

Golden ichor trickled from a wound on his right arm. His shroud of darkness thinned. Hazel could see the murderous expression on his face.

You, Clytius growled. *You worthless –*

'Worthless?' Hecate asked quietly. 'I'd say Hazel Levesque knows a few tricks even *I* could not teach her.'

Hazel stood in front of her friends, determined to protect them, but her energy was fading. Her sword was already heavy in her hand, and she hadn't even swung it yet. She wished Arion were here. She could use the horse's speed and strength. Unfortunately, her equine friend would not be able to help her this time. He was a creature of the wide-open spaces, not the underground.

The giant dug his fingers into the wound on his biceps. He pulled out a diamond and flicked it aside. The wound closed.

So, daughter of Pluto, Clytius rumbled, *do you really believe Hecate has your interests at heart? Circe was a favourite of hers. And Medea. And Pasiphaë. How did they end up, eh?*

Behind her, Hazel heard Annabeth stirring, groaning in pain. Percy muttered something that sounded like, 'Bob-bob-bob?'

Clytius stepped forward, holding his sword casually at his side as if they were comrades rather than enemies. *Hecate will not tell you the truth. She sends acolytes like you to do her bidding and take all the risk. If by some miracle you incapacitate me, only then will she be able to set me on fire. Then she will claim the glory of the kill. You heard how Bacchus dealt with the Alodai twins in the Colosseum. Hecate is worse. She is a Titan who betrayed the Titans. Then she betrayed the gods. Do you really think she will keep faith with you?*

Hecate's face was unreadable.

'I cannot answer his accusations, Hazel,' said the goddess. 'This is *your* crossroads. You must choose.'

Yes, crossroads. The giant's laughter echoed. His wounds seemed to have healed completely. *Hecate offers you obscurity, choices, vague promises of magic. I am the anti-Hecate. I will give you truth. I will eliminate choices and magic. I will strip away the Mist, once and for all, and show you the world in all its true horror.*

Leo struggled to his feet, coughing like an asthmatic. 'I'm loving this guy,' he wheezed. 'Seriously, we should keep him around for inspirational seminars.' His hands ignited like blowtorches. 'Or I could just light him up.'

'Leo, no,' Hazel said. 'My father's temple. My call.'

'Yeah, okay. But –'

'Hazel . . .' Annabeth wheezed.

Hazel was so elated to hear her friend's voice that she almost turned, but she knew she shouldn't take her eyes off Clytius.

'The chains . . .' Annabeth managed.

Hazel inhaled sharply. She'd been a fool! The Doors of Death were still open, shuddering against the chains that held them in place. Hazel had to cut them free so they would disappear – and finally be beyond Gaia's reach.

The only problem: a big smoky giant stood in her way.

You can't seriously believe you have the strength, Clytius chided. *What will you do, Hazel Levesque – pelt me with more rubies? Shower me with sapphires?*

Hazel gave him an answer. She raised her *spatha* and charged.

Apparently, Clytius hadn't expected her to be quite so suicidal. He was slow raising his sword. By the time he slashed, Hazel had ducked between his legs and jabbed her Imperial gold blade into his *gluteus maximus*. Not very ladylike. The nuns at St Agnes would never have approved. But it worked.

Clytius roared and arched his back, waddling away from her. Mist still swirled around Hazel, hissing as it met the giant's black smoke.

Hazel realized that Hecate *was* assisting her – lending her the strength to keep up a defensive shroud. Hazel also knew that the instant her own concentration wavered and that darkness touched her, she would collapse. If that happened, she wasn't sure Hecate would be able – or willing – to stop the giant from crushing her and her friends.

Hazel sprinted towards the Doors of Death. Her blade shattered the chains on the left side like they were made of ice. She lunged to the right, but Clytius yelled, *NO!*

By sheer luck, she wasn't cut in half. The flat of the giant's blade caught her in the chest and sent her flying. She slammed into the wall and felt bones crack.

Across the room, Leo screamed her name.

Through her blurry vision, she saw a flash of fire. Hecate stood nearby, her form shimmering as if she were about to dissolve. Her torches seemed to be flickering out, but it might just have been that Hazel was starting to lose consciousness.

She couldn't give up now. She forced herself to stand. Her side felt like it was embedded with razor blades. Her sword lay on the ground about five feet away. She staggered towards it.

'Clytius!' she shouted.

She meant it to sound like a brave challenge, but it came out as more of a croak.

At least it got his attention. The giant turned from Leo and the others. When he saw her limping forward, he laughed.

A good try, Hazel Levesque, Clytius admitted. *You did better than I anticipated. But magic alone cannot defeat me, and you do not have sufficient strength. Hecate has failed you, as she fails all of her followers in the end.*

The Mist around her was thinning. At the other end of the room, Leo tried to force-feed Percy some ambrosia, though

Percy was still pretty much out of it. Annabeth was awake but struggling, barely able to lift her head.

Hecate stood with her torches, watching and waiting – which infuriated Hazel so much, she found one last burst of energy.

She threw her sword – not at the giant but at the Doors of Death. The chains on the right side shattered. Hazel collapsed in agony, her side burning, as the Doors shuddered and disappeared in a flash of purple light.

Clytius roared so loudly that a half-dozen stelae fell from the ceiling and shattered.

'That was for my brother, Nico,' Hazel gasped. 'And for destroying my father's altar.'

You have forfeited your right to a quick death, the giant snarled. *I will suffocate you in darkness, slowly, painfully. Hecate cannot help you. NO ONE can help you!*

The goddess raised her torches. 'I would not be so certain, Clytius. Hazel's friends simply needed a little time to reach her – time you have given them with your boasting and bragging.'

Clytius snorted. *What friends? These weaklings? They are no challenge.*

In front of Hazel, the air rippled. The Mist thickened, creating a doorway, and four people stepped through.

Hazel wept with relief. Frank's arm was bleeding and bandaged, but he was alive. Next to him stood Nico, Piper and Jason – all with their swords drawn.

'Sorry we're late,' Jason said. 'Is this the guy who needs killing?'

LXXVI

HAZEL

HAZEL ALMOST FELT SORRY FOR CLYTIUS.

They attacked him from every direction – Leo shooting fire at his legs, Frank and Piper jabbing at his chest, Jason flying into the air and kicking him in the face. Hazel was proud to see how well Piper remembered her sword-fighting lessons.

Each time the giant's smoky veil started creeping around one of them, Nico was there, slashing through it, drinking in the darkness with his Stygian blade.

Percy and Annabeth were on their feet, looking weak and dazed, but their swords were drawn. When did Annabeth get a sword? And what was it made of – *ivory*? They looked like they wanted to help, but there was no need. The giant was surrounded.

Clytius snarled, turning back and forth as if he couldn't decide which of them to kill first. *Wait! Hold still! No! Ouch!*

The darkness around him dispelled completely, leaving nothing to protect him except his battered armour. Ichor oozed from a dozen wounds. The damage healed almost as fast as it was inflicted, but Hazel could tell the giant was tiring.

One last time Jason flew at him, kicking him in the chest, and the giant's breastplate shattered. Clytius staggered backwards. His sword dropped to the floor. He fell to his knees, and the demigods encircled him.

Only then did Hecate step forward, her torches raised. Mist curled around the giant, hissing and bubbling as it touched his skin.

'And so it ends,' Hecate said.

It does not end. Clytius's voice echoed from somewhere above, muffled and slurred. *My brethren have risen. Gaia waits only for the blood of Olympus. It took all of you together to defeat me. What will you do when the Earth Mother opens her eyes?*

Hecate turned her torches upside down. She thrust them like daggers at Clytius's head. The giant's hair went up faster than dry tinder, spreading down his head and across his body until the heat of the bonfire made Hazel wince. Clytius fell without a sound, face-first into the rubble of Hades's altar. His body crumbled to ashes.

For a moment, no one spoke. Hazel heard a ragged, painful noise and realized it was her own breathing. Her side felt like it had been kicked in with a battering ram.

The goddess Hecate faced her. 'You should go now, Hazel Levesque. Lead your friends out of this place.'

Hazel gritted her teeth, trying to hold in her anger. 'Just like that? No "thank you"? No "good work"?'

The goddess tilted her head. Gale the weasel chittered – maybe a goodbye, maybe a warning – and disappeared in the folds of her mistress's skirts.

'You look in the wrong place for gratitude,' Hecate said. 'As for "good work", that remains to be seen. Speed your way to Athens. Clytius was not wrong. The giants have risen – *all* of them, stronger than ever. Gaia is on the very edge of waking. The Feast of Hope will be poorly named unless you arrive to stop her.'

The chamber rumbled. Another stela crashed to the floor and shattered.

'The House of Hades is unstable,' Hecate said. 'Leave now. We shall meet again.'

The goddess dissolved. The Mist evaporated.

'She's friendly,' Percy grumbled.

The others turned towards him and Annabeth, as if just realizing they were there.

'Dude.' Jason gave Percy a bear hug.

'Back from Tartarus!' Leo whooped. 'That's my peeps!'

Piper threw her arms around Annabeth and cried.

Frank ran to Hazel. He gently folded her arms around her. 'You're hurt,' he said.

'Ribs probably broken,' she admitted. 'But, Frank – what happened to your arm?'

He managed a smile. 'Long story. We're alive. That's what matters.'

She was so giddy with relief it took her a moment to notice

Nico, standing by himself, his expression full of pain and conflict.

'Hey,' she called to him, beckoning with her good arm.

He hesitated, then came over and kissed her forehead. 'I'm glad you're okay,' he said. 'The ghosts were right. Only one of us made it to the Doors of Death. You . . . you would have made Dad proud.'

She smiled, cupping her hand gently to his face. 'We couldn't have defeated Clytius without you.'

She brushed her thumb under Nico's eye and wondered if he had been crying. She wanted so badly to understand what was going on with him – what had happened to him over the last few weeks. After all they'd just been through, Hazel was more grateful than ever to have a brother.

Before she could say that, the ceiling shuddered. Cracks appeared in the remaining tiles. Columns of dust spilled down.

'We've got to get out of here,' Jason said. 'Uh, Frank . . . ?'

Frank shook his head. 'I think one favour from the dead is all I can manage today.'

'Wait, what?' Hazel asked.

Piper raised her eyebrows. 'Your *unbelievable* boyfriend called in a favour as a child of Mars. He summoned the spirits of some dead warriors, made them lead us here through . . . um, well, I'm not sure, actually. The passages of the dead? All I know is that it was *very, very* dark.'

To their left, a section of the wall split. Two ruby eyes from a carved stone skeleton popped out and rolled across the floor.

'We'll have to shadow-travel,' Hazel said.

Nico winced. 'Hazel, I can barely manage that with only myself. With seven more people –'

'I'll help you.' She tried to sound confident. She'd never shadow-travelled before, had no idea if she could, but after working with the Mist, altering the Labyrinth – she had to believe it was possible.

An entire section of tiles peeled loose from the ceiling.

'Everyone, grab hands!' Nico yelled.

They made a hasty circle. Hazel envisioned the Greek countryside above them. The cavern collapsed, and she felt herself dissolving into shadow.

They appeared on the hillside overlooking the River Acheron. The sun was just rising, making the water glitter and the clouds glow orange. The cool morning air smelled of honeysuckle.

Hazel was holding hands with Frank on her left, Nico on her right. They were all alive and mostly whole. The sunlight in the trees was the most beautiful thing she'd ever seen. She wanted to live in that moment – free of monsters and gods and evil spirits.

Then her friends began to stir.

Nico realized that he was holding Percy's hand and quickly let go.

Leo staggered backwards. 'You know . . . I think I'll sit down.'

He collapsed. The others joined him. The *Argo II* still floated over the river a few hundred yards away. Hazel knew that they should signal Coach Hedge and tell him they were alive. Had they been in the temple all night? Or *several* nights? But at the moment the group was too tired to do anything except sit and relax and marvel at the fact that they were okay.

They began to exchange stories.

Frank explained what had happened with the ghostly legion and the army of monsters – how Nico had used the sceptre of Diocletian and how bravely Jason and Piper had fought.

'Frank is being modest,' Jason said. 'He controlled the entire legion. You should've seen him. Oh, by the way . . .' Jason glanced at Percy. 'I resigned my office, gave Frank a field promotion to praetor. Unless you want to contest that ruling.'

Percy grinned. 'No argument here.'

'*Praetor?*' Hazel stared at Frank.

He shrugged uncomfortably. 'Well . . . yeah. I know it seems weird.'

She tried to throw her arms around him, then winced as she remembered her busted ribs. She settled for kissing him. 'It seems *perfect*.'

Leo clapped Frank on the shoulder. 'Way to go, Zhang. Now you can order Octavian to fall on his sword.'

'Tempting,' Frank agreed. He turned apprehensively to Percy. 'But you guys . . . Tartarus has to be the *real* story. What happened down there? How did you . . . ?'

Percy laced his fingers through Annabeth's.

Hazel happened to glance at Nico and saw pain in his eyes. She wasn't sure, but maybe he was thinking how lucky Percy and Annabeth were to have each other. Nico had gone through Tartarus *alone*.

'We'll tell you the story,' Percy promised. 'But not yet, okay? I'm not ready to remember that place.'

'No,' Annabeth agreed. 'Right now . . .' She gazed towards the river and faltered. 'Uh, I think our ride is coming.'

Hazel turned. The *Argo II* veered to port, its aerial oars in motion, its sails catching the wind. Festus's head glinted in the sunlight. Even from a distance, Hazel could hear him creaking and clanking in jubilation.

'That's my boy!' Leo yelled.

As the ship got closer, Hazel saw Coach Hedge standing at the prow.

'About time!' the coach yelled down. He was doing his best to scowl, but his eyes gleamed as if maybe, just maybe, he was happy to see them. 'What took you so long, cupcakes? You kept your visitor waiting!'

'Visitor?' Hazel murmured.

At the rail next to Coach Hedge, a dark-haired girl appeared wearing a purple cloak, her face so covered with soot and bloody scratches that Hazel almost didn't recognize her.

Reyna had arrived.

LXXVII

PERCY

PERCY STARED AT THE ATHENA PARTHENOS, waiting for it to strike him down.

Leo's new mechanical hoist system had lowered the statue onto the hillside with surprising ease. Now the forty-foot-tall goddess gazed serenely over the River Acheron, her gold dress like molten metal in the sun.

'Incredible,' Reyna admitted.

She was still red-eyed from crying. Soon after she'd landed on the *Argo II*, her pegasus Scipio had collapsed, overwhelmed by poisoned claw marks from a gryphon attack the night before. Reyna had put the horse out of his misery with her golden knife, turning the pegasus into dust that scattered in the sweet-smelling Greek air. Maybe not a bad end for a flying horse, but Reyna had lost a loyal friend. Percy figured that she'd given up too much in her life already.

The praetor circled the Athena Parthenos warily. 'It looks newly made.'

'Yeah,' Leo said. 'We brushed off the cobwebs, used a little Windex. It wasn't hard.'

The *Argo II* hovered just overhead. With Festus keeping watch for threats on the radar, the entire crew had decided to eat lunch on the hillside while they discussed what to do. After the last few weeks, Percy figured they'd earned a good meal together – really anything that wasn't fire water or drakon-meat soup.

'Hey, Reyna,' Annabeth called. 'Have some food. Join us.'

The praetor glanced over, her dark eyebrows furrowed, as if *join us* didn't quite compute. Percy had never seen Reyna without her armour before. It was onboard the ship, being repaired by Buford the Wonder Table. She wore a pair of jeans and a purple Camp Jupiter T-shirt and looked almost like a normal teenager – except for the knife at her belt and that guarded expression, like she was ready for an attack from any direction.

'All right,' she said finally.

They scooted over to make room for her in the circle. She sat cross-legged next to Annabeth, picked up a cheese sandwich and nibbled at the edge.

'So,' Reyna said. 'Frank Zhang . . . praetor.'

Frank shifted, wiping crumbs from his chin. 'Well, yeah. Field promotion.'

'To lead a different legion,' Reyna noted. 'A legion of ghosts.'

Hazel put her arm protectively through Frank's. After an hour in sickbay, they both looked a lot better, but Percy could tell they weren't sure what to think about their old boss from Camp Jupiter dropping in for lunch.

'Reyna,' Jason said, 'you should've seen him.'

'He was *amazing*,' Piper agreed.

'Frank is a leader,' Hazel insisted. 'He makes a great praetor.'

Reyna's eyes stayed on Frank, like she was trying to guess his weight. 'I believe you,' she said. 'I approve.'

Frank blinked. 'You do?'

Reyna smiled dryly. 'A son of Mars, the hero who helped to bring back the eagle of the legion . . . I can work with a demigod like that. I'm just wondering how to convince the Twelfth Fulminata.'

Frank scowled. 'Yeah. I've been wondering the same thing.'

Percy still couldn't get over how much Frank had changed. A 'growth spurt' was putting it mildly. He was at least three inches taller, less pudgy and more bulky, like a linebacker. His face looked sturdier, his jawline more rugged. It was as if Frank had turned into a bull and then back to human, but he'd kept some of the bullishness.

'The legion will listen to you, Reyna,' Frank said. 'You made it here alone, across the ancient lands.'

Reyna chewed her sandwich as if it were cardboard. 'In doing so, I broke the laws of the legion.'

'Caesar broke the law when he crossed the Rubicon,' Frank said. 'Great leaders have to think outside the box sometimes.'

She shook her head. 'I'm not Caesar. After finding Jason's note in Diocletian's Palace, tracking you down was easy. I only did what I thought was necessary.'

Percy couldn't help smiling. 'Reyna, you're too modest. Flying halfway across the world by yourself to answer Annabeth's plea, because you knew it was our best chance for peace? That's pretty freaking heroic.'

Reyna shrugged. 'Says the demigod who fell into Tartarus and found his way back.'

'He had help,' Annabeth said.

'Oh, obviously,' Reyna said. 'Without you, I doubt Percy could find his way out of a paper bag.'

'True,' Annabeth agreed.

'Hey!' Percy complained.

The others started laughing, but Percy didn't mind. It felt good to see them smile. Heck, just being in the mortal world felt good, breathing un-poisonous air, enjoying actual sunshine on his back.

Suddenly he thought of Bob. *Tell the sun and stars hello for me.*

Percy's smile melted. Bob and Damasen had sacrificed their lives so that Percy and Annabeth could sit here now, enjoying the sunlight and laughing with their friends.

It wasn't fair.

Leo pulled a tiny screwdriver from his tool belt. He stabbed a chocolate-covered strawberry and passed it to Coach Hedge. Then he pulled out another screwdriver and speared a second strawberry for himself.

'So, the twenty-million-peso question,' Leo said. 'We got this slightly used forty-foot-tall statue of Athena. What do we do with it?'

Reyna squinted at the Athena Parthenos. 'As fine as it

looks on this hill, I didn't come all this way to admire it. According to Annabeth, it must be returned to Camp Half-Blood by a Roman leader. Do I understand correctly?'

Annabeth nodded. 'I had a dream down in . . . you know, Tartarus. I was on Half-Blood Hill, and Athena's voice said, *I must stand here. The Roman must bring me.*'

Percy studied the statue uneasily. He'd never had the best relationship with Annabeth's mom. He kept expecting Big Mama Statue to come alive and chew him out for getting her daughter into so much trouble – or maybe just step on him without a word.

'It makes sense,' Nico said.

Percy flinched. It almost sounded like Nico had read his mind and was agreeing that Athena should step on him.

The son of Hades sat at the other end of the circle, eating nothing but half a pomegranate, the fruit of the Underworld. Percy wondered if that was Nico's idea of a joke.

'The statue is a powerful symbol,' Nico said. 'A Roman returning it to the Greeks . . . that could heal the historic rift, maybe even heal the gods of their split personalities.'

Coach Hedge swallowed his strawberry along with half the screwdriver. 'Now, hold on. I like peace as much as the next satyr –'

'You *hate* peace,' Leo said.

'The point is, Valdez, we're only – what, a few days from Athens? We've got an army of giants waiting for us there. We went to all the trouble of saving this statue –'

'*I* went to most of the trouble,' Annabeth reminded him.

'– because that prophecy called it the *giants' bane*,' the

coach continued. 'So why aren't we taking it to Athens with us? It's obviously our secret weapon.' He eyed the Athena Parthenos. 'It looks like a ballistic missile to me. Maybe if Valdez strapped some engines to it –'

Piper cleared her throat. 'Uh, great idea, Coach, but a lot of us have had dreams and visions of Gaia rising at Camp Half-Blood . . .'

She unsheathed her dagger Katoptris and set it on her plate. At the moment, the blade showed nothing except sky, but looking at it still made Percy uncomfortable.

'Since we got back to the ship,' Piper said, 'I've been seeing some bad stuff in the knife. The Roman legion is almost within striking distance of Camp Half-Blood. They're gathering reinforcements: spirits, eagles, wolves.'

'Octavian,' Reyna growled. 'I *told* him to wait.'

'When we take over command,' Frank suggested, 'our first order of business should be to load Octavian into the nearest catapult and fire him as far away as possible.'

'Agreed,' Reyna said. 'But for now –'

'He's intent on war,' Annabeth put in. 'He'll have it, unless we stop him.'

Piper turned the blade of her knife. 'Unfortunately, that's not the worst of it. I saw images of a possible future – the camp in flames, Roman and Greek demigods lying dead. And Gaia . . .' Her voice failed her.

Percy remembered the god Tartarus in physical form, looming over him. He'd never felt such helplessness and terror. He still burned with shame, remembering how his sword had slipped out of his hand.

You might as well try to kill the earth, Tartarus had said.

If Gaia was that powerful, and she had an army of giants at her side, Percy didn't see how seven demigods could stop her, especially when most of the gods were incapacitated. They had to stop the giants *before* Gaia woke, or it was game over.

If the Athena Parthenos was a secret weapon, taking it to Athens was pretty tempting. Heck, Percy kind of liked the coach's idea of using it as a missile and sending Gaia up in a godly nuclear mushroom cloud.

Unfortunately, his gut told him that Annabeth was right. The statue belonged back on Long Island, where it might be able to stop the war between the two camps.

'So Reyna takes the statue,' Percy said. 'And we continue on to Athens.'

Leo shrugged. 'Cool with me. But, uh, a few pesky logistical problems. We got what – two weeks until that Roman feast day when Gaia is supposed to rise?'

'The Feast of Spes,' Jason said. 'That's on the first of August. Today is –'

'July eighteenth,' Frank offered. 'So, yeah, from tomorrow, exactly fourteen days.'

Hazel winced. 'It took us *eighteen* days to get from Rome to here – a trip that should've only taken two or three days, max.'

'So, given our usual luck,' Leo said, '*maybe* we have enough time to get the *Argo II* to Athens, find the giants and stop them from waking Gaia. *Maybe.* But how is Reyna supposed to get this massive statue back to Camp Half-Blood before the Greeks and Romans put each other through the blender? She doesn't even have her pegasus any more. Uh, sorry –'

'Fine,' Reyna snapped. She might be treating them like allies rather than enemies, but Percy could tell Reyna still had a not-so-soft spot for Leo, probably because he'd blown up half the Forum in New Rome.

She took a deep breath. 'Unfortunately, Leo is correct. I don't see how I can transport something so large. I was assuming – well, I was hoping you all would have an answer.'

'The Labyrinth,' Hazel said. 'I – I mean, if Pasiphaë really has reopened it, and I think she *has* . . .' She looked at Percy apprehensively. 'Well, you said the Labyrinth could take you anywhere. So maybe –'

'No.' Percy and Annabeth spoke in unison.

'Not to shoot you down, Hazel,' Percy said. 'It's just . . .'

He struggled to find the right words. How could he describe the Labyrinth to someone who'd never explored it? Daedalus had created it to be a living, growing maze. Over the centuries it had spread like the roots of a tree under the entire surface of the world. Sure, it could take you anywhere. Distance inside was meaningless. You could enter the maze in New York, walk ten feet and exit the maze in Los Angeles – but only if you found a reliable way to navigate. Otherwise the Labyrinth would trick you and try to kill you at every turn. When the tunnel network had collapsed after Daedalus died, Percy had been relieved. The idea that the maze was regenerating itself, honeycombing its way under the earth again and providing a spacious new home for monsters . . . that didn't make him happy. He had enough problems already.

'For one thing,' he said, 'the passages in the Labyrinth are way too small for the Athena Parthenos. There's no chance you could take it down there –'

'And even if the maze *is* reopening,' Annabeth continued, 'we don't know what it might be like now. It was dangerous enough before, under Daedalus's control, and he wasn't evil. If Pasiphaë has remade the Labyrinth the way she wanted...' She shook her head. 'Hazel, *maybe* your underground senses could guide Reyna through, but no one else would stand a chance. And we need you here. Besides, if you got lost down there –'

'You're right,' Hazel said glumly. 'Never mind.'

Reyna cast her eyes around the group. 'Other ideas?'

'I could go,' Frank offered, not sounding very happy about it. 'If I'm a praetor, I *should* go. Maybe we could rig some sort of sled, or –'

'No, Frank Zhang.' Reyna gave him a weary smile. 'I hope we will work side by side in the future, but for now your place is with the crew of this ship. You are one of the seven of the prophecy.'

'I'm not,' Nico said.

Everybody stopped eating. Percy stared across the circle at Nico, trying to decide if he was joking.

Hazel set down her fork. 'Nico –'

'I'll go with Reyna,' he said. 'I can transport the statue with shadow-travel.'

'Uh . . .' Percy raised his hand. 'I mean, I know you just got all eight of us to the surface, and that was awesome. But a year ago you said transporting just *yourself* was dangerous and unpredictable. A couple of times you ended up in China.

Transporting a forty-foot statue and two people halfway across the world –'

'I've changed since I came back from Tartarus.' Nico's eyes glittered with anger – more intensely than Percy understood. He wondered if he'd done something to offend the guy.

'Nico,' Jason intervened, 'we're not questioning your power. We just want to make sure you don't kill yourself trying.'

'I can do it,' he insisted. 'I'll make short jumps – a few hundred miles each time. It's true, after each jump I won't be in any shape to fend off monsters. I'll need Reyna to defend me and the statue.'

Reyna had an excellent poker face. She studied the group, scanning their faces, but betraying none of her own thoughts. 'Any objections?'

No one spoke.

'Very well,' she said, with the finality of a judge. If she'd had a gavel, Percy suspected she would have banged it. 'I see no better option. But there will be *many* monster attacks. I would feel better taking a third person. That's the optimal number for a quest.'

'Coach Hedge,' Frank blurted.

Percy stared at him, not sure he'd heard correctly. 'Uh, what, Frank?'

'The coach is the best choice,' Frank said. 'The *only* choice. He's a good fighter. He's a certified protector. He'll get the job done.'

'A faun,' Reyna said.

'Satyr!' barked the coach. 'And, yeah, I'll go. Besides,

when you get to Camp Half-Blood, you'll need somebody with connections and diplomatic skills to keep the Greeks from attacking you. Just let me go make a call – er, I mean, get my baseball bat.'

He got up and shot Frank an unspoken message that Percy couldn't quite read. Despite the fact that he'd just been volunteered for a likely suicide mission, the coach looked *grateful*. He jogged off towards the ship's ladder, tapping his hooves together like an excited kid.

Nico rose. 'I should go, too, and rest before the first passage. We'll meet at the statue at sunset.'

Once he was gone, Hazel frowned. 'He's acting strangely. I'm not sure he's thinking this through.'

'He'll be okay,' Jason said.

'I hope you're right.' She passed her hand over the ground. Diamonds broke the surface – a glittering milky way of stones. 'We're at another crossroads. The Athena Parthenos goes west. The *Argo II* goes east. I hope we chose correctly.'

Percy wished he could say something encouraging, but he felt unsettled. Despite all they'd been through and all the battles they'd won, they still seemed no closer to defeating Gaia. Sure, they'd released Thanatos. They'd closed the Doors of Death. At least now they could kill monsters and make them *stay* in Tartarus for a while. But the giants were back – *all* the giants.

'One thing bothers me,' he said. 'If the Feast of Spes is in two weeks, and Gaia needs the blood of two demigods to wake – what did Clytius call it? The blood of Olympus? – then aren't we doing exactly what Gaia wants, heading to Athens? If we don't go, and she can't sacrifice any of us, doesn't that mean she can't wake up fully?'

Annabeth took his hand. He drank in the sight of her now that they were back in the mortal world, without the Death Mist, her blonde hair catching the sunlight – even if she was still thin and wan, like him, and her grey eyes were stormy with thought.

'Percy, prophecies cut both ways,' she said. 'If we *don't* go, we may lose our best and only chance to stop her. Athens is where our battle lies. We can't avoid it. Besides, trying to thwart prophecies never works. Gaia could capture us somewhere else or spill the blood of some other demigods.'

'Yeah, you're right,' Percy said. 'I don't like it, but you're right.'

The mood of the group became as gloomy as Tartarus air, until Piper broke the tension.

'Well!' She sheathed her blade and patted her cornucopia. 'Good picnic. Who wants dessert?'

LXXVIII

PERCY

AT SUNSET, PERCY FOUND NICO tying ropes around the pedestal of the Athena Parthenos.

'Thank you,' Percy said.

Nico frowned. 'What for?'

'You promised to lead the others to the House of Hades,' Percy said. 'You did it.'

Nico tied the ends of the ropes together, making a halter. 'You got me out of that bronze jar in Rome. Saved my life yet again. It was the least I could do.'

His voice was steely, guarded. Percy wished he could figure out what made this guy tick, but he'd never been able to. Nico was no longer the geeky kid from Westover Hall with the Mythomagic cards. Nor was he the angry loner who'd followed the ghost of Minos through the Labyrinth. But who was he?

'Also,' Percy said, 'you visited Bob . . .'

He told Nico about their trip through Tartarus. He figured

if anyone could understand, Nico could. 'You convinced Bob that I could be trusted, even though *I* never visited him. I never gave him a second thought. You probably saved our lives by being nice to him.'

'Yeah, well,' Nico said, 'not giving people a second thought . . . that can be dangerous.'

'Dude, I'm trying to say thank you.'

Nico laughed without humour. 'I'm trying to say you don't need to. Now I need to finish this, if you could give me some space?'

'Yeah. Yeah, okay.' Percy stepped back while Nico took up the slack on his ropes. He slipped them over his shoulders as if the Athena Parthenos were a giant backpack.

Percy couldn't help feeling a little hurt, being told to take a hike. Then again, Nico had been through a lot. The guy had survived in Tartarus on his own. Percy understood firsthand just how much strength that must have taken.

Annabeth walked up the hill to join them. She took Percy's hand, which made him feel better.

'Good luck,' she told Nico.

'Yeah.' He didn't meet her eyes. 'You, too.'

A minute later, Reyna and Coach Hedge arrived in full armour with packs over their shoulders. Reyna looked grim and ready for combat. Coach Hedge grinned like he was expecting a surprise party.

Reyna gave Annabeth a hug. 'We will succeed,' she promised.

'I know you will,' Annabeth said.

Coach Hedge shouldered his baseball bat. 'Yeah, don't

worry. I'm going to get to camp and see my baby! Uh, I mean I'm going to get this baby to camp!' He patted the leg of the Athena Parthenos.

'All right,' said Nico. 'Grab the ropes, please. Here we go.'

Reyna and Hedge took hold. The air darkened. The Athena Parthenos collapsed into its own shadow and disappeared, along with its three escorts.

The *Argo II* sailed after nightfall.

They veered southwest until they reached the coast, then splashed down in the Ionian Sea. Percy was relieved to feel the waves beneath him again.

It would have been a shorter trip to Athens over land, but after the crew's experience with mountain spirits in Italy, they'd decided not to fly over Gaia's territory any more than they had to. They would sail around the Greek mainland, following the routes that Greek heroes had taken in the ancient times.

That was fine with Percy. He loved being back in his father's element – with the fresh sea air in his lungs and the salty spray on his arms. He stood at the starboard rail and closed his eyes, sensing the currents beneath them. But images of Tartarus kept burning in his mind – the River Phlegethon, the blistered ground where monsters regenerated, the dark forest where *arai* circled overhead in the blood-mist clouds. Most of all, he thought about a hut in the swamp with a warm fire and racks of drying herbs and drakon jerky. He wondered if that hut was empty now.

Annabeth pressed next to him at the rail, her warmth reassuring.

'I know,' she murmured, reading his expression. 'I can't get that place out of my head, either.'

'Damasen,' Percy said. 'And Bob . . .'

'I know.' Her voice was fragile. 'We have to make their sacrifice worth it. We have to beat Gaia.'

Percy stared into the night sky. He wished they were looking at it from the beach on Long Island rather than from halfway around the world, sailing towards almost certain death.

He wondered where Nico, Reyna and Hedge were now, and how long it would take them to make it back – assuming they survived. He imagined the Romans drawing up battle lines right now, encircling Camp Half-Blood.

Fourteen days to reach Athens. Then one way or another, the war would be decided.

Over in the bow, Leo whistled happily as he tinkered with Festus's mechanical brain, muttering something about a crystal and an astrolabe. Amidships, Piper and Hazel practised their swordplay, gold and bronze blades ringing in the night. Jason and Frank stood at the helm, talking in low tones – maybe telling stories of the legion or sharing thoughts on being praetor.

'We've got a good crew,' Percy said. 'If I have to sail to my death –'

'You're not dying on me, Seaweed Brain,' Annabeth said. 'Remember? Never separated again. And after we get home . . .'

'What?' Percy asked.

She kissed him. 'Ask me again, once we defeat Gaia.'

He smiled, happy to have something to look forward to. 'Whatever you say.'

As they sailed further from the coast, the sky darkened and more stars came out.

Percy studied the constellations – the ones Annabeth had taught him so many years ago.

'Bob says hello,' he told the stars.

The *Argo II* sailed into the night.

Glossary

Achelous a *potamus*, or river god

Aegis Thalia Grace's terror-inducing shield

Aeolus god of all winds

Akhlys Greek goddess of misery; goddess of poisons; controller of the Death Mist; daughter of Chaos and Night

Alcyoneus the eldest of the giants born to Gaia, destined to fight Pluto

Alodai twin giants who attempted to storm Mount Olympus by piling three Greek mountains on top of each other. Ares tried to stop them, but he was defeated and imprisoned in a bronze urn, until Hermes rescued him. Artemis later brought about the giants' destruction when she raced between them in the form of a deer. They both took aim with their spears, but missed and instead struck each other.

Aphrodite the Greek goddess of love and beauty. She was married to Hephaestus, but she loved Ares, the god of war. Roman form: Venus

Aquilo Roman god of the North Wind. Greek form: Boreas

Arachne a weaver who claimed to have skills superior to Athena's. This angered the goddess, who destroyed Arachne's tapestry and loom. Arachne hung herself, and Athena brought her back to life as a spider.

arai female spirits of curses; wrinkled hags with bat-like wings, brass talons and glowing red eyes; daughters of Nyx (Night)

Archimedes a Greek mathematician, physicist, engineer, inventor and astronomer who lived between 287–212 BCE and is regarded as one of the leading scientists in classical antiquity; he discovered how to determine the volume of a sphere

Ares   the Greek god of war; the son of Zeus and Hera, and half-brother to Athena. Roman form: Mars

argentum   silver; the name of one of Reyna's two metallic greyhounds that can detect lies

Argo II   the fantastical ship built by Leo, which can both sail and fly and has Festus the bronze dragon as its figurehead. The ship was named after the *Argo*, the vessel used by a band of Greek heroes who accompanied Jason on his quest to find the Golden Fleece.

Argonauts   in Greek mythology, a band of heroes who sailed with Jason on the *Argo*, in search of the Golden Fleece

Ariadne   a daughter of Minos who helped Theseus escape from the Labyrinth

Arion   an incredibly fast magical horse that runs wild and free, but occasionally answers Hazel's summons; his favourite snack is gold nuggets

astrolabe   an instrument used to navigate based on the position of planets and stars

Athena   the Greek goddess of wisdom. Roman form: Minerva

Athena Parthenos   a giant statue of Athena, the most famous Greek statue of all time

augury   a sign of something coming, an omen; the practice of divining the future

aurum   gold; the name of one of Reyna's two metallic greyhounds that can detect lies

Auster   Roman god of the South Wind. Greek form: Notus

Bacchus   the Roman god of wine and revelry. Greek form: Dionysus

ballista (**ballistae**, pl.)   a Roman missile siege weapon that launched a large projectile at a distant target (*see also* **scorpion ballista**)

barracks   the living quarters of Roman soldiers

Bellona   a Roman goddess of war

Boreads   Calais and Zethes, sons of Boreas, god of the North Wind

Boreas   god of the North Wind. Roman form: Aquilo

braccae   Latin for *trousers*

Bunker Nine   a hidden workshop Leo discovered at Camp Half-Blood, filled with tools and weapons. It is at least two hundred years old and was used during the Demigod Civil War.

Cadmus   a demigod whom Ares turned into a snake when Cadmus killed his dragon son

Calypso   the goddess nymph of the mythical island of Ogygia; a daughter of the Titan Atlas. She detained the hero Odysseus for many years.

Camp Half-Blood   the training ground for Greek demigods, located on Long Island, New York

Camp Jupiter   the training ground for Roman demigods, located between the Oakland Hills and the Berkeley Hills, in California

catapult   a military machine used to hurl objects

Celestial bronze   a rare metal deadly to monsters

centaur   a race of creatures that is half human, half horse

centurion   an officer of the Roman army

Ceres   the Roman goddess of agriculture. Greek form: Demeter

charmspeak   a blessing bestowed by Aphrodite on her children that enables them to persuade others with their voice

chiton   a Greek garment; a sleeveless piece of linen or wool secured at the shoulders by brooches and at the waist by a belt

Circe   a Greek goddess of magic

Clytius   a giant created by Gaia to absorb and defeat all of Hecate's magic

Cocytus   the River of Lamentation in Tartarus, made of pure misery

cohort   one of ten divisions in a Roman legion, a group of soldiers

Colosseum   an elliptical amphitheatre in the centre of Rome, Italy. Capable of seating fifty thousand spectators, the Colosseum was used for gladiatorial contests and public spectacles, such as mock sea battles, animal hunts, executions, re-enactments of famous battles and dramas.

cornucopia   a large horn-shaped container overflowing with edibles or wealth in some form. The cornucopia was created when Heracles (Roman: Hercules) wrestled with the river god Achelous and wrenched off one of his horns.

Cupid   Roman god of love. Greek form: Eros

Cyclops   a member of a primordial race of giants (**Cyclopes**, pl.), each with a single eye in the middle of his or her forehead

Daedalus   in Greek mythology, a skilled craftsman who created the Labyrinth on Crete in which the Minotaur (part man, part bull) was kept

Damasen   giant son of Tartarus and Gaia; created to oppose Ares; condemned to Tartarus for slaying a drakon that was ravaging the land

Demeter   the Greek goddess of agriculture, a daughter of the Titans Rhea and Kronos. Roman form: Ceres

denarius (denarii, pl.)   the most common coin in the Roman currency system

Diocletian   the last great pagan emperor, and the first to retire peacefully; a demigod (son of Jupiter). According to legend, his sceptre could raise a ghost army.

Diomedes   a principal Greek hero in the Trojan War

Dionysus the Greek god of wine and revelry, a son of Zeus. Roman form: Bacchus

Doors of Death the doorway to the House of Hades, located in Tartarus. The Doors have two sides – one in the mortal world, and one in the Underworld.

drachma the silver coin of Ancient Greece

drakon a gigantic yellow and green serpent-like monster, with frills around its neck, reptilian eyes and huge talons; it spits poison

dryads tree nymphs

Earthborn *Gegenees* in Greek; monsters with six arms that wear only a loincloth

eidolons possessing spirits

Elysium the section of the Underworld where those who are blessed by the gods are sent to rest in eternal peace after death

empousa a vampire with fangs, claws, a bronze left leg, a donkey right leg, hair made of fire and skin as white as bone. *Empousai* [pl.] have the ability to manipulate the Mist, change shape and charmspeak in order to attract their mortal victims.

Epirus a region presently in northwestern Greece and southern Albania

Eris goddess of strife

Eros Greek god of love. Roman form: Cupid

faun a Roman forest god, part goat and part man. Greek form: satyr

Favonius Roman god of the West Wind. Greek form: Zephyros

Fields of Asphodel the section of the Underworld where people who lived neither a good nor a bad life are sent after death

Fields of Punishment the section of the Underworld where people who were evil during their lives are sent after death to face eternal punishment for their crimes

Furies   Roman goddesses of vengeance; usually characterized as three sisters – Alecto, Tisiphone and Megaera; the children of Gaia and Uranus. They reside in the Underworld, tormenting evildoers and sinners. Greek form: the Erinyes

Gaia   the Greek earth goddess; mother of Titans, giants, Cyclopes and other monsters. Roman form: Terra

Geras   goddess of old age

Geryon   a monster with three bodies that was slain by Heracles/Hercules

gladius   a short sword

Graecus   the word Romans used for *Greek*

greaves   shin armour

Greek fire   an incendiary weapon used in naval battles because it can continue burning in water

gris-gris   In this New Orleans Voodoo practice named after the French word for grey (*gris*), special herbs and other ingredients are combined and put into a small red flannel bag that is worn or stored to restore the balance between the black and white aspects of a person's life.

gryphon   a creature with the forequarters (including talons) and wings of an eagle and the hindquarters of a lion

Hades   the Greek god of death and riches. Roman form: Pluto

Hannibal   a Carthaginian commander who lived between 247–183/182 BCE and is generally considered to be one of the greatest military strategists in history. One of his most famous achievements was marching an army, which included war elephants, from Iberia over the Pyrenees and the Alps into northern Italy.

harpy   a winged female creature that snatches things

Hecate   goddess of magic and crossroads; controls the Mist; daughter of Titans Perses and Asteria

Hemera   goddess of day, daughter of Night

Hephaestus   the Greek god of fire and crafts and of blacksmiths; the son of Zeus and Hera, and married to Aphrodite. Roman form: Vulcan

Hera   the Greek goddess of marriage; Zeus's wife and sister. Roman form: Juno

Heracles   the Greek equivalent of Hercules; the son of Zeus and Alcmene; the strongest of all mortals

Hercules   the Roman equivalent of Heracles; the son of Jupiter and Alcmene, who was born with great strength

Hermes   Greek god of travellers; guide to spirits of the dead; god of communication. Roman form: Mercury

Hesiod   a Greek poet who speculated that it would take nine days to fall to the bottom of Tartarus

Horatius   a Roman general who single-handedly held off a horde of invaders, sacrificing himself on a bridge to keep the barbarians from crossing the Tiber River. By giving his fellow Romans time to finish their defences, he saved the Republic.

House of Hades   a place in the Underworld where Hades, the Greek god of death, and his wife Persephone rule over the souls of the departed; an old temple in Epirus in Greece

Hyperion   one of the twelve Titans; Titan lord of the east

Hypnos   Greek god of sleep. Roman form: Somnus

hypogeum   the area under a coliseum that housed set pieces and machinery used for special effects

Iapetus   one of the twelve Titans; lord of the west; his name means *the Piercer*. When Percy fought him in Hades's realm, Iapetus fell into the River Lethe and lost his memory; Percy renamed him Bob.

ichor   the golden fluid that is the blood of gods and immortals

Imperial gold   a rare metal deadly to monsters, consecrated at the Pantheon; its existence was a closely guarded secret of the emperors

Janus   Roman god of doorways, beginnings and transitions; depicted as having two faces, because he looks to the future and to the past

Juno   the Roman goddess of women, marriage and fertility; sister and wife of Jupiter; mother of Mars. Greek form: Hera

Jupiter   the Roman king of the gods; also called Jupiter Optimus Maximus (the best and the greatest). Greek form: Zeus

Kampê   a monster with the upper body of a snake-haired woman and the lower body of a drakon; appointed by the Titan Kronos to guard the Cyclopes of Tartarus. Zeus slew her and freed the giants from their prison to aid him in his war against the Titans.

katobleps   a cow monster whose name means 'down-looker' (***katoblepones***, pl.). They were accidentally imported to Venice from Africa. They eat poisonous roots that grow by the canals and have a poisonous gaze and poisonous breath.

Katoptris   Piper's dagger

Kerkopes   a pair of chimpanzee-like dwarfs who steal shiny things and create chaos

Khione   the Greek goddess of snow; daughter of Boreas

Koios   one of the twelve Titans; Titan lord of the north

Krios   one of the twelve Titans; Titan lord of the south

Kronos   the youngest of the twelve Titans; the son of Ouranos and Gaia; the father of Zeus. He killed his father at his mother's bidding. Titan lord of fate, harvest, justice and time. Roman form: Saturn

Labyrinth   an underground maze originally built on the island of Crete by the craftsman Daedalus to hold the Minotaur (part man, part bull)

Laistrygonian giant   a monstrous cannibal from the far north

Lar   a house god, ancestral spirit (**Lares**, pl.)

legionnaire   Roman soldier

lemures   Roman term for angry ghosts

Leto   daughter of the Titan Koios; mother of Artemis and Apollo with Zeus; goddess of motherhood

Lotus Hotel   a casino in Las Vegas where Percy, Annabeth and Grover lost valuable time during their quest after eating enchanted lotus blossoms

Mansion of Night   Nyx's palace

manticore   a creature with a human head, a lion's body and a scorpion's tail

Mars   the Roman god of war; also called Mars Ultor. Patron of the empire; divine father of Romulus and Remus. Greek form: Ares

Medea   a follower of Hecate and one of the great sorceresses of the ancient world

Mercury   Roman messenger of the gods; god of trade, profit and commerce. Greek form: Hermes

Minerva   the Roman goddess of wisdom. Greek form: Athena

Minos   king of Crete; son of Zeus; every year he made King Aegus pick seven boys and seven girls to be sent to the Labyrinth, where they would be eaten by the Minotaur. After his death he became a judge in the Underworld.

Minotaur   a monster with the head of a bull on the body of a man

Mist   a magic force that disguises things from mortals

Mount Tamalpais   the site in the Bay Area (northern California) where the Titans built a palace

naiads   water nymphs

Necromanteion   the Oracle of Death, or House of Hades in Greek; a multilevel temple where people went to consult with the dead

Neptune   the Roman god of the sea. Greek form: Poseidon

New Rome   a community near Camp Jupiter where demigods can live together in peace, without interference from mortals or monsters

Notus   Greek god of the South Wind. Roman form: Auster

numina montanum   Roman mountain god (***montana***, pl.). Greek form: *ourae*

nymph   a female nature deity who animates nature

nymphaeum   a shrine to nymphs

Nyx   goddess of night; one of the ancient, firstborn elemental gods

Odysseus   legendary Greek king of Ithaca and the hero of Homer's epic poem *The Odyssey*. Roman form: Ulysses

Ogygia   the island home – and prison – of the nymph Calypso

ourae   Greek for mountain god. Roman form: *numina montanum*

Ouranos   father of the Titans

Pasiphaë   the wife of Minos, cursed to fall in love with his prize bull and give birth to the Minotaur (part man, part bull); mistress of magical herbal arts

Pegasus   in Greek mythology, a winged divine horse; sired by Poseidon in his role as horse-god, and foaled by the Gorgon Medusa; the brother of Chrysaor

Periclymenus   an Argonaut, the son of two demigods, and the grandson of Poseidon, who granted him the ability to change into various animals

peristyle   entrance to an emperor's private residence

Persephone the Greek queen of the Underworld; wife of Hades; daughter of Zeus and Demeter. Roman form: Proserpine

phalanx a compact body of heavily armed troops

Phlegethon the River of Fire that flows from Hades's realm down into Tartarus; it keeps the wicked alive so they can endure the torments of the Field of Punishment

pilum (*pila*, pl.) a javelin used by the Roman army

Pluto the Roman god of death and riches. Greek form: Hades

Polybotes the giant son of Gaia, the Earth Mother

Polyphemus the gigantic one-eyed son of Poseidon and Thoosa; one of the Cyclopes

Porphyrion the king of the giants in Greek and Roman mythology

Poseidon the Greek god of the sea; son of the Titans Kronos and Rhea, and brother of Zeus and Hades. Roman form: Neptune

praetor an elected Roman magistrate and commander of the army

Proserpine Roman queen of the Underworld. Greek form: Persephone

Psyche a young mortal woman who fell in love with Eros and was forced by his mother, Aphrodite, to earn her way back to him

quoits a game in which players toss hoops at a stake

Riptide the name of Percy Jackson's sword; *Anaklusmos* in Greek

River Acheron the fifth river of the Underworld; the river of pain; the ultimate punishment for the souls of the damned

River Lethe one of several rivers in the Underworld; drinking from it will make someone forget his identity

Romulus and Remus the twin sons of Mars and the priestess Rhea Silvia. They were thrown into the River Tiber by their human father, Amulius, and were rescued and raised by a she-wolf. Upon reaching adulthood, they founded Rome.

Saturn the Roman god of agriculture; the son of Uranus and Gaia, and the father of Jupiter. Greek form: Kronos

satyr a Greek forest god, part goat and part man. Roman equivalent: faun

Scipio Reyna's pegasus

Sciron an infamous robber who ambushed passers-by and forced them to wash his feet as a toll. When they knelt, he kicked his victims into the sea, where they were eaten by a giant turtle.

scorpion ballista a Roman missile siege weapon that launched a large projectile at a distant target

Senatus Populusque Romanus (SPQR) meaning 'The Senate and People of Rome', refers to the government of the Roman Republic and is used as an official emblem of Rome

shadow-travel a form of transportation that allows creatures of the Underworld and children of Hades to travel to any desired place on earth or in the Underworld, although it makes the user extremely fatigued

Sibylline Books a collection of prophecies in rhyme written in Greek. Tarquinius Superbus, a king of Rome, bought them from a prophetess named Sibyl and consulted them in times of great danger.

spatha a heavy sword used by Roman cavalry

Spes goddess of hope; the Feast of Spes, the Day of Hope, falls on August 1

stela (**stelae**, pl.) an inscribed stone used as a monument

Stygian iron a magical metal, forged in the River Styx, capable of absorbing the very essence of monsters and injuring mortals, gods, Titans and Giants. It has a significant effect on ghosts and creatures from the Underworld.

Tantalus   In Greek mythology, this king was such a good friend of the gods that he was allowed to dine at their table – until he spilled their secrets on earth. He was sent to the Underworld, where his curse was to be stuck in a pool of water under a fruit tree, but never to be able to drink or eat.

Tartarus   husband of Gaia; spirit of the abyss; father of the giants

telkhine   a sea demon with flippers instead of hands, and a dog's head

Tempest   Jason's friend; a storm spirit in the form of a horse

Terminus   the Roman god of boundaries and landmarks

Terra   the Roman goddess of the earth. Greek form: Gaia

Thanatos   the Greek god of death; servant of Hades. Roman form: Letus

Theseus   a king of Athens who was known for many exploits, including killing the Minotaur

Three Fates   In Greek mythology, even before there were gods, there were the Fates: Clotho, who spins the thread of life; Lachesis, the measurer, who determines how long a life will be; and Atropos, who cuts the thread of life with her shears.

Tiber River   the third-longest river in Italy. Rome was founded on its banks. In Ancient Rome, executed criminals were thrown into the river.

Tiberius   was emperor of Rome from 14–37 CE. He was one of Rome's greatest generals, but he came to be remembered as a reclusive and sombre ruler who never really wanted to be emperor.

Titans   a race of powerful Greek deities, descendants of Gaia and Uranus, who ruled during the Golden Age and were overthrown by a race of younger gods, the Olympians

Triptolemus   god of farming; he aided Demeter when she was searching for her daughter, Persephone, who was kidnapped by Hades

trireme   an Ancient Greek or Roman warship, having three tiers of oars on each side

Trojan Horse   a tale from the Trojan War about a huge wooden horse that the Greeks built and left near Troy with a select force of men inside. After the Trojans pulled the horse into their city as a victory trophy, the Greeks emerged at night, let the rest of their army into Troy, and destroyed it, decisively ending the war.

Trojan War   In Greek mythology, the Trojan War was waged against the city of Troy by the Achaeans (Greeks) after Paris of Troy took Helen from her husband, Menelaus, king of Sparta.

venti   air spirits

Venus   the Roman goddess of love and beauty. She was married to Vulcan, but she loved Mars, the god of war. Greek form: Aphrodite

Vulcan   the Roman god of fire and crafts and of blacksmiths; the son of Jupiter and Juno, and married to Venus. Greek form: Hephaestus

Wolf House   where Percy Jackson was trained as a Roman demigod by Lupa

Zephyros   Greek god of the West Wind. Roman form: Favonius

Zeus   Greek god of the sky and king of the gods. Roman form: Jupiter

Keep reading

for an **EXCLUSIVE** sneak peek

at the thrilling final instalment of

RICK RIORDAN'S

latest series

THE BLOOD
OF OLYMPUS

JASON

JASON HATED BEING OLD. His joints hurt. His legs shook. As he tried to climb the hill, his lungs rattled like a box of rocks.

He couldn't see his face, thank goodness, but his fingers were gnarled and bony. Bulging blue veins webbed the backs of his hands.

He even had that old-man smell – mothballs and chicken soup. How was that possible? He'd gone from sixteen to seventy-five in a matter of seconds, but the old-man smell happened instantly, like *Boom. Congratulations! You stink!*

'Almost there.' Piper smiled at him. 'You're doing great.'

Easy for her to say. Piper and Annabeth were disguised as lovely Greek serving maidens. Even in their white sleeveless gowns and laced sandals, they had no trouble navigating the rocky path.

Piper's mahogany hair was pinned up in a braided spiral. Silver bracelets adorned her arms. She resembled an ancient statue of her mom, Aphrodite, which Jason found a little intimidating.

Dating a beautiful girl was nerve-racking enough. Dating a girl whose mom was the goddess of love . . . well, Jason was always afraid he'd do something unromantic, and Piper's mom would frown down from Mount Olympus and change him into a feral hog.

Jason glanced uphill. The summit was still a hundred yards above.

'Worst idea ever.' He leaned against a cedar tree and wiped his forehead. 'Hazel's magic is too good. If I have to fight, I'll be useless.'

'It won't come to that,' Annabeth promised. She looked uncomfortable in her serving-maiden outfit. She kept hunching her shoulders to keep the dress from slipping. Her pinned-up blonde bun had come undone in the back and her hair dangled like long spider legs. Knowing her hatred of spiders, Jason decided not to mention that.

'We infiltrate the palace,' she said. 'We get the information we need, and we get out.'

Piper set down her amphora, the tall ceramic wine jar in which her sword was hidden. 'We can rest for a second. Catch your breath, Jason.'

From her waist cord hung her cornucopia – the magic horn of plenty. Tucked somewhere in the folds of her dress was her knife, Katoptris. Piper didn't look dangerous, but if the need arose she could dual-wield Celestial bronze blades or shoot her enemies in the face with ripe mangoes.

Annabeth slung her own amphora off her shoulder. She too had a concealed sword, but, even without a visible weapon, she looked deadly. Her stormy grey eyes scanned the surroundings, alert for any threat. If any dude asked Annabeth for a drink, Jason figured she was more likely to kick the guy in the *bifurcum*.

He tried to steady his breathing.

Below them, Afales Bay glittered, the water so blue it might've been dyed with food colouring. A few hundred yards offshore, the *Argo II* rested at anchor. Its white sails looked no bigger than postage stamps, its ninety oars like toothpicks. Jason imagined his friends on deck following his progress, taking turns with Leo's spyglass, trying not to laugh as they watched Grandpa Jason hobble uphill.

'Stupid Ithaca,' he muttered.

He supposed the island was pretty enough. A spine of forested hills twisted down its centre. Chalky white slopes plunged into the sea. Inlets formed rocky beaches and harbours where red-roofed houses and white stucco churches nestled against the shoreline.

The hills were dotted with poppies, crocuses and wild cherry trees. The breeze smelled of blooming myrtle. All very nice – except the temperature was about a hundred and five degrees. The air was as steamy as a Roman bathhouse.

It would've been easy for Jason to control the winds and fly to the top of the hill, but *nooo*. For the sake of stealth, he had to struggle along as an old dude with bad knees and chicken-soup stink.

He thought about his last climb, two weeks ago, when Hazel and he had faced the bandit Sciron on the cliffs of Croatia. At least then Jason had been at full strength. What they were about to face would be much worse than a bandit.

'You sure this is the right hill?' he asked. 'Seems kind of – I don't know – *quiet*.'

Piper studied the ridgeline. Braided in her hair was a bright blue harpy feather – a souvenir from last night's attack. The feather didn't exactly go with her disguise, but Piper had earned it, defeating an entire flock of demon chicken ladies by herself while she was on duty. She downplayed the accomplishment, but Jason could tell she felt good about it. The feather was a reminder that she wasn't the same girl she'd been last winter, when they'd first arrived at Camp Half-Blood.

'The ruins are up there,' she promised. 'I saw them in Katoptris's blade. And you heard what Hazel said. "The biggest –"'

'"The biggest gathering of evil spirits I've ever sensed,"' Jason recalled. 'Yeah, sounds awesome.'

After battling through the underground temple of Hades, the last thing Jason wanted was to deal with more evil spirits. But the fate of the quest was at stake. The crew of the *Argo II* had a big decision to make. If they chose wrong, they would fail, and the entire world would be destroyed.

Piper's blade, Hazel's magical senses and Annabeth's instincts all agreed – the answer lay here in Ithaca, at the ancient palace of Odysseus, where a horde of evil spirits had gathered to await Gaia's orders. The plan was to sneak among them, learn what was going on and decide the best course of action. Then get out, preferably alive.

Annabeth re-adjusted her golden belt. 'I hope our disguises hold up. The suitors were nasty customers when they were alive. If they find out we're demigods –'

'Hazel's magic will work,' Piper said.

Jason tried to believe that.

The suitors: a hundred of the greediest, evilest cut-throats who'd ever lived. When Odysseus, the Greek king of Ithaca, went missing after the Trojan War, this mob of B-list princes had invaded his palace and refused to leave, each one hoping to marry Queen Penelope and take over the kingdom. Odysseus managed to return in secret and slaughter them all – your basic happy homecoming. But, if Piper's visions were right, the suitors were now back, haunting the place where they'd died.

Jason couldn't believe he was about to visit the actual palace of Odysseus – one of the most famous Greek heroes of all time. Then again, this whole quest had been one mind-blowing event after another. Annabeth herself had just come back from the eternal abyss of Tartarus. Given that, Jason decided maybe he shouldn't complain about being an old man.

'Well . . .' He steadied himself with his walking stick. 'If I *look* as old as I feel, my disguise must be perfect. Let's get going.'

As they climbed, sweat trickled down his neck. His calves ached. Despite the heat, he began to shiver. And, try as he might, he couldn't stop thinking about his recent dreams.

Ever since the House of Hades, they'd become more vivid.

Sometimes Jason stood in the underground temple of Epirus, the giant Clytius looming over him, speaking in a chorus of disembodied voices: *It took all of you together to defeat me. What will you do when the Earth Mother opens her eyes?*

Other times Jason found himself at the crest of Half-Blood Hill. Gaia the Earth Mother rose from the ground – a swirling figure of soil, leaves and stones.

Poor child. Her voice resonated across the landscape, shaking the bedrock under Jason's feet. *Your father is first among the gods, yet you are always second best – to your Roman comrades, to your Greek friends, even to your family. How will you prove yourself?*

His worst dream started in the courtyard of the Sonoma Wolf House. Before him stood the goddess Juno, glowing with the radiance of molten silver.

Your life belongs to me, her voice thundered. *An appeasement from Zeus.*

Jason knew he shouldn't look, but he couldn't close his eyes as Juno went supernova, revealing her true godly form. Pain seared Jason's mind. His body burned away in layers like an onion.

Then the scene changed. Jason was still at the Wolf House, but now he was a little boy – no more than two years old. A woman knelt before him, her lemony scent so familiar.

Her features were watery and indistinct, but he knew her voice: bright and brittle, like the thinnest layer of ice over a fast stream.

I will be back for you, dearest, she said. *I will see you soon.*

Every time Jason woke up from that nightmare, his face was beaded with sweat. His eyes stung with tears.

Nico di Angelo had warned them: the House of Hades would stir their worst memories, make them see things and hear things from the past. Their ghosts would become restless.

Jason had hoped that *particular* ghost would stay away, but every night the dream got worse. Now he was climbing to the ruins of a palace where an army of ghosts had gathered.

That doesn't mean she'll *be there*, Jason told himself.

But his hands wouldn't stop trembling. Every step seemed harder than the last.

'Almost there,' Annabeth said. 'Let's –'

BOOM! The hillside rumbled. Somewhere over the ridge, a crowd roared in approval, like spectators in a coliseum. The sound made Jason's skin crawl. Not so long ago, he'd fought for his life in the Roman Colosseum before a cheering ghostly audience. He wasn't anxious to repeat the experience.

'What was that explosion?' he wondered.

'Don't know,' Piper said. 'But it sounds like they're having fun. Let's go make some dead friends.'

Coming Autumn 2015

MAGNUS CHASE
AND THE
GODS OF ASGARD

THE SWORD OF SUMMER

www.rickriordan.co.uk

HORROR SHOWS, BLOODBATHS, LYING AND STEALING

WHO BETTER TO TELL THE TRUE STORIES OF THE GODS OF OLYMPUS THAN EVERYONE'S FAVOURITE DEMIGOD HERO?

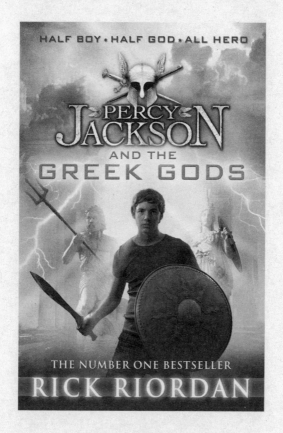

LOOK OUT
FOR ALL THE
GRAPHIC
NOVELS
FROM
RICK RIORDAN

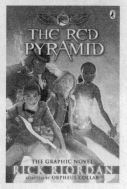

WHEN PERCY MET CARTER

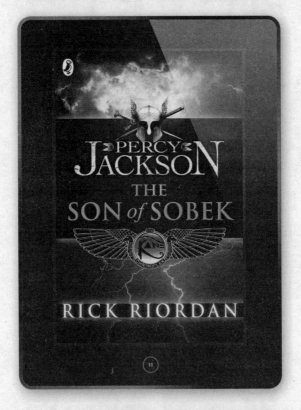

A SHORT STORY BRINGING TOGETHER THE WORLDS
OF PERCY JACKSON AND CARTER KANE!

www.rickriordan.co.uk

WHEN ANNABETH
MET SADIE

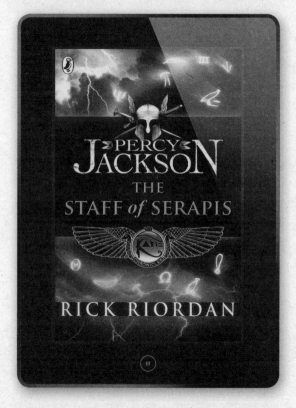

A SHORT STORY BRINGING TOGETHER THE WORLDS
OF ANNABETH CHASE AND SADIE KANE!

www.rickriordan.co.uk

RICK RIORDAN

EPIC HEROES.
LEGENDARY ADVENTURES.

PERCY JACKSON FOUGHT GREEK GODS.
NOW THE GODS OF EGYPT ARE WAKING IN
THE MODERN WORLD. . .

www.rickriordan.co.uk